Home

<u>ALSO BY TRINITY LEMM</u>

Fingerprints

The Forever Series:

Forever Burn
Forever Frozen
Forever & Ever

Trigger Warning:

This story contains descriptions of near-death experiences, car accidents, grief, death of a family member, some references to religion, and other topics that may be sensitive to some readers.

4

To all those who find it hard to forgive— sometimes life is too short not to.

Playlist

"Love in the Dark" – Adele

"BLUE" – Troye Sivan & Alex Hope

"What A Time" – Julia Michaels & Niall Horan

"Ocean Eyes" – Billie Eilish

"Malibu" – Miley Cyrus

"Die First" -Nessa Barrett

"My Tears Ricochet" – Taylor Swift

"Something to Someone (Acoustic)" – Dermot Kennedy

"Dark Paradise" – Lana Del Ray

"If the World Was Ending" – JP Saxe & Julia Michaels

"Only Love Can Hurt Like This" -Paloma Faith

"San Francisco" -Niall Horan

"Still" -Niall Horan

Home

a novel

Trinity Lemm

Chapter One
Kamryn

It was hot out. Too damn hot for my liking.

I looked up at the sky, squinting at the sun as it beat down with no mercy, perched above the buildings. Even though I was sitting against a building, shaded by its small, overhanging arch, it wasn't enough to stop me from sweating.

I was thirsty. Really thirsty. Like *insanely* thirsty and possibly dying from it, but I didn't have it in me to go on the trek to find more water.

San Francisco was busy, and there were endless amounts of people walking up and down the street, wearing everything from business attire to sundresses and tote bags. Some of them dropped money by my feet, but I still didn't move.

My old house was only a few miles away, but I refused to return there. Even if it meant saving my own life.

I knew I needed a job. A month on the street was a long time for a twenty-year-old. But not many people were willing to hire someone with little job experience and no reliable way to get to work.

I'd applied at various restaurants around the corner I'd claimed, but it was also hard for people to get a hold of someone who didn't have a phone or computer.

I reached over into my small duffel bag, the only bag I had. I dug through my clothes, and a small burst of excitement rippled through me when I found the small box of granola bars, but when I lifted the box, it was empty.

I groaned, tossing the box on the other side of me.

I often used the money people graciously left me to go to the grocery store a few blocks down to get some cheap snacks. Even though fast food was the cheapest option, eating it multiple times a day made me feel sick, so I tried my best to even it out with whatever other food I could afford.

My bottom lip trembled, and I knew that if I had enough water in my body right now, I would cry.

I studied my surroundings, trying to do whatever it took to get my mind off myself. I caught sight of a young girl walking between her parents. She was holding their hands, swinging them back and forth as she looked around at the buildings, her pink dress swaying.

A twinge of anguish grew in the pit of my stomach, and I forced myself to look away. Within another minute, the anguish was accompanied by jealousy.

If my parents were here, I wouldn't be sleeping on this raggedy blanket.

I shook my head, forcing those thoughts away. I didn't want to allow myself to become more miserable, but misery was impossible to avoid when nothing had gone right in my life since I was sixteen.

Just then, I could see a man out of the corner of my eye, heading in my direction. I didn't have to look directly at him to know it was the same man that had walked by numerous times since I'd made this corner my new home.

I kept my head down as he approached and took his keys out. I was trying my best not to look up at him, to avoid showing him the despair on my face, but I could feel his eyes on me, and for some reason, I wondered what color they were.

Curiosity won, and I looked up at the man. Sure enough, his eyes were on me, and luckily for me, I got the answer to my question.

Brown eyes.

Specifically amber brown.

But it wasn't how beautiful his eyes were that made me continue to study them. It was the overwhelming amount of pity lingering behind them.

I blinked at him, watching as he fidgeted around with his keys. He glanced back and forth between the door and me as he stuck his key in the lock and turned it.

And just like that, he was gone.

I dropped my head down again, almost disappointed that he was no longer there. Because once again, the crushing sense of loneliness entered my lungs.

The image of the man was burning into my mind, but when my stomach rumbled again, I couldn't think of anything besides my hunger.

I wiped my forehead with the back of my hand, squeezing my eyes shut. I shifted around uncomfortably. I wanted to change. To get out of my damp clothes. But unfortunately, all the other clothes in my bag were dirty too.

I finally forced myself to stand. I looked down at myself, my eyes skimming over the rip in my cream t-shirt and my dirty pajama shorts. The nicest article of clothing on me were my flip flops and they were from the Dollar Store.

I sighed and stepped over to the crosswalk, waiting for the light to signal that it was okay to walk. I didn't bother bringing my stuff with me. The only people who would steal a homeless girl's belongings were other homeless people, and there wasn't a single other homeless person in sight. Even if my things did get stolen, I wouldn't really care at this point. I was running out of motivation to try or to care. It was hard to live a life on the street, but it was harder doing it alone.

The light finally turned, allowing me to snap out of my pathetic thoughts. I trudged across the street and up to the door of the coffee shop. I grabbed the door handle as my eyes landed on the sign that read *Bathrooms for paying customers only.*

I sighed to myself again, praying that Lydia would be working so I could use the restroom.

When I opened the door, there she was, standing behind the counter. Relief flooded through me at the sight.

Lydia was young, only sixteen. The same age I was when my life began falling apart. Fortunately, Lydia had a bright future ahead.

She was a very pretty girl, and she looked exactly her age. Her brown hair was always up in a ponytail and her *Joe's Coffee* hat covered all her hair besides the very few strands that framed her face.

Lydia shot me a shy smile. "Hi, Kamryn."

"Hi, Lydia," I said, returning the smile. I pointed down the hall towards the bathroom. "Can I?"

Her brown eyes filled with compassion, her face scrunching together, as if in pain. "My manager found out I've been letting you use it... He wasn't very happy about it."

My shoulders slumped. "Oh."

She glanced around, eyeing the empty shop. "You can use it today, but I probably won't be able to let you use it anymore after that," she said with a wince.

"Okay," I nodded towards the floor. "Did you by any chance get to ask if there are job openings available?"

Lydia pulled one side of her mouth over with regret. "I did ask, but apparently there won't be any openings until some of the other baristas leave next month for college."

"Oh," I nodded, rubbing my tired eyes.

"But if you want, I can tell my manager you're interested when there are openings."

I gave her a thankful, yet timid smile. "That's okay. Thanks though."

She nodded apologetically.

I cocked my head towards the hall. "I'll be back."

"Okay. It doesn't look like anyone will be coming in soon, so take your time."

"Thanks," I said, heading into the bathroom.

I closed and locked the door behind me. I stood there for a moment, tipping my head back as I felt the cool AC blow on my face.

I jumped when there was a knock on the door. "Kamryn?" Lydia said. "Would you like some water?"

I swung the door open at the sound of the word, my eyes wide in excitement. Lydia held out a cup of water, and I gladly took it, bringing it straight to my mouth. I chugged. And I chugged. And I didn't stop chugging until the cup was empty.

"Do you want some more?"

"Yes please," I nodded eagerly.

She gave a reassuring grin as she took the cup and walked off to refill it.

Thank God for Lydia. Her kindness was truly a blessing. For the past two weeks, she'd been allowing me to use the bathroom here, and even gave me water or cookies when the shop wasn't busy. But most of all, she was the only friend I had.

Within thirty seconds, Lydia was back with a refill. "I'll give you a few minutes to yourself," she said, handing the cup over.

"Thank you."

After she walked off, I closed the door again. I took a small gulp of water and placed the cup beside the sink. I shifted my weight, nervous to look in the mirror and see my reflection.

But finally, I did.

And I couldn't help but regret it.

I looked like a worn out, knock-off version of my beautiful mother.

My face was dirty, and the French braid that I had my hair in was more than messy. Platinum blonde strands were sticking out everywhere. I was fairly skinnier than I used to be. Embarrassment washed over me knowing that this was what the man had seen. Or better yet, what everyone had been seeing.

Worst of all, the part of me that I hated looking at most was the grief in my eyes.

Losing my parents at sixteen was a tragedy.

Losing my fiancé to another woman at twenty was a catastrophe.

But losing myself over the past month was the most painful loss of all.

I shook my head at my reflection as I turned the warm water on, using it to splash my face. It felt refreshing. I took my time washing up, not stopping until I was sure all the dirt on my face was gone. I swished around a mouthful of water, wishing I had toothpaste, but thankful for the water, nonetheless.

I made sure to use the toilet, not knowing when the next time I'd be able to use one would be. The last thing I did was redo my braid. I spent my time on it. If this was the last time that I'd have a mirror in front of me for a few days at the least, then I may as well use it.

Once I was *slightly* more confident than I was when I first walked in, I finished the cup of water and met Lydia back out front. Once again, she was standing behind the counter. Her kind smile radiated through the shop, allowing the somber air to thin.

"How was your freshening up?" she asked.

"Wonderful," I said, grabbing a seat from the nearest table and scooting it up to the counter.

"Good!" She reached below the counter, pulling out a small baggy and sliding it over to me.

"Are those..."

"Yes," she smiled.

I snagged the bag faster than the speed of light, not hesitating to rip it open. The smell of chocolate chip cookies wafted through the air. I happily breathed it in, grabbing a cookie and shoving it in my mouth.

Lydia let out a laugh. "Good?"

"Mhmm," I hummed with a nod. I downed the first two cookies and saved the last one, intending for it to be my dinner later.

Lydia gave another chuckle as she grabbed her cleaning supplies and made her way out to the seating area. I watched as she began washing down tables, her normal closing process.

I shifted around in my seat. "Closing soon?"

"Yeah," she said.

"What time is it?"

"Almost five."

"Damn," I muttered under my breath. Closing time meant that I'd have to get out soon. At this point, I knew the shop was always busiest during the morning and early afternoon, but once three o'clock hit, there weren't many people in need of coffee. I really should've taken better advantage of the two-hour time gap, where I probably could've sat around in the shop, accompanied by Lydia and the AC, but the problem was that I didn't have a watch. I never knew what time it was. On top of that, Lydia didn't work every day. I was always worried that I'd walk into the shop to see Joe, the owner, or some employee that would rat me out.

But I guess none of that mattered since Lydia wasn't going to let me in from now on either.

"How was your day?" Lydia asked.

I shrugged. "Same old," I murmured. "You?"

"Same old," she repeated.

I dropped my chin to my chest, soaking up the last few minutes of cool air. My eyes aimlessly followed Lydia around the room as she began sweeping the floor.

"Do you start school soon?" I asked.

"On September first."

"Oh, so you've still got what? Over a month?"

"Yeah," she nodded.

"What's the date anyway?"

"July twenty-ninth."

I sighed under my breath. I was supposed to be getting married on August first. I should've spent the past month preparing for the wedding, but instead of worrying about last minute dress alterations and decorations, I was worrying about when my next meal would be.

My mind shifted onto Ryan. I gritted my teeth together, hoping Lydia wouldn't notice the change in my attitude as my mind wandered off.

I wondered how he and Sadie were doing. Living in *our* house. Sleeping together in *our* bed. Not worrying about a single thing under *our* roof.

I was still in shock about it all, but who wouldn't be? Not everyone's fiancé comes to them two months shy of their wedding and admits to knocking up another woman.

"Kamryn?" Lydia said, snapping me out of my thoughts.

My head shot up. "Yeah?"

Her face melted. "I have to close now."

I nodded, taking a deep breath as I stood. "Okay." I put the chair back where I got it from and allowed Lydia to lead me out of the shop.

I stood beside her as she locked the door. "Thanks for letting me in again," I said.

She put her keys back in her small purse. "No problem."

My eyes saddened, but I looked everywhere other than at her so that she wouldn't see. "Well, I guess I'll see you around," I said, turning on my heels.

"Wait, Kamryn."

I looked over my shoulder.

"I mean... I guess if you occasionally come in when no one else is in the shop then it's okay."

A tiny grin tugged on the corners of my lips. "Really?"

"Yeah. We'll just have to be careful, so I don't get caught," she laughed.

"Okay," I chuckled with a nod. "Thank you."

"Of course. Have a good night."

"You too." With that, I turned back around, but before I began walking, I froze, squinting as I looked across the street.

The man from earlier was walking up to the door of his apartment again. I stared at the back of his head, taking in his dusty blonde hair. I almost wished he was facing me so I could take another look at his eyes, but just before I got the chance to cross the street, he slipped inside.

I waited impatiently for the light to turn and once it did, I jogged across the street and towards my tattered blanket, but my steps slowed when I caught sight of a small Tupperware box and a water bottle sitting beside it.

I glanced around quickly, but I was less curious about where it came from and more curious about what was inside. I darted for it, opening it to reveal chicken, rice, and some vegetables.

I was an eighth of a second away from using my hands to shovel it into my mouth when I noticed some plastic silverware on the other side of the water bottle. I grabbed it and dug in.

The second a bite of chicken was in my mouth, my entire body relaxed with satisfaction, and once I started, I didn't stop until every last bite was gone.

***

The next few hours passed by slowly, and I spent most of it braiding and unbraiding my hair just for the sake of having something to do. Before I knew it, it was dark out.

There was a light breeze that came and went, and each time it did, a shiver scurried down my spine. I reached into my duffel bag and took out a sweatshirt—the only one I had—and slipped it over my head.

I curled up into a ball on my blanket and closed my eyes. I could feel a tear forming behind my lids, but I refused to let it fall as I shivered once more.

That was the worst thing about San Francisco. The days were so hot, and the nights were so cold, but no matter what time of day it was, the loneliness stayed the same.

Chapter Two
Decker

I groaned as I turned my alarm off. Rolling over, I rubbed my eyes.

Seven a.m.

"Ugh," I grumbled, sitting up. I sat there for a moment, dreading getting out of bed, but I knew that I had to.

I sighed as I tossed the covers off me and headed into the bathroom, turning on the shower. I stood in front of the mirror as I waited for the water to get hot. My hands found their way to the edge of the sink, and I leaned into it as I studied my reflection.

My hair was a mess, of course, and I let out another sigh at the sight of stubble on my chin. I brought a hand up, rubbing it along my jaw. I'd have to shave before work.

I stepped out of my basketball shorts and right as I opened the shower door to step in, the girl outside of my apartment wandered into my mind. I wasn't sure why she did at that very moment, but I quite honestly wasn't surprised about it. She'd been popping into my head at random times throughout the day ever since she showed up on that corner.

I wondered about her as I showered. I wanted to know how she ended up homeless. What was her story? She looked young, possibly around my age, but it was hard to tell.

Yesterday was the first day she actually looked back at me, the first day I got a good look at her face.

Her ivory skin was coated in dirt, but even without the opportunity of getting a clear picture of each and every one of her features, it was her baby blue eyes that had me caught.

Their color was bright, but they screamed misery.

I couldn't help but imagine myself in her shoes. Even though I didn't know how she ended up there, I could tell by one look that she didn't deserve to be there.

I thought about her for the remainder of the shower, plus the entire time I was shaving. By the time I headed into the kitchen to make breakfast, the wonder was killing me. I leaned over the kitchen sink and peeked through my window blinds, hoping to get a glimpse of her, but I couldn't see her from that angle.

My mouth pulled to the side in disappointment as I tread over to the fridge. I grabbed all the ingredients needed for scrambled eggs and got to work. As I was mixing everything together, I paused, my hand dropping the whisk into the bowl. I took my bottom lip between my teeth and without another thought, I added two more eggs.

When I glanced up at the clock on the wall, I grew panicked. I only had twenty minutes to eat, brush my teeth, and get dressed before I needed to head to work. I moved faster, desperately rushing to get everything done.

Once the eggs were done, I pushed half of them onto a plate and the other half into a Tupperware box. I grabbed a piece of toast out of the toaster and carefully laid it in. I shut the box right after, trying to keep the food warm while I ate and got dressed quickly.

I glanced in the mirror after getting dressed and brushing my teeth, reassuring myself that I looked professional enough. I pushed a hand through my hair, ensuring that the front was gelled upwards the way I liked it, not a hair out of place. I touched my chin, satisfied with how well I'd shaved it. Then after giving myself a convincing smile, I speed-walked back into the kitchen, grabbing some plastic silverware and lying it across the top of the Tupperware.

Just as I was about to grab my work stuff and head out the door, I backtracked to the fridge. Tugging it open, my eyes skimmed over everything as I wondered what to give her to drink. I grabbed a water bottle and a juice box. Yes, I was a twenty-two-year-old man, but who the hell didn't love juice boxes?

Once I was one hundred percent sure I had everything, I headed out the door. I peeked over at the corner and sure enough, there she was, sleeping in a ball.

I knew if I didn't leave the food now and sprint to work that I'd probably be late, yet I couldn't help but stand there for a moment and study her. Even asleep atop a dirty blanket, she was pretty. *Really* pretty.

The hood of her sweatshirt was up, but I could still see strands of her platinum blonde hair sticking out. Her facial features were delicate, and I wondered if her skin was as soft as it looked. I almost wished she was awake so that I could get another look at her eyes.

I walked over as quietly as I could. I wasn't sure if she knew I was the one that left food yesterday, but we still hadn't been formally introduced and this definitely wasn't the way I wanted to do it.

I placed the food about a foot away from her, taking one last glimpse at her before forcing myself to head to work.

But I was embarrassed to admit that the entire walk was spent thinking about her.

***

"It's a Thursday night. I have work tomorrow," I said through the phone.

"Dude," Benny said, "I haven't seen you in weeks. Come out with us tonight."

Benny was one of the only people I still talked to regularly from high school. I wasn't a big fan of everyone from high school, and after senior year, most of them weren't fans of me either.

I sighed. "Who's all going?"

"Myra and me for sure. I don't know who else."

I sighed again, louder this time as I dodged through people on the sidewalk. "I don't want to drink."

"You never wanna drink."

"Exactly." I raised a displeased brow even though he couldn't see it.

"C'mon bro. Myra really wants to see you."

"So?"

He scoffed through the phone. "What do you mean *so?* She's hot and she likes you and if you hadn't already banged her, I would've done it myself."

"Go ahead," I said. "I don't care."

A small herd of nerves began dancing through me when I turned down my street. I picked up the pace a little, both nervous and excited to see the girl on the corner.

Was it messed up that I was eager to see a homeless girl that lived outside my apartment?

Definitely.

But could I help it?

No.

"Decker? *Hellooo?*" Benny said, snapping me out of my thoughts.

"What?"

"Geez, did you not hear anything I just said?"

"Nope."

He groaned. "Just come out tonight."

"When are you guys going?"

"Around eight."

I chewed on the inside of my cheek. "I'll think about it."

"Well, let me know soon."

"Alright, alright," I said, hanging up the phone.

My eager pace slowed when I saw the last thing I wanted to see. Benny stood in front of my apartment, shooting me a smug grin.

"Aye, Decks!"

"Dear Lord," I muttered to myself as he approached. He was in my damn way, blocking my view of the girl. I tried to peer around him, but it seemed to be no use. "What are you doing here? We were literally just on the phone."

"Well, you see," he said, throwing an arm over my shoulder, "I knew you'd have that reaction over the phone, so I figured I'd wait here and come drag you outta your apartment myself."

I shimmied his arm off me. "Well, now it's a definite no."

"C'mon," Benny pushed, "we can grab some food beforehand, and everyone else can meet us for drinks after."

I glanced back and forth between him and my apartment door. I swallowed. "I was gonna make dinner here."

He tilted his head towards his shoulder, disappointed. His voice turned flat, an immense difference from his usual, chirpy tone. "I haven't seen you in forever."

I gritted my teeth together, taking in his pleading expression. "Fine," I finally agreed. "But I'm leaving by eleven."

"Atta boy!" he exclaimed, his smile reappearing as he snaked his arm around me once again and led me away from the only person I wanted to see.

***

Dinner with Benny went fine. It was the *aftermath* of dinner that caused me to get agitated.

Being the only sober one at the table was not fun at all. Although, drinking probably wouldn't have been that much fun either.

I sat across from Myra, feeling her small feet purposely kick me under the table. My eyes trailed up to her face and I took a good look at her.

No doubt was she beautiful. With her alluring features and voluminous brown locks, she was a sight to be seen, for sure. She had been ever since high school.

But she didn't have the same striking blue eyes as the girl outside my apartment.

I wondered about the girl once more, worried about her. I kind of felt like shit knowing that I was probably her only source of dinner, and I didn't even give her that tonight.

It was strange to be so concerned about someone you had never met, but regardless, there was something that pulled me towards her. Something deep within me made me care about her even though I still didn't know her name.

"Decks," Myra said, leaning into the table.

"Yeah?"

"What've you been up to? I haven't heard from you lately."

"Not much," I shrugged. "You?"

She lifted a shoulder. "Nothing new."

I nodded, bored.

"How's the internship?" she asked, sipping on her vodka lemonade.

"It's good. How's your..." I trailed off, forgetting whatever it was that she did.

"Salon?" She lifted a sassy brow.

"Yes, that! How's your salon?"

"Pretty good," she nodded, tilting her head towards her shoulder. "We're thinking about relocating to a bigger space."

"That's great," I said.

Before she could answer, our conversation was cut short when Nolan and Alaina came back from the bar with their drinks.

Nolan and Alaina were so physically different, but their personalities were very similar. Either way, they still looked like a perfect couple.

Nolan was African American with a buzzcut. He'd been one of my best friends since sophomore year, and even though I'd known Benny for longer, most of the time, I liked Nolan more. He was laid-back and carefree, the complete opposite of Benny. And best of all, he was one of the funniest people I'd ever met.

Alaina was a small redhead. Her porcelain skin was covered in freckles, and she always wore a bright smile.

"Decks," Nolan said, nodding to me across the table, "why aren't you drinking?"

"Because he's a wuss," Benny intervened.

I shot Benny a glare before turning back to Nolan. "I have work tomorrow."

Nolan nodded, seemingly relieved by my answer.

Myra held up her empty glass and shook it around, causing the ice to clink against the glass. "Empty," she said, standing. "I'm gonna go get a refill. Decks, come with?"

I eyed her with a blank expression. I could see Benny staring at me out of the corner of my eye. He nudged me under the table. I let out a sigh under my breath as I stood and followed Myra over to the bar.

We stood side by side as we waited for the bartender to head over to us. "So," Myra said, "what are you doing this weekend?"

"I'm not really sure yet," I said, avoiding eye contact with her.

"Do you want to hang out?"

I stayed quiet for a moment, probably a moment too long. Myra was a smart girl, smart enough to understand what the silence meant.

"Decks, you can say no," she said with a friendly grin. "I just..."

Myra glanced up at me quickly before dropping her head and sighing. "It's okay," she muttered.

Before thinking, my mouth started moving, for some reason asking the one question that I didn't really care to know the answer to. "What are you looking for?"

Her head darted back up to me. "Nothing in particular. I just feel like I only know the high school version of you. I want to know you beyond..." she trailed off and I was thankful she did.

I took in her pleading expression, but the image of the blonde girl's pleading expression overtook my thoughts. I slyly glanced past Myra's head at the clock on the wall.

Ten-twenty.

"Myra," I started, "it's not that I don't think you're a great girl. There's just a lot going on, so I'm not sure if now—"

"I get it," she cut me off, but her tone was less aggravated and more understanding, which made me relieved. Myra had always been kind and soft-spoken. She was never the pretty girl in high school that was a bitch to everyone else, which was exactly why it made me feel even worse rejecting her.

I was grateful the bartender finally noticed us, and as she headed over to take Myra's order, I zoned out, my thoughts roaming directly back to the blonde girl.

God, I wished I knew her name so I could stop thinking of her as *the blonde girl* or *the homeless girl.*

I wondered if she was already asleep or if she'd be awake by the time I got back. I wanted to meet her. I wanted her to know me as more than the guy whose apartment she stayed outside of, as more than the guy that left her food, if she even knew it was me doing so. I internally cursed myself at the fact that I could've left a note with the food, at least leaving my name.

Myra's voice snapped me out of my thoughts. "Ready?" she asked with a new drink in her hand.

I nodded, following her back to the table. But instead of sitting down, I stayed standing. "I'm gonna head out."

"What!" Benny whined. "But we just got here."

"You and I got here *hours* ago."

"It's not even eleven yet," he argued.

"I said I would leave *by* eleven, not *at* eleven," I said. "And dude, I'm literally still in my work clothes. I wanna go home and change and—"

"Benny, don't be an ass," Alaina added in, tilting her head at him.

Nolan draped his arm around her shoulder. "If he's ready to go, let him go."

Benny sighed. "Fine."

I made my way around the table saying goodbye to everyone. When I got to Myra, I gave her a hug.

"And hey, if you change your mind about this weekend, let me know," she said.

I gave her a friendly grin. "Will do." I waved as I walked off, and the second I was outside, I picked up the pace. I was glad the bar was only a few blocks from my place.

It was fairly quiet, but it was still San Francisco, and cars never stopped driving up and down the street no matter what time of the night it was.

Once I approached my apartment, I slowed my steps down. I glanced around, but there wasn't a person in sight as I neared the girl.

I guess it was just her and me.

I peeked around the corner carefully, trying my best to make sure I wouldn't scare her. But when I caught sight of her, she was curled up in a ball, sound asleep.

I could hear her peacefully drawn-out breaths as I took a step closer, just close enough to see her body shiver ever so slightly.

My mouth formed a hard line and I turned on my heels, heading inside. I strode directly over to the small chest in the living room where I kept extra blankets and pillows, plucking out a blanket with baseballs on it from when I was younger. I didn't hesitate to walk back out to the corner.

I carefully and quietly laid the blanket over her small body. I couldn't help but stand for a moment and take in the sight of her.

My lungs filled with as much air as they could hold before I blew a long breath out my nose. I felt like a creep just standing there, watching her sleep. My head dropped towards the ground as I went back inside.

After brushing my teeth and changing, I collapsed into bed. I stared at the ceiling, wondering what the best way to introduce myself would be.

Because no matter what, I was determined to know her name.

Chapter Three
Kamryn

When my eyes fluttered open, I immediately brought my brows in from the fact that I was warmer than I normally was each morning.

My hands skimmed over the blanket that was draped across my body. I shot up to get a better look. It was a fleece blanket with baseballs on it. There was a tiny tag sticking out on the corner. I took it between my fingers and read the name scribbled across the top.

Decker

I stared at it for a few minutes, probably a few minutes too long, but it wasn't like I had anything better to do anyway.

I didn't have to be told that it belonged to the man I saw each day, the man whose apartment I slept outside of. I just somehow knew.

"Decker," I whispered the name to myself.

I held onto the tag with one hand and used the other to feel along the blanket once more. It was soft. Without a doubt softer than any of the clothes I had, which led me to wonder why this man that I'd never met before was giving his nice, soft blanket away to the homeless girl outside his apartment.

Just as I was about to lay back down and bask in the warmth once again, a shadow approached.

My eyes darted up to meet his amber brown ones and I held my breath as he stood there, a few feet away.

He had a startled expression on his face, as if he hadn't expected for me to be awake. My eyes trailed down to the Tupperware box in his hands and my shoulders relaxed.

We were staring at each other for another moment too long before I finally conjured up enough courage to speak.

"Hi," I said.

There was a flicker of a smile that danced across his face at the sound of my voice. "Hi."

I pointed to the name on the tag as I lifted a brow, all my previous nerves somehow disappearing. "I'm assuming you're Decker?"

He nodded, staring down at the top of the Tupperware box. "Yeah." He plucked a tiny piece of paper off it, crumbled it up and stuck it in his pocket.

"And I'm also assuming you're the one that's been bringing me food?"

"Yeah," he repeated, inhaling deeply.

I smirked lightly. "Do you say anything other than *yeah*?"

"Yeah," he chuckled with a nod, causing my laughter to follow suit. His eyes found mine again as he asked, "Are you hungry?"

I wanted the food, *of course I wanted it,* but part of me felt bad taking from this man who'd already given me so much before he even knew my name.

"It's okay," I shook my head. "You really don't have to—"

"No, it's alright. I already ate, so I wasn't gonna eat it anyways."

I tipped my chin towards my chest. "Are you sure?"

"Yeah, absolutely," he said, closing the gap between us. I was expecting him to drop the food and leave, but to my surprise, he sat down on the corner of my tattered blanket. He handed me the Tupperware box and plastic silverware, along with a juice box.

"Thank you," I smiled at him.

"You're welcome."

I didn't want to look away from his face, but I did, turning my attention to the box and popping it open. On one side, there was a bagel, lightly toasted with cream cheese. The other side was filled with fresh strawberries.

I dug right in, going for the strawberries first. After a few bites, I glanced back up. Decker's eyes were on the blanket beneath us, seemingly taking in every rip and tear in the fabric. I took the opportunity to glance him over, noting his nice suit and dress shoes.

"Where are you going?" I asked shyly. His head shot up and he brought his brows inwards, confused. "You're all dressed up," I said with a grin.

"Oh," he smiled back, glancing down at his suit. "I have work today."

"Where do you work?"

"I have a paid internship at a law firm."

I raised an impressed brow. "Fancy," I said. I could've sworn I saw him smirk in the slightest, but I pretended like I hadn't caught it. I continued speaking between bites. "So, an internship? Are you still in school or something then?"

"Yeah, I'll be starting my second semester of law school in the fall."

I took a gulp of juice before I spoke again. "You seem young to be in law school already. Did you finish your undergrad early or something?"

"Surprisingly, yeah," he chuckled.

I wanted to ask why it was surprising to him, but my mouth was full, and the subject got changed before I had the chance.

"Are you from around here?" he asked.

I nodded again. "I went to Parkersville High School."

His brows shot up. "Oh, that's not far from me at all. I went to Lane North."

"Oh," I smiled. "You were only like twenty minutes away from me."

"Who knows? Maybe I knew you," he shrugged.

"There's no way," I said as I glanced past his shoulder. "I would've remembered you."

He grinned, shifting his weight around. It wasn't until then that I realized I probably smelled bad. Embarrassment flooded over me, and I scooted over just enough to create a little more distance between us. Decker didn't seem to notice though, and if he did, he didn't seem to care. His smile hadn't faded.

"I still haven't gotten your name," he said with a smirk.

"Kamryn," I replied, placing the empty Tupperware box beside me.

"Kamryn," he repeated.

"Yep," I grinned. A tiny smile tugged on his lips as he looked at me and I couldn't help but notice the surge of butterflies that flew within me at the sight.

Finally, his eyes fell to the watch on his wrist, and he sighed. "I should probably get going." He stood and dusted off his suit.

"Okay." I gave a sad nod. "Thank you again for the food. I'll see you around."

"You're welcome." He nodded once. "Bye Kamryn."

"Bye," I said in a small voice as I waved.

I wished our conversation would've lasted longer. I wasn't sure if it was because I'd hardly had anyone to speak to in the past month or if it was Decker himself, but there was a swarm of bliss that ran through my bloodstream.

For whatever the reason was, I felt like I had some motivation today. Motivation to do something besides sit here and bask in my sorrow like I had for countless days prior.

I didn't know what time it was, but by the amount of traffic and people walking, I assumed it was eight or nine.

I grabbed my duffle bag and stuck my hand all the way to the bottom, digging until I found the small pile of money I'd been saving.

I took out every coin and every bill that'd been dropped by my feet over the past however many days and began counting it.

Nineteen dollars.

A hopeful smile lingered on my face, and I shoved all the money into the pocket of my sweatshirt before hopping onto my feet and heading towards the store.

***

Even though it was just Walmart, I still felt out of place. Everyone around me was wearing clean clothes, while I hadn't changed out of mine in God knew how long.

Everyone else was carrying a purse or wallet for their belongings, while I had my only belongings stuffed into the pocket of my sweatshirt.

Everyone else was pushing a shopping cart, filling it with their weekly groceries, while I wandered through the store with a tiny basket, buying whatever small items I could afford with my nineteen dollars.

I trekked around the store in search of food that I knew wouldn't go bad. I grabbed a small box of granola bars and tossed them into my basket before doing the same with a box of fruit snacks.

Thirteen dollars left.

My eyes lit up when I turned down the bottled water aisle. I knew there was no way I could physically drag an entire case of water three blocks back to my corner by myself, so I settled for a gallon instead, which was fine with me because it was cheaper anyway.

I continued roaming through the store, taking my sweet time since there was nowhere else I needed to be today. I made my way up and down each aisle just for the hell of it. When I turned down the candy aisle, I held my breath.

I'd always had a sweet tooth ever since I was little. My mom used to buy me these little chocolate candies that had caramel inside of them. When I was young, I used to steal them off the kitchen counter when she wasn't looking. And as I grew into my early teen years, once my parents stopped caring about having dessert before dinner, I would binge eat them until dinner was ready. I always had a bag of them hidden in my nightstand drawer.

After my mom passed, I refused to eat them for over a year, but once I eventually got myself to start eating them again, they brought me comfort, reminding me of my mother's caring touch, kind smile, and beautiful blue eyes.

I eyed the bag from across the aisle and wandered over, standing directly in front of it as I took in its every detail.

30

There was a throb coming from within me, one that was so deep I could feel it in my bones. It felt as though it was part of me, as if it was inside my genetic make-up.

My eyes began to water, and I inhaled deeply as the image of my beloved parents popped into my head. I stood there, wondering for the millionth time in my life where I would be if they were still alive. If they hadn't left that gala when they had. If it wasn't New Year's Eve. If there hadn't been snow on the ground. *If that drunk driver hadn't hit them.*

I shook my head as I dropped it, allowing those thoughts to fade away. When I glanced back up at the chocolates, I was surprised when my mother didn't pop back into my head. This time, Decker did.

Even though the brown of the bag didn't match the brown of his eyes, I thought of them. Of those amber irises staring back at me.

I hoped he would bring me dinner. Not specifically because I wanted the food, but because I simply wanted to see him again.

Our conversation this morning was a mere five minutes long, but it was so enjoyable, nonetheless.

I was tempted to grab the bag of chocolates and toss it in my basket, but instead, I turned on my heels and headed into the beauty department.

If I couldn't shower, the least I could do was put on some damn deodorant.

I picked out the cheapest one that still smelled nice. The last thing I grabbed was an apple to eat for lunch before I headed to check out.

I was pleased when the total came out to be fifteen dollars, allowing me to save the remaining four dollars for my next grocery trip. Whenever that would be.

Once I had everything settled, I set back out into the busy streets of San Francisco.

Chapter Four
Decker

I was practically running, zigzagging in and out of people on the sidewalk as I raced home. The second my boss said I could leave early, I rushed out the door.

It was shy of four in the afternoon, and I was anxious to get home and make dinner so that I could bring some to Kamryn again.

The moment she said her name this morning, it kept going through my head all day long.

Kamryn, Kamryn, Kamryn, Kamryn.

Even though I knew she could tell I was nervous in her presence, there was this unsaid comfort between us. Before officially meeting her, there had been something gravitating me towards her, and now that I'd seen her face up close, heard her voice, and learned her name, that gravitation had grown stronger.

By the time I got onto my own block, I was noticeably out of breath. My fast pace slowed to a casual walk. The last thing I wanted was to run into Kamryn while out of breath and breaking a sweat. That would've been embarrassing as hell.

I walked as nonchalantly as possible to the corner, and when I peeked around it, my eager smile flipped, replaced by a long frown.

All of Kamryn's belongings were there, but she wasn't.

I spun around myself, glancing up and down the street for her, but she was nowhere in sight. Disappointment traveled through me, and I sighed heavily as I turned towards my apartment door.

I wondered where she was, what she was doing, and if she was okay. For a moment, I considered that maybe she was just avoiding me. Maybe she thought it was creepy that the guy whose apartment she stayed outside of had been bringing her food and covering her with blankets while she slept. Let's face it. It was a little creepy when you worded it that way.

But when I remembered how much she was smiling this morning, I knocked the creep theory out of my head. She couldn't have been avoiding me, considering how talkative she was earlier. Right?

I had never been so concerned over what a girl thought about me before, especially when I'd technically only known the girl for half a day.

My dress shoes scuffed against the wooden floor, carrying me all the way to my bedroom. I slipped the shoes off and tossed them carelessly into the closet. I changed into a t-shirt and basketball shorts before lying down in bed and using the TV remote to click the power button on.

I usually watched TV on the couch in the living room, rather than on the small TV in my bedroom, but for some reason, I was feeling lazy. Maybe it was because of my disappointment. Or maybe I was just being dramatic.

There was a Marvel movie marathon on, so I clicked on that and tossed the remote beside me. I couldn't go twenty minutes without my mind wandering back to Kamryn, and I squeezed my eyes shut in frustration.

I considered peeking outside again to see if she was back from wherever she'd been, but I stopped myself, determined to avoid the creep theory.

But sometime between that second and the next, I passed out.

***

There was a crash louder than a bomb, firetruck, and fireworks combined. I immediately shot up in bed and looked around in a panic. It wasn't until there was a bright flash outside my window that I realized it was storming.

I breathed a sigh of relief that that's all it was before falling back against the mattress. I rolled over and grabbed my phone off the nightstand to check the time. It was nine at night.

Goddamn. I was passed out for over four hours? What the fuck?

My stomach rumbled, screaming at me because it hadn't been filled since noon. I groaned, tossing around in bed. I knew I'd just overslept and would most definitely not be able to fall asleep when I normally would, but that didn't encourage me to get up. Not at all. I was way too comfortable.

The TV was still on, and I immediately recognized *Captain America.* I studied the blue of his shield. It was so bright, an electrifying shade. I stared at it, unsure of why I couldn't stop staring at it until it finally occurred to me.

Kamryn.

I shot out of bed and sprinted out of my bedroom. I glanced out my front window, and when I saw nothing but a blur of rain, I rushed faster, slipping on the first pair of shoes I saw and grabbing an umbrella out of the storage closet.

The rain was loud, *annoyingly loud,* but my heartbeat still managed to be louder as I scrambled out the door and around the corner.

Chapter Five
Kamryn

San Francisco was always busy, but right now, there wasn't another person or a car in sight.

It was just the storm and me.

My face was buried into my knees, but that didn't keep me from shivering. The rain was beating down with bruising force, and although time always seemed to go by slower in my corner, it seemed especially slow right now.

How long could this storm possibly last?

I'd do anything to be in warmth right now. Or at least somewhere that wasn't *wet*. Hell, I'd take the harsh sun in a heartbeat over this weather.

I was trying to concentrate on anything other than how cold I was, but I was trembling so heavily that I couldn't get my thoughts past it.

I wrapped my arms tighter around my knees, burying my face deeper.

"Kamryn!" someone yelled.

My head shot up, recognizing the voice. "Decker?"

He held an umbrella above his head, standing a few feet from me. "Do you wanna come in?" he asked.

"Are you sure?"

"Yes," he immediately nodded.

I knew the invitation was him pitying me, and as much as I wanted to decline just for that reason alone, I knew I couldn't. I'd freeze to death out here otherwise.

There was next to no hesitation in my voice as I responded. "Please," I gave a nod.

He closed the gap between us and leaned down, holding the umbrella above me while he grabbed my blanket and duffel bag.

"Oh, you don't have to—"

"It's okay," he softly said, getting drowned out by the rain.

I followed him inside, and the moment the warmth hit my skin, my entire body relaxed. I glanced around the apartment quietly.

It was very spacious, with what looked to be one bedroom and one bathroom. The kitchen was straight ahead of where I stood, lined with granite countertops and an island in the center. On the opposite side of the kitchen, there was a small seating area with a flat screen TV mounted to the wall.

It was a stark difference from what I was used to, much newer and nicer than my old house with Ryan.

It seemed like Decker was well-off, and although I should've been scared to be walking into the apartment of a man that I barely knew, I somehow felt calm and comfortable.

Everything in the space gave off a cozy vibe, Decker included. I should've been worried. I should've been running over to the kitchen to grab a knife in case this were some kind of clever kidnapping, but instead, I just stood still. My eyes followed Decker with more curiosity than caution as he set my belongings next to the couch and placed his umbrella in a nearby closet.

My pulse galloped as he stepped towards me, stopping shy of a few feet once again.

Before he had the chance to look at me, I swallowed a sigh, my head falling to the floor as I wondered who was going to be the first to speak.

Chapter Six
Decker

She was drenched in water from head to toe with her eyes dropped towards the ground, water dripping off her delicate chin.

When she looked up at me, I forced myself to look away because I didn't want her to catch me staring. I was pretty sure she still did, though.

I finally gained the nerve to look back at her. Our eyes locked, and I was surprised when neither of us looked away, but I was also relieved that we didn't.

I liked looking at her, and even more so, I liked when *she* looked at *me*.

Regardless of the fact that she was standing there with messy hair, no makeup, and in a wet, oversized hoodie and pajama shorts, there was something about seeing her in her purest form that made her so attractive.

Her bright blue eyes, the ones that matched Captain America's shield, bore into me. We stood in silence for a moment longer before there was a small rumbling noise coming from her.

She covered her stomach with both hands and we each let out a chuckle at the same time. "Sorry," she said in a small voice.

"Hungry?"

She glanced back up at me, her eyes filled with innocence.

"I still haven't eaten dinner," I said. "I can make us something."

"Okay," she grinned.

I pointed. "And do you wanna get out of those clothes?" My eyes widened when I realized how that question came out. "I didn't mean..."

Kamryn broke out in laughter. "It's okay. I know what you meant." She looked down at herself. "I don't really have any other clean clothes though."

"Well, you can't stay in wet clothes. You could borrow some of mine."

"You think they'd fit?"

My eyes trailed down her body, taking in her small frame. She was half my size. "Definitely not," I chuckled. Her mouth dropped into a light frown. "But I could give you the smallest clothes I have?"

Kamryn's mouth tugged upwards. "I'd really appreciate that."

I returned the smile and cocked my head towards my bedroom, prompting her to follow. "You know," I said as I picked through my dresser, "you probably shouldn't walk into strangers' apartments."

The tiniest chuckle sounded through her lips. "Why? Are you gonna kill me?"

"No," I replied, "but the next stranger might."

"Who said you were a stranger? I met you this morning."

I stopped rummaging through the drawer for a moment to shoot her a smile. "I'm not quite sure if twelve hours is a long enough time to consider someone to *not* be a stranger."

She shrugged. "Debatable."

"Didn't your parents ever teach you about stranger danger?" I joked.

Kamryn's smile instantly dropped, replaced with a heartbroken frown. "Yeah," she muttered quietly. "Yeah, they did."

Her sudden change in mood made me once again curious as to what her story was. I wanted to know why the mention of her parents made her so sad. Did they kick her out or something? Was that why she was living on the street?

Her frown caused my heart to turn somber, and my first reaction was to find a way to make her happy again. I wasn't sure why, but it felt like her feelings were contagious. Every time she smiled, it was nearly impossible not to. And every time she frowned, I could feel it in my chest.

"Do you like French toast?" I asked.

She tipped her head. "Yeah."

"Do you like bacon?"

"Yeah," she repeated, her frown coming up in the slightest.

"Do you like chocolate milk?"

Her mouth finally flipped the rest of the way, returning to a warm grin. "Love it."

"Then I know what we're having for dinner," I said, pulling out a t-shirt and the smallest pair of drawstring shorts that I had and handing them over.

"Thank you," she said as she took them. "I really owe you."

I shook my head. "You don't owe me anything."

I could pick out a small trace of a blush as she glanced down at her feet. "I know you've already done so much for me, but can I ask for one more thing?"

I eyed her in curiosity. "What is it?"

"Could I please use your shower?"

I nodded. "Of course."

***

I flipped the French toast over, listening to Kamryn humming a song in the shower. The sound brought a light smile to my lips. She'd already been in there for almost twenty minutes, but I didn't mind. I had no idea when the last time she got a shower was, but either way, I would've done the exact same thing if I was in her shoes.

The water finally turned off. Excitement wiggled through me. I was eager to have her out here by me, to be able to talk to her and see her face again.

"Decker?" her sweet voice called.

I turned, and when I caught sight of her peeking her head out of the bathroom, covering her body with a towel, I gulped.

Was it bad that I wanted the towel to accidentally fall?

I inhaled deeply, and when I reminded myself that I'd been staring at her for thirty seconds without responding to her, I rushed to speak. "Y—yeah?"

She covered her face with her hand. "I forgot the clothes in your room. Could you grab them for me?"

"Yeah, sure. One second," I said, tossing the finished French toast onto a plate. I turned the stove off and walked into my room, focusing on my pace so that I didn't seem so eager and awkward, even though I *was* eager and awkward.

The clothes were sitting on the edge of my bed, and as I walked over to the bathroom door with them, Kamryn held her hand out, reaching for the clothes. As I handed them over, I could feel her fingers lightly brush against mine.

There was a spark that flickered between our skin, so tangible that I was almost certain I could see it in the air.

A delicate smile lingered upon her lips, and I was tempted to ask if she felt it too. If she *saw* it too. But at a loss of words, I took a step backwards.

"Thank you," she murmured quietly before closing the door.

I blew out a long breath and stood there for another eighth of a second before forcing myself to head back into the kitchen. I planted my hands on the countertop and leaned into them, staring down at the granite as I tried to recover from whatever the hell that was.

I shook my head. "Chill out," I muttered to myself before putting together both of our plates. I put three pieces of French toast and three pieces of bacon onto each plate. Then, I began pouring glasses of chocolate milk just as Kamryn walked out of the bathroom.

Seeing her in my clothes made me do a double take, causing me to miss the second glass and send the chocolate milk streaming across the countertop.

40

"Damnit," I groaned. Kamryn's laughter echoed through the air. "Don't laugh at me," I smiled, grabbing a handful of paper towels.

"You're clumsy," she giggled. She reached over the counter and grabbed some paper towels to help me clean.

"Thanks," I said.

"Next time, you should probably watch where you pour it," she teased.

"I was distracted."

"By?"

I shook my head but couldn't contain my grin.

"*By?*" she repeated, raising a curious brow.

I mumbled my words so quietly and jumbled that it sounded like gibberish. "You walking out of the bathroom."

"Huh?" she chuckled. "English, please?"

My shoulders rose and fell as I took a deep breath. I glanced up at her, knowing that my smirk still hadn't disappeared. "You."

The same shade as pink cotton candy washed over her face and she broke eye contact with me. Her eyes roamed around and landed on one of the plates. "Is this for me?"

The fact that she felt the need to change the subject made me think she either felt embarrassed by my comment or she thought it was weird. The creep theory crawled back into my mind, but I ignored it.

"Yeah," I replied. I pushed one of the glasses of chocolate milk over to her.

"Thanks," she grinned. "I really, really appreciate this."

I kept my eyes on her, unable to stop watching her every move. "You're welcome."

I didn't have a dining area, just stools around the island in the center of the kitchen. She took a seat on one and I stayed standing directly across the island from her.

Thunder sounded from outside and I saw Kamryn jump in the slightest as she picked up her fork. I wondered how many times she'd been caught in a storm, forced to sleep in the rain. I internally cringed, remembering how cold and helpless she'd been when I found her outside.

We both fell silent. Thankfully, our silence was overtaken by the rain, but it didn't last more than a few bites before Kamryn spoke. "Tell me more about yourself."

"What would you like to know?"

"Well, I already know where you're from," she said, taking a bite of bacon. "But I don't want just surface level stuff. That kind of stuff is boring."

"Um," I thought, "I played baseball throughout high school?"

"I played softball." Her smirk reappeared. "But that's sorta surface level. Tell me something more interesting."

"Is this an interrogation?" I raised a joking brow.

"I'm just trying to not consider you as a stranger anymore."

"Hey," I pointed at her with a piece of bacon, "you already claimed I wasn't a stranger."

She bobbed her head side to side. "Maybe I was just trying to make myself feel better for willingly entering a man's apartment that I barely knew."

"Ouch," I grinned. I dropped my bacon and glanced back up at her. I'd only ever seen her hair in a messy braid, but since she just showered, it was down and straightened. She was focused on her food, and I used her distraction to study her face, every square inch of it. I'd only ever truly studied her eyes before, but now that I was looking closer at her other features, I noticed she had the cutest little button nose, resting in the center of her face. There were a few freckles underneath her eyes, just a few, so subtle that if I wasn't staring directly at them, I wouldn't have noticed them. My gaze dropped down to her full lips. And just as I began imagining what they tasted like, Kamryn looked back up at me.

I snapped my eyes upwards, hoping she didn't catch me in the act.

"Let's play a game," she said after swallowing a bite of French toast.

"What game?" I asked.

She shot me a devilish smirk. "Twenty questions."

Chapter Seven

Kamryn

Decker lifted a brow. "I don't even remember how to play that game."

I gave a small chuckle. "Honestly, neither do I."

He laughed, picking up his glass of chocolate milk and taking a long gulp of it.

I took the final bite of French toast that was on my plate and once I swallowed, I rubbed my full stomach under the island, grateful that Decker couldn't see. It felt so nice to have a belly full of food.

"Fine. We'll just ask each other some questions," I said.

"Okay," he nodded once. "You start."

"You don't have a girlfriend, right?"

One side of his mouth turned upwards. "I feel like some could consider that question as surface level, but no, I don't."

I ignored the first half of his response and only focused on his answer to the question. "Why not?" I asked quietly.

His brows crinkled, seemingly confused, as if the answer was obvious.

It wasn't obvious to me, though. He seemed like perfect boyfriend material. Sweet. Caring. Good sense of humor. *Pretty face.* And don't even get me started on what he probably looked like under that t-shirt.

Decker's amber eyes bore into me. "I could ask the same thing about you."

I gasped under my breath. *Good with words*, I added to the list. But I tilted my head with a smile, determined not to blush again. I raised a joking brow. "Probably because I collect my toenails in a jar."

He chuckled lightly, reaching over the island and retrieving my empty plate. "Good one." He turned towards the sink, and I watched in awe as his back muscles tightened in the slightest under his shirt while he cleaned the dish off and placed it in the dishwasher. My mouth was parted and as he swung back around, I snapped it shut. "Unless?"

"No, I don't actually do that!" I shook my head, laughing. "But to answer your question... I, uh, did have a boyfriend. A fiancé actually. But that ended, so..." I trailed off.

The look in Decker's eyes was a strange mixture of compassion and relief. "Can I ask what happened?"

I bobbed my knee up and down. "He..." I glanced down at the countertop, thinking about Ryan. My mind quickly played back our entire relationship, and I couldn't help but wonder how five years went down the drain. After going through so much together— from my parents' passing, finishing high school together, moving in together at eighteen, and getting engaged at nineteen, it felt like it was all for nothing. "He, uh," I spoke again, "well, I guess I sorta left." I shrugged.

Decker's face fell, his mouth parting open. "Why?"

I looked away from him as I spoke. There was absolutely no way in hell I could look him in the eye as I explained this. I didn't *want* to explain this, but I was also the one who insisted on getting deeper than surface level, so I guess I asked for it. "He knocked up another girl a few months ago and we called off the wedding."

Decker's face twisted into anger. His jaw twitched in the slightest. "That's messed up."

"I know."

"Well, fuck that guy," he said, straightening. "You deserve better than that."

"Thank you," I grinned lightly.

His expression turned playful again and right as he began speaking, the air in the room shifted back to its lighthearted vibe. "Aren't you a little too young to be getting married anyway?"

I couldn't hold my smirk back. "Aren't you a little too young to work at a law firm?"

He shook his head lightly, scrunching his face together. "I don't work there. I'm an intern."

"Paid intern," I corrected him. "I'd consider that a job. You even said this morning that you were going to *work*."

"Touché," he nodded.

We stared at each other as a short moment of silence passed. His fixated gaze caused a spark to travel from the tips of my fingers up to my shoulders and all the way down to the soles of my feet. I hadn't worn makeup in months, but there was something about his gaze that made me feel like I didn't need it. As if he was whispering compliments to me through his eyes.

The intensity subsided as I looked away. "It's your turn by the way."

"For?"

"To ask a question," I smiled.

"Okay, okay," he nodded. "Let me think of a good one." He pushed his lips into a hard line as he stared off in thought. A part of me wished his stare was resting on me again, but it gave me a chance to admire the side of his face. I swore his jawline had the ability to cut diamonds. I couldn't be sure though unless I touched it. *Which I wanted to do so damn badly.*

"Alright," he finally said, turning his attention back onto me. "I've got a good one that's not surface level."

"Let's hear it."

"If you could be anywhere in the world right now, where would you be?"

I raised my brows in surprise. Damn, that *was* a good one. "Um, I don't really know. I feel like everyone has a favorite place or even a person they would go to, but I don't have a place or a person that feels like home, so I guess I don't really have an answer."

Decker's brows wiggled and his voice turned soft. "Not even like your childhood home?"

"That depends," I said, once again avoiding eye contact with him. "Would my parents be alive or not?"

He froze, and I could physically see his chest stop expanding for a solid ten seconds. "Kam," he delicately said, shaking his head. "I'm so sorry. I—"

"It's okay, it's okay," I replied, looking down. But when I looked back up, Decker's eyes were apologetic. His sympathy was radiating off him, and by his utter silence, I could tell he was at a complete loss of how to make it better. "Just do something to make me smile," I quietly said.

He blinked at me a few times, letting my words soak in. "Okay," he nodded frantically. He swallowed a massive gulp of air. "Um... well first, is it okay if I call you Kam?"

"Yes," I giggled. I was amazed by how quickly he had the ability to change my mood. I was absolutely certain that I hadn't smiled or laughed this much in months.

Maybe even years.

Decker shot me a grin so subtle, yet so charming at the same time. "Are you tired, Kam?"

Every time he said my name, it sent a current of elation through me. I gave him a one-shoulder shrug. "Not really. Are you?"

"Well considering I napped for over four hours, no, not at all." He laughed, and once again, my laughter followed. "Guess we're gonna be up all night."

"Guess so," I smirked. "How will we keep ourselves occupied? We already played twenty questions."

"Played it horribly," he corrected me with a smile. "But there's a Marvel movie marathon on."

I could feel my entire face light up. "I love those movies."

"Me too. I'll turn them on." He made his way around the island and towards the living room. "Wanna grab some snacks?" he asked over his shoulder.

We'd just ate, but after going without food for so long, I didn't mind the thought of eating again. It was as if my stomach had turned into a bottomless pit over the past month. "Sure. Where are they?"

"Well unfortunately," Decker said, flipping through channels on the TV, "for how damn expensive this apartment is, it doesn't come with a pantry." I could spot his playful grin from across the room, causing another ripple to flow through me, but this ripple was different. Instead of just elation, this time, desire was added. "So, they're in the top two cabinets on the far side of the kitchen."

I forced myself to look away from his marvelous grin as I hopped off the stool. I opened the cabinets, scanning through the snacks. When my eyes landed on the same brown bag that I stared at earlier in Walmart, my entire body stiffened for the slightest moment. I reached up and right as I touched the bag, every muscle within me relaxed.

I pulled the bag out. "You like these?" I asked, staring at it.

"Love 'em," Decker said, placing the TV remote on the coffee table in the living room and strolling over to me. I couldn't take my eyes off the bag, as if staring at it would make my mother burst into the room and demand I share the candy with her.

But when I felt how close Decker was standing behind me— close enough to feel his body heat combine with mine, I held my breath. Held it just with the intent of having the ability to listen to his.

His hand slid onto my lower back as he scooted around me. "Sorry," he muttered.

"You're good," I murmured back, shifting over to get out of his way.

He grunted, clearing his throat. "You want popcorn?"

I blinked away the longing in my eyes. "Sure."

Chapter Eight
Decker

When my eyes flickered open, I was lying on the couch. I had the urge to get up and stretch, but I didn't move. Not a single inch.

Because Kamryn was *sprawled out on top of me.*

Her face was nuzzled against my chest, platinum blonde hair draped across me. I held my breath, afraid that breathing would wake her. But when my lungs started struggling, I gave in to the oxygen.

I slowly brought my arms up and around her, holding her to me since I was too much of a pussy to do it while she was awake.

She was still wearing my clothes, and I silently cursed myself because I told myself last night that I was going to throw all her clothes in the wash. Not that I minded her wearing my clothes. I didn't mind at all. I just figured she'd prefer her own clothes over mine.

Kamryn stirred, and I shut my eyes to pretend like I was sleeping, but I worried that the sporadic thumping of my heart would give me away.

She let out a tiny groan of exhaustion, and I used it as my excuse to slowly open my eyes.

"Oh," she whispered, looking up at me. "I'm sorry, did I wake you?"

I took a deep breath, relieved that she wasn't fazed by the fact that only two thin pieces of fabric separated our bare chests.

"No," I said. I cleared my throat, attempting to get rid of the raspy sound in my voice.

"Okay, good," she quietly said, dropping her head back onto my chest.

Yes, yes, yes, my mind reeled. *Wait— no no no. She's gonna hear my frantic heartbeat.*

She sighed, melting against me. "You're warm."

I chuckled lightly. "So are you. My own personal blanket."

We laid there in silence for a few minutes before Kam practically jumped off me. She rubbed her forehead. "I—I'm sorry. I'm sure you have a bunch of stuff to do today, and I already overstayed my welcome, and—"

I sat up. "Kam, you're fine. I have nothing to do today and if I didn't want you here, then I wouldn't have invited you in."

I wasn't sure where these thoughts of hers had come from, but it probably had to do with the idea she had in her head that the world was against her. I read it all over her face last night when we were talking. Her parents passed. She recently went through a messy breakup. She didn't mention having any other family or friends.

She was lonely. But I didn't think it occurred to her that even though I had more tangible things than her, that I was just as lonely.

Kamryn's face melted like an ice cube on a hot day. "Really?"

"Yes," I assured her.

"Well," she paused, sitting down next to me, "you're sure you're not busy today?"

"I'm sure," I nodded, giving her a fragile grin. I grabbed my phone off the coffee table and checked the time. "Damn. It's almost eleven already."

"Well, we did stay up until three-thirty," she said.

"True." I dropped my phone and turned to look at her. "Wanna go out for brunch?"

I stared at her lips as she tried to suppress a grin. A single laugh escaped out of her mouth. "Brunch?"

"You know..." I said, talking with my hands, "brunch. Breakfast-lunch."

"I know what brunch is," she smiled. Her blue eyes brightened for a moment before her face fell altogether. "But I don't have money." She shook her head.

I gave a shrug. "It's fine. I've got it."

When her face melted again, something inside of me melted with it. There was something so intoxicating about her smile that every time it disappeared, it caused a pang within my chest. As she took a deep breath, preparing to speak, I could feel my heartbeat accelerate again. I'd never been so scared to hear the word *no*.

"Decker, no..." she shook her head lightly. "You've already done so much for me. I can't let you do more."

All in the matter of ten seconds, at least a dozen things came to mind as to how I should convince her to go out with me. I'd never been a very flirtatious guy. I wasn't the super outgoing guy that walked up to the pretty girl at the bar and got her number. But if pretending to be that guy would persuade Kamryn to stick around for the day, then I was all for it.

"Okay, how about this," I said, focusing hard to ensure that my voice didn't shake as I spoke. "I'm assuming you only feel that way because you think friends shouldn't always pay for each other's stuff, right?"

She bobbed her head side to side. "Yeah, I guess."

"Then how about we make it a date?"

She stared at me quietly, and as silence overcame us for a few moments, I started to internally panic. *What was she thinking right now? Did I just ruin my chance?*

Just as I was about to accept that she was going to turn me down, her cheeks flushed lightly, and the corner of her mouth lifted in the slightest. She blinked rapidly as her gaze stayed on me. "A date?" she asked, her voice as soft as silk.

"Yeah," I nodded, my eyes glued to her.

Her smirk grew. "A date," she repeated. "Hmm, might have to think about it."

I could pick out the playfulness in her tone, and I couldn't help but smile in reaction. "Oh, really?"

She gave a light shrug. "I suppose I'll go on a date with you."

It was too easy to be playful with her. Too easy to get lost in our teasing or flirtation or whatever the hell this was. Even though being around her made me nervous as hell, I somehow never had to think about the next thing to say.

"Oh, you suppose?" I asked with one brow raised high, falling back against the couch. "Well, if you're gonna lie, then I'll lie too." Her face twisted into confusion, but her smirk never wavered. "I *don't* wanna go on a date with you."

She tipped her chin towards her chest. "How do you know I'm lying?"

I studied her baby blue eyes before sitting back up and leaning in so close that our breath was blending together. "I just know," I softly said.

She gulped, then sat up straighter, keeping her face close to mine. "Fine. I would like to go on a date with you."

I smiled. "Good. Because I know the perfect place for brunch."

Chapter Nine
Kamryn

Brunch.
Every time Decker said it, I couldn't help but giggle. There was something about a six-foot muscular man saying such a cutesy word that made me laugh.

I'd never gone on a date with anyone besides Ryan before, so I was doing my best to hide my nerves, but I could feel my heartbeat accelerating faster by the second as I got dressed.

Decker was nice enough to let me wash some of my clothes in his washer. Thank God, because there was no way I was wearing his huge t-shirt and drawstring shorts to *a date*, no matter how comfortable they were or how much I didn't give a shit about what other people thought about my appearance.

I cared about what Decker thought, though.

I always used to care about how I looked, especially in high school after my parents passed. After losing them and giving up softball, I didn't have much left to care for besides Ryan and my appearance. My hair was usually in a French braid, but I used to do my makeup a lot. I used to get dressed up a lot too. But ever since the only things on my mind became food and water, I didn't care about my appearance.

But going to a nice restaurant in a man's oversized clothing was still a no-no. Especially since Decker looked so nice.

In reality, he was only wearing a white t-shirt and blue jeans, but somehow, he made it look fancy.

I put on the only pair of jeans and the only decent shirt that I had— a plain black top.

Since the restaurant was only a few blocks away from Decker's apartment, we walked. When we got there, Decker jogged a few steps ahead of me, shooting me a smile as he opened the door for me.

"Wow," I smirked with a lifted brow as I walked through the door. "A gentleman."

"Well," he said as he followed inside, "gotta make a good impression."

You already have, I thought to myself, but there was no way I'd say that aloud. I was sure Decker knew I liked him, but I liked him so much that I didn't want to scare him off, and I was worried that if he knew every thought that went through my mind about him, that it really *would* scare him off.

The hostess led us to a table in the far corner of the restaurant. Decker and I scooted into our seats, sitting across from each other.

Our waitress was on top of everything, taking our order shortly after we sat down. Right after I handed her my menu and looked back at Decker, he was grinning wide.

"What?" I asked, trying to ignore the ball of jitters in my stomach.

"Nothing," he shook his head, breaking eye contact. His voice dropped a little. "I'm just glad you agreed to go out with me."

I was still in shock that he asked me to go out with him in the first place. I didn't think there were many guys that would jump at the opportunity of going out with a homeless girl.

"Well, I figured it would be a good way to get to know you better," I said.

Decker brought a brow upwards. His tone was nothing less than teasing. "Am I still a stranger? Even after last night?"

"I still don't even know how old you are."

He smiled. "I'm twenty-two. And you are?"

"Twenty," I answered, taking a sip of water. "Last name?"

"Shepley."

"Decker Shepley," I said.

"That's right," he grinned with a single nod.

"Middle name?"

He scrunched his face together.

"What? Not a fan of your middle name?"

"Eh, my parents could've done better."

I eyed him, lifting a brow.

He sighed. "It's Lincoln."

"That's not even bad," I shrugged. "Definitely could be worse."

"What's yours?" he asked.

"Elizabeth."

"Kamryn Elizabeth..."

"Arliss," I finished for him.

"Arliss?" he questioned, his voice cracking in the slightest as he stared off.

"What?"

"Nothing," he shook his head, shifting around in his seat.

When his eyes met mine again, I couldn't help but smirk, running a hand over my braid. "What's your zodiac sign?"

"My zodiac sign?" he said with a chuckle.

"Wait! Let me guess." I leaned forward. I eyed him while he eyed me, and I got so lost in studying him that I almost forgot what I was supposed to be doing. I had to glance away in order to clear my mind again. "Um," I started, "are you a Leo?"

He shook his head. "Not even close."

"Damn" I muttered.

"I'm a Capricorn."

"Damn!" I said louder. "I'm usually pretty good at guessing."

It was impossible not to notice the glimmer in his brown eyes as he smiled. "Alright, let me guess yours," he said, leaning across the table.

54

He reached over and touched my hand gently, causing my breath to hitch. He spoke slowly, lost in thought. "Either... a Capricorn or an Aquarius."

I leaned forward, matching him. "Neither."

"Shit," he said as he sat back in his seat. But thankfully, he kept his hand faintly touching mine. "What are you then?"

"Sagittarius."

"That would've been my next guess."

"Yeah, right," I laughed.

"You know," he said, "a lot of people say Capricorns and Sagittariuses have good compatibility."

There I was again— blushing. Goddamn that was like the third time in less than twenty-four hours. And the thing was, he didn't come across as a flirt, not intentionally at least. He didn't seem like the guy that had a long list of pickup lines in his back pocket. Didn't seem like the type to spit out whatever he could to impress a girl. He seemed calm, laid-back, and surprisingly a little shy sometimes. The type that got nervous to ask a girl on a date or to ask her to come into his apartment in the middle of a thunderstorm.

"Really?" I responded, raising a flirty brow. "Because I've heard otherwise."

His mouth pulled over to a sexy, inviting grin, and knowing that he definitely didn't do it on purpose only made it more attractive. "Guess we'll see about that."

Chapter Ten
Decker

After spending the entire day together, I was absolutely terrified.

Because I liked her *so damn much*.

I felt like it was obvious she was going to spend the night here again, but I didn't know how to ask. I wanted her to know she was welcome here and that she could sleep here for weeks on end if she wished, but my nerves were holding me back from telling her that. Because what if she didn't want to stay here? What if she didn't like me as much as I liked her?

All day long, I'd been forcing myself to be more outgoing and flirtatious, because I was constantly yearning to see her blush. I loved watching her mouth pull up into a shy smile. I loved the way her eyes gleamed like the ocean when she was content or laughing. Seeing her happy made me feel wholesome and it sure as hell was addicting.

We made pasta together for dinner. We took our time eating and doing the dishes, neither of our smiles disappearing while we did so.

Once we were done, I finally built up the courage to ask her if she wanted to stay the night. "Kam?" I spoke.

Her sweet eyes darted over to me. "Yeah?"

"Did you w—"

But I was interrupted by a knock on the door. My face fell and I sighed as I strolled over to answer it.

When I swung the door open, Nolan and Alaina were standing there, smiling at me.

"Hey, Decks!" Alaina said.

"Hey," I said. They both noted the displeased look on my face and their smiles dropped slightly.

"Is this a bad time?" Nolan asked, bringing his brows in.

I glanced over my shoulder at Kamryn. She was sitting on one of the stools in the kitchen, looking back and forth between the countertop and me.

When I turned back around, Alaina was peeking around me, trying to get a glimpse into the apartment. Her face lit up and she spoke quietly. "Do you have a girl here?"

I widened my eyes, trying to signal for them to keep their cool and not make a big deal about it. I gave a tiny nod.

"Oh my gosh," she whispered. "Can we meet her?"

I took in their eager expressions and let out a sigh, stepping to the side to allow them in. Kamryn did a double take, her face twisting into fear for just a moment before going back to her normal, friendly expression.

"Hi," Kamryn greeted them, hopping off the stool.

"Hi," Alaina said with a smile. She held her hand out and Kamryn shook it. "I'm Alaina."

"Kamryn." She turned to Nolan with her hand stretched and he gave her a warm smile as he shook it.

"Nolan."

"Kamryn," she repeated with a smile.

Sure, I was nervous for them to meet Kamryn, but I was more nervous for *Kamryn* to meet *them*. Because honestly, I didn't care about what anyone thought of Kamryn. I knew how I felt about her, and those feelings only grew each time I looked at her, which was scary considering we'd only officially known each other for a day and a half.

On the other hand, I did care what Kamryn thought about them. I didn't want her impression of them to affect her impression of me.

But I was fairly confident that I didn't need to worry too much about Nolan and Alaina. I was just glad it wasn't Benny that knocked on the door.

Alaina and Kamryn got to chit-chatting and even though I was standing in the kitchen talking to Nolan, I couldn't help but glance over at the girls every few minutes. Each time I did, they seemed to be smiling and laughing, so that was a good sign.

"Dude, calm down," Nolan said with a laugh. "I can tell you're freaking out. It's all over your face."

"Just a little," I said, peering over at the girls again.

He raised a brow as he leaned against the counter. "You must really like this girl."

I sighed. "I do."

"Well, I think we're gonna go to Westside tonight if you guys wanna come."

I cringed. "She's not twenty-one."

His eyes widened. "How old is she?"

"Twenty."

"Oh," he said, relieved. "I thought you were gonna say like seventeen or something." He chuckled.

"Definitely not." I let out a laugh.

Nolan stared off in thought for a moment before his entire face lit up in realization. "It's Saturday, right?"

"Yeah."

"We can totally get her in. We'll know the bouncer that's working tonight."

My brows wiggled. "Who?"

"Tommy Pry."

The second that name came out of his mouth, my brows shot straight up, and I belted out a laugh. "You mean Tommy 'Pries-into-everyone's-business' Tommy Pry? Like from high school?"

Nolan gave a slow nod. "That's the one."

"You really think he's gonna do *me* a favor?" I asked skeptically.

Nolan shrugged. "Worth a shot, right?"

I looked over at Kamryn again. She was still smiling, caught up in a conversation with Alaina. I felt like it would be good for Kamryn to make some new friends, and since the girls seemed to be getting along, it might make Kam more likely to stick around tonight if she knew we would be spending it with Nolan and Alaina.

"Alright," I said, turning back to Nolan. "I'll ask her if she would wanna go."

"Cool," Nolan said with a friendly smile. He checked the time on his watch. "It's a little past six. Alaina and I were on our way to dinner when we stopped over. Do you wanna meet up around nine and head to Westside together?"

"I'll talk to Kam first and text you guys?"

"Okay," he nodded. "That works."

Nolan and Alaina said their goodbyes for now, and I was a little appeased when Kamryn seemed upset about their departure.

She had a long frown on her face as I walked over. Our hands once again brushed against each other lightly, causing another trail of electricity to ripple between our skin.

Kam's eyes shot up to look at me, filled with a mixture of satisfaction and passion. My heartbeat paused for just a second before picking up with intensity. I had no more doubts that she felt the connection between us. Something in her eyes whispered that not only did she feel it, but that she *liked* it.

"Um," I started, scratching the back of my head, "Nolan and Alaina are going out tonight and asked if we'd wanna go with."

A pleased expression surfaced on her face, and she smiled lightly. "Really?" she asked, as if she couldn't believe anyone wanted to spend more time with her.

"Yeah. Would you wanna go?"

"Sure," she nodded rapidly. "Where are we going?"

"There's a bar down the street that we usually go to."

Her shoulders slumped as her smile disappeared. "You know I'm not twenty-one."

"It's alright," I assured her. "We know the bouncer."

She tipped her head at me doubtfully. "And he'll let me in?"

"Yeah."

"You're sure? I just don't wanna get in trouble for trying to sneak into a bar," she said with a chuckle.

"Yeah," I gave a nod. "I'll make sure you get in just fine."

"Okay," she murmured, her smile reappearing.

And just from that sight alone, my butterflies reappeared with it.

Chapter Eleven
Kamryn

When Alaina brought over an entire bag of clothes to let me choose from to borrow, I was overwhelmed with gratitude.

Decker's kindness and open arms had been such a breath of fresh air over the past few days, not to mention the relief it was to not be constantly worrying about when my next meal would be. But now that I'd made a new girlfriend, I was even more excited than before.

I'd only ever had one close girlfriend before. Arianna and I were close throughout middle school and high school. I considered her my best friend and she considered me hers, but she absolutely hated Ryan. Looking back on it, she had been a great judge of character, but at the time, I was wedged between a rock and a hard place because the two of them always made me feel the need to choose between them.

I hadn't spoken to Arianna in a little over a year. We'd gotten into an argument after I got engaged and hadn't spoken since. I considered trying to contact her after leaving Ryan, but not only was I unsure of where she was now, I knew it would've looked terrible for me to show up on her doorstep after everything. I didn't want the whole "I told you so" spiel, and plus, I didn't think there was any way to fix our friendship after what we'd said to each other. After all, there was no taking back poison once it's been spewed.

The guys were hanging out in the living room while Alaina and I got ready together in the bathroom.

"Here, here, here!" she exclaimed with excitement.

"What?" I giggled, picking through her clothes.

She pulled a makeup bag out of her backpack. "We can do your makeup."

I let out a tiny gasp in excitement. "I haven't done my makeup in so long."

"Well, now's the perfect time," Alaina smirked. "Do you want to do it, or do you want me to?"

I gave a sheepish look. "Can I?"

"Of course!" she broke into a smile. "We have about the same skin tone, so all this stuff should work on you."

"Thank you," I smiled as she handed the bag over.

"You're welcome," she said softly, her friendly smile never fading. She studied me in the mirror, her brows coming in in the slightest as she tilted her head towards her shoulder. "What was your last name again?"

"Arliss," I replied.

"Arliss..." she repeated. "Hmm... I feel like I've heard that name before."

I gave a tiny shrug. "Maybe from high school?"

"What did you do during high school?"

"I played softball."

Her mouth dropped open. "Me too!" Alaina cheered. She swiped her hand through the air, waving it off. "That's probably where I've heard your name."

I gave her a light chuckle. "Probably. We used to play against you guys all the time."

"Yeah," she said. "You guys were always better though." I laughed as she pulled the toilet seat down and took a seat on it, rummaging through the bag of clothes at her feet. "Did you find anything you liked in here?"

I spoke as I began applying concealer, pleased that it matched my skin tone. "I didn't look through it all yet, but I really like the black top in there."

She poked around in the bag and pulled out the top I was referring to. "This one?"

"Yep!"

"I feel like this will look really good on you."

"Thanks." I turned and gave her a grateful smile.

"Yeah, for sure," she smiled back. "Now hurry up and get ready so we can take some pictures!"

***

One makeover and a lot of bathroom selfies later, Alaina and I finally stepped out of the bathroom. Immediately, Decker's and my eyes locked, and I watched as a teeny tiny grin tugged at the corners of his lips.

Alaina headed straight over to Nolan, and he welcomed her with open arms and a smile before gently kissing the top of her head.

They were such a cute couple. They were the type of couple where you could physically see their love for each other linger throughout the air.

I forced myself to look away from their adorable display of affection as I walked over to Decker.

The black top I was wearing was short sleeved and crossed over in the front and the dark blue jeans I was wearing were skin-tight.

His shoulders rose and fell with a deep breath as his eyes glanced me over. "You look incredible."

I couldn't suppress the blush and grin that overcame my face. I inhaled deeply through my nose as my eyes trailed down his body. "You too," I quietly muttered, just loud enough for him to hear.

We eyed each other for a moment until Nolan's voice caused us to break our stare.

"Ready to go?" he asked the group.

Everyone nodded and a swarm of gratification traveled through me as we made our way out the door.

***

I stayed close to Decker as we walked towards the bouncer. I could feel the jitters inside of me about to burst out, my nerves threatening to get the best of me. I knew I needed to calm down or I'd look out of place.

Decker could sense my tenseness. Without looking at me, he grabbed my hand and laced our fingers together.

Somehow, his skin was enough to slow my heartbeat down, which I thought was odd considering that every time we had touched prior to right now, it was always the reason for the *acceleration* of my heartbeat.

I guess his touch just had control of my heart, period.

Nolan and Alaina walked in front of us and the second the bouncer caught sight of them, he shot them a friendly smile.

"Well, well, well, look who we've got here," the bouncer said.

Nolan gave him a nod. "Tommy."

The bouncer looked back and forth between Nolan and Alaina. "You two are still together?"

"Going on five years," Alaina smirked, reaching for Nolan's hand.

He happily accepted her gesture, giving her a warm grin before turning back towards Tommy.

"Are we good to go in?" Nolan asked.

Tommy shrugged. "Yeah, you two are good."

Nolan and Alaina made their way past him, and as Tommy's gaze shifted over to us, his eyes hardened, zeroing in on Decker.

"Shepley," he said flatly.

"Pry," Decker said, lifting a brow lightly.

"You're at a bar?"

"Well, I am twenty-two," Decker responded.

Tommy's eyes flickered over to me. His hard gaze diminished as one side of his mouth lifted. "Did you go to high school with us? I don't remember you."

I shook my head. "I went to Parkersville."

Tommy nodded. "Do you have an ID on you?"

I broke eye contact with him as Decker leaned forward. "Just let her in, Pry." But by the tone of his voice, it sounded more like a warning than a request.

Tommy studied Decker, his face as hard as stone. His eyes slowly made their way back over to me. He glanced me up and down, stopping for a moment too long on my chest before returning to my face.

"Fine," Tommy said. "You better not cause problems though, Shepley."

Decker ignored his comment as his hand rested on my lower back, guiding me inside. I let out a deep breath as he led me up to the bar.

"That was a close one," I said.

Decker gave me a coy grin. "Told you that you wouldn't have a problem getting in."

I wiggled a single brow. "I barely got in."

"Well, you're in now," he said, sitting down at the bar and motioning to the stool beside him. I took a seat. "Do you want something to drink?" he asked.

I pulled my mouth over to one side. "Um, I don't really know what to order. I've never been to a bar."

He faced me, positioning himself so that our knees were touching. "Well, what do you usually drink?"

"I don't drink often," I admitted.

"So, you're a lightweight?" he teased with a smile.

"Probably," I giggled. "But I'm pretty sure I've only ever had like seltzers and wine before."

"So, do you like sweet drinks, then?" he asked.

I gave a one-shoulder shrug. "Yeah, I guess so."

He nodded before turning back towards the bar and waving down a bartender. I zoned out while he ordered our drinks, twisting around in my seat as I took in the scene.

Nolan and Alaina were off in the corner, dancing. The bar was packed and there was a small stage on the opposite side of the room where a local band was playing.

"Kam," Decker said, causing my head to snap back over to him. He pushed a glass towards me.

"Thank you," I smiled, looking down at it. The drink was a light-yellow color, and my brows creased in the slightest. "What is it?" I asked curiously.

"Vodka sour."

"What's that?"

His grin expanded, and under the harsh bar lights, I could easily make out the glimmer in his eyes. "It's vodka with some sour juice they use. It's what Alaina gets sometimes. She says it tastes like candy."

I grinned at him thankfully, pulling the glass closer to me. "Sorry I'm clueless."

He chuckled. "Don't be. I kinda like it."

I stuck the tiny straw in my mouth, hoping that it would somehow take away the light burn in my cheeks. The drink did taste like candy, and I found myself taking a few long sips. "It's good," I nodded. "What did you order?"

He held up a bottle. "Just beer."

"I've never had beer."

"Wanna try it?" he offered.

"Sure." I brought it up to my lips and took a small, experimental sip. My face screwed into disgust as I handed it back.

"Don't like it?" he said with a laugh.

"No," I shook my head, scrunching my face together. "I'll stick with my candy drink." He grinned as he took another swig.

"Guys!" Alaina shouted, running over to us. "Come dance!"

Decker frowned. "You know I'm a terrible dancer."

"So am I," I added. I lifted a flirty brow, shooting Decker a challenging smirk as I hopped off the bar stool, drink in hand. "But I'm gonna dance anyways."

"Yay!" Alaina shrieked.

I took a few steps before turning back around. "You coming?"

Decker eyed me, his beguiling smirk never disappearing. But as Nolan approached, Decker's attention shifted onto him. He glanced back at me quickly. "I'll be there in just a bit, I promise!" he shouted to me.

I gave him a nod as I followed Alaina the rest of the way to the dance floor. At first, I was a little embarrassed to dance in front of so many random people, given that I could not dance for my life. But Alaina was jolting her body around, clearly not giving a damn that she looked ridiculous, which helped me let loose.

I sipped on my drink as we shimmied around. For the first time in months, I felt so free. To go from having no one to having three new friends was not only fulfilling, but it was a blessing. Even though I was dancing in a bar, somewhere I was legally not supposed to be, I still somehow felt like I belonged.

Alaina pointed towards my glass. "What are you drinking?"

I shrugged. "Decker said it was a vodka-something."

She brought her brows inwards. "A vodka sour?"

I nodded. "Yes, that!"

Her mouth dropped open. "Me too!" she squealed.

I smiled wide as we clinked our glasses together and brought them to our mouths.

Within another five minutes, our drinks were gone, and although it wasn't my first time drinking alcohol, I definitely *was* a lightweight.

I hadn't had a drink in over six months, but my tolerance hadn't been high to begin with.

Alaina sipped on her drink until all that was coming through her straw was air. She frowned at the empty glass. "Do you wanna go get another drink?" she asked over the music.

I turned, glancing in the direction of the bar and spotting Nolan and Decker, still chatting. I was slightly bummed that Decker hadn't come over to dance with us. The idea of being near him was so damn tempting, and the alcohol running through my bloodstream only amplified the temptation.

"Sure," I finally answered.

She smiled, cocking her head towards the bar. I began following her, and when she suddenly stopped and faced me, the straightened look on her face made me a little worried.

"Actually," she spoke, "do you wanna take a shot?"

My eyes widened. "A shot? I've never taken one before."

"You'll either love it or hate it."

As we approached the guys, their conversation seemed to come to a halt. They both looked at us, and Decker's smile grew as we got closer.

Right when we were in arms reach, his arm snaked around my waist and he pulled me in, holding me beside him. I couldn't suppress the pleased grin that was threatening to break my face in half. His arms were so warm, so comfortable. It felt normal to be this close to him even though we'd only known each other for a few days.

"Finished your drink already?" Decker asked.

"Yeah," I said sheepishly.

"Do you want another one?"

I studied his kind eyes as I responded. "Alaina wants to take shots."

"Shots, shots, shots!" Alaina shouted. "Nolan will be taking one with us and Decker..." she trailed off, looking over at him.

"Do you wanna take one with us?" I asked innocently, resting a hand on his thigh.

His eyes dropped down to my hand. When he looked back up at me, there was a peculiar gleam in his eye. It almost looked like a strange mixture of an apology and lust.

His mouth formed a hard line. "I don't really drink hard liquor."

"Oh c'mon," I melted into him. "Are you sure?"

He broke eye contact with me, glancing back down at my hand and covering it with his free one. "Yeah, it just... makes me feel sick."

"Oh, okay," I shrugged.

"So, I'll order three lemon drops, then?" Alaina asked.

"I don't know what that is, but sure!" I said in excitement.

Alaina ordered the shots and within a few minutes, one was in my hand. There was a tiny ball of nerves sitting in the center of my stomach as I held it, staring at it. I'd never taken a shot before, but I heard they tasted terrible. Knowing that Alaina had a similar taste in drinks as me made me slightly more reassured that whatever this was wouldn't be awful.

Alaina and Nolan raised their shots, prompting me to do the same. The second the glasses touched, we each brought them to our mouths, and I squeezed my eyes shut as I let the liquid fall down my throat.

My brows crunched together as I stepped over and set the empty shot glass on the bar.

"Did you like it?" Alaina asked.

"I think so."

"You *think* so?" she laughed.

I smirked. "I might need another one to make sure."

Her eyes widened. "Another one?"

"We can wait a bit," I said.

"Okay good," Alaina nodded. She leaned towards me. "Because I'm already feelin' it a little."

My head fell back as I let out a laugh, grabbing Alaina's hand and tugging her back to the dance floor.

Chapter Twelve
Decker

I was watching her closely.

I wasn't doing it to be creepy or anything. We all knew I wanted to avoid the creep theory at all costs. But I was watching because I knew *other* people were watching.

Besides the fact that I was on high alert for some guy to try to pull something on Kamryn, I also couldn't look away from her massive smile. It was impossible not to notice how much fun she was having. Just the sight itself made me satisfied.

The first few times I ever saw her, before I was even bringing her food, she looked so miserable. With dirt upon her skin and sadness in her eyes, I never would've guessed that that was the same Kamryn who was living it up on the dance floor.

I spoke to Nolan without taking my eyes off Kam. "I just wanna say thank you guys for tonight. From what I know so far, Kam hasn't had it easy, and it really looks like she's having fun tonight, so thanks."

Nolan gave me a friendly pat on the shoulder. "No problem, man. I'm glad the girls are getting along so well."

"Same," I said. "I'll have to thank Alaina too when I get the chance."

"I feel like we should go join them."

"Probably," I agreed, setting my empty beer on the bar. "I'm gonna take a leak and then I'll meet you guys out there."

Nolan nodded, walking towards the girls while I headed to the bathroom.

I stepped up to the urinal and started to go, and the second Pry appeared next to me, doing the same, I sighed to myself.

"Shepley," he acknowledged me, staring straight ahead.

"Pry," I said flatly.

A moment passed before he spoke again. "So, who's the girl?"

I responded as I zipped my pants back up. "None of your business." I turned towards him, my tone warning. "And stop eyeing her. She's not a piece of candy. Especially not for *you*."

I didn't give him the chance to respond, just stepped over to the sink and began washing my hands. By the time I was drying my hands, he was once again next to me.

I could feel his eyes on me, and even though I was far from being drunk, the beer definitely wasn't helping to slow the temptation of punching him.

"I was just asking out of curiosity," he muttered.

"Sure you were," I nodded. I gave him a hard glare. "I mean it, Pry. Stay away from her."

"Or what?" he dared.

"Or I'll beat your ass just like I did in high school." I turned on my heels and shoved open the bathroom door.

Agitation circled through me as I walked towards the dance floor, but right when Kam came into view, all the annoyance left my body.

I stood behind her, but slightly off to the side. I didn't even have to think about it before my arm looped around her waist.

She jumped with a startled look on her face, but when she turned to see me, her body relaxed, and her mouth swiveled up into a smile.

I leaned in, placing my mouth close enough to her ear so that she could hear me over the music. "Are you having fun?"

She nodded rapidly. "Yes!" Her face melted, and under the soft touch of my hand, I could feel her body melt along with it. "Thank you so much for bringing me. Thank you for everything, really."

I brought my lips to the fragile skin of her temple and placed a light kiss. "You're welcome."

She looked at me under her long lashes, her bright blue eyes piercing through me. "Dance with me?" she requested.

"Fine," I smiled. "But I can't dance, so if I accidentally step on your toes, don't be mad."

Kam giggled. She turned towards me and grabbed my hands, clearly having no idea what she was doing, which made me more comfortable since I had no idea either.

I began spinning her around, and somehow, it felt like everything around us disappeared for a moment. As if I wasn't who I knew I was— wasn't anything or anyone other than the person *she* saw me as.

And it sure as hell felt good.

We danced for a few songs before Alaina tugged on my arm.

"What?" I asked sharply, but when I glanced over to see the nervous look on her face, my hardened expression faded. "What?" I asked again, softer this time.

Her eyes darted around the bar. "I could've sworn I saw Benny and Myra."

I raised my brows, keeping my hands on Kam's waist as she swayed side to side. I was just glad she was so occupied by the music that she wasn't listening to Alaina's and my conversation.

"Are you sure?" I asked Alaina.

"Pretty sure," she said.

"Well hopefully they don't—"

"Decks!" Benny's voice called.

I dropped my head and let out a sigh as I turned over my shoulder, keeping one hand planted on Kam's waist.

"Hey," I said, not at all surprised to see him standing right behind me.

Kam finally noticed that one of my hands was missing. She stopped dancing and looked around with confused eyes as Benny's gaze shot past me and straight onto her.

He nodded once. "Who's this?"

"Kamryn," I responded.

Kam leaned forward and held her hand out as she gave a kind smile. "Kamryn," she repeated.

Benny's dazed expression twisted into a friendly grin. "I'm Benny," he said, shaking her hand.

"Nice to meet you. Are you another friend of Decker's?"

"Yeah!" he shouted over the music. "Since first grade!"

Her eyes widened a bit. "Oh, wow! Very long time."

"Yep," he grinned, patting me on the back. "Hey, uh, Myra's here too."

I tilted my head at him, studying the culpable look in his eye. "Did you follow us here?"

He gave a single chuckle. "No, of course not!" he said, swiping his hand through the air as if the idea was ridiculous. "We just checked Nolan and Alaina's location."

I rolled my eyes. "Of course."

Benny shrugged. "We didn't know *you'd* be here. Be careful though."

"Why?"

"I mean... Myra asked you to hang out this weekend and you turned her down. If she sees you here with another girl, she might get upset."

Shit.

I immediately felt like an asshole for rejecting Myra and then taking a different girl out instead, but in all honesty, I'd completely forgotten she asked me in the first place. I'd been so distracted by Kamryn that it completely slipped my mind.

The worst part was that Myra had been so nice about it on Thursday that I just felt like more of an asshole. She was my friend, and it would've been wrong to try to hide from her all night. I knew the right thing would be to say hello, but I didn't want her to catch sight of Kamryn and get her feelings hurt.

But before I could figure out what to do, Myra appeared next to Benny.

Too late.

"Hey," she said, disappointment thick in her voice and clear on her face.

Kamryn's friendly smile never faded as she shifted her attention onto Myra. "Hello! Are you also a friend of Decker's?"

Myra eyed me for a moment, but what made it worse was that her eyes were full of anguish rather than anger. The second her eyes fell onto Kamryn, and she caught sight of Kam's contagious smile, Myra couldn't help but smile back.

"Yeah," Myra said. She stuck her hand out. "I'm Myra. It's nice to meet you."

Kam gladly shook her hand. "You too. I'm Kamryn."

The tension started to subside, and I was able to relax when all six of us began dancing with no issues. I'd admit that I still felt a little awkward dancing between the girl I was crushing hard on and the girl I used to hook up with. But Kamryn didn't seem to suspect that anything happened between Myra and me in the past, which made me relieved.

I still felt bad, though. About *both* of them.

Even though I hadn't actually lied to Kam, it somehow felt like I was lying. Myra and I had never been anything besides hook-up buddies in the past, but was I supposed to tell Kamryn that?

And on the other hand, I felt bad for Myra for obvious reasons. Thankfully though, it seemed like her mood had flipped around. For a while at least.

When I saw Myra stalk towards the bar by herself, I sighed under my breath and figured that I should take the opportunity to at least apologize.

I grabbed Kam's hand, my thumb lightly brushing over it as I leaned forward. "I'll be right back, okay?"

"Okay!" she nodded.

I darted in and out of people until I spotted Myra at the bar. I took a deep breath through my nose as I walked up and stood next to her. I could tell she knew I was there by the side eye she gave me, but she refused to meet my gaze.

"Myra," I said gently.

"Yes?" she said, staring forward.

"Well for starters, I'm sorry. I know it's shitty that I told you no and then came out with someone else."

Her brows came inwards as her head jerked over to look at me, but what caught me so off guard was how soft her voice came out. "Decker," she started, lightly shaking her head, "it wasn't that you came here with another girl. It's that you *lied* to me about it."

I brought my hands up in front of me. "In all honesty, I didn't have these plans until a couple hours ago."

She sighed, looking down. "You could've just told me that you were talking to someone else."

I nodded lightly. "I could've... but I didn't meet her until yesterday," I admitted.

Myra tilted her head towards her shoulder in doubt. "Actually?"

"Yes," I nodded firmly.

She studied me for a moment, and when she finally decided I was telling the truth, she brought a hand up and dropped it down onto the bar, letting out a light chuckle. "I can't even stay mad at you."

I laughed. "Good," I said. "I don't like when my friends are mad at me."

The corners of her mouth lifted into the tiniest of smiles. "She seems very sweet."

"She is," I agreed. "At least so far."

Both of us chuckled and as a bartender approached, Myra shot me one last smile. "You should probably get back to your date."

The remorse that I'd been feeling finally fell off my shoulders. "Thank you for being so understanding."

Her warmhearted expression never faded. "You're welcome, Decks."

I gave her one last nod and with that, I walked off, heading straight to the person that I wanted to see most.

Chapter Thirteen
Kamryn

It was getting late, but I wasn't tired at all. The alcohol, the excitement, and the music were keeping me going.

All the boys were once again seated at the bar while Myra, Alaina, and I were still lighting up the dance floor. As much as I wanted to be by Decker every damn second, I was having just as much fun with the girls.

"I'm sweating," Alaina said, out of breath as she swayed side to side.

"Me too," I said. Myra nodded beside me in agreement.

"Do you guys wanna sit down for a few?" Alaina asked.

Both Myra and I nodded rapidly, following Alaina over to the nearest table. But right as we all sat down, Alaina sprang right back up.

"Actually, I'm about to piss my brains out. I'll be right back." She strode off before either of us could respond.

Myra let out a laugh, lightly shaking her head. "She is something special."

"Yeah, she is," I laughed in agreement.

It fell silent between us and just as I was about to make conversation by asking her how she knew everyone, she pretty much beat me to it.

"So, Decker mentioned that you guys recently met?" she said kindly.

"Yeah," I said with a light grin. "We just met like... a day ago." I looked down at the table as a blush overcame my face. I could feel the warmth of the blood circling around in my cheeks, and I couldn't help but wonder how Decker's name itself had this effect on me. God, I mean, I literally met him *yesterday.* Or I supposed that it was two days ago now if it was currently past midnight.

When I glanced up at Myra, a strange sense of nerves began rising in my gut. I could feel the jealousy lingering through the air like cigarette smoke, but for some reason, I didn't feel the need to worry about it. I wasn't sure what it was about Myra that made me so cautious yet settled at the same time. It was a strange feeling that I'd never encountered before, but nonetheless, her friendly smile still hadn't wavered.

Her voice was full of genuine curiosity, coming out so soft that if I wasn't giving her every ounce of my attention, I definitely wouldn't have heard it. "How'd you guys meet?" she asked.

I didn't want to explain it to her, given that I didn't know her at all and wasn't completely sure what her intentions were, but when I looked directly at her and saw nothing on her face besides courtesy, I didn't feel right lying.

So, I did what I always did when telling someone something that I didn't want to. *I looked away.*

"Um..." I started, "I didn't have anywhere to go, and... I was staying outside Decker's apartment, and... he invited me inside the other night during the storm."

My eyes carefully shifted back onto Myra, expecting to see some sort of resentment, yet her face showed anything but. She smiled delicately before leaving forward a bit. "Decker is a really great guy," she said with a nod.

"Yeah," I agreed. "I mean, I don't know him super well yet, but he's been very welcoming and I'm grateful for that."

Myra tilted her head in the slightest. "He really likes you."

"Really?" I asked, leaning forward to match her. "Did he tell you that?"

She nodded firmly. "He did."

I nervously rubbed my thighs underneath the table. "That makes me nervous," I admitted.

"Why?" she chuckled.

"I don't know," I said, shaking my head.

She shrugged. "Just be yourself. That's why he likes you in the first place."

I didn't get the chance to respond before Alaina plopped down next to me.

"Phew," she shook her head. "For a second I didn't think I'd make it to the bathroom. My bladder was about to explode."

I laughed. "I surprisingly haven't had to go yet."

"I've already gone three times," Myra said.

Laughter filled our table, but the laughter came to a halt when Benny appeared.

"Hey," he greeted us before turning to Myra. "Are you ready to go? It's getting late. I'll walk you home."

"Oh," she said, taken off guard.

"What time is it?" I quietly asked.

"A little past one," Benny replied.

"Damn," I muttered under my breath. I hadn't realized how late it was.

I swiveled around in my seat, looking for Decker. Even though the bar was finally starting to clear out a little bit, it was still full enough to make it difficult to spot him.

Each moment that passed made me more and more nervous to find him because I didn't know what was supposed to happen now. Was he going to let me sleep at his apartment again? Was I supposed to go back to my wretched corner?

Alaina's voice snapped me back to reality. "Well, get home safe, guys!"

"You too," Myra said, giving Alaina a hug. The second she let go, Myra stepped over to me and leaned down, wrapping her arms around me. I stiffened for a moment, taken off guard before I did the same. I hoped she didn't notice my hesitation, but even if she did, she didn't seem to react to it.

"It was nice meeting you guys," I said as she pulled away. Myra gave me a smile as Benny nodded.

"You too," they said in unison, turning on their heels and walking out in sync.

Alaina sighed. "Nolan will probably want to go soon."

I nodded slowly, staring off. My head was reeling, jumping through every way that tonight could end. When the thought of finally seeing what was under that damn shirt of Decker's popped into my mind, my hands started to shake.

All at once, my thoughts came to a stop, and I zipped over to face Alaina. "Can I ask you something?"

I seemed to catch all of her attention, because her drunken eyes zoned in on me. "Sure," she said.

"Can we take another shot?"

She chuckled, standing. "Absolutely."

***

Another hour passed, and Nolan and Alaina had already left. The bar had cleared out a significant amount, and even though I was pretty sure they'd be closing shortly, Decker didn't seem to notice.

Because all his attention was on me.

"I'm sorry that I wasn't by you more tonight," Decker said as we sat at the bar. "You just seemed like you were having a lot of fun with the girls, so I wanted to give you some distance."

I shook my head. "That's okay. I appreciate that."

Decker's eyes never left my face as he reached for my hand and carefully picked it up. I wondered what he was doing, but I couldn't ask. My breathing had escalated to an unhealthy amount, and I couldn't seem to drag in enough air to speak.

He brought my hand up to his mouth and ever so softly touched his lips to my skin. I swallowed, absorbing how his lips felt softer than rose petals. But the second we parted, and he delicately placed my hand back onto the bar, a small hole formed in the center of my chest from immediately missing his touch.

"I hope you had a good night," he said.

I opened my mouth to respond, but at first, nothing came out. I dug my nails into my thigh to snap me out of my trance. "Yeah," I assured him. "I had a great night."

"Good," he said, sipping his beer.

I finally regained my composure, feeling as though my soul had been pushed back into my body. "Can I ask you something?" I blurted out.

He kept his eyes on me as he set his beer down. "Of course. What is it?"

For a second, I regretted speaking in the first place, but my mind had been finding its way back to the question for hours now.

"What's up with Myra?"

Decker's body noticeably froze as he blinked at me with a startled expression. "What do you mean? Did she say something to you?"

I anxiously swiveled around on the bar stool. "Not exactly. I mean... sorta." I shrugged.

"Sorta?"

"She seemed very interested in hearing about how we met."

Decker nodded as he inhaled deeply, filling his lungs with enough air for an army of people. "Okay."

I raised a brow, becoming more anxious, which I didn't think was even possible. "Okay?"

Decker stared past my shoulder. "Okay," he repeated, finally looking back at me. "I'm just gonna tell you the truth."

My heart began thumping so sporadically that I was convinced there was a jackhammer inside my chest. I blinked rapidly at Decker, impatiently waiting for whatever explanation he was about to give.

"Apparently she likes me," Decker said in a shaky voice, avoiding eye contact with me. "And we have hooked up in the past, but that was months ago."

"Hooked up as in..." I paused, peering at him aimlessly. "As in sex?"

His chest was expanding extensively. "Yeah," he admitted. "It only ever happened a few times, but it hasn't happened in like three months."

I bit the inside of my cheek so hard that I thought it might start bleeding. Myra had been so sweet all night that I'd *almost* convinced myself that the jealousy drifting through the air was just part of my imagination. *Almost.*

But now that I knew I read it right, I wasn't sure what to think of Myra. Even though she was jealous, she hadn't been treating me with disrespect. She seemed so genuine that it made it hard to be mad at her.

And that was the biggest issue. *I didn't have a reason to be mad at her.*

Decker wasn't mine. I met him like thirty-six hours ago. And even though I had a fat crush on him already, it would've been ridiculous to be jealous.

Even though I was jealous. Because Myra had seen exactly what was under that shirt.

"Are you mad?" Decker asked. Then he suddenly shook his head back and forth. "I swear I didn't know that her and Benny were going to show up tonight."

"I'm not mad," I said, but quite honestly, I couldn't even decide if it was a lie or not. I didn't have the right to be mad at Decker when we weren't together. Just because we went on one date *yesterday* didn't mean we were a couple. Even if we had been a couple, I couldn't be mad at him for things that happened before he met me.

"Really?" he asked, relieved.

"Yeah. Why would I be mad?"

"I don't know," he softly said, running his tongue over his lips quickly. "She... wasn't being mean to you or anything though, right?"

"No," I shook my head. "She was really nice, actually."

Decker let out another sigh of relief. "Good," he grinned. He patted me on the leg. "I'm gonna run to the bathroom really quick. I'll be right back."

"Okay," I said as he connected his lips to the side of my head before dashing to the bathroom.

Seconds after Decker was out of sight, a man sat down beside me. I could see him looking at me out of the corner of my eye. The stranger's glare made me shift around uneasily, but when he spoke, I immediately recognized his voice.

"So, what's a nice girl like you doing with Shepley?" the bouncer asked curiously.

I tipped my head towards my shoulder, just enough to look back at him. He was eyeing me sharply, waiting for an

answer, but I couldn't shake off the feeling of needing to defend
Decker.

"What's your problem with him?" I asked.

"I just don't think he's the best guy."

I sat up straight. "Whatever you think you know about
him, you're wrong."

"Maybe," he shrugged. His stare became harder. "I
guess either *I* don't know enough about him, or *you* don't."
With that, he shot me a charismatic smile before hopping off
his stool and walking off.

What a weird way to end a conversation. What a weird
way to *start* a conversation in the first place. My brows crinkled
inwards, but I shook it off as Decker approached.

His eyes were fixated on the bouncer across the room,
staring him down with fire behind his eyes. He nodded once.
"What did Pry want?" he asked.

"Pry?"

"That's his last name."

"Suits him well," I murmured.

Decker glanced back and forth between the bouncer
and me before ultimately landing on me. His expression
softened. "Are you ready to go home?"

"You're forgetting I don't have a home," I reminded
him.

His eyes found mine. "You're welcome to stay with
me."

There was something so enchanting about those words,
and I gave a grateful smile as I followed him out of the bar.

Chapter Fourteen
Decker

I locked the apartment door behind me once we got back. Right as I turned over my shoulder, Kam was standing on the far side of the room, eyeing me with a dazed look on her face, as if she were unsure of what was supposed to happen next.

My head dropped to the ground and my eyes slowly scanned up her body, studying every inch of her from her feet to her thighs to her hips to her chest to her pretty face.

She crossed one of her legs behind her as she pointed to the couch, pretending like she hadn't noticed. "I'll sleep on the couch."

"No," I shook my head as my brows came in. "I can sleep on the couch. You can have my bed."

One of her shoulders dipped down. "We can share the bed. I wouldn't mind sleeping next to you." The second the words left her mouth, she covered her face with her hand, but her hand was so small that it didn't fully mask the flush of pink that encompassed her face. "I mean..." she corrected herself, "I wouldn't mind sharing the bed. That's what I meant."

I tried to suppress my laughter.

Her expression flipped from embarrassed to bold. "What?"

I finally let a small chuckle escape as I turned my head to the side.

"What?" she demanded, placing a hand on her hip.

My eyes peeked over to look at her. She pushed her head forward, waiting for my answer.

God, she was adorable.

I assumed it was the booze that suddenly gave me the courage to stride over to her. I stepped towards her until I was only inches away.

She gazed at me silently with those big blue eyes as her chest began taking deep, shallow breaths.

I hadn't drunk enough to consider myself to be wasted, but my brain felt foggy, and because of that, I was seeing everything differently. Her eyes had all my attention at the moment, and the more I studied them, the more confused I got.

Because for some reason, they looked familiar. Looked as if I'd seen them somewhere before. But instead of trying to pinpoint it, I brought my hand up to her cheek and rested it there softly. My thumb trailed over her delicate skin as I watched her eyes change from blue skies to sapphires—becoming harder, more focused.

I took a deep breath, tilting my head lightly. "I like you," I admitted.

Her mouth parted and something akin to fascination flashed across her face. "I like you too."

I grinned as I leaned forward and connected our lips, content when she immediately relaxed against me, placing her hands on my chest.

Our lips moved rhythmically together, and I couldn't help but acknowledge that I'd never felt like my lips fit so perfectly against another.

Everything about her screamed blue. From her eyes to the way her lips felt. *Depth. Trust. Sincerity.*

There was a sort of tender curiosity racing through me, wondering what her skin felt like. And the longer my lips were against hers, the stronger the curiosity got.

I wanted to know.

I clutched her waist and lifted her, pleased when her legs wrapped around my back. I led her into my bedroom and placed her gingerly on the mattress before positioning myself above her.

It felt natural to be against her, to be breathing with her, kissing her as though I'd known her for half my life.

Her hands slipped underneath my t-shirt and crawled along my back as mine slowly trailed under her black top, starting at the base of her belly and traveling all the way up to her breasts.

Our mouths parted as I pulled back and lifted her shirt just enough to place a warm kiss in the center of her chest, and when I decided that wasn't enough, I let my tongue escape to stream across her skin.

If a color could have flavor, her skin was exactly what blue would taste like.

Kam let out a tiny moan, sending me into a frenzy as I gripped her shirt and guided it over her head. She impatiently grabbed my face and brought it right back onto her lips, and I let her.

Her hands slid under the waistband of my pants, lingering for a moment before she pulled away from me completely.

"Decker?" she said, bringing her hands over her chest.

"Yeah?" I said, out of breath.

"I really like you..." she said, "but I want to know you better first."

I nodded, taking in her earnest expression as I pulled back, creating space between us. "That's okay."

Her mouth formed a hard line before falling into a frown. "Are you disappointed?"

Kam's beautiful eyes were clouded with worry, and once again, I felt the need to brighten her mood. "No," I immediately said, shaking my head. "No, not at all."

Was I disappointed that we wouldn't be having sex? No. But was I disappointed that I wouldn't get to explore every part of her? Yes.

I reached over to the bottom of the bed and grabbed her shirt. "Here," I said softly, handing it to her.

"Thanks," she said. But instead of putting it back on, she just held it over her chest, keeping her focus on me. "It's just that I've only ever slept with my ex before, and I've known him since I was fifteen. So, I guess I just—"

"Kam," I gently interrupted her, "you don't have to explain anything."

Her frown lifted into a fragile grin.

"I'm sorry if I went too far," I said.

"Don't be." She shook her head as she lightly bit her lip. "I didn't say I didn't like it."

My mouth curled into a satisfied smirk as I planted a hand on the bed, leaning forward to connect my lips to her forehead. "I'll step out so you can change into your pajamas." I stood, turning towards the door.

"Decker?"

"Mhmm?" I peeked over my shoulder.

Her hands nervously fumbled around with the blanket as she spoke. "Can I sleep in some of your clothes? They're a bit more comfortable."

My smile grew inevitably. "Of course."

Chapter Fifteen
Kamryn

Sunday went by quickly, consisting of a lazy day with waffles in bed and movies all day long. The more time I spent with Decker, the more I realized how much I enjoyed his company. There was never a dull moment when we were together and being with him made me forget about everything bad in my life.

When Monday morning rolled around, the sound of footsteps awoke me.

My eyes slowly peered open, just enough to spot Decker's bare back, standing in nothing but a towel around his waist as he dug through his dresser.

The second I saw him begin to turn towards me, I snapped my eyes shut, pretending to be asleep. I did my best to keep my breathing even, regardless of how fast my heart was truly beating.

I kept my eyes sealed until I heard Decker leave the room and head into the kitchen. I groggily rolled over and checked the time on the alarm clock that Decker had on his nightstand.

Seven-thirty.

My eyes didn't hesitate to close again, and I laid there, losing track of time. I didn't hear Decker coming this time, but I *felt* it.

There was a crowd of butterflies that appeared in my stomach, and it was their fluttering that gave Decker's presence away. It was strange to me that without actually seeing or touching him, my body still reacted to him.

I didn't dare move as I felt his warmth hovering above me, and when his lips met the top of my head, I was tempted to open my eyes, to twist around and connect our mouths instead, but I didn't.

It wasn't until the butterflies disappeared and I heard the front door shut that I finally opened my eyes, getting a glimpse of Decker's empty room. My shoulder's slumped, wondering where Decker went so early in the morning before I realized that he most likely went to work.

After all, it was Monday.

I groaned as I threw the comforter off me and swung my legs over the side of the bed. I dragged myself out of the bedroom and when my eyes landed on the piece of paper that was hanging onto the refrigerator with a baseball magnet, I practically ran to it and snatched it off the fridge.

Kam,

Help yourself to anything in the kitchen or really anything in the apartment for that matter. I can't wait to see you when I get home from work.

-Decker

A smile surfaced on my lips. The type of smile that you could feel all over your face.

I placed the note on the kitchen counter and maintained a grin as I opened the fridge, grabbing the carton of milk. I left it on the counter next to the note before picking out some cereal and pouring myself a bowl.

I sat on one of the stools at the island while I ate, once again overwhelmed with gratitude from having food in front of me. I just wished Decker was here though.

After eating, I took a seat on the couch and turned the TV on. But as the minutes passed, there was an unsettled feeling that was swelling in my gut. I took a look around the apartment and couldn't shake the sense that it was wrong for me to be here without Decker, as if I was taking advantage of his kindness.

I felt almost guilty about it, and after a few more hours went by, that guilt became more defined.

I sighed to myself and turned the TV off as I stood. I went into Decker's room and grabbed the small duffel bag of mine that was sitting in the closet. Without another thought, I dolefully made my way outside, back to my forlorn corner.

***

I wasn't sure how many hours went by before a tall figure was standing before me.

My shy eyes slowly trailed upwards to meet Decker's. His brows came together, and I studied his lips as he spoke. "Hey," he said gently, "what are you doing outside?"

"I just..." I gave a tiny shrug with one shoulder. "You weren't home."

I could see his amber brown eyes soften, changing to liquid gold as he squatted down to meet my level. "That doesn't mean you had to go back outside," he said.

"I feel bad," I admitted quietly.

"Kam," he said, "it's really nothing. I don't mind. Like I said the other night, you're welcome to stay here."

I gazed at him with doubtful eyes as my uncertainty hovered over both of us like an umbrella.

Decker's focus didn't stray away from me. "I want you here," he said sternly.

There was warmth growing from the center of my chest, spreading throughout my whole body. My mouth slowly tugged upwards, causing Decker's to as well, as if it were a chain reaction.

"C'mon," he stood, cocking his head towards the apartment. "Let's go make dinner." His hand extended towards me, and the second I accepted the gesture, every ounce of doubt vanished.

Chapter Sixteen
Kamryn

Every time Decker was at work, I was left with nothing but reality and my own thoughts, which were two things I hated.

Now that Decker was in my life, everything was less painful. My life didn't seem so pointless anymore. I didn't feel alone anymore. But when he wasn't around, I missed him.

When I was dating Ryan, I didn't know what I was doing. I didn't have a plan for myself. I didn't have a solid job. I wasn't in school. It just seemed like my purpose was to float through life by Ryan's side.

He was still in school to become a financial advisor, and after my aunt used all the money my parents had left for my college fund, I'd practically stepped into the stay-at-home wife role before I was even Ryan's wife. I had jobs every now and then, but I hated all of them and never seemed to stay at one for longer than a few months at a time.

I roamed through downtown San Francisco, job-hunting once more. I'd been going almost every day, trying to find anything available. I came across a small ice cream shop, but rather than go inside, I simply stared at it.

Its familiarity was all too much for me. I'd been here more times than I could even count.

Ryan and I used to go on weekly dates here ever since we were in high school. I sucked in a sharp breath, feeling a small twinge of sadness wash over me.

I missed Ryan. But it wasn't the same feeling of loss that I got when it came to Decker. It wasn't the overwhelming disappointment and ache in my chest that I felt every time Decker wasn't around. It was simply a recognition, a small emotion rather than a physical response. I missed Ryan the same way I missed Arianna— like I'd lost a friend rather than a soulmate.

"Where are you going?" Ryan asked, following me as I jogged upstairs and into our bedroom.

I scoffed. "You not only slept with another woman, but you knocked her up," I said, grabbing a duffel bag out of the closet. "That's plenty of reason to call off a wedding if you ask me."

"B—but you're leaving?"

I brought my brows in as I threw as many clothes as I could into the duffel bag. "Why would I stay?"

"Well, where are you gonna go?" he wondered, concern thick in his voice.

My fiancé just cheated on me and knocked up another woman and all I could feel about it was anger. There was no sadness, no heartbreak, just annoyance. Every time he spoke, I seemed to get more annoyed. "Don't worry about it."

Ryan's voice turned stern, but all he did was stand there, continuing to watch me grab my shit. "I will worry about it."

I dropped my packed bag on the bed, my teeth clenched as I finally looked up at him. "It's none of your business!"

"I care about you, so actually, it is *my business!"*

"Yeah?" I challenged, eyeing him. "You care about me so much that you slept with another woman?"

He took a step backwards, running both hands stressfully through his hair. "Kam," he said, his voice going hoarse again, "I'm sorry. I know that probably doesn't mean shit and you have every right to call off the wedding, but please don't leave."

I narrowed my eyes at him, leaning forward. "You really have the nerve right now to ask me to stay here with you?"

He dropped his arms in front of him helplessly. "I'm not asking you to stay here for my sake. I'm asking you to stay here for your own!"

My mouth parted and I shook my head as I grabbed the duffel bag, flying past him. "You're an idiot," I muttered.

I knew he was following me as I descended the stairs, but I refused to look back at him.

"Kamryn," he hissed behind me.

I was pretty sure the duffel bag weighed a quarter of my body weight, but as heavy as it was, I kept walking towards the front door.

"Oh, here," I said as fearless as possible. I tugged my engagement ring off and tossed it to him. "You can have that back."

He caught it and stepped forward, reaching for my elbow. "Can we please just sit down and talk about this?"

"What is there to talk about?"

He looked away, blowing a frustrated breath out his nose. "Fine," he mumbled. "Go then."

I raised a brow. "Oh, so now you're kicking me out?"

His mouth dropped and he let out a miffed chuckle. "Are you serious?"

"Do you want me to leave?"

"I'm not letting you end up on the street and I'm not making you show up on your crazy aunt's doorstep."

"That wasn't what I asked," I seethed. "Do you want me to leave?"

He stared at me in silence for a moment too long, and to me, that was enough of an answer. "I don't want it to be like this between us from here on out."

I clutched the duffel bag over my shoulder. "Bye Ryan," I said, walking out.

***

"How was your day?" Decker asked as we ate dinner together.

I gave a bummed shrug. "Alright, I guess. How about you?"

Concern creased his features as he eyed me. He carefully laid down his fork. "You seem upset," he said gently. "Is everything okay? What's on your mind?"

I rested my hands on my lap, looking down at the countertop. "Just thought a lot about my life today, I guess."

"Okay," he nodded once, "and what were you thinking?"

"Mostly about how I ended up on the street." I shrugged again.

His eyes flashed compassion. "Do you wanna talk about it?"

I looked at him from under my lashes, considering it.

Decker still had no idea about the details of my life. Not Ryan or my parents or my aunt. None of it. My parents were a topic that I rarely discussed with anyone, even with Ryan, and he'd been around long enough to *know* them.

But I didn't want Decker to feel like I was hiding from him. He'd taken me in without a second thought and I felt like I owed him some sort of explanation in return.

"Um," I started, shifting around on my stool, "as you already know, my parents passed. Since my dad didn't have any siblings and my mom only had one sister, my Aunt Karen got custody of me, but we did not get along in the slightest. No matter what I did, she always had a problem with it. I always kinda thought it had more to do with my mom than with me. She hated my mother," I explained, shaking my head as I stared off. "I think it was a jealously thing. My mom was always the favorite growing up, and when they got older, my mom got married and had me and my aunt never did any of those things. She was just a grouchy, bitter lady."

Decker hadn't picked his fork back up. He hadn't taken a sip of chocolate milk. It was as if his energy refused to go anywhere other than towards me.

I looked back and forth between him and the refrigerator behind him as I spoke. "When I turned eighteen and graduated and went to move out, I found out she used all the money that my parents had left for me. Literally everything besides a few hundred dollars was gone." I blew out a disheartened sigh. "That's when Ryan and I got a house together, which he primarily paid for obviously since I had no money."

Decker's eyes seemed to change from hearing Ryan's name. It wasn't just compassion that crossed his features. A spark of jealousy lingered as his jaw shifted back and forth in the slightest.

But he still didn't look away from me. He still didn't interrupt. I considered stopping there just for the sake of sparing him whatever he may be feeling right now, but when he gave me a small nod, prompting me to continue, I did.

"Obviously, you know what happened with that. After I left, I stayed in a hotel for a few nights, using the money I did have at the time. But everything was so expensive and before I knew it, I was almost out of money. I tried contacting my aunt at that point because I was desperate, but I couldn't get a hold of her. She moved to a different house last year and didn't tell me where. After another week or two, I sold most of the stuff I'd brought with me like my phone, some clothes, and some random jewelry I had and..." I paused, swallowing. "You know the rest."

In the blink of an eye, Decker made his way around the island and took me in his arms. He rested his cheek on top of my head, his thumb trailing across the exposed skin of my shoulder. "I'm sorry," he said.

All I could do was nod.

And all he could do was hold me.

"I didn't even realize until today that I left some of my mother's things behind," I said.

"Do you think..." he stuttered, "*he* did anything to any of it?"

I pulled my mouth over to the side. "No," I admitted. "I don't think so. He's not cold-hearted like that."

Decker slowly nodded against me, but I couldn't tell if the jealousy had returned or not.

"I'll go back for it all eventually, I'm sure," I said.

He carefully brought his hand to my cheek, skimming his fingers across my skin before tracing my jawline. "Thank you for telling me all that. I know it was probably hard for you."

94

“Thanks for asking. It felt kinda good to get some of it off my chest.”

He gave me a modest smile. “Good,” he said, toying with my braid, “it’s what I’m here for.”

Chapter Seventeen
Decker

The past two weeks had been nothing less than fulfilling. Kam was still staying with me and after each day that passed, it seemed like she was becoming more accepting of the fact that I wanted her here.

I was trying my best to remind her of it every day, whether by words or by actions. And every time I did, that captivating smile of hers appeared, tempting me to do everything I could to keep it there.

When Monday morning came around and my alarm clock sounded, I smacked it as quickly as possible, turning it off before it had the chance to wake Kam.

Even though it had been two weeks of going to work every day while Kam stayed at the apartment, it never got easier. The more time I spent with her, the more I wanted to be around her. Going eight hours every day without seeing her was a harsh beating but coming home to her was the only thing that made the eight-hour days worth it.

I groaned as I pulled myself out of bed and went through my regular morning routine. Once I was ready for work, I tiptoed back into the bedroom, and right as I bent down to kiss Kam's forehead, her blue irises gazed at me as she laid there, snuggled in the blankets.

"Did I wake you?" I asked, running my hand over the top of her head.

"No," she said quietly. "I just felt like you weren't in the bed anymore and it woke me up."

If I hadn't known exactly what she meant, I would be utterly confused right now. But somehow, it was as if we both knew when the other was around— and when the other was not. Even with my eyes closed, I could still feel when her presence was across the room.

My hand trailed from the top of her head to her cheek. I brushed my thumb across her soft skin, giving her a loving grin. "I gotta head to work."

"Okay," she said sadly. "I'm probably gonna job-hunt some more today."

"Good luck," I said, carefully placing my lips against hers. I basked in the warmth of them for a moment, memorizing the feeling. Right as I pulled away, I regretted it. "I'll see you after work, okay?"

She nodded lightly. "Have a good day."

"You too," I said gently, turning on my heels and trudging out of the apartment.

***

"Decker," a voice called.

I sighed under my breath as I turned over my shoulder, shooting a fake grin to the man in the suit that was walking directly towards me.

"Yeah, boss?"

He raised a displeased brow. "You know I hate when you call me that."

I sighed again. "Sorry, *Dad*."

"Better," he said, fingering through a folder of papers. "We have a new client, new case."

"Okay," I shrugged. "What is it?"

"Man charged with stalking his ex-girlfriend. Says he wasn't stalking her, blah, blah, blah. You know how it goes," he summarized, shuffling through the rest of the papers. He snapped the folder shut and handed it over. "Here."

My expression remained dull, but I didn't hesitate to take it.

"You know the drill. Read through it, front to back, then start building a case."

"What are you gonna be doing?"

He sighed, shifting his weight onto one foot. "Apparently there's an issue with Reese that I need to go address."

My brows scrunched together. "Reese? The receptionist?"

"Yeah," he sighed. "I don't really know what's going on. I'm gonna go figure it out while you start working on that case."

I nodded lightly. "Alright." I slowly backed away from him, retreating to my small office. I tossed the folder on my desk and sighed as my eyes traveled over to the phone.

God, I wished I could call Kamryn, but she didn't have a phone. Just hearing her voice would make the day go by so much quicker.

I grabbed the blue post-it notes from the far side of my desk and held them in my hand for a second, staring at the shade that resembled Kam's eyes.

I blew out a long breath, shaking off the longing as I turned my attention onto the folder. I flipped it open and began reading, using the post-it notes to mark important details.

Right before I got to the end of the papers, my father's voice overtook the office. He wasn't necessarily yelling, but his disappointed tone was echoing.

I pushed myself out of my seat, my brows furrowing as I headed towards the front, following my father's voice. Just before I rounded the corner, I stopped, tuning into the conversation that my father was having with what sounded like Priya, one of the younger lawyers.

"Sir," she spoke calmly, "I—I'm really not sure what happened. She just said she was quitting and left."

"She didn't give any reason?" my dad asked sharply.

"No," Priya said.

My dad gave out a lengthy, frustrated sigh. "Well, now what? We have no receptionist and Monday is one of our busiest days."

Priya stammered. "I—I mean, I can work the phone for the next hour or so, but I'm supposed to meet with a client later."

Without another thought, I stepped around the corner. I knew my father would know I'd been eavesdropping, but I didn't care. I had one thing on my mind, and I was going to make sure I got it.

"Dad," I said firmly.

Both my dad and Priya turned, noting my arrival. My dad gave Priya a single glance, but it was enough for her to get the hint to step out.

She nodded once and walked off, seemingly thankful that I'd intervened in the conversation.

Once she was out of sight, I got straight to the point. "I know someone that can replace Reese."

His brows shot up, immediately interested. "Who?"

"Her name is Kamryn. She's super smart. Easy to talk to. Very kind. She'll do the job well."

He nodded along, crossing his arms against his chest. "And how do you know her?"

I bit the inside of my cheek for half a second as I stood up straighter, refusing to let my confidence drop. "I've been seeing her."

His hard expression softened quite a bit, turning from a lawyer to my father. "Oh," he said. "Since when?"

"It's only been a few weeks," I said. "But I know she needs a new job, so..."

He tipped his head side to side in thought, studying me. I waited what felt like hours for him to respond, even though I knew it had only been seconds.

"Alright," he finally said with a stern nod. "If you think this girl will do a good job, then I trust you. Bring her in tomorrow and we'll get her trained."

"Will do," I agreed, keeping my composure. But the truth was, I was freaking out in the best way possible. Because I knew that when I told Kamryn, she would lose her shit *in the best way possible.*

And that was a sight I needed to see.

***

I speed-walked all the way home, too damn excited to not only see Kamryn, but to tell her the news.

By the time I got to the apartment door, I was slightly out of breath. I fumbled around with my keys, my hands shaking too much to cooperate.

Finally, when I got the key in the lock and swung the door open, my heart was overwhelmed with adoration, taking in the sight of Kamryn cooking in the kitchen.

"Hi," she greeted me with a smile.

I smiled back wildly, unable to control the glee within my body. I trekked over, standing behind her and wrapping my arms around her middle. I rested my chin on her shoulder. "Hey," I said.

"How was work?"

"It was pretty damn awesome."

She turned to look at me with wrinkled brows, smirking as she did so. "Pretty damn awesome? Why?" she asked. "You're usually not so happy when you come home from work."

I kissed her temple before letting her go and pushing myself onto the island, taking a seat on the counter. "Well, let's get one thing straight. I'm always happy to see *you* after work," I declared. "But," I paused dramatically, "today I'm extra happy."

She stirred the alfredo sauce that was cooking on the stove as she glanced back at me. I took in how perfectly pieced together her braid was and how well the few loose strands of hair that had fallen framed her face.

Kam took a minute to respond. "Well? Are you gonna tell me why or not?" she laughed.

"Our receptionist quit today."

She laughed again. "Why does that make you happy? Did you not like them or something?"

"No, not necessarily that. But then my da— boss," I corrected myself, "was super pissed off and stressed about not having a receptionist... So, I told him I knew the perfect girl for the job."

She swung around to face me, disbelief striking her. "Decker..."

100

"Yes?" I smirked.

"Are you saying you got me a job?"

I nodded firmly. "That's exactly what I'm saying."

Her jaw dropped. "Oh my God," she said, covering her mouth with her hand. "Are you serious?"

"Dead serious."

Kam squealed, jumping up and down as if she were on a pogo stick. She hopped over and wrapped her arms around me. I welcomed it without a doubt and held onto her tightly, nuzzling my face into the crook of her neck.

She let go, standing between my legs. "So, do I have to do like a job interview?"

"Nah," I shook my head. "You'll just come to work with me tomorrow and they'll get you trained right away."

Kam's hand flew up to shield her giant smile. She bounced up and down on her toes. "Ahh!" she exclaimed, jumping into me again.

I chuckled lightly, but Kam gasped while she pulled away rapidly this time. "Wait."

"What?"

She chewed on her finger nervously. "I don't have anything to wear."

"Shit," I muttered, scratching the back of my neck. "Um," I shook my head in thought. "I mean, you could wear that nice top and the jeans you have?"

She bobbed her head side to side. "I could..." she said in a troubled tone. "But it's a law firm. Do you think that outfit is like... professional enough?"

I shrugged lightly. "I mean, I would consider it business casual."

Her face fell, still unsettled. "I'm just worried," she admitted. "I wanna make a good first impression."

I knew the only person who would potentially say anything would be my dad, but I honestly didn't give a shit about his opinion of Kam's outfit. Then again, I didn't really think he would say anything since he knew she was the girl I'd been seeing. Either way, I wanted Kam to feel confident going into the office tomorrow morning.

"We can run to the mall after dinner," I said.

Her chin fell towards her chest. "Decks... I know what that means."

I gave her a mischievous grin as I shrugged. "Either you let me buy you an outfit or you wear what you have."

She narrowed her eyes at me in thought. "Ugh," she mumbled. "Fine."

I grinned, content with her decision. I kicked my legs, still seated on the counter. "Is dinner almost done?"

"Yeah," she said, stepping over to check the sauce and pasta again. She turned back to me with a heartwarming grin. "I used my mom's old recipe for the sauce."

I hopped off the counter and stepped beside her. I placed a hand on her hip as I left a small kiss on top of her head. "I'm sure it'll be wonderful."

Chapter Eighteen
Kamryn

I was already awake when Decker's alarm went off. I'd been so anxious that I woke up countless times in the middle of the night, anticipating the alarm clock.

After eating breakfast with Decker and taking turns showering, I applied some of my new mascara and braided my hair before making my way to the bedroom closet.

The second I caught sight of the outfit that Decker bought for me yesterday at the mall, I stared at it, feeling physically unable to reach for it.

I glanced over my shoulder, reading the clock on the nightstand.

We only had fifteen minutes before we needed to leave.

I exhaled deeply, filled with nerves as I turned back to the closet. I didn't allow myself to think about it anymore before I snatched the clothes off the hanger.

I got dressed and headed into the bathroom to make sure I looked alright. I stood in front of the mirror, smoothing out my red blouse and blazer before moving down to my pencil skirt and smoothing that out as well.

"Decker?" I called out.

He appeared in the doorway within seconds. "Almost ready?"

"Do I look okay?" I asked.

His smirk slowly grew as he looked me up and down. "Yes. You look great."

I cringed, still doubtful. "Are you sure?"

"Yes," he said with a confident nod.

"Okay... I'm ready then."

He held his hand out. My hand shook as I reached for his, but the second our skin touched, the doubt went away and comfort soaked in.

The walk was even shorter than I expected, which was both a blessing and a curse.

A blessing because I didn't have to go long overthinking about walking into the building. And a curse because I didn't have nearly enough time to prepare myself.

When we got there, Decker opened the door for me. We took the elevator to the fourth floor and the second we stepped out of it, the nerves reappeared. I stayed close, knowing that being near him would ease my rapid heartbeat.

A woman appeared from the hallway. She was fairly short with tan, gleaming skin and straightened dark hair that rested at her shoulders. Right as she spotted us, she gave a warm smile. I didn't hesitate to give one back.

"Decker," she greeted him with a nod.

"Priya," he acknowledged her.

Priya turned towards me. "You must be our new receptionist."

"Yes," I nodded excitedly. "I'm Kamryn."

She held a hand out and I shook it gently. "Nice to meet you."

"You too."

"I was asked to train you today."

"Oh, great!"

"You don't have any clients to meet with today?" Decker asked.

"Not until this afternoon," Priya responded. Decker nodded as Priya gestured towards the front desk. "Right this way."

Decker winked at me. "Good luck."

I gave him an eager smile as I followed Priya.

She brought me around the front desk and the second I was able to see what was behind it, my eyes bulged out of their sockets. Folders and papers were scattered across the desk, most of them covered with bolded or highlighted words, which made me assume they were all important. I gulped, intimidated.

I needed this job. I wanted to do it well. And above all, how embarrassing would it be if the girl Decker was dating was a terrible receptionist?

My mind circled through negative thought after negative thought, but right when Priya began speaking, I made sure to give her all my attention.

"So, I know it probably looks scary at first," she said with a laugh. "I used to be the receptionist a while ago, actually."

"Really? What do you do now?"

"Well, since I *finally* finished law school, I'm a full-time lawyer here," she smiled.

"That's amazing," I said. "Congratulations."

"Thank you," she grinned.

"Did you have an internship when you were still in law school? Like Decker?"

She sat down in the office chair as she replied, letting out a tiny scoff. "I did have an internship, but half of it was being the receptionist. Decker is a little different, obviously." She gave a playful eyeroll.

I noticed how much I'd calmed down since walking into the office and meeting Priya, and I took the comfort as my cue to ask her why Decker was different, but before I could speak, she beat me to it.

"Speaking of the boss," she said, "do you wanna meet him?"

"Oh," I straightened, nerves immediately returning. "R—right now?"

"Yeah," she stood. "I should probably take you to meet him before he gets busy."

"Oh," I repeated. "Okay."

"Plus," she added, "I know he's very excited to meet you."

"He is?"

She nodded with a grand smile.

"Alright..." I muttered, following her.

We walked silently to his office. There were a handful of cubicles where people didn't seem to pay us any attention as we passed. The clicking of computer keys could be heard, along with hushed chattering, but other than that, it was quiet.

There were a few doors side by side, and I dug my heels into the floor, avoiding knocking into Priya as she abruptly halted in front of one of the doors. She gave a small knock.

"Come in!"

Priya quietly opened the door and stuck her head in. "Hi, sir. I have Kamryn here if you'd like to meet her."

"Yes, bring her in."

She held the door open for me, and right then, I realized she wasn't coming in with me. She gave me a reassuring look as I swallowed hard, walking past her.

My new boss was sitting at his desk, his gaze rising from the paper in his hands to me.

"Hello," I greeted him with a smile.

"Kamryn," he smiled back, standing.

"It's nice to meet you, Mr." I paused, glancing down at the nametag on his desktop, "Shepley?" my brows came in.

He nodded once, extending his hand out. I fidgeted as I stepped forward, reaching for his hand for a firm shake.

"Shepley as in... Decker's..."

He chuckled at my surprise. "He didn't tell you I was his father, did he?"

"No, he did not."

"Of course, he didn't." He shook his head with a chuckle. He gestured to the seat in front of his desk. "Go ahead and take a seat."

I gave a nervous smile as I sat, once again smoothing out my pencil skirt as I did so.

"Excited for your first day?"

"Yeah," I nodded briefly. "A bit nervous though, being honest."

He waved it off. "Don't be. I'm sure it's nothing you can't handle. Has Priya started training you yet?"

"No," I said. "She wanted me to meet you first before you got busy. She did show me the front desk, though." I

106

wasn't sure if it was the nerves radiating off me or the fear in my eyes that gave me away.

"Don't be intimidated by that thing. Our old receptionist left it a mess." He folded his hands on the desk. "Anyway, I just wanted to go over a few things with you." He waited until I nodded to continue. "Your starting pay will be sixteen dollars an hour. You'll get some paid time off and other benefits as well. Priya will give you the employee handbook when you see her again. They're up front."

"Sounds great!" I smiled, prompting him to continue.

"She also doesn't have any clients to see until later so she'll have all morning to train you and answer any questions you may have."

I smiled wider with a nod. "Thank you very much for this opportunity. I really, really appreciate it."

"You're welcome," he said with a kind grin. "But you should thank Decker. He spoke very highly of you yesterday." He stood, so I followed his lead.

"I'll be sure to thank him again. It was nice meeting you Mr. Shepley."

"You too, Kamryn."

Chapter Nineteen
Decker

"You did great today," I smiled at Kam as we rounded the corner, approaching the apartment.

"You think so?"

"Definitely," I said. "Tuesdays tend to be busy, and you seemed to handle it really well even though it was your first day."

"Well, I had Priya's help for most of the day."

I shrugged as we stepped up to the door. "Still."

We walked in and each headed straight for the bedroom to change. I snatched some pajamas out of my drawer, happy to throw them on even though it was only five o'clock. But instead of changing right then and there, I retreated to the bathroom to give Kam her space.

I'd be lying if I said that each time I did this, it didn't poke at my impatience. Because it *did*. It sure as hell did. But I wasn't impatient because I hadn't gotten laid in months. I was impatient because I was dying to see every inch of her skin, to learn more about her, to feel even closer to her than I already did.

I peeled off my suit and instead of tossing my pajama shirt on, I stopped. I bit the inside of my cheek as I read the devastating word on my chest that was supposed to represent a new beginning.

Redemption.

Etched into my skin. Hovering over my heart. A promise I swore to keep the second the world gave me another chance.

It was also the only reason why I was thankful Kam hadn't seen me shirtless yet. Because I knew that once she did, she would ask questions.

And those weren't questions that I was ready to answer.

I swallowed so hard that my Adam's apple bobbed, and I looked away from the mirror as I gripped my t-shirt, my knuckles turning white as I lifted it over my head.

Once I was dressed, I picked up my suit and walked out of the bathroom. It always felt strange knocking on my own bedroom door, but I did it anyway.

"Kam?"

"Yeah," she answered. "You can come in."

I twisted the knob and stepped inside, grabbing a hanger and slipping my suit onto it.

"What do you wanna do for the rest of the night?" Kam asked, seated with her legs crossed on the bed.

I grinned, placing the hanger in the closet. "Anything."

"I have a question."

I stiffened, taken off guard at the change of topic. "Yeah?" I asked, turning towards her.

She brought her knees up to her chest, hugging them to her. "Why didn't you tell me about your father?"

My shoulders wiggled around slightly, uneasily, before shrugging altogether. "I don't know," I admitted. "I guess I didn't want you to think you got the job just because my dad is the boss."

Her voice dropped a little. "That is why I got the job though, isn't it?"

My face fell, matching hers, and I took a seat beside her on the bed. "No matter what, you got the job. You've been great at it so far and I know you're going to keep doing amazing."

Her eyes brightened and before I could even blink, she jumped into me, wrapping her small arms around me as she nuzzled her face into my neck. "Thank you," she whispered.

I took her in my arms, breathing in her sweet scent. "You're welcome."

She pulled away, waving her hands around as she talked. "I promise that once I have enough money, I'll find my own place."

A light swarm of dizziness overcame me. I didn't want her to leave. I wasn't letting her stay here just to let her stay here. She was here because I wanted her here. At this point, I'd gotten used to waking up next to her every day. It made me start off each day in a better mood. I didn't want to lose that.

"You..." I started. "You don't have to..."

"Decker... I can't keep interrupting your life."

"You're not," I shook my head desperately.

"I just..." she looked away, "I have nothing to give back to you."

"I don't need anything," I assured her. "Besides you."

"You don't think this is weird though? Living together right off the bat?" She paused, standing up and walking across the room. Her back was facing me, but I could see her shoulders rise and fall with a sigh.

"Like... you think we're moving too fast?"

Kam turned, facing me once again. "I mean, most couples don't live together until they've been dating for a few years." She rocked her weight side to side. "Which, I don't even know if that's what we are."

I stared at her blankly.

"A couple, I mean," she clarified.

"I want to be," I admitted. I'd already had it drilled into my mind that we were a couple, and I thought she'd felt the same way, but now I wasn't so sure. I guess we never really had the conversation to make it official though. Not until now at least.

Kam was just eyeing me, staring me down with a specific yearning. But I couldn't tell if the look she was giving me was because she liked what I'd said or because she didn't.

I gulped, waiting for her to say something. *Anything.* The silence was making panic build up in my gut, and if my rapid breathing was the only sound in the air for another second, I was going to lose my mind.

"Kam?" I quietly asked.

"I do want that," she said, taking a tiny step closer. "I do."

I wasn't sure if I should go to her or not, wasn't sure if she wanted to feel my touch right now, but I stood anyway, reaching for her.

I ran my fingers down her arm, gripping her hand once I got to it. "Is that what you want?" I asked, fearfully waiting for her to change her mind.

But her voice was nothing less than confident. "Yes."

"Then we're a couple?" I asked with a hopeful grin.

Her voice fell to a whisper. "Yeah."

My smile grew and I wrapped my arms around Kam's waist, lifting her into the air. She squealed as I carefully tossed her onto the bed and climbed on to join her. She laughed as I smuggled her with kisses around her face, tickling her sides as I did so.

Finally, I drew back, hovering above her to get a better look at her. "Don't move out," I said. "Ever."

Kam ran her hand through my hair. "Don't ever give me a reason to and I won't."

"Deal," I grinned.

Chapter Twenty
Decker

Kam and I had gotten into a daily routine, and I'd never felt so comfortable in my own skin. For the first time in years, I wasn't alone, and I wasn't drenched in self-hatred.

I sat in my office, working on the same case my father had given me at the beginning of the week. After I finished reading through it and marking the important details, I was given the task of starting the defense for my father to use in court. I was still surprised that he trusted me with so much of his job, and as grateful as I was for that, it also put a lot of pressure on my back.

There was a light knock on my door, and I didn't even have the opportunity to tell the person to come in before the door opened. My father peeked his head inside.

"How's it going?" he asked.

"Fine," I said. "Are you gonna come in?"

He stepped inside and closed the door behind him. "A few things."

"Yeah?"

My dad strode over and took the seat in front of my desk. "First, I just wanted to say I think Kamryn is doing a great job so far."

I couldn't hold my smile back. "She is, isn't she?"

"She is," he agreed with a strong nod. "And second... your mother and sister wanna meet her."

I dropped my head back and rolled my eyes. "Ugh, Dad. Why'd you tell them?"

"Well," he shrugged, "it slipped."

"Slipped," I repeated sarcastically.

"I was just... excited for you."

I folded my arms on the desk, leaning forward in the slightest. I raised a brow at my father.

"You haven't seen someone since—"

"I get it," I cut him off.

His voice became quieter. "Does she know anything?"

I eyed him in silence for a moment before looking away disgracefully. "No, she doesn't. So please don't say anything."

"I promise I won't," he agreed. "You do know you'll have to tell her eventually though, right?"

"Dad, please..." I shook my head. "I really, *really* don't want to even think about that right now."

"Alright," he sighed.

"Thank you."

"But your mom and sister still wanna meet her."

I clenched my teeth together. "When?"

"This weekend would be ideal," he said.

I let out a heavy sigh, rubbing the light stubble on my chin. "Alright," I said in an agitated tone. "Under two conditions."

"Which would be?"

I tapped my fingers, counting them off as I spoke. "One, no one mentions anything about you know what. And two, no one asks about Kam's parents because they passed when she was younger and talking about it makes her upset."

He gave a nod in understanding. "I hear you loud and clear."

***

I swallowed hard, scrubbing a plate before handing it over to Kam to put in the dishwasher. "So, um," I said, clearing my throat, "my parents invited us over for dinner this weekend."

I watched her freeze out of the corner of my eye, stopping halfway to the dishwasher. "Okay," she said gently, finally bending the remainder of the way to put the plate in.

"Do you want to go?"

"Yeah," she nodded nervously. "Yeah, we should go."

"Cool." I gave her a reassuring smile, handing over another plate. "My mom and sister are excited to meet you."

She smiled back, taking the plate. "How old is your sister again?"

"Eighteen."

"Is she still in school?"

"Yeah," I nodded. "She just started her first semester at Stanford."

Kam's brows shot up. "Wow. She must be a genius."

I fidgeted, reaching for silverware to scrub. I gulped down more shame. "Yeah, Emmy's the smart one of the family."

Kam playfully nudged me. "Says the one who comes from a family of lawyers."

I pushed out a chuckle. "She's still the smarter one. Trust me."

She stood beside me, close enough so that our arms were touching. "Well, I'm excited to meet them too."

I pushed down all the shame I'd been feeling, forcing myself to look at her. "Me too," I said.

Chapter Twenty-One
Kamryn

I was trying to breathe, but my nerves were making it really damn difficult to. Since neither of us had a car and Decker's family lived twenty minutes outside the city, his sister was going to pick us up. And she was supposed to be here any minute.

"Kam," Decker smiled, grabbing my hand and pulling me to him. "It's gonna go just fine. Stop stressing."

I sighed, tilting my head in worry. "I know, I know. I just want them to like me."

"They will," he said without a trace of doubt. His voice was so comforting, so caring. My lashes fluttered as I glanced up at him, craning my neck far back enough to look him right in the eye. His eyes were brown and sweet like cinnamon, but I could pick out the sliver of fear behind them that he was trying so hard to hide.

I sucked in a sharp breath. "Why are *you* nervous?"

Decker's gaze shifted over my shoulder. His mouth opened, but no words came out. He licked his lips and tried again. "I just don't want my family to say anything stupid."

The corners of my mouth lifted subtly knowing that he cared so much about his family's behavior around me. My fingertips trailed along the soft skin on his wrist. "I'm sure they'll be fine."

Decker blew out a worried breath before raising his hand and brushing it across my cheek. "God, I hope so," he whispered.

I could feel the aftermath of his touch as the electricity reached the center of my body. His stare only added to the passion in the air, draping over both of us like a blanket.

A knock sounded on the door, and nothing followed it for a moment besides the sound of our own silence.

Decker cleared his throat as he stepped backwards away from me, instantly causing my body to feel the space created between us.

"Coming!" Decker called out as he rubbed the back of his neck.

"Hurry up!" a female voice yelled back. "My car is running!"

Decker rolled his eyes. "We're coming!"

We'd made brownies to bring to dinner. I grabbed the baking pan that was covered in tinfoil, clutching it tightly as I followed Decker towards the door.

When he swung the door open, a young girl in a sundress stood in the doorway with crossed arms, her weight shifted over to one side in a sassy stance, eyes landing on Decker.

"I texted you like five minutes ago," she said. She sighed as her eyes wandered over to me. Her expression softened. "Hi," she said with a tiny nod. "I'm Emmy."

I could feel my face brighten. "Kamryn," I smiled back.

She swayed gleefully. "Nice to meet you."

"You too," I nodded.

Decker's shoulders lifted as he pushed his hands into his jean pockets. "Are we... ready?"

"Yeah," Emmy and I said in unison.

We followed Emmy to her car, and I happily let Decker take the passenger seat while I slid into the backseat.

Everyone was quiet at first, silence overtaking the car other than the faint sound of the radio turned down low. I inhaled deeply through my nose, but just as I was beginning to relax within the silence, Emmy broke it.

116

"Where have you been?" she asked Decker, turning her attention back and forth between him and the road. "You haven't been home in a while."

Decker had been speaking more about his family ever since we were asked to come over for dinner, but it wasn't until now that I realized how much he hardly spoke of them beforehand. I wasn't quite sure how often Decker used to go home for visits, but if he used to go home as often as Emmy was making it sound, then I could only assume I was the reason why he stopped.

I glanced down at the brownies in my lap, waiting to hear whatever Decker's answer was going to be. I kept my head low, my eyes shifting upwards just enough to see Decker lightly shrug.

"Just got busy," he said. "I know you just started school. How's it going?"

"It's good," Emmy said. I could see a light hint of pink brush over her cheeks through the rearview mirror. "I met a boy."

Decker's brows came inwards as far as they possibly could. "A boy? No. Absolutely not."

Emmy sighed, rolling her eyes. "I thought you'd be happy about it considering *you're* dating again."

Again?

I zoned out for a moment, dwelling on the word. Decker had never mentioned anything about an ex-girlfriend before. A hint of anger bubbled to the surface of my skin because I'd been so transparent about Ryan with him, yet he apparently hadn't been fully transparent with me.

Myra's face flashed into my mind, and I wondered if there was something Decker was leaving out. Had Myra been more than a hookup buddy in the past or was I just out of the damn loop altogether?

Decker's voice snapped me out of my thoughts. "Emmy," he said firmly through gritted teeth.

"Sorry," she whispered. "I'm just excited about meeting someone new."

"You just started college. Boys can wait."

She sighed again, but this sigh was more saddened than anything. "He doesn't even know that I like him as more than a friend anyway, so don't worry."

"Good," Decker said.

Before thinking, I interrupted, rushing to Emmy's defense. "Hey," I said, pulling my brows in. Decker twisted around in the passenger seat to look at me. "Be nice. Let her be excited."

A faint smile touched Emmy's lips as she glanced at me in the rearview mirror. "Thanks."

I nodded to her with a smile as she pulled into the driveway. The house was huge, bigger than the one I used to live in with my parents. The outside of the house was made of yellow tinted bricks and a stone walkway lined the front, leading up to the door.

Emmy pulled her car into one of the spots in the two-door garage. I gulped down sand as I undid my seatbelt and scooted out of the backseat.

My nerves were once again threatening to overpower me, but the second that Decker's hand was on my lower back, guiding me towards the house, I relaxed under his touch.

When we got to the front door, Emmy walked right in, allowing Decker and me to trail behind.

"Mom, Dad," Emmy called out, "we're back."

I took in every inch of the foyer, studying the cream-colored walls and beautiful paintings that could be nothing less than originals. The floors were lined with mahogany wood. There was a small chandelier hanging from the ceiling and a grand piano off to the right. It was so classical, yet somehow modern looking at the same time. Nevertheless, I was not at all surprised that this was what a well-known lawyer's house looked like.

I could've continued studying the house if Decker's parents hadn't strolled in. His mom's arms were already extended, reaching for her son with the same look on her face that people gave to babies or puppies— the expression that they were looking at the cutest thing on the planet.

"Aw, Decks!" she exclaimed, hugging him tight. He towered over her, and his long arms delicately wrapped around her back as if she were fragile. But she didn't hold back,

118

squeezing him as if all our lives depended on it. Mr. Shepley and I gave each other a quick greeting in the midst of it all.

When his mom pulled away, she held him by his forearms to look at him. "I missed you. It would be nice if you visited your *mother* every once in a while."

"Sorry, Mom," Decker smiled.

"Your lucky father gets to see you every day." She rolled her eyes. "It's not fair." Finally, her attention shifted onto me and her smile returned. "Oh!" she cheered. "You must be Kamryn."

"Yes, hi," I smiled. "It's nice to finally meet you."

"You as well! Oh, give me a hug," she insisted with her arms out. Decker took the brownies out of my hands as I wrapped my arms around his mom. We smiled at each other as we pulled away.

"Here, Mom," Decker said, handing over the pan.

"What's this?" she asked.

"We made brownies," I said.

"Oh, lovely! Now we've got dessert." She smiled wider as she turned on her heels, heading into another room. The rest of us followed, and once again, I was astounded by the house as we entered the kitchen. It was filled with white cabinets and black granite countertops with an island in the center.

The delicious aroma of lasagna wafted through the air, and I took a deep whiff, inevitably being brought back to my childhood.

Just being in a nice house with a set of parents was enough to make me think of my own. Even though it had been years since they passed, I never missed them any less. Internally, I was hurting, but I pulled myself together as best as I could.

The oven timer beeped, and Decker's mom rushed over to turn it off. "Perfect timing," she said, slipping an oven mitt on.

"Mom, do you need help with anything?" Decker asked.

A tiny grin tugged upwards on my lips, watching how sweet Decker was to his mother. But I still couldn't shake the idea that there was something he hadn't told me. Whatever it was, I needed to have faith in him. If it was something important, something that mattered, then I was sure he would've told me. If he had dated someone before, maybe the relationship just wasn't serious enough for him to have mentioned it. I shook off all the doubts and insecurities that had surfaced since the car ride, taking a deep breath as I relaxed in my skin.

"That's okay honey," she said, shooing him away. "You guys can go take a seat in the dining room. The food will be ready in just a minute."

"You sure?" Decker asked, raising a brow.

"Yes," she insisted. "I'll have your father help."

Decker nodded to his mother, then cocked his head to the side, gesturing for me to follow.

There was a long table in the dining room with a tiny chandelier hanging above it. Decker sat at the head of the table, and I sat on his right, Emmy beside me.

Within a few minutes, Decker's parents came in, carrying the lasagna, a bowl of salad, and a plate of breadsticks.

"Here we go," Mrs. Shepley said, getting everything situated in the center of the table.

"It smells amazing," I said as Decker handed me a plate. "Thank you for dinner, Mr. and Mrs. Shepley."

"You're welcome, honey. I'm glad you and Decker could make it. We've been so excited to meet you and get to know you more," Mrs. Shepley smiled as everyone piled food onto their plates. A jitter of nerves slid down my spine. I knew going into dinner that his family would ask me questions about myself, but I was unprepared. There was nothing about my life worth boasting about. Everyone else my age already had impressive achievements, jobs, or college scholarships. Whereas all I had was a history of living on the street, a failed engagement, and parents that I emotionally couldn't afford to speak of aloud.

"And please," Mrs. Shepley added, "feel free to call me Shannon."

"And you can call me Scott," Mr. Shepley joined. "Outside the office that is," he said with a teasing grin.

"So, Kamryn," Shannon started, patting her mouth with a napkin, "Decker mentioned you're from Parkersville?"

"Yeah," I responded between bites. "I went to high school there."

Shannon gave a warm grin as she chewed and swallowed. "Is that when you two met? In high school?" she asked, her eyes bouncing back and forth between us.

I gave Decker a worried side eye, embarrassment crossing my face. He caught my gaze, reading my mind with perfect clarity, and just as I opened my mouth to speak, Decker did for me.

"Yeah," he lied, lightly touching my knee under the table. "We met through Alaina. They both played softball."

Shannon's smile grew wider. "Awe, Alaina is the sweetest."

"She really is," I agreed.

I felt bad for lying to Decker's parents. *I really did.* But walking into the house of a wealthy family and explaining to them that you met their son when he saved you from living on the street wasn't exactly an easy thing to do.

I wished the truth was as simple as the lie.

"Have you always lived in Parkersville then?"

"For the most part," I said. "My parents and I moved there when I was about three."

"Do your parents still live there?"

There was a loud clash and everyone's heads turned to the head of the table. Decker's hand covered his face, his fork lying on the side of his plate where he'd dropped it.

"*Mom*," he warned, his shaking hand covering his face.

Everyone was silent, clueless, confused.

Everyone besides me, of course.

"My..." I paused, forcing myself to speak, "parents passed when I was younger."

Shannon's hand shot up to her mouth. Her eyes turned sullen, screaming apologies. "I'm so sorry," she muttered beneath her hand. "I—I didn't know."

"It's okay," I assured her, shaking my head.

"I'm really sorry to hear that," Scott added.

"Me too," Emmy whispered beside me.

"It's alright," I said.

Decker finally dropped his hand onto the table, his eyes darting over to me. "I'm so sorry."

"Really, it's okay."

His eyes didn't leave mine though. Because he knew I *wasn't* okay.

Decker still didn't know what happened to my parents. He never asked, and at this point, he knew better than to ask. It's not that I would've gotten angry if he had, but it always hurt so much to talk about the two people in the world that you loved the most but lost too soon.

I took a quick glance over at Decker, just enough to catch the hard glare that he shot at his father when he wasn't looking.

There was an unsaid tension between the two, the type that you couldn't decipher, but the more you paid attention to it, the stronger it seemed to get.

We ate in silence for a few minutes as the awkwardness subsided.

"Well," Scott finally spoke, dropping his napkin onto his clean plate, "Kamryn has been doing great at the office so far."

"Thank you." A tiny grin surfaced on my face. I guess that was one thing I could boast about.

Decker swallowed his last bite of lasagna. "Told you she would."

"Yeah," Scott nodded, a mischievous grin appearing as he turned towards Decker. "And how's that case that *you've* been working on?"

"Oh, Scott," Shannon rolled her eyes. "Let's not talk about work stuff right now."

Scott sighed. "Alright."

Decker's eyes seemed to look everywhere other than at his father, ultimately landing on his mother instead. "How are you, Mom?"

"Good, oh, I'm good!" she exclaimed. "Speaking of good," she stood, "why don't we pop open some of that fantastic wine we've got?"

"Mo—" Decker started, but before he could even finish his thought, Shannon had left the dining room. He sighed.

"Don't want any?" Scott asked, lifting a brow.

"I want some," Emmy interrupted.

"No," Scott and Decker said in unison before shooting another glare at each other.

Decker broke his gaze away from his father. Instead, he turned his head towards the wall and stared at it.

This time, *I* touched *him* under the table. My touch seemed to snap him out of whatever haze he was in. His warm hand found mine and squeezed.

"Would you guys like a glass?" Shannon reappeared, holding a bottle of wine in one hand and a few wine glasses in the other, clutching onto them with the stems between each of her fingers.

"Oh, uh, I'm not twenty-one yet," I admitted.

"You're not?" Emmy asked, her brows meeting.

"I'm twenty."

Shannon waved it off. "You're almost there. And it's not like we all magically become mature enough at midnight on our twenty-first birthdays." She poured a glass and pushed it over to me. I didn't hesitate to lift it to my lips and take a sip.

"You're breaking the law," Scott teased.

"Good thing she knows a defense lawyer," Shannon joked.

Decker let out a huff, cursing under his breath.

I turned towards him as I set the glass down. "You okay?" I whispered.

"Yeah," he responded, his jaw lightly twitching.

"Decks, honey, do you want one?" Shannon asked as she handed Scott a glass.

"Sure, Mom," he muttered unenthusiastically.

Emmy crossed her arms. "Great, so I'm the only one who can't have one."

"I won't have one if it makes you feel better," Decker said.

Emmy sighed. "No, it's fine." She turned to me. "Do you wanna come see my room? I just redid it. I can show you the rest of the house too."

"I can show her around," Decker said defensively.

"No, no," Scott said. "Why don't you let Emmy show her?"

Decker gritted his teeth together as he eyed his father. "Fine."

I took another gulp of wine before standing and giving Decker a reassuring glance as I followed Emmy out of the dining room. I studied the family photos that lined the walls, leading all the way up the stairs. When I caught sight of a photo of Decker, kneeling with a baseball bat in hand and a bright smile on his face, I paused. He was definitely in high school during it. His jersey had Lane North's colors and right beside the frame, there was a medal hung up.

Most Valuable Player.

A smile tugged on the corners of my lips as I continued trudging up the stairs, turning the corner to follow Emmy.

Her room was a light blue. Photos of Emmy and her friends were scattered along the walls, decorations surrounding them. All her furniture was bright white, even her comforter, which made the room look like the sky.

"So, this is my room," she said.

My eyes wandered around, reminded of my own room way back when.

"It's really cute," I said.

"Thanks," she smiled, plopping down on her bed. "I have a question."

Nerves immediately danced within my stomach. "Yeah?" I gulped.

Her eyes became softer, and in that moment especially, she looked so much like Decker. They had the same dusty blonde hair and compassionate brown eyes. But whereas Decker's facial features were hard and defined, Emmy's were soft and delicate.

"How did you and Decker actually meet?"

My eyes blinked rapidly, and my mouth parted. "How did we..." I trailed off.

She gave me a subtle, inviting grin. "I know he was lying downstairs."

I exhaled heavily and sat down beside her. "How'd you know?"

She shrugged. "He's my brother. I always know if he's lying. He does this weird thing when he lies where he looks down and then his eyebrow kinda twitches."

I laughed, relieved to hear Emmy's laughter mix with mine. But as our laughter subsided, my nerves reappeared.

There was a light sting piercing my core, threatening to force my lasagna back up, but I breathed heavily through my nose.

"Um," I started, sitting cross-legged, "long story short," I paused again, staring down at the comforter, "I didn't have any place to stay, and Decker saw me on the street and invited me in."

Her eyes widened before softening once again. "You were homeless?"

"Yeah," I confessed.

"How?" she whispered. "What happened?"

Typically, I didn't like talking about my past. I didn't like talking about Ryan or living on the street, and I *especially* did not like talking about my parents— their death at least. But when I glanced back up at Emmy, there was a peculiar sense of comfort that eased me. And if I had to guess why, I'd say it was simply the fact that she was Decker's sister.

Not only did they look so much alike and give off the same soothing vibe, but they obviously *shared blood*. Which meant that Emmy was pretty much just another version of Decker— the female version I supposed.

I pushed myself a bit farther back onto her bed. "Like I said downstairs, I lost my parents when I was younger, so I lived with my only aunt for a while, but we didn't get along. So, I moved in with my boyfriend right after high school. Then eventually a bunch of bullshit happened, and yeah..." I trailed off.

Emmy gasped. "I'm so sorry," she winced. "I cannot imagine going through all that, especially since I'm assuming that's the *summarized* version."

"Yeah," I chuckled, even though no part of this conversation was funny. "Yeah, it's the summarized version."

She exhaled sympathy with every breath, filling every crevice of the room with it. "I'm sorry," she said again quietly. "If it helps at all," she paused, a light smile crossing her lips, "I can tell Decker cares about you a lot."

"You think so?"

"A thousand percent," she nodded firmly. "He looks at you like you're a fucking queen." She let out a laugh. "I've never seen him look at *anyone* like that."

Satisfaction shot through me like a lightning bolt hitting a tree. A massive smile overtook my face, wiping away every somber feeling that I previously had.

"He's the most incredible guy I've ever met," I admitted. "Such a step up from my ex." Emmy and I both laughed, and even her laughter somehow reminded me of Decker. "But I..." I hesitated, my gaze wandering.

"Yeah?"

"I wasn't going to say anything, but since we are talking about Decker, I have a question."

She rubbed one of her hands atop the other, almost anxiously. "Okay," she said in a small voice.

"I really should be asking him this, but... I heard you mention in the car that Decker was dating *again*," I said, putting emphasis on the word. "But he hasn't mentioned any past relationships to me."

Emmy's shoulders dropped drastically with a calm exhale. "Oh," she nodded. "Um, honestly, it doesn't even really matter. He dated a girl in high school named Casey, but it was a long time ago."

A wave of relief overtook my worry faster than a river flooding into the ocean. "So, it's nothing to worry about?"

Emmy broke eye contact with me, studying the other side of her room. "No."

"Okay good," I said. "So, who's this new guy you met at school?"

Her lips curled upwards. "His name is Jordan. He's super cute and he's in one of my classes."

"Ooo," I teased lightheartedly. "Why don't you ask him out?"

Emmy's mouth formed a hard line and she shrugged helplessly. "I just get so shy."

A small laugh tumbled out of my mouth. "Wow," I said, "you really are like your brother."

"Really?" she snickered.

"Yep. He—"

But I was interrupted by Decker appearing in the doorway. He leaned against the doorframe, crossing his arms. His trademark grin surfaced. "I what?" he asked, raising a brow.

126

There was something about him right now that made me want to run over and throw myself at him. I wasn't sure if it was the way he was standing as if he didn't have a care in the world or if it was the raspy tone of his voice, but either way, I might've done it if Emmy wasn't there.

"Nothing," I insisted.

His eyes drilled into me, as if we were having the same thoughts. "Are you ready to head home?"

I gave him a glance over. "Yeah."

He nodded. "Emmy, could you drive us?"

"Sure," she said, hopping off the bed. She waited a moment for Decker to give an appreciative nod and start heading down the hallway before turning to me. Her voice dropped to a whisper, and she held her pinky out. "And I promise I won't say anything to my parents."

"Thank you," I smiled, hooking our pinkies together.

Chapter Twenty-Two
Decker

Kam and I waved goodbye to Emmy as she drove off and as we turned towards the apartment, a smug grin crossed my lips.

"Oh look. Our package came." I nodded once towards the small box sitting atop the doorstep.

Kam's brows creased and she let out a small chuckle, sounding sweeter than sugar. "What package?"

I leaned down and grabbed it, shoving it under my arm as I shimmied my key out of my pocket and jammed it into the lock. I gave her a crooked grin over my shoulder. "You're gonna have to open it and see."

She sighed. "No more gifts!"

My smile grew as we walked in, and it grew even more when Kam pretended to angrily flick her shoes off. "What if this one is a gift for both of us?"

Her eyes shot over to me. "How so?"

I shrugged. "Open it and see."

She sighed again, louder this time. "Fine," she said.

I held the box out with one hand, and she stomped over, using both of her tiny hands to snatch it from me. "You're the worst," she mumbled with a grin, heading over to the couch. I sat directly beside her, close enough for our thighs to touch.

There was a bolt of warmth that shot through me, traveling from my thigh through my dick and all the way up to my stomach. I gulped down the desire that arose within me, turning my attention back to the box in Kam's hands. I handed her my keys and she used the edge of one to cut apart the tape on the box.

She pulled the top open and her face immediately twisted from curiosity to confusion to disbelief. "Decker..." she started, judgment overtaking her tone. "You didn't."

"I had to," I said as a ball of jitters began forming in the pit of my stomach. Was she mad? Or was she just in such disbelief that she sounded mad?

She pulled the brand-new phone out of the box, her mouth agape. Her shoulders slumped as she stared at it.

"Do you..." I spoke. "Are you mad?

Her head shook rapidly. "No," she said. "Of course I'm not mad. I just... hate that you've spent so much money on me." Her head shook again, and she held the phone towards me. "I can't accept this."

My pulse quickened and I sprung into reassurance mode. "Listen, baby," I said softly, sliding my arm over hers, "I knew it would be helpful. Do you have any idea how much I *hate* not being able to talk to you when we're apart?"

She frowned, eyeing me in silence.

I sighed quietly, feeling the need to *quite literally* turn her frown upside down. "Ever since we met, all I've wanted to do is be with you. Talk to you. Be near you in any way possible. Before working together, I fucking *hated* not being able to talk all day long. And yeah, we work together now, but I barely get to see you throughout the day. Now that you have a phone, we can talk any time we aren't together."

One corner of her lips quivered, sliding upwards and taking the other side with it. She dived into me, wrapping her arms around me so tight that I was nearly gasping for air. I chuckled against her hair. "Still mad about it?" I teased.

"No," she said, and even though I couldn't see her face, I could *hear* her smile. "Thank you, Decker."

"You're more than welcome," I sputtered against her. My lips began burning, longing for her to put out the fire among them.

The second she pulled away, I grabbed her head and pulled her back to me, bringing our mouths together. But the burning sensation didn't cease. It simply slithered down my throat and didn't stop migrating downwards until it was settled in my groin.

She let out the tiniest moan against me and the parting of her lips allowed me to stick my tongue inside her mouth to explore. Her hand ran up my thigh, and the lustful friction created sparks that flew off our skin like a sparkler on the goddamn Fourth of July.

I ran my hand through the hair on the back of her head as I kissed her harder. She didn't allow our lips to part as she climbed onto my lap, straddling me. I gripped her hips, pinning her against me, unwilling to let us separate an inch.

Kam was kissing me hungrily, greedily, as if she owned me. Her hands cupped my jaw tightly as another moan escaped out of her mouth, vibrating against my lips. My hands ran up and down her back before ultimately resting on her ass and squeezing.

She pulled away from me sharply. "Do you wanna go in your room?"

I sucked in a sharp breath. I was more than surprised that she asked to take it to the bedroom, but there was no way in hell I was going to turn her down.

"Yeah," I said quietly, brushing my lips against hers once again. She was so close that I could feel her eyelashes flutter against my cheek as I gripped underneath her thighs and lifted her, carrying her into the bedroom.

I laid her down gently on the bed, standing at the end of it with one knee on the mattress. Kam watched me intently as I reached behind me and gripped the back of my shirt, yanking it over my head.

Her gaze shot directly to the black ink above my heart, and just as I thought she was going to ask about it, her eyes drifted back to my face without saying anything.

She sat up and tugged her shirt off, tossing it on the floor. "Come here," she muttered. Pure temptation set my body on fire as I glanced over her chest.

Her breasts were even bigger than I'd thought, resting admirably on her chest, but that wasn't what was causing my dick to harden more. It was the rapid rise and fall of her chest that was causing me to sizzle with lust. It was the way she was looking at me with so much passion and anticipation that was making me want to touch every single part of her body.

And suddenly, I couldn't get to her fast enough.

I pushed myself onto the bed and positioned myself above her. I nudged her head with my own, tossing it to the side to gain access to her neck. My lips swept across her skin, tasting every inch of blue that she had to offer.

I reached between her legs and rubbed gently. Kam's breathy moans filled the room, and her hands trailed down my arms and found their way to the waistband of my pants.

I happily helped her yank them off before slipping my thumb into her jeans. Before I tugged them down, I pulled away and steadied myself above her just enough to look at her face.

"Are you sure?" I asked.

She bit her lip and nodded.

I dropped my forehead onto hers. "Kam," I whispered, "I need to hear you say it."

"Yes," she immediately said. Her blue eyes turned hazy, burning into me with intensity. "Yes, I'm sure. I'm so, *so* sure."

I gave a subtle nod before carefully planting my lips against hers once more, holding myself up with one elbow and using my other hand to help her shimmy her pants off.

I traced my fingertips from the side of her boob all the way down to her hip before lingering over her crotch. I pushed a finger inside of her, pleased to find how wet she already was.

Her hips rocked against my hand as I pumped my finger in and out of her. She reached down and grabbed my length, gripping it as tight as possible before sliding her hand up and down.

I groaned lightly as she quickened her pace. "Feel good?" her throaty voice asked.

I couldn't help but grin as I peered down at her. "You're drivin' me fuckin' crazy."

"Good," she muttered with a sexy smirk. Thankfully, she didn't let go of me as I reached over and fished a condom out of the nightstand.

I slid it on in seconds and brought my dick to her opening. My eyes stayed glued to her face as I slowly pushed myself inside of her, earning a soft gasp from her soft lips.

The moment I kissed her again, the rest of the world turned to dust. There was nothing else that mattered besides her, besides the feeling of our bodies together.

Her hands clawed at my back as I plunged myself deeper inside her, overwhelmed with how damn good she felt. It was like she was made for me.

Her insides clutched onto me so tightly that every inch of me was pulsing with pleasure, but no way was I going to allow myself to finish anytime soon.

I wanted to take my time with her. Feel her. Make it last. And above all, I wanted *her* to finish first.

I kept rocking into her, losing track of time as the minutes ticked by. Kam wrapped her legs around my back, allowing me to hit at a different angle. I held on for as long as possible, waiting until she cried out in pleasure and her eyes rolled into the back of her head until I let myself go with her.

Chapter Twenty-Three
Kamryn

We laid there. Completely engulfed in silence. Both too stunned to speak.

My head was resting on Decker's chest, my body exhausted, but satisfied. His heartbeat flickered beneath my touch and as my eyes shifted upwards in response to the sound, I once again noticed his tattoo.

My slim fingers reached for it, trailing across the ink as if it were treasure. "I didn't know you had a tattoo," I said softly.

Decker's breathing suddenly quickened. "Yeah," he murmured. "Got it not too long ago."

"What does it mean?"

I knew what the word *redemption* meant. I wasn't an idiot. But why that word? Why did that specific word matter so much to Decker that he wanted it tattooed on his chest?

Decker took a breath so deep that his chest carried my head up and down with it. His heartbeat accelerated, pounding into my ear like a fast drumbeat.

"I, uh," he started, his voice trembling in the slightest, "I didn't really make the best decisions my senior year of high school."

Curiosity flooded through me. *I wanted to ask.* God, I *really* wanted to ask. But would it be wrong of me to ask him about something that clearly made him so uneasy? The same way that I got uneasy when people asked me about my parents or living on the street?

Everyone had things about their past that shaped them into the person they were. And everyone had things about their past that they weren't proud of— things that were better off left in the past.

"Well, good thing it's in the past then," I said.

A relieved grin spread across his mouth, stretching so wide that the smile reached his eyes. But the smile fell when he spoke again. "I'm sure I'll explain it to you someday."

And now, *I* was grinning. Because it was the way he said "someday" that insinuated that he planned on staying together for a long time.

I nodded. "Someday, then."

"You don't have any tattoos, right? I didn't see any when I was..." he trailed off with a light blush, once again becoming the shy Decker that I knew and loved.

I froze for a moment at the thought.

Loved.

Did that word really just go through my mind?

I cleared my throat, shaking it off. "I have a small one," I said as I pushed myself up. I sat cross-legged, turning my body towards him. I lifted my right arm. Decker accepted the invitation to touch the delicate ink along my rib cage.

His hands memorized my skin, causing my heart to damn near explode. "What kind of flowers are they?"

"Daisies," I said, a current of both sadness and comfort running through me, creating a strange mixture in my bloodstream.

"Are they for..." he trailed off, his eyes jumping over to me.

"My parents," I nodded. "Every time my dad bought flowers for my mom, they were always daisies."

The tattoo only had two small daisies with their stems intertwined. One of them had pink petals and the other, blue, symbolizing my parents and their favorite colors. Shortly after their passing, I knew I needed something to remind me of them. Something that would be with me wherever I went. So, I got the tattoo on my eighteenth birthday.

Decker's quiet voice came out gravelly as he admired it. "It's beautiful."

"Thank you," I got out, carefully dropping my arm. The second it was beside me, Decker's hand gently pushed at my shoulder, pressing me against the mattress once again.

He smiled as he hovered above me, but instead of making a move, he just eyed me, studying my face as if it were his job.

His amber brown eyes melted to gold and the butterflies within me didn't just swirl around this time— they completely took flight throughout me.

It still astonished me how just one look from him could be felt all over my body, as if his gaze had the power to ignite every cell of mine.

Decker's face slowly approached mine, almost in slow motion. His lips caressed mine, passion burning so deep that they branded me.

His lips belonged on mine. That, I was more than sure of.

Chapter Twenty-Four
Decker

I let out a depleted sigh as I shifted around in my seat, staring at the file in my hands.

I'd been working on the same case for weeks now, the same one my father had given me about the stupid ass guy that was stalking his ex-girlfriend. The guy could deny it all he wanted, but he clearly did it. Either way, it wasn't my job to point out the obvious. My job was to defend him whether he was guilty or not.

I never wanted to become a lawyer, but when it became the only option I had, it became a pretty good option. Not to say that being a lawyer would be all that bad. The money was good. The work was annoying, and sometimes damn near impossible, but each case was different, which always kept things interesting.

I was trying to see the light in it all, but this was never my plan.

On the other hand, if I had stuck to my original plan, then I never would've met Kamryn.

She was the light in it all.

I dropped the file on my desk and reached for my phone instead. Kam's phone number was already programmed into my favorites, making it easy to pull up her contact.

Me: Having fun?

Her: I'll be having fun when I get my first paycheck this weekend.

I smiled, clutching onto my phone. I took my bottom lip between my teeth and chewed on it as I typed out another message.

Me: Are you thinking about me over there?

She was only twenty steps away from my office, but she still felt so far away. Being able to text her every day this week made being at work much more bearable though. Now I had a way to talk to her other than only when we were on our lunch break.

Her: Sure, baby. Whatever floats ur boat!

Me: U float my boat

The rest of the office was so quiet that I could've sworn I heard her giggle.

Her: How romantic!

Another smirk lingered on my face, and the smirk only grew when I envisioned the tight pencil skirt Kam put on this morning. I glanced down at my lap, noticing the unavoidable bulge in my pants.

Me: How bout you come into my office for a bit?

Her: So ur dad can catch us sucking faces during work hours? No thx!

Me: Damn. I'll try again tmw

Her: Good luck trying. You've asked me every day this week and got the same answer every time.

Me: I'm a very motivated guy

I couldn't wipe the stupid grin off my face. Part of me didn't understand how a simple conversation over text with her could make my mood do a complete one-eighty.

But the other part of me knew exactly why. I knew without a doubt that I was in love with her. *Disgustingly* in love. The type of mushy love that people cringed at.

I couldn't help myself. She was saintly, a true angel in my world of demons. She was so addictive in every type of way that I honestly couldn't imagine myself ever being able to go without her again.

I'd only known her for hardly over a month at this point, but it felt like we were already on the path to building a life together, a *world* together, where there was no shame. No guilt. No sins.

I was obsessed with the way she looked at me like I could do no wrong. She thought I was better than I was. I knew I should've told her the other night. *I knew I should've.* But I just wasn't ready. The same way I knew she wasn't ready to talk more about her parents.

There were just some boundaries that neither of us wanted to cross yet.

***

There was the lightest of knocks on my office door. "Decker?" Kam's voice echoed.

"Come in, baby."

The door opened and she closed it behind her. "Hey," she smiled, but as she realized that none of my things were packed up yet, her smile faded. "Are you ready to go home?"

I checked the small digital clock on the corner of my desk. It was already a few minutes past five. "Ugh," I grumbled, rubbing my forehead. "Did my dad already leave?"

"I think so," she nodded. "The rest of the office is empty. From what I could tell, at least."

I sighed again, dropping my head back. Kam made her way around the desk and spun my chair around, just enough to give herself the room to straddle me.

I drew in a sharp breath, a rush of blood heading straight towards my dick, breathing life into it.

Kam ignored the protrusion that was jamming into her crotch, her head glancing over at my messy desk. "I'm assuming you're not ready to go?"

"No," I shook my head disappointedly. "I have to finish writing these direct-examination questions."

Her brows came together as she adjusted herself on my lap. Little did she realize that the small movement in itself was making me hornier than I already was. "Why did your dad make you prep the whole trial for him?"

I shrugged. "He wants me to get as much experience as possible, so he gave me this case while he works on a more advanced one."

Her arms casually rested around my neck. "He's working on another case right now?"

I nodded, biting the inside of my cheek.

"What is it?"

My shoulders rose as I took a deep breath, the question resurrecting the discomfort in me as I spit out the words. "A murder case."

Kam's eyes widened. "No way," she muttered.

"Yeah." I shook my head as I gestured to all my papers. "This trial starts next week though. Same with my classes for the semester," I sighed.

She nodded lightly, then planted a swift kiss on my lips before climbing off me, leaving my lap cold and lonely. "Well, how long do you think you'll be?"

I groaned as I took another look at my desk. "Probably a little over an hour."

"Okay. I'm gonna head home then and let you get back to work so you can finish."

"Alright," I nodded reluctantly. She gave me a shy smile before turning on her heels. "Wait," I demanded.

"Yeah?"

"Come here," I insisted with a tight grin.

She tilted her head towards her shoulder, and as if she read my mind, wandered right over. Her breasts came into perfect view as she leaned down and traced her lips over mine.

She pulled away, biting her lip as she did so. "See you at home, handsome."

Chapter Twenty-Five
Kamryn

Forty-five minutes later, I was already on my way back to the office, clutching a brown bag with two meals in it. I hadn't been planning on going back, but once I got to the apartment and realized that I'd be eating dinner by myself, I couldn't help but wince.

I figured I'd grab our leftovers from last night and bring them to Decker so we could eat together. Even though we'd each be sitting there in silence while we ate and Decker worked more, it was still better than being separated.

Thankfully, the building was still unlocked when I got there. I made my way up the elevator. The floor was uncannily quiet and empty as I sauntered towards Decker's office. I used my free hand to knock and waited a moment for Decker to tell me to come in.

But when that moment didn't come, I faltered. My mouth formed a hard line as I took a single step backwards.

Just as I was about to pull my phone out and give Decker a call, the office door cracked open. Decker's troubled facial expression matched mine.

His face lightened. "Holy shit," he laughed. "I thought you were a ghost."

"Did I scare you?" I laughed as I stepped inside and took a seat.

"Yes," he admitted with a chuckle, making his way back to his seat. "I wasn't expecting you to come back, so when I heard a knock, I legitimately thought it was a ghost." His eyes landed on the bag that I'd set on the table. "Whatcha got?"

I unrolled the brown paper bag and began taking out the small Tupperware boxes. "I prepared a delicious dinner for us."

Decker raised a brow, his mouth twitching as he tried to hold in laughter. He pointed a sluggish finger. "Are those our leftovers?"

"Yes."

His laughter finally slipped out. "What a chef," he teased.

I giggled as I popped the top off one of the boxes. "Well, I wanted to get here quickly so I could eat with you." I shrugged lightly as I piled some chicken into my mouth.

Decker's teasing tone turned sincere. "Well, thank you."

I grinned. "You're welcome."

The room went silent for a few ungodly minutes. I ate quietly while Decker scribbled on the paper in front of him, taking a bite of food occasionally.

His eyes danced back and forth between the desk and me as a slow, inevitable grin came across him. "You don't have to sit there in silence, you know."

"Well, I don't wanna interrupt you."

"I'm almost done, don't worry."

My eyes skimmed along the floor to ceiling bookcase on the far side of the room. I stood and made my way over. I brought my hand up, my fingers grazing over the spines of the hundreds of books filled with boring information.

I could feel his eyes on me, and when I peeked over my shoulder, I wasn't surprised to see his gaze stuck in my direction. His stare electrocuted me with a bolt of fervor, pure warmth and passion.

There was a peculiar gleam in his expression— a crossover between lust and love.

"What?" I asked so quietly that I was sure if the office wasn't empty right now, it wouldn't have been heard.

"I love you," he blurted out. There was no shake in his voice, no uncertainty behind the words.

I turned to fully face him, my mouth slightly agape. When I realized I'd been standing there, staring at him for thirty seconds and still hadn't said anything, I finally spit the words out. "I love you too."

The second he stood, heat flooded my core. Even though I saw him in a suit every single day, there was something about right now that made my insides pulse.

My breathing picked up as he walked towards me, then hitched altogether when his hand cupped my cheek. I could visibly see his Adam's apple bob as he gulped.

This time, I didn't have to think about the words in order for them to fly out. "I love you."

A wolfish grin stretched across his face as his thumb trailed along my jaw. He leaned in, his lips grazing against my ear. "I love you too, Kam."

He stepped forward, forcing my steps backwards until I hit the bookshelf. And just like that, he had me pinned me into place.

Decker's chest rose and fell heavily as he stared at my mouth. As my lips parted, waiting for his next move, I realized just how heavily I was breathing too.

He reached for the back of my thigh, gripping it tightly before his hand slipped underneath my pencil skirt and gradually moved upwards. His touch lit my skin on fire, but I didn't mind the burn. I welcomed it. Wished for it. Waited for it to ignite further.

His voice came out sounding husky as he tugged at the hem of my skirt. "I want this off."

"Then take it off," I muttered.

Clearly, I didn't have to tell him twice because he didn't hesitate to yank it down. I stepped out of the skirt and kicked it away.

Decker's hands immediately clutched my waist, holding me tight against him, tight enough to roll his hips against mine. His erection was threatening to burst through his dress pants, his hot breath making me feverish.

I needed him to kiss me. I needed him to kiss me *now*. What was he waiting for? Each second that ticked by made the insides of my thighs tingle more.

His delicate touch across my bare skin was taunting me, making me ache more for him. He gave a crooked smile, sexy-as-sin.

And that's when I lost my patience.

I gripped the back of his neck and pulled him into me, slamming our lips together. He didn't falter for a single moment, catching right on to create a steady rhythm of our mouths moving together.

When my lips parted again, he used the opportunity to slip his tongue inside my mouth. The kiss was otherworldly, bringing my heartbeat to a pace so fast that I was sure it should've killed me.

I clawed at him, hungry for him. His mouth broke away from mine, just enough to unbutton my shirt and drop it to the floor. His greedy eyes found mine as his hands slipped behind my back and unclasped my bra. "I love you so much," he said.

"I love you." I moaned as he squeezed my breasts. "More."

"More talking or more touching?"

"Both," I demanded, tugging off his suit jacket.

His hot breath hit my neck as he went in for the kill, his mouth warm against my throat. He spoke between kisses. "I fucking love you." A kiss. "You're beautiful... so beautiful." Another kiss.

I tipped my head back against the bookshelf, nearly gasping for air even though he wasn't inside me yet. Hell, he didn't even have his pants off yet.

"You love me?" I questioned.

"Of course."

"Then show me," I ordered.

Within sixty more seconds, all of Decker's clothes were off as well. He took a condom out of his wallet and slipped it on in record time.

Decker's attention zipped back onto me. He grabbed my leg and hiked it upwards. I followed his lead, hooking my

144

leg behind his backside as his lips found their way back to my neck, sucking gently.

I reached down and gripped his length, impatiently guiding it to my opening. Decker did the rest, driving his hips forward to push himself inside me.

I sucked in a sharp breath, my mind roaming into Nirvana at the feeling. He rocked against me, each thrust sending me into the bookshelf. I knew I was going to have a bruise on my tailbone by tomorrow, but I didn't give a shit.

I let out a whimper, clutching onto Decker for stability as my legs weakened with each thrust. "Decker," I cried.

His breaths turned ragged, drilling into me harder and harder. I basked in the feeling, memorizing what it felt like to have him inside me as our moans filled the air.

And eventually, when my fingers dug into his shoulders and I let out a satisfied cry, he knew I'd reached my breaking point and he did the same.

My legs buckled from the climax and Decker laughed as he caught me. "You alright?" he chuckled.

"More than alright," I murmured, out of breath.

"Maybe we should stay after hours more often," he joked.

"I wouldn't complain if we did."

Chapter Twenty-Six
Decker

Kam's smile was at a record length, stretching from ear to ear as she bounced up and down on her toes.

I swore that smile had the ability to move mountains.

She clutched onto her envelope with so much strength that I could see her knuckles turning white.

"Ahh!" she shrieked, shoving the envelope in my face.

I dodged it with a chuckle, trying to avoid getting a paper cut in my eye.

She finally stood flat on her feet, her eyes fixated on the envelope as if she was afraid it would vanish between her fingers. Her smile hadn't faltered a single centimeter. If anything, it'd somehow grown bigger.

I waited a moment to allow her to bask in her joy before I spoke. "Well, are you gonna open it?"

Kam let out a squeak of excitement, holding the envelope against her chest. "Okay, okay," she said. "Here I go..." She thumbed it open and pulled the check out. Her eyes widened with amazement as she studied it. "Wow," she muttered in disbelief.

"Happy?"

"Absolutely!"

"Good." I tilted my head towards my chest, my eyes softening. If someone had told me a month ago that the homeless girl that lived outside my apartment would become the very best thing in my life, I never would've believed them. And now here she was, her dirt-covered face replaced with a radiant one. Her empty stomach replaced with a full one. Her broken heart replaced with a sewn one.

"Oh my gosh!" she screeched. "We have to celebrate!"

"Yeah?" I raised a brow. I stepped forward, lightly gripping her forearm and tugging her towards me. Once she was close enough, I wrapped my arms around her lower back and swayed her for a moment before leaning in close. "How so?"

Her voice was wary, as if trying too hard to control what was coming out of her mouth. "We could go out with everybody?"

I tipped my head side to side, pretending to be in thought. My hands slipped lower, and the second I grabbed her ass, her spine stiffened. "Or I have a better idea."

She leaned back to get a better look at my face. "Let me guess," she said, raising a joking brow. "You're trying to get laid?"

I bit my tongue, trying to suppress the massive grin that was threatening to give me away.

"Hmm?" she pushed.

I stifled a laugh, looking down at her ocean eyes. "Don't act like you don't want to."

"What makes you so sure that I *do* want to?"

My face turned deliberate, focused. All I had to do was chase my fingertips across the top of her arm and she shivered beneath me.

"That," I said surely. "Your body always reacts to mine. *That's* how I know."

She dragged in a deep, careful breath. "Fine," she agreed. "But we're going out after. And I'm paying."

"No way." I shook my head once.

Kam lifted a brow, a flirty smirk rising with it. "Then no deal."

I chewed on my bottom lip in thought.

"Oh, c'mon, Mr. Big Ego. Let me pay for once."

I waved it off. "We'll talk about it after."

"No. Do we have a deal or not?"

"This is coercion."

She gave a shrug, her breasts bouncing up and down as she did so. The sight was mouthwatering. I swallowed.

"Fine," I agreed.

"Good." She cocked her head towards the bedroom with a smirk. "Lead the way."

***

Nolan, Alaina, Benny, Myra, Kam, and I all walked up to Westside collectively.

The second I spotted Pry at the door, my teeth grinded together. I squeezed Kam's hand a little harder, making sure to keep her close so that it was clear to him to back the fuck off.

There were a few people in line ahead of us, but Pry's eyes skimmed over our group, and when his gaze shifted between Kam and me, a menacing smirk appeared on his face.

My jaw shifted beneath my skin. As much as I wanted to turn around and go somewhere else, I couldn't. Tonight was Kam's night to celebrate her first paycheck, to celebrate her life heading in a new direction. And unfortunately, since she wasn't twenty-one yet, this was the only place we could get her into.

"You okay? You're squeezing my hand really hard," Kam laughed.

"Yeah, sorry," I said, loosening my grip.

The line finally shortened. Pry didn't even bother checking our IDs as we all strolled inside, but his eyes focused too much on Kam for my liking. I could pick out the yearning in his expression, causing my muscles to tighten. I shot him a warning glare, but he didn't seem to notice.

I swore to God if he made any sort of slimy move towards my girl, he'd be leaving on a stretcher.

Again.

I tried to shake off my annoyance as we made our way towards the bar, and right when Kam's dazzling smile appeared, mine couldn't help but follow suit. I thrived off her happiness.

The six of us gathered around the bar, and even though we'd only been there for thirty seconds, Kam didn't hesitate to get shit started.

"Okay!" she announced, waving her hands around excitedly. "A round of shots on me!"

The group exploded in cheers. All besides me, of course. My satisfied grin was still lingering though as I leaned against the bar, watching Kam's reaction to everyone's excitement.

Her elation was lighting up the whole building. It was as if she had a bright glow above her head, inevitably brightening everyone and everything around her.

She stepped through everyone to reach me. "I'm assuming you don't want one?"

"No thanks, baby."

"Okay," she smiled, shrugging it off. She leaned over the bar, trying to wave down a bartender. My eyes dropped to her ass jutting out as she bent forward.

Goddamn.

She just looked so freaking good. Not that she ever looked bad, but she looked phenomenal tonight in her ocean blue, low cut top and white jeans. The outfit was courtesy of Alaina, of course.

Thank you, Alaina.

The color brought out her striking eyes, and her platinum hair rested in waves past her shoulders. I took a moment to stare at her, taking in every detail of the masterpiece that she was.

When the bartender came back with a small tray of shots, I stepped out of the way as five hands reached in to grab one.

Benny's brow lifted as he gave a sly smile. "Wanna sip?" he asked, pushing his shot glass towards me.

My face twisted into disgust as the smell of liquor wafted in my direction. I brought my elbow up, blocking him from getting any closer. "Don't be an asshole."

"Alright, alright," he said, pulling the glass away. "I'm sorry. That was a dick move."

"Yeah, it was," I muttered. I was surprised the smell itself didn't send me to the bathroom barfing.

"Okay, wait," Nolan said. Once he had everyone's attention, he continued. "Let's make a toast to Kam... for kicking life's ass!"

"To Kam!" everyone shouted.

Her face flushed, her addictive smile wiggling across her face. I watched as she pounded the shot back like a champ before slamming the empty glass on the bar.

"Woo!" she cheered. "Let's do another one!"

Oh gosh. This was going to be a long night.

***

I sat at the bar, swiveling back and forth in my seat next to Benny. Kam and the other girls were taking selfies on the far side of the room. Nolan was off somewhere talking to some guys he knew.

I let out a heavy sigh as I took another glance at Kam. I rubbed the stubble on my chin. "I need to tell her, man."

Benny's head snapped over to me, his beer halfway to his mouth. "She doesn't know?"

I gulped. *Hard.* "No."

"What, you think she'll freak if you tell her?"

"Probably," I sighed, running my hands up and down my thighs restlessly. "I mean what girl wouldn't freak out after finding out her boyfriend's a criminal?"

Benny's expression softened in the slightest. "You're still beating yourself up over it, aren't you?"

"How could I not?"

He sighed, setting his beer on the bar. "Well, you should definitely tell her soon. The sooner, the better, really."

I bit my lower lip so mercilessly that I was surprised it didn't start spurting blood. "The worst part is that I feel like I've had a few opportunities to tell her, and I totally choked." Benny eyed me, waiting for an explanation. "Like when she saw my tattoo for the first time," I said.

"She asked?"

"Of course," I said. "I could've told her right then and there. I *should've* told her right then and there." I sighed again. "But I pussied out."

Benny was rarely the type of friend that you went to for advice. He was the friend that was always looking to have a good time. The friend that hated the sappy moments or deep

150

talks. But when you did catch him in a serious conversation, he was always there for you.

"I don't blame you," he said softly. "You don't even talk about that night with any of us."

I winced.

"Sorry," he said, wincing alongside me. Then he muttered, "In more ways than one," as he raised his beer back up to his mouth, pretending like that was supposed to create a curtain to hide his words.

"Stop," I demanded, peering up at him. The mood between us had turned somber, which was what this subject usually did.

"What?" Benny shrugged, avoiding eye contact with me.

My tone was so anguished, so defeated. "You're blaming yourself again."

He finally managed to meet my gaze. "Well, it's partly my fault."

"It's no one's fault but mine," I assured him.

His voice fell further. "I could think of one more person at fault."

I sucked in a deep breath, reading his mind. Yeah, I guess I could think of one more person too. But then again, she didn't force me to do what I did that night. As much as I wanted to blame it on her, I couldn't.

It was my fault. And we all knew it.

Chapter Twenty-Seven
Kamryn

I'd never been this drunk before.

Two mixed drinks and four shots was definitely not a good idea for a lightweight. But at the same time, I was having so much fun.

It was a good thing that tomorrow was Saturday, so that I'd have all day to lay in bed and nurse off the hangover that I was bound to have.

I let out a shriek of laughter as Decker's hands wrapped around me from behind. I melted against him, his head resting on my shoulder. We swayed side to side like this on the dance floor, earning a satisfied smile from Alaina.

Decker turned his head so that his mouth was merely touching my ear. "I love you," he said, the words tickling my earlobe like raindrops.

I twisted to look at him. "I love you too," I grinned.

His charming smile lit up the bar, staying there for only a moment before the smile turned smug. He leaned back in. "You look so good tonight. We're going straight to the bedroom when we get home."

A laugh popped out of my mouth, even though his words were the farthest thing from humorous. My core began throbbing uncontrollably, and when his thumb trailed along the exposed skin between my crop top and jeans, a little shiver raced up my spine.

As much as I wanted to drag him into the bathroom and take him there, I straightened, taking a deep breath through my nose to keep my self-control.

I swallowed, then licked my lips before answering. "Well, you'll have to wait," I teased.

He let out a frustrated groan, but his smile never faded.

"Hey!" Benny shouted at the group. "Will someone go outside with me while I have a smoke?"

Nolan's brows came in. He had one arm draped around Alaina, the other holding a beer. "I'm going to get another beer. Go by yourself," Nolan said, prancing off.

"No," Benny whined to the rest of us.

"You're like a girl that can't go to the bathroom by herself," Myra taunted.

He smirked at her. "Come with me?" he asked, lifting a brow.

Myra smirked back, but it was impossible not to catch the difference in their eyes. She smirked at him like a sister that was teasing her younger brother. But he smirked at her the same way Decker smirked at me.

Full of adoration.

"Nope," she replied, giving him a playful cold shoulder as she turned and began dancing again.

Decker scoffed. "I can't believe you're still smoking anyway."

Benny shoved his hands in his pockets, shifting his weight back and forth. "I'll quit at some point."

"Yeah," Decker rolled his eyes. "Sure, you will."

"Decks, come with me?" Benny pleaded with a puppy dog expression. "C'mon, don't leave a brother hanging."

Decker eyed him for a moment, ultimately before sighing. "Fine," he grumbled. "You better make it a quick one though." He turned to me, his arm still wrapped around my waist. "Will you be okay for a few?"

"Yeah," I assured him.

"Alright," he murmured with a side grin, planting a kiss on my forehead before following Benny out of the bar.

The second Decker was no longer in the room, my entire body shuddered from the lack of closeness. He was just too addictive to be away from.

Decker was right. Benny had better make it a fast one.

When my mind finally snapped back to reality instead of being focused on Decker's departure, I realized that Alaina was laughing like a hyena.

Myra crossed her arms as she attempted to smother Alaina with a hard glare, but her playful grin gave her away.

"What?" I asked.

Alaina's laughter halted just enough to respond. "Benny."

"What? His smoking?"

"No, no, no," Alaina waved it off. "Myra, you wanna fill her in?"

Myra sighed, dropping her arms back at her sides. "Benny is..." she started, pushing her mouth into a hard line as she tried to think of how to explain, "one of my best friends. I mean, I've known the guy since junior year of high school, but he—"

"Has feelings for you and you don't reciprocate?" I finished for her.

Her shoulders slumped as she blew out a loud breath. "Is it really that obvious?"

"Yeah," I cringed. "Have you told him you only like him as a friend?"

Her mouth pulled over to one side in dissatisfaction. "See, that's the thing. I've tried to make it super clear to him, but he's also never straight up asked me on a date or confessed that he had feelings. He's never even tried to make a move. Like how do you reject someone before they even make a move?"

"Yeah," I agreed with another wince.

"I don't wanna just out of the blue be like *Hey, I know you like me, but it's never gonna happen.* That would make things so awkward!"

"And you would break his little heart," Alaina added.

Myra lolled her head to the side to look at her. "Exactly."

I could see Myra's dilemma. Benny made it more than obvious that he was into her. He was constantly wanting to be around her, not to mention the way he *looked* at her. I didn't blame her for not telling him her truth before he even confessed his. Nobody wanted to break their friend's heart.

"Kamryn, right?" a deep voice came from behind me, making me jump and step closer to the girls.

Myra rolled her eyes. "Tommy," she groaned in annoyance.

He lifted an impish brow at her, but it wasn't hard to catch the way his eyes kept flickering back to me. "Did I interrupt something?"

"Yes," Alaina said.

"I just wanted to come over and say hello."

Myra clearly caught his wandering eyes as well, because she was quick to step forward. "Well, you've done it now, so I suggest you walk off before Decker gets back," she warned.

"Why?" his brows shot inwards. "I'm not afraid of Shepley."

Myra's voice was laced with skepticism. "Well, you probably should be."

I glanced over at Alaina with a muddled expression, willing her to look back at me and give me answers, but she was still focused on Tommy.

Alaina shook her head. "We don't need to repeat high school right now, okay?"

Tommy shrugged. "I'm not trying to."

"What *are* you trying to do?" I blurted out.

His rock-like stance softened, but for some reason, his eyes were still on me, as if I was the only one he was talking to. "Look, I—"

"You what?" Decker spat from behind him.

Tommy turned, taking a step backwards to create distance between them. "Shepley," he said through gritted teeth.

There was no ounce of patience in Decker's voice or body for that matter. Every single muscle of his was as stiff as a board. "What are you doing, Pry?" he seethed, his jaw shifting beneath his skin.

"Nothing," Tommy insisted with a hardness in his tone.

"Nothing?" Decker doubted. He began slowly stepping towards Pry like a lion closing in on its prey. "I thought I told you to stay away from her."

Tommy took a step back with each step that Decker took forward, and although he wasn't letting the intimidation show on his face, his body language screamed *fear*.

What the hell was I missing here, though? These two clearly had a history, bad blood dating back to high school, but why? I wasn't oblivious to the fact that Decker always got tense whenever Tommy came around, but he never explained the reasoning behind it, and honestly, I'd never thought too much into it to ask.

I glanced at the girls, and of course, they didn't look confused at all. They knew exactly why Decker had flipped a switch.

I'd never seen this fire in his eyes before. He didn't just look bitter. He didn't just look angry. He looked completely *outraged*.

"So, *why*?" Decker questioned, his hands drawing into fists at his sides. "Why is it always mine?"

My brows came in, focusing on Decker's words. *"Why is it always mine?"* What the hell did that mean? Has this happened before?

My mouth parted in realization. *This must've happened before.*

Emmy's voice rang in my head. *"He dated a girl in high school named Casey, but it was a long time ago."*

I didn't have to hear anyone say her name in order to put the pieces together.

"Don't make me throw you out, Shepley," Tommy threatened, but his threat wasn't intimidating considering his shaky voice. Either way, Decker still didn't look fazed in the slightest.

Tommy's space to step away was running out as Decker continued to stalk forward, standing tall as if he were indestructible.

I felt like I should step in and stop him, but for some reason, my body wouldn't cooperate. I wasn't sure if it was the liquor or the unease within me.

"Decker," Myra warned, taking a wary step forward.

But it was as if he couldn't hear her. His eyes didn't stray away from Tommy, zoned in on him like a gun aiming at its target. His clenched fists were visibly shaking, overtaken with fury.

Just as Decker was about to raise his fist in the air, Nolan lunged between him and Tommy, his beer slightly spilling over from the act.

"Whoa, whoa, whoa," Nolan said, planting his free hand on Decker's chest.

Decker immediately halted under his touch, his clenched fists slowly coming undone.

"Let's all chill out," Nolan insisted, looking back and forth between the two.

"I didn't need you to save me, Nolan," Tommy countered.

Nolan pulled back. "I'm sorry," he said sarcastically. "Did you *want* another broken nose?"

Tommy let out a huff, his gaze shifting off, but this was also the first moment that his body had somewhat relaxed since Decker's voice emerged from behind him.

It was crystal clear Tommy was relieved about Nolan butting in, but his ego was far too big to admit it. Either way, I didn't really care about how Tommy was feeling. I only cared about Decker.

I stared at him with worried eyes, waiting for him to look back at me. As if my stare was screaming at him, his eyes slowly shifted onto me. I could see his entire body relax with a deep breath as we kept eye contact, every hardened muscle finally softening.

My mouth formed a long frown, and without a second thought, I stepped over to him with my arms extended.

Decker's eyes never left me, completely forgetting that everyone, including Tommy was still standing there. He walked forward, closing the gap between us and taking me tightly into his arms. Our bodies relaxed against each other, and he buried his head into the crook of my neck.

"I'm sorry," he croaked into my ear.

"Let's just go home," I said in a quiet voice, squeezing him tighter.

"Okay," he breathed out.

Chapter Twenty-Eight
Decker

"Are you gonna tell me what that was all about?" Kam asked gently as we got tucked under the covers.

Our walk home had been quiet, but I held Kam's hand tightly the whole way. When we got back, she still hadn't said anything or asked questions up until now. I couldn't even tell if she was mad about what happened. She didn't sound mad, but I wasn't quite sure.

I took a deep breath, rolling over to look at her. "I'm sorry," I started off with.

She didn't accept nor deny my apology. She just moved right past it— another reason why I couldn't tell if she was mad at me. But her voice stayed calm, gentle, loving.

"Has it happened before?"

I squeezed my eyes shut as I let out a sigh. "Yeah."

She spoke quietly, as if in a whisper. "What happened?"

I shivered beneath the sheets as I began speaking. "I was dating someone in high school and Pry made a move on her and... I lost my shit."

"You broke his nose?"

"Yeah," I admitted, ashamed, as if I weren't about to do it again an hour prior.

"And you were dating Casey?"

I froze, fear casting over me like a shadow. My mouth opened but nothing came out at first. Reluctance was jammed in my throat. "U—um, yeah..." I stuttered. "How did you..."

"Emmy told me."

The fear ignited into terror. Did she know? What did Emmy tell her?

I was too scared to ask the most important question on my mind. I stared at her, trying to read a trace of how much she knew.

What do you know, Kamryn?

As if she read my mind, she spoke, still unfazed by my deafening silence. "She only said that you dated someone named Casey. She didn't tell me anything else. Quite honestly, I'm pretty sure she only told me because I asked."

I tipped my head down, letting out a sigh of relief. "Oh."

Kam's blue irises were peering into me silently, and I blew out another breath with the realization that I needed to at least explain myself further.

I hadn't spoken her name aloud in years. It felt like I was spitting out poison. "Casey and I dated for a little over a year, but it seemed like every time I turned around, she was cheating and lying."

Kam's eyes widened, sympathy flooding out of them like rivers. "Is that why you broke up?"

I bobbed my head side to side against my pillow. "For the most part, yeah," I said.

God, I hated giving her half-truths, but even if I wanted to give her the full truth now, I was one-hundred percent sure that I physically wouldn't be able to get it out. Talking about Casey was enough torture for now.

"Hey," Kam said faintly, scooting closer to me. Her hand cupped my face before her thumb swiped over my cheek. "Hey, it's okay."

I hadn't even realized I was crying. Little did she know the real reason why.

I wasn't crying over Casey. I was crying from what I did *because* of Casey.

"We don't have to talk about it anymore," she said.

"I'm sorry."

"For what?"

Feeding half-truths to you. Circling around my sins like I was dancing around a campfire. For not telling you what I really am.

"I just..." I muttered, but before I could continue, she stopped me.

"Decks... don't be sorry," she assured me, tangling our legs together underneath the covers. "Just know that I would never, *ever* cheat on you."

"I know," I whispered with a faint smile. "I would never cheat on you either."

Her sweet grin stretched a little. "And I'd never lie to you."

I could feel a rocket of pain physically pounding inside me, spreading throughout my body like lethal injection as it headed towards the heart.

Because I wished I could say the same, Kam. I really wished I could.

Chapter Twenty-Nine
Kamryn

The second I opened my eyes, I saw Decker's. His amber irises were on me, but it was the bags beneath them that caught my eye.

Had he not slept at all last night?

"Good morning," his raspy voice called out, drenched in an underlying layer of devastation.

"Good morning," I said back.

His hand reached towards me, gently taking a strand of my loose hair between his fingers and toying with it. "You're so beautiful in the morning."

A fragile smile touched my lips, but the smile was quickly replaced with a wince. I cupped my forehead. "Baby hangover," I said, squeezing my eyes shut.

Decker hopped out of bed. "Let me get you some water."

I could hear him rustling around in the kitchen for a few minutes after he disappeared, but I kept my eyes closed, currently preferring the darkness over the light that was casting through the blinds.

I barely heard him enter the room, but I *felt* when he did before he even spoke.

"Here you go," he said softly, sitting on the edge of the bed with a glass of water held out to me.

I took my time sitting up. "Thank you." I clutched the glass with two hands like a toddler and brought it up to my mouth.

"I'm sorry again about last night," Decker said, sorrowful. He looked down at the comforter.

I shook my head. "Decks, it's okay. Really. You have nothing to be sorry for."

He kept his head dropped towards the mattress, but his eyes peered up to look at me. "Yes, I do," he whispered.

But the fact of the matter was that I honestly didn't care. I wasn't upset in any type of way. I knew what it felt like to be cheated on, and I understood more than anyone that jealousy was a powerful beast. If the roles were reversed, I would've reacted the same way.

I didn't want Decker feeling bad about something that I'd quite honestly already forgotten. The only thing that was currently on my mind was the aching migraine taking over.

"Decks," I sighed, placing the glass on the nightstand, "please, it's okay. Can we just forget about it? I've got a killer headache."

I rubbed my forehead again, peeking up at him through heavy lids. He nodded as his hand found its way to my thigh, gently caressing it. I knew the gesture was only meant to comfort me, but migraine or not, his touch still sent a jolt of lust through me.

"You want some breakfast?" he asked.

"Please," I requested. "And then afterwards, I want you to come back to bed. I could tell you didn't sleep well last night."

He gave a tiny nod in agreement before leaning in, his hand planted on my waist as he left the gentlest kiss on my forehead. I closed my eyes as his lips lingered there, memorizing how it felt to have them against my skin. I breathed in deeply until my lungs were filled with him, sucking in so much of his presence that I was getting high from it.

When his lips left, he didn't pull away completely. Instead, he brought his forehead to mine while his hand lightly gripped the back of my neck, holding me close.

"I want you to know that you're the best thing that's ever happened to me," he said. "And you have no idea how scared I am of losing you."

Despite my growing headache, I didn't want to close my eyes. My hand slowly trailed over his sharp jawline, tracing from the edge all the way to his chin. "You won't."

He clenched his eyes shut as if he were in pain. "I really, really hope not."

"Hey," I muttered, "look at me." I waited until his eyes popped open before I continued. *"You won't,"* I repeated.

***

When I woke back up, Decker was still asleep, finally getting some rest after staying up all night, beating himself over things that didn't matter.

I studied him. The way the black ink on his chest was peeking out from underneath the covers. The way his ashy hair was askew against his pillow. The way his breaths were peacefully drawn out.

Everything about him was intoxicating, down to the smallest of details, and I couldn't help but wonder— how could Casey ever cheat on *him*?

I sat there for minutes on end, admiring him. I wanted to touch him. To snuggle up beside him. Whisper in his ear how thankful I was for him and how much I loved him.

But I didn't want to wake him.

Instead, I grabbed my glass of water off the nightstand and pounded down the rest of it. At this point, I was pretty sure I'd slept, eaten, and hydrated the hangover out of me. But honestly, I could go for a coffee right now.

I carefully climbed out of bed and threw leggings on, not bothering to change out of my pajama shirt. I grabbed my phone and my wallet with my new debit card in it and slipped my shoes on before heading outside into the sun.

It was seventy degrees out, which immediately made me regret wearing leggings, but since I was only going across the street, there was no point in running back inside to change.

I stepped over to the crosswalk and waited for the little man to appear that told me it was safe to walk. There was a bundle of nerves and excitement racing through me at the thought of seeing Lydia.

I hadn't seen her in so long and so much had changed since then that I was nervous how she would react when she saw me. Would she notice a difference? Would she be able to differentiate my clean face from my dirt-ridden one?

I wasn't even sure if she still worked at the coffee shop. I ran a hand over the messy French braid that I hadn't bothered redoing after I woke up. It didn't really matter to me though, because no matter how bad I may have looked right now, I was a hundred percent sure I still looked better than I did two months ago.

The bell atop the door rang as I swung it open. My eyes glanced around for Lydia, checking every face in the shop. It was only noon and right now, the shop was as lively as I'd ever seen it.

I stumbled over to the end of the line to order, my eyes still peering around for Lydia.

I played on my phone as I waited in line, checking my new Instagram account that I'd recently made for myself. My first post was a selfie of Alaina, Myra, and me from last night. I grinned as I looked at it.

One of the most painful parts of being homeless was being lonely. I had no one to talk to. No one to share my time with. That in itself was brutal— because all I *had* was time. I didn't have a home or clean clothes or food. I didn't have a phone or an accessible bathroom or water. All that I had was time. And when you had no one to share the only thing that you had with, things got pretty lonely.

I never expected to lose my parents at such a young age. I never expected to end up being homeless. I never expected to be absolutely *miserable*. But now I had everything I could've possibly needed. I had *more* than what I needed, and I couldn't be more grateful. Decker had given me the tools that I needed to get my life back on track and now I finally felt like I had a fighting chance to kick life's ass.

I remained patient as the line dwindled down and finally, it was my turn to step up to the counter. The second I looked up from the ground, Lydia's disbelief sat clear on her face.

"Kamryn," she smiled.

"Hi," I said, an inevitable smile growing.

Her fingertips touched her lips. "Oh my gosh. You look so good!"

"Thank you," I grinned.

"Not that you didn't look good before!" she said, quick to correct herself.

I chuckled. "It's okay. I know what you mean."

"How are you?" she asked, leaning over to check how long the line was behind me. I peeked over my shoulder. There were only a few people behind me, but still, I didn't want to hold up the line.

"I'm good," I answered with a strong nod. "I'm really good."

"That's so great." Relief coated her voice, her eyes, her smile. "Look, I really wanna catch up, so could you stick around for a bit after the line is gone? I have my break coming up so we can chat for a while? I shouldn't be longer than twenty minutes."

"Yes, absolutely."

"Okay, great," she nodded. "What can I get you then?"

"Can I please have a medium caramel Frappuccino?"

"Sure thing."

"And a chocolate chip cookie," I added, handing over my debit card, which felt so damn good to be able to do.

"Of course," Lydia laughed, swiping my card. "Coming right up."

"Thanks." I put the card back in my wallet and stepped over to the side as Lydia took the next customer's order. There was another barista making drinks at record speed, pumping out what seemed like numerous orders at a time.

I swear it had only been sixty seconds when my drink and cookie were in front of me. I thanked the unknown barista as I grabbed them and headed over to a small empty table in the corner by the front window.

I took a sip of coffee, letting out a soft hum from how good it tasted. It wasn't until then that I realized my smile had hardly left my face ever since stepping out of the apartment.

Every time Decker wasn't next to me, I missed him like crazy. It was undeniable that he was my favorite person. At this point, he was part of me. The one pulsing through my blood. The one keeping my gravity centered. The one who had absolute control over my heart.

But through loving Decker, I was finally learning to love myself again. As much as I missed him each time we were apart, I was still enjoying myself when we weren't together. It was the little things that gave me little victories each day. Like being able to walk across the street and grab a coffee by myself without feeling lonely.

When a shadow stood over me, my eyes hesitantly trailed upwards. I could feel my muscles tense beneath my skin as I held my breath, choking back disgust.

"Kamryn," my aunt said, sounding just as appalled as I felt.

"Aunt Karen," I gritted between my teeth.

"Where have you been?" she asked, sipping on her drink.

I rolled my eyes. "Where have *you* been?"

"Don't roll your eyes at me," she snapped. "I asked you a question."

I wanted to roll my eyes again, but I managed to hold myself back. "I've just been... around," I said, trying not to let my resentment shine through. "What are you doing here?"

She shrugged casually. "Stopped to grab coffee on my way back from book club."

I gave a nod, pretending to care. "Nice."

I hated how she was just standing there, hovering above me. If she was going to stay and "chat," then she should've at least sat down. There were plenty of things I disliked about my aunt, but this was one of the most— she always felt the need to make you feel like you were less than her. Whether that meant saying it straight to your face or standing above you like you were a child.

No way in hell was I going to offer her a seat though.

"So really," she began again, "where have you been? Because I know you haven't been staying with Ryan."

My eyes narrowed in the slightest as I stared at her incredulously. "And how would you know that?"

Nonchalantly, she took another sip of coffee. "He stopped by."

My hands strained atop the table. "What?"

She spoke as if none of this conversation were important in the slightest, as if we were just discussing the goddamn book at her book club. "Yep. Tracked down my new address and came by looking for you. Said he wanted to make sure you were okay."

"And what did you tell him?"

She shrugged. "I told him you were fine."

I scoffed, nearly breaking out in laughter from disbelief. The fact that my ex-fiancé showed up on her doorstep, claiming he had no idea where I was, yet she didn't bat an eyelash with concern, showed exactly how much she cared about me.

"When was this?" I demanded.

"A few months ago."

I bit my lip as I nodded, holding back a scream. "Well, great. Thanks for letting me know," I said sarcastically.

She tilted her head as she eyed me with a tight-lipped smile. "You look exactly like your mother. Especially with those blue eyes."

Her dark brown eyes were so dark that they were nearly black, matching her soul. Her nose was oddly arched like a witch, and her graying hair did not help her cause.

She didn't look the slightest bit like my mother. No wonder why she was so jealous of her.

I lifted a brow. "I know."

This time, she rolled her eyes. "Don't flatter yourself, Kamryn. Your mother wasn't a superstar or anything."

I leaned towards her, refusing to back down. "She could've been."

Her glare hardened. "Not anymore," she said, spitting envy.

It took everything in me not to stand up and start screaming in her face while I wrapped my hands around her neck and squeezed the life out of her.

My jaw was so tight, like it was made of steel. I stared at her as if my glare itself could kill her.

Finally, a small figure approached, standing on the opposite side of the table.

My aunt saw Lydia out of the corner of her eye. She let out a small sigh, sounding bored as she checked her watch. "Well, it was nice seeing you, sweetie. Let me know if you need anything," she said with a deceptive smile, lightly squeezing my shoulder before walking off.

"Bitch," I muttered under my breath. I shook off my irritation as Lydia slid into the seat across from me. Animosity was still fresh in my blood, but I refused to let my aunt ruin my time with Lydia.

"Hey," Lydia said, "thanks for waiting."

"Yeah, of course."

"So," she smiled, stirring her coffee, "tell me everything."

I pushed a loose strand of hair behind my ear, blowing out a breath. "I don't even know where to start."

"I haven't seen you in so long. I think since the summer. It was definitely before school started for me."

"Oh yeah! How is school?"

"It's good," she shrugged. "Nothing quite interesting about it." She propped her elbow up on the table and rested her chin on her hand. "I wanna hear about you."

I took my bottom lip between my teeth for a moment, attempting to shield my massive, embarrassing smile. "I've been staying with someone."

Lydia's eyes grew wide. "It's not your ex, is it?"

"No, no!" I assured her. "It's a new guy actually."

"Name?"

"Decker."

"Decker," she repeated. "That's an interesting name. I've never heard it before."

I tilted my head in thought. "Neither have I, actually."

"Decker," she said again, staring off. "What does that name even mean?"

"I'm not sure," I said, intrigued. "I'm gonna look it up." My phone was already lying face up on the table, so all I had to do was give it a few taps to get our answer.

The second the search results came up, I bent over laughing.

"What?" Lydia asked. "What's it mean?"

My laughter was loud enough to be heard across the room, but I couldn't contain myself. I couldn't even spit the words out to tell her. I was laughing so hard that my abdomen was on fire.

"What!" Lydia said again through a smile. But when it was clear to her that I would need another minute before I'd be able to answer her, she sighed. "Let me see that." She grabbed the phone off the table, bringing it up to her face. "Ditch digger?" she read with a laugh.

Her reading it aloud only caused me to laugh more. I toppled over in my chair, envisioning Decker digging ditches for a living instead of becoming a lawyer.

Once we both finally caught our breaths and I used a napkin to pat down the wet corners of my eyes that resulted in our Laugh Fest, Lydia finally spoke again.

"Well, do you have a picture of you and Mr. Ditch Digger?"

I giggled, picking up my phone and scrolling through my camera roll. I didn't have a lot of photos on there since it was still so new, so I pulled one up that Decker and I took last night at Westside.

"Woah," her eyes grew. "He is a *very* handsome dude."

I tried to push my mouth into a line to hide my smile, but I could still feel it peeking through. I gave a strong nod. "He is."

She tipped her head towards her shoulder, her eyes still grazing over the photo. "He looks kinda familiar."

"He lives across the street."

Lydia's head popped up, her face distorting into a scowl. "You've been across the street this whole time and haven't come to visit me!"

I covered my face with both hands. "I know, I know! I'm the worst."

Her palm flew over her chest as she used her other hand to give my phone back. "Gosh, Kamryn. You disappeared for so long that there was a point in time where I thought something really bad happened to you."

I winced. "I should've thought about that. I'm sorry."

She blew out a long breath, her pleasant smile slowly coming back to the surface. "It's okay," she said. "But tell me more."

Chapter Thirty
Decker

I groggily rolled over, letting out a sigh as my eyes blinked open. I reached beside me, only to feel nothing but the comforter, then immediately shot up.

"Kam?" I called out. I waited a moment but there was no response. "Kam?" I said, a little louder this time.

Still nothing.

I jumped out of bed, my breathing picking up as I tread into the kitchen. "Kam?" I checked the living room. The bathroom. Even the damn supply closet.

And still... nothing.

The worry in the air was thick enough to tighten my throat, cutting off my air supply.

Where did she go? Did last night truly bother her and she wanted to leave because of it?

I spun around myself, my heart painfully flipping at the thought. She couldn't have left though, right? Not after the way she was reassuring me this morning that I wouldn't lose her... right?

Did she know how much I needed her? How over the course of a few months she'd become the entire focal point of my world?

I blew out a heavy breath, jogging back into our bedroom to call her. Thank God, I got her that phone. What the hell would I have done if this happened beforehand?

My hand shook as I grabbed it off the nightstand and when I unlocked it to see a text from Kam, my body calmed.

Kam: Ran across the street to grab some coffee with an old friend and catch up. See you when I get home, handsome! Love you <3

My hand fell over my chest as I caught my breath, the anxiety slowly leaving my body. I reread her text, staring at the end of it as a smirk tugged on the corners of my mouth.

Me: Take your time, beauty queen. I love you.

Another huge sigh of relief climbed out as I took a seat on the bed. I chewed on my bottom lip, staring off in thought.

I needed to figure out what the fuck I should do. It was obvious that the truth was the best route, but would it be acceptable if I waited longer to go down that route? Would it be wrong to stay quiet about my demons even though they had nothing to do with Kam?

I felt like a liar. But was I one? Was I a liar for taking my time to explain to her the worst parts of myself?

I snatched my phone off the bed, dialing the one person's number that I trusted to give me the right answer.

It rang once. Twice. Three times. I bobbed my leg up and down in anticipation. *C'mon. Pick up the phone.*

"Hey, Decks," Alaina answered. "What's up?"

"I need your advice."

"*My* advice?" Alaina questioned. "Must be pretty serious..." she joked. "What's up?"

"Well..." I started, tripping over the words, "Kam still doesn't know."

"Doesn't know about..." she trailed off, unsure.

"You know," I said, my teeth lightly clenching.

"Oh."

"I know I need to tell her, but I just can't get myself to do it and it's eating me alive and—"

"*Decker*," she cut me off. "It's okay."

I sighed. "I feel like it's not."

"Does she know *anything* at all?"

"Yeah, she knows there's something I've been struggling to talk about, and she knows a little bit about Casey at least."

"Well, I'd freaking hope you told her a little about Casey after last night," Alaina blurted. She sighed, her voice softening. "But she didn't push for any details?"

"No."

"Then it's fine for now. Clearly none of your past is a make-it-or-break-it for her. Trust me. I see the way she looks at you. When you eventually tell her, she's not going to look at you any differently." Silence overtook us for a moment. I could tell Alaina was waiting for me to respond, but my mind was on a loop, thinking of a million different ways that Kam could react. But not a single way I imagined ended with her seeing me the same way she does now. "Well, that's what you're worried about, isn't it?" Alaina finally broke the silence. "That she'll see you differently?"

"Yeah," I admitted. "And that she'll leave me."

"She's certainly not going to leave you based off decisions you made when you were *seventeen*."

"I just feel like I'm leaving out such a huge part of my life."

"I'm sure there are things she hasn't told you about her life either."

"Yeah..." I said. "I guess you're right."

"Just give yourself more time and stop obsessing over it. When you do finally tell her, she doesn't need to know every single detail. You don't need to put yourself through that. Hell, *I* don't even know every single detail and I was there that night."

I closed my eyes, but instantly regretted it as flashbacks of that night sat right behind my lids. "You weren't..."

She sighed. "You know what I mean."

I didn't respond, too shaken from the images that could never be erased from my memory.

Thankfully, Alaina once again cracked the silence on my behalf. "Be patient with yourself," she said softly. "You have trauma from that night. There's no need to force yourself to talk about it before you're ready. Kam loves you. And she's going to love you regardless of what or when you tell her."

"But what if I'm never ready to tell her?"

"You will be. You'll know when you are."

I sighed, nodding to myself. "You're right. Thanks, Alaina."

When I hung up, I didn't bother moving just yet. My mind was still reeling, unable to get the nightmarish reality out of my head.

Just like I had ten-thousand times over the past four years, I couldn't help but let all the what ifs soak in.

What if I hadn't walked into the room when I had? What if I hadn't caught Casey in the act? What if I just listened to Benny? What if I hadn't gotten so mad that I—

Stop, I demanded myself.

I rolled my shoulders back as I moped into the bathroom. I twisted the shower valve until it was practically all the way cranked, the water becoming scorching hot in seconds.

For some reason, I stepped in front of the mirror. As I rested my hands on the sink, my reflection gave me conflicting feelings.

On one hand, I wanted to believe I deserved Kamryn, that I could be good enough for her. But then again, part of me just couldn't accept the idea that I was worthy of her when I was what I was.

Even if that night never happened, I probably still wouldn't be worthy of her. Maybe in another life, I could've been.

I pushed myself off the sink, slipping my sweatpants off and stepping into the shower. When the hot water hit my skin, I didn't even flinch. And neither did my thoughts. They just kept coming.

My hands ruffled through my hair underneath the water. The bar of soap almost slipped out of my hand when I grabbed it, but I managed to catch it, which surprised me considering how far away my mind was. I barely even felt like I was in my own body as I began washing myself.

You spent the past four years reliving every moment of that night. It's time to focus on the present, not the past.

I nodded slowly to myself, trying to encourage the new direction that my mind had somehow wandered towards.

I closed my eyes, a light smirk inevitably taking over my lips from the picture of her face that was forever engrained into my wounded mind. I focused on her blue eyes, clear and pure.

The image created a surge of need and inspiration and love that was desperate to overtake the ruthless ways of my thinking.

No more obsessing over the past. It's time for redemption and redemption starts with loving her.

No more obsessing over the past.

No more.

***

"Decks?" Kam called out as I wrapped a towel around my waist.

My heart soared at the sound, another smile surfacing. I didn't hesitate to swing open the bathroom door. "Hey," I beamed.

Kam swiveled around at the sound of my voice. Her eyes immediately dropped down to my chest and her throat visibly dipped as she gulped.

"Eyes are up here," I teased with a grin.

She gave a pompous smirk but didn't bother to glance away from my bare skin. "I'll look where I please."

My brows flew up. "Whatever you say, boss."

Her baby blues swept up to my face. My entire focus seemed to get trapped in her gaze, willingly being held captive.

"How was your coffee hangout?" I asked.

"Good," she nodded. But after another moment, a tiny snicker left her mouth.

"What?"

Her small snicker grew louder, becoming a rich giggle. She muttered something between laughs, but I couldn't decipher it.

"What?" I asked again, dipping my head down.

"Ditch digger," she chortled.

Confusion draped over me, my brows wiggling as I eyed her. Her laughter still hadn't ceased as she pulled her phone out of her pocket, unlocked it, and held the screen up to me.

I warily plucked it out of her small hands, my brows once again crunching together. *Ditch digger?*

"No way," I denied. "This has gotta be wrong."

"I don't think it is," she snorted.

My mouth formed a hard line. "There's no way my parents named me *Ditch Digger*."

Kam finally kept her composure long enough to get out a full sentence. "They didn't. They just named you something that *means* Ditch Digger." She exploded in another whoop of laughter.

"Yeah? Is that just *so* funny?" I challenged.

"It is."

"Hmm," I murmured, typing her name into the search bar. Right as the results popped up, I let out a hoot. "Oh, yeah? Well your name means *Crooked Nose*."

That caught her attention.

"What! No, it doesn't."

"Oh yes, it does."

She snatched her phone out of my hand in denial, taken aback as she read the screen. "Whatever!" she whined. "That's still not as bad as Ditch Digger."

"I feel like it is."

"It's *not*."

Her defensiveness brought a tiny grin to my lips. And just then, my heart once again fell right into her hands. The urge to kiss her was humming through me, even stronger than usual. I zoned in on her lips that were straightened in stubbornness.

I kept gazing at her until a comfortable, yet familiar silence fell between us. Her lips twitched, struggling to fight back the urge to smile.

Finally, when she did, my breath hitched in the slightest. No matter how many times I'd seen her smile, the sight still managed to knock the breath out of me.

176

Just as I was about to close the gap, cradle her face between my hands and kiss her crazily, she beat me to it, lunging into me and smashing her lips against mine.

I kissed her back until we were both gasping for air. My hands found their way to the back of her thighs, and I scooped her up bridal style, carrying her into our room.

Kam let out a giggle as I playfully tossed her onto the bed. A small snort fell from her mouth as she covered her face with her hands. "Your towel fell."

I shrugged, amused. "Why are you hiding?" I laughed.

She innocently peeled her hands away from her face. "You're naked."

"You've seen me naked dozens of times," I laughed. "You want me to put clothes on?"

"No," she blurted out.

I chuckled, falling onto the bed beside her. My fingers made their way to her sides, tickling her until her laughter filled every corner of the apartment.

"Decks," she struggled to get out between laughs, attempting to push me away. "Stop... I can't... breathe."

I snickered, pulling my hands away. "Whatever you say, Crooked Nose."

Her eyes narrowed. "Ditch Digger."

I jokingly rolled my eyes, pushing myself off the bed to grab my towel off the floor. The second I stood, I got a hard smack over my ass.

"Hey!" I shrieked, twisting around.

Kam was lying horizontally on the bed as she dropped her hand against the mattress, once again engulfed in laughter. "Nice ass," she gave a sly smile.

I abandoned my previous task and climbed back onto the bed, hovering over her. I slipped a hand beneath her, clinging onto her round ass through her leggings. "Nice ass," I muttered.

Her laughter abruptly halted, replaced with curiosity of what I was about to do next. I could see the hunger swimming in her eyes, could hear a stunned breath leave her mouth in a rush.

I pushed my hardness against her as I went straight for her throat, sweeping my mouth against it. She let out a soft hum as her blue eyes peered around, their sharpness weakening. I had her right where I wanted her. Right where I needed her.

I was obsessed with the way her skin tasted, irrevocably hooked like an addict. I couldn't seem to pull myself away as I kissed the rapid pounding of her pulse beneath her skin, content when it kissed me back. This tiny stretch of her throat was her sweet spot, feeling like both silk and sin against my lips.

I could feel my back muscles unavoidably tighten as her hands traced over them, and when her nails dug into my skin, a pleased sigh left my mouth and vibrated against her throat.

Kam's hands snaked to my chest, gripping my shoulders tightly. Before I knew it, she'd managed to flip me over, taking control as if she were a racecar driver and my lap was the driver's seat.

Her fingers raked over my abs, caressing each ridge. She brought her mouth down, her tongue lightly brushing over the pathway that her fingers had just traveled.

She had complete and utter power over me right now, and she knew it too. Her eyes glanced up, flaring a deep shade of the ocean as she sunk lower and lower towards my groin.

The spell she was casting over me was dominating in every type of way. I could feel my body temperature spike, my blood hammering harder underneath my skin as Kam slowly took my dick into her mouth, pumping it in and out.

My head fell back against the mattress and a desperate noise came from the back of my throat. I was close to panting, my lungs working hard to maintain a proper airflow. The addict within me pulsed with pleasure at the feeling of her lips wrapped around me.

I brought my head up just enough to be able to witness what she was doing to me. When her eyes popped open to watch me watching her, the drug that she put into my system amplified so much that I was quite certain I was on the brink of an overdose.

I basked in the euphoria for minutes on end until Kam rose back up to sit atop me once more. Instinctively, my fingers found their way to her skin, lingering beneath the hem of her shirt.

And just like that, I had all the power again.

Her alluring expression had shifted to a pleading one. Her chest was now the one taking shallow breaths. She was the addict now.

Or perhaps, we were both still addicts, considering the way my dangerous high hadn't worn off by the feel of her velvet skin.

The cloud of lust in Kam's eyes vanished as a light buzzing noise came from the nightstand. She let out a deep gust of air under her breath. "Your phone's ringing."

I shook my head, my focus still on her and her only.

She leaned forward, taking a peek at my phone screen. "It's your mom."

"She can wait," I murmured softly.

Kam's mouth formed a hard line, seemingly in an internal plight. "What if it's something important?"

I sighed as Kam climbed off me. I hurriedly grabbed a pair of basketball shorts from my dresser and threw them on before reaching for the phone, because there was no way in hell that I would sit here talking to my mother while I was buck naked.

"Hello?"

"Decks!" she exclaimed excitedly. "Hi, my little sunshine. How are you doing?"

My eyes skimmed over Kam, a complacent smirk lighting up my face. "I'm good, Mom. How are you?"

"I'm good!" I could practically hear her smiling through the phone, per usual. My mother was the happy angel in the family, whereas my father had always been the grumpy one. "So, I was just going to call and talk to you about the wedding. Are you guys planning on carpooling with us?"

My eyes widened to a record size. "The wedding," I repeated.

"Yes..." she said, then sighed. "Decker, you forgot, didn't you?"

"Um..." I stalled, "well, I mean, I—I guess it kinda sorta slipped my mind."

"You forgot."

I sighed to myself. "Yes, I forgot," I admitted.

"Decker Lincoln," she chided, causing me to wince. "Well, you better call Sara up and see if there's a way you can still bring Kamryn."

"Alright, I will."

"I mean, now," she demanded. "Like right now. Don't wait."

"Okay, I'll call her now."

"Good. Call me back after and let me know what she says."

I nodded. "Love you, Mom."

"Love you too, sweetie."

I sighed again, scrolling through my contacts to find my cousin's name.

"Is something wrong?" Kam's delicate voice asked.

I pivoted around to take in her troubled expression. Her eyes were so innocent, so unbelievably harmless after the way she just had me in her mouth less than five minutes ago.

"I just... forgot to do something. I'll be right back."

"Okay," she quietly said as I stepped out of the room.

I wasn't necessarily trying to hide the conversation from her. But if my cousin wasn't going to allow me to bring Kam last minute, then I wasn't going, and if Kam knew I was skipping my cousin's wedding, she would make me go.

I brought the phone up to my ear, shifting my weight side to side as it began ringing.

"Hey, Decker," Sara answered.

"Hey," I started, "how's it going?"

"Good. Stressed with some last-minute wedding bullshit, but it's good," she laughed. I gave a small wince from her words. If she was already stressed, then I was about to add more stress to her plate, which was not at all what I wanted to do.

"Yeah, I can imagine," I said, mindlessly scuffing my feet on the floor. "I, um... I actually called because I have a question."

"Okay, shoot."

"So, I know I already sent in my RSVP over the summer, but I've been seeing someone for a while now and I know it's last minute to ask, but—"

"Yes."

180

"What?"

"Yes, you can bring her. If this is the same girl your parents have been talking nonstop about, then I wanna meet her."

Of course, my parents had been talking nonstop about Kam. We'd been over for dinner a few more times since the first time, not to mention my father's daily praising that she's the best receptionist we'd ever had. Her desk was always the neatest in the office and she brought a sweet smile to work every day, a stark difference from everyone else's scowls. On top of that, she'd somehow managed to snag us more clients than ever before.

"You're sure?" I asked. "I don't wanna make things more difficult for you guys."

"Really, it's fine. Aaron and I will take care of it."

I smiled coyly. "Thanks, Sara. I owe you big time."

An untouchable amount of satisfaction and excitement consumed me. The first thing that Kam did when I walked back into our bedroom was point out my grin.

"Why're you so smiley?" she beamed.

"We're going to a wedding."

Her face flashed a dozen emotions at once, from confused to exuberant. "Huh?"

"My cousin is getting married in a few weeks in Malibu."

Her eyes lit up at the end of my sentence. "We're going to Malibu?"

I gave a content nod. "We're going to Malibu."

Chapter Thirty-One
Kamryn

"You're sure you don't want me to come with you?" Decker asked, wincing through his words.

"I'm sure," I nodded confidently.

"Okay..." he agreed reluctantly. "But please be careful and make sure you stay away from weirdos."

I chuckled. "Decks, I'll be fine. It's just the mall."

"I know, but psychos go to the mall too."

"I'll be okay," I assured him.

"Call me if you need anything. I'll run there if I have to."

I let out a laugh, causing Decker's pearly whites to appear in a small smile.

"I'm serious," he said. "I'll invent teleportation on the spot if necessary."

"Okay, sure," I rolled my eyes jokingly. I went on my tippy toes to plant a kiss on his lips. "I love you. See you later."

"Be careful!" he shouted as I closed the front door behind me.

I took a taxi to the mall, which was about a fifteen-minute drive. It felt good to walk into the mall for the first time in over six months. Although my primary focus was to find a dress to wear to the wedding, there was a rush of satisfaction from knowing that if I found something else I liked, then I

182

could buy it. If I wanted to stop in the food court and buy something to eat, then I could. If I got thirsty and wanted to use it as an excuse to buy a smoothie, then I would.

These were all the little things I'd missed while living on the street. The small luxuries that people took for granted every day. I would never take them for granted ever again.

The first few stores I went into had absolutely nothing worth looking at twice. I didn't have a specific color or style of dress that I wanted. I'd be fine with anything that wasn't ugly. Hell, at this point, I might be stuck with something ugly considering that I waited until the last minute to look for a dress.

I'd known about the wedding for the last two weeks and waited until two days before we left to go shopping.

Smart move, Kamryn.

The next store I went into looked a little more promising. There was a wider selection of dresses to look at. I skimmed through them until one caught my eye. I tilted my head towards my shoulder, rubbing the fabric between my fingers as I stared at it.

It was a blush pink maxi dress with a halter neckline. There was a subtle, yet sexy slit in the left leg.

I tried to envision it on me and couldn't at first, but the more I tried, the clearer the vision became. I knew I still needed to try it on, though. I was an average height for a woman, but it was quite possible that it would still be too long on me. The last thing I needed was for Decker's entire family and then some to see me trip over my own dress.

I double checked the size to make sure it was the right one before grabbing it by the hanger and folding the bottom half of the dress over my forearm. I headed towards the fitting rooms and just as I was a few feet short of them, a hand gripped my shoulder and whipped me around.

I jumped, fear getting caught in my throat, but relief followed at the sight of who stood before me.

"Oh my God. I can't believe it's actually you." Arianna's mouth was still propped open in shock as she grabbed me by the shoulders and pulled me into a hug.

"Hey," I managed to mutter.

She gave a tight squeeze before finally letting go. "How are you? Where have you been?"

I was still a little startled from the surprise encounter, but I felt a strange sense of comfort from seeing my old friend. At the same time, I was confused why she seemed happy to see me after the way we left things. The last words I heard from her echoed in my head.

When he breaks your heart, don't come crying to me.

I shifted my weight around. "I'm good," I finally nodded. "How are you?"

Her voice came out gently, still in awe. "Good," she shrugged subtly. "Where have you been?" she asked again, hurt behind her voice. "I haven't seen you in over a year."

I didn't want to tell her. I didn't want her to know every horrid detail of what happened over the past year. "Just around," I said, my gaze dropping to the floor.

Her voice was a little harder this time. "Kam."

I glanced up at her, somehow brave enough to meet her gaze.

"I heard about what happened with Ryan."

"Oh."

I was expecting to hear her give me the whole spiel about how she'd always been right about him and how I should've listened to her from the beginning, but surprisingly, Arianna's entire demeanor, especially her eyes, softened. "I'm so sorry."

I blinked at her, dazed. "It's alright."

"It's not," she shook her head. "Where have you been staying?"

Arianna had been my best friend since middle school. She knew all my favorite foods, movies, and songs. She knew my weird mannerisms and funny quirks. She was there with me on the night my parents died and every night after. She knew me forwards and backwards, well enough to know that after leaving Ryan, I had nowhere else to go.

My silence took her for a turn. Her brows drew closer. "Or was he the one to leave the house?"

"No," I corrected her. "Since, you know," I sighed, "the house was under his dumbass name."

"Oh right," she whispered, bringing her fingers up to her lips for a moment. "Have you been staying with your aunt then?"

"No," I said again. I gulped as I looked at her. "I didn't have anywhere to stay for about a month, but I have a place now."

A puzzled expression trailed across her face. She tipped her chin towards her chest. "Kam..."

I just looked at her helplessly.

There was a moment of silence hovering between us as she tried her hardest to read my face. "Are you saying..." she shook her head, abandoning the thought.

"Yeah."

Arianna's face fell even further, her eyes glossing over. "Why didn't you call?" her voice broke. "You would've been more than welcome to stay with me."

My gaze strayed away from her, knowing that if I looked at her sorrowful eyes any longer, mine would follow suit completely. "I just figured you hated me after that last argument we had and—"

"Hey," she cut me off, "I know that fight was ugly, but I could never hate you. I've tried texting and calling you a few times over the past few months, actually."

"I got a new number."

"Oh," she said. "Can I... can I have it?"

I gave an appreciative grin as I nodded. "Of course."

"Cool," she smiled, pulling her phone out and handing it over. "Are you, um, busy for the rest of the afternoon?"

I responded as I added my number into her phone. "Um, I have a wedding to go to, so I need to try this dress on, but..." I brought my attention back up to her, giving the phone back. "Would you want to come over and hang out? You can meet my boyfriend."

Her eyes bulged as she smiled. "Um, yes! You have a new boyfriend?"

"Yeah." I could feel the color staining my cheeks as Decker's face popped into my mind.

"You're blushing," she smirked.

I turned away. "Stop," I grinned.

"Wow, Kam. He must be special if the thought of him makes you blush."

"He is special."

Her eyes lit up. She bobbed up and down on her toes a few times. "Well, let's hurry up and have you try this dress on then."

***

An hour and a half later, I cracked open the apartment door. "Decks?"

"Yeah, baby?" he called back.

"I have a friend with me."

Arianna followed in slowly behind me, her eyes snooping around every detail of the apartment.

Decker appeared from our bedroom with a bright smile. "A friend?" he asked before his eyes swept over to Arianna. "Hello."

I couldn't quite read the look on her face, but whatever it was, it was beyond amusing. It was like a mixture of bewilderment, nervousness, and fascination.

"Hi," she let out, stepping forward to shake Decker's hand when he held his out. A tiny snicker snuck out of my mouth at her reaction.

"Old friend?" Decker asked.

"Very old," Arianna said. "Friend, I mean. Not my age. I'm not old."

Decker and I both laughed. "You're embarrassing yourself," I teased.

"I know," she agreed.

"Friends from high school?" Decker asked.

"Since middle school, actually," Arianna said.

"Did you guys just run into each other?" he wondered, glancing back and forth between us.

"Yep," I said. "At the mall. Where all the psychos run around."

Decker's charming smile didn't falter as he rolled his eyes.

"What?" I joked. "Are you surprised I came back in one piece?"

"Surprised? Not necessarily. Happy about it? Absolutely."

I giggled. "Well, just so you know, I found a dress."

"Can I see it?"

"Mmm, not right now," I said, stepping over to wrap my arms around him for a hug. His strong arms bundled me up.

Home.

"Arianna and I are gonna have some girl time. We've got some catching up to do."

Decker didn't release me from his warm grasp. He let out a husky chuckle, sending a vibration through my cheek and all the way down to my toes. "Are you kicking me out?"

I finally pulled away to look at him. I gave him a playful tap on the nose with the tip of my finger. "Yes."

Another deep chuckle sounded through those perfect lips of his. "Alright. I'll be watching TV in our room if you guys decide I'm cool enough to hang out with you."

"Highly unlikely," I joked as he walked off towards our room, letting out another laugh.

The second I turned back to Arianna, I was taken aback by the amount of joy and amusement she had on her face. Her mouth was bouncing back and forth between a wide smile and being smack dab open. Just speechless.

"What?" I snickered.

"Well first," she said, lowering her voice, "holy shit. He's gorgeous. Where did you *find* him?"

I couldn't contain the burst of delight in my heart. I pointed to the front corner of the apartment. "Right out there."

She tipped her head. "Huh?"

"We've got lots to catch up on." I cocked my head to the living room couch. "I'll start."

Chapter Thirty-Two
Kamryn

I watched Decker's muscles bulge through the sleeves of his navy-blue t-shirt as he lifted our luggage out of the trunk of the car. We carpooled with Decker's parents and Emmy for the six-hour car ride, almost half of which I slept on Decker's shoulder for.

I grabbed the handle of my suitcase and began wheeling it towards the hotel, following everyone else. I took everything in as we walked inside.

Even though it was October, the sun was still beating miraculously as if it were July. I could smell the saltwater from here, could hear the laughter of children playing on the beach as a light sea breeze was sent our way. My eyes wandered around aimlessly, desperately trying to get a glimpse of the ocean.

"Is the beach close?" I asked.

"Yeah, it's right behind the hotel," Decker said. I followed him off to the side as his parents went to the front desk to check us in.

"Where's the wedding at?"

"It's going to be on the beach."

"Really?" I said excitedly. "That'll be pretty. I've always wanted a beach wedding."

Decker's brilliant eyes zipped over to me, a playful grin tugging on the corners of his lips. "You want a beach wedding, huh?"

I nudged him with a grin. "Maybe."

He smirked charmingly. "We could arrange that."

My face flushed and I dropped my head, letting my hair create a curtain between us.

"You're blushing."

"No, I'm not."

"I love when you blush."

I peeked upwards, a warm feeling bubbling through my core as I caught Decker's intent gaze. If we were on this subject for any longer, my face was going to be pink all damn day. "What are we doing for the rest of the day?"

"Anything you want."

"Let's go to the beach."

***

The sun was out to play, and I couldn't be happier.

We lived in California. I was used to the sun. But I hadn't been excited about it in God knew how long. I couldn't even remember the last time I went to the beach.

Decker and I were sprawled out on a massive beach blanket, soaking in every ounce of Vitamin D that the sun had to offer. My entire body was relaxed, in the best state of zen imaginable.

I could feel the blanket rustle in the slightest and I opened my eyes, peeking up at Decker just enough to see that he'd sat up. I followed his lead as his award-winning grin slowly began drawing upwards.

"What?" I asked.

"Your bathing suit matches the ocean, which matches your eyes."

I looked down at my suit, then over at the water. "I guess you're right," I smiled.

He ran a hand through his soft hair. "Are you gonna go in the water?"

"It's probably cold."

"Wanna find out?"

"Ugh," I grumbled lazily, squinting from the sun. "Why don't you go test it out first?"

"Fine," Decks puffed, pushing himself to stand. I leaned forward as he walked towards the water, my tongue unavoidably trailing over my bottom lip as I studied him from head to toe. His black swim trunks hugged his ass without being freakishly tight on his legs, back muscles pulling together in the slightest with each step. His golden skin glowed healthily as he dipped his toe into the water. He turned. "It's not too bad." Within an instant, a pompous smirk settled on his face. "Are you checking me out?"

I wiped the lustful look off my face, abruptly leaning back into my hands. "No."

He raised a confident brow. "I think you were."

"I was looking at the ocean."

A husky laugh rolled off his tongue. He pointed at me. "You were just giving me sex eyes."

"I was *not* giving you sex eyes."

"Oh, yes you were."

I crossed my arms as he began walking towards me. "Uh, no I wasn't." Before I knew it, Decker lifted me from behind, his arms wrapped around my middle. "What the *hell*!" I screeched through a laugh.

I wiggled around in his arms, knees lifted towards my chest as he carried me to the base of the water. "Decker!"

"Admit you were checking me out or I'm throwing you in," he laughed, his chest vibrating against my back.

"No, no, *no!* Decker, there are sharks!" I squealed.

He gave another snicker. "There are no sharks around here."

"There will be after I punch you and your nose is bleeding."

"That was aggressive!" he laughed.

"So are sharks!"

"You're feisty today," he said with amusement. "Might have to do something about that."

I froze in his grasp, my mind heading to the dirtiest places. "What did you have in mind?" I wondered aloud.

A wave of laughter just as strong as the waves before us rippled out of his mouth. "I didn't mean it sexually!"

190

"Oh."

"See, I knew you were giving me sex eyes!"

"I wasn't," I choked through a laugh.

Decks stepped deeper into the water until it was at his knees. "I'll drop you right now."

"Don't you *dare*."

He slowly started loosening his grip on me.

"Okay, okay!" I shrieked. "I was checking you out!"

"Now was that so hard?" he teased, dropping me.

A shrill yelp flew out of my mouth as my legs were immersed in cold water. "Decker Lincoln!" I gritted through my teeth. "It's *freezing*!"

"Oh, c'mon," he held his arms out with a charming grin.

I skimmed my hand across the water, sending it splashing in his direction.

"Hey!" he laughed, stepping backwards.

I did it again.

"You do not wanna start splash wars right now," he warned blithely.

Another splash.

But instead of splashing back, Decker paused, glancing past my shoulder.

I eyed him for a moment. "What?"

He squinted into the distance. "Is that a fin?"

"What?" I screeched, jumping over to him.

He bent over, enveloped in laughter. "I can't believe you fell for that."

I let out a huff. "I should've known you were lying when your eyebrow twitched."

"What?" he chuckled.

"Nothing," I said, pushing his shoulder. "You're mean."

His arms wrapped around me once again, holding me tightly as the waves rocked us side to side. His lips found the top of my head. "It's all out of love, baby."

Chapter Thirty-Three
Kamryn

Seeing Decker in a suit always fucking got to me.

Sara and Aaron's wedding ceremony was absolutely beautiful, and I enjoyed every second of it. The reception, which we were currently at, was even better. But I'd be lying if I said taking that suit off of Decker wasn't a recurring thought through it all.

I felt kind of obscene for it considering we were surrounded by his family, but I couldn't help myself. His steel blue suit hugged him in all the right places and the fact that his tie was a dusty pink that matched my dress just made him even more irresistible.

It was currently dusk, and the sun was lowering over the ocean, illuminating a pink and orange hue. The reception was on the beach, so there was a large wooden floor laid out across the sand as a makeshift dance floor.

Decker had one hand on my lower back, a beer in his other. I stood beside him, holding a glass of wine.

"Kamryn!" Shannon exclaimed with a smile, making her way over. "Come meet everyone." She grabbed my hand, dragging me away.

"Mom!" Decker called.

"Oh, shush," she rolled her eyes. "You'll be fine for a few minutes without her."

I looked back at Decker with a tight-lipped smile as he groaned. I let out a tiny giggle, following Shannon over to a small group of people.

Their heads slowly turned as we approached, and one by one, each of their smiles appeared.

"Alright," Shannon said to the group, "we've gotta be quick over here because I'm sure Decker will lose his mind if she's gone for longer than two minutes."

I let out a laugh. Little did she know that I'd go just as crazy.

Shannon gestured to me, signaling for me to introduce myself.

I nodded to her with nervousness, turning to the group. "Hi," I said almost breathlessly, "I'm Kamryn, Decker's girlfriend."

I held my hand out to each of them, overwhelmed as I collected a handful of names that I immediately couldn't keep straight.

"Nice to meet you. I'm Hallie."

"Johnathon."

"Lucy!"

"Amelia."

"Rueben."

"Zoey!"

"Max."

I nodded at them after getting through the group, trying to contain my puzzled look.

"These are all of Decker's cousins," Shannon explained. "Aside from the bride, of course, but we'll go meet her soon."

"Oh!" I smiled. "It's nice to meet you all."

One of the girls touched my arm kindly, and I quietly struggled to remember if she was Lucy or Amelia. "How long have you and Decker been together?"

"About three months," I said.

"That's so exciting!" one of the other girls jumped in. "Where is Decker, anyway? I haven't seen him yet."

I was sure two minutes had passed by now, and it seemed like I was suddenly so aware of his absence. I inhaled deeply, but it seemed to burn.

"I heard my name?"

My curled hair whipped over my shoulder as I spun around. "Hey," I said, my grin nearly breaking my face in half at the sound of his voice.

"Yeah, you heard your name," one of the boys said. "We were just talking about how much you suck."

Decker lifted a joking brow, smirking as he brought his drink up to his mouth and took a sip. "Yeah?" he joked.

My God, was he sexy.

I stiffened beside him for a moment, squeezing my thighs together to try to eliminate the tingling sensation between them.

"Yeah," his cousin taunted.

"Suck this," Decker said, bringing a finger into his mouth and sucking in his cheeks before plopping his middle finger out and holding it up to his cousin.

"Original," his cousin mocked. "Pretty sure I invented that move."

Decker chuckled. "Fuck off, Rueben. You didn't invent shit."

Rueben, I repeated in my head, doing my best to match each face to their name.

Decker snaked his free arm around my waist, pulling me closer. "Have you met Sara yet?"

I shook my head. "Your mom said she was going to take me there next, I think."

Shannon was talking up a storm with a few of the cousins— of course, I wasn't sure of their names.

"Mom," Decker said.

Shannon turned with a bright smile. "Yes, honey?"

"I'm gonna take Kam to meet Sara."

She nodded, waving us off.

Decker intertwined our fingers, leading us toward the bride and groom. By now, they'd changed into more comfortable attire, but nonetheless, they still looked flawless.

Sara caught us out of the corner of her eye, shooting us a smile and stepping towards us. Her arms went outwards, and Decker accepted her gesture, giving her a warm hug.

"Congratulations," he said.

"Thanks, little cuz!" The second they disconnected, Sara's eyes slid over to me. I glanced her over, keeping a friendly grin.

Her brown hair was in an elegant up-do, makeup looking beautifully natural. She was wearing a lavish white romper, her veil still perfectly intact.

"Kamryn?"

"Yes," I smiled. "Congratulations."

"Thank you!" She wrapped her arms around me, and I kept my wine glass as far away from her body as I hugged her back because no way in hell was I going to accidentally spill all over the bride.

"The wedding was absolutely stunning," I said.

"Thank you. I'm glad you guys could make it."

"Well, we endured a six-hour car ride with my parents for this, so really, you owe me one," Decker joked.

I rolled my eyes with a smile. "It wasn't that bad."

"Maybe not for you considering you slept the whole time," he countered.

"You could've slept too."

"Nah, I've never been able to fall asleep in the car."

"That sounds like a you-problem," I teased.

Sara erupted in laughter. "I see why your parents love her so much!" she said. "I like her. She's funny."

Decker sighed with a crooked smile, pulling me to him once again. "I guess I like her too."

"You guess?" I lifted a playful brow, facing him.

His lips wavered, trying to fight his smile, but it was no use.

"You guys are adorable," Sara said. "Makes me wanna throw up."

I laughed as Decker turned towards her. "Says the one who just had the most extravagant wedding of the century."

She shrugged with a grin, sipping on her wine.

"I'm sure Uncle Tom just loved spending his whole retirement fund on all this," Decker joked.

"Hey asshole," she pointed with a smile, "Aaron and I paid for a lot of it ourselves actually. And just for that comment, I'm getting you the shittiest gift I can find when you two get married."

The thought of marrying Decker rolled through my mind, and the more I let the idea linger there, the more I liked it. Because really, I wouldn't mind marrying Decker. I wouldn't mind at all.

"Whatever," Decker spoke. "Our wedding is gonna top your wedding anyway."

"Yeah?" she stepped back with a chuckle. "You think you can top this?" She held her arm out, gesturing to the ocean, the sunset, and every beautiful detail in between.

"I don't know, Decks," I chimed in. "I don't think it gets much better than this."

"We'll find a way," he assured me, lightly brushing his thumb over my cheek. "We'll find a way."

Chapter Thirty-Four
Decker

It was already dark out. The string lights on the surrounding palm trees were lit up, the temperature had gone down to a comfortable sixty degrees, the ocean waves were still lively below the glowing moon, and I was thoroughly enjoying myself.

But I wasn't going to last much longer.

I wasn't sure what it was about weddings that always made people so damn horny. Maybe the whole "love is in the air" saying was true.

Whatever the reason was, I was aching to go back to our hotel room and be alone with Kam.

A slow song came on, and Kam extended her hand to me with a sweet smile. There was no hesitation before I accepted her gesture.

I pulled her in, bringing my hands to her waist as hers snaked around the back of my neck. We swayed together with perfect precision, two hearts connected.

My lips curved upwards as I looked at her. "You look beautiful."

It may have been dark, but under the hundreds of lights illuminating the beach, there was plenty of light to make out her cheeks turn from ivory to pink like a cherry blossom flourishing.

But she didn't shy away from it like she had many times before. Her eyes didn't stray from me. "That's like the hundredth time you've told me tonight."

I lifted one shoulder. "Just wanted to remind you," I said. "I don't want you to forget."

Her shy grin remained as her eyes danced at me. "You don't look too bad yourself."

I could feel her finger trail casually across the back of my neck, and the simple touch brought a bolt of heat from the top of my spine to the very bottom of it.

I lightly licked my lip, my gaze hovering past her for a moment before jumping straight back to her. "I want this with you."

She tipped her head. "Want what?"

I lifted one hand off her waist just enough to motion around us. "All this."

Her expression matched mine— hopeful and wistful. "I've been thinking the same thing all night."

I grinned at her, right as the song came to an end. I cleared my throat, attempting to get her attention, but failing. My grip on her waist tightened and I pulled her close enough to bring my mouth to her ear, brushing against it as I spoke. "Are you ready to go back to the room?"

I didn't miss the breathy note in her voice. "I was starting to think you'd never ask."

Chapter Thirty-Five
Kamryn

I'd always wondered what having a big family would be like, and after being surrounded by Decker's huge family during the wedding, I felt less alone, and I felt a sense of belonging I'd never experienced before.

On top of that, it all solidified how much I wanted a big family in the future.

Two weeks had already passed since the wedding, and Thanksgiving would be here in just one more.

I took a sip of my iced coffee as I stood at the crosswalk, waiting once again for my okay to cross the street.

I'd been stopping by *Joe's Coffee Shop* every Sunday morning to pay a quick visit to Lydia and grab some coffee. Luckily, I hadn't run into my wicked aunt again.

At this point, I'd grown accustomed to this healthy routine. Work during the week. Hang out with Decker and our friends on the weekends. Grab some coffee and relax on Sundays. Repeat.

I'd even had the opportunity to see Arianna a couple of times since we first ran into each other at the mall. I felt like I finally had a grip on my own life, and it couldn't have felt any damn better.

I crossed the street and headed up the short steps to the apartment door, but when I went to turn the knob, all it did was jiggle. My brows creased as I fished my keys out of my pocket and walked in.

My eyes immediately landed on the bouquet of blue and pink daisies on the kitchen counter. I strode over to it and brought my nose down, taking a deep whiff of their sweet smell.

There was a small card lying beside the vase. My fingers traced over the black ink written across it.

Date night?

I could feel my heart turn from a solid to a liquid before aching from Decker's missing presence. Wherever he'd gone, I wanted him back now. It'd only been a few hours since I'd seen him, but a few hours felt like too long without your favorite person.

My fingers brushed over the soft flower petals as a warm flush overcame my cheeks.

Goddamn it. It was ridiculous how he had the power to make me blush when he wasn't even here.

I gave the daisies another sniff and as if I'd manifested it, the apartment door swung open.

Decker strolled in with a few bags of groceries. "Hi, gorgeous," he greeted me, dropping the bags and sauntering over.

"Hi," I grinned, wrapping my arms around him. "Thank you for the flowers."

"You're welcome."

"They're daisies."

He chuckled lightly. "I know."

"You remembered."

He pulled back to look at me, but his hand remained steady on my hips. One thumb traced along my tattoo over my shirt. "Of course, I did."

Decker's kind eyes didn't leave mine, and when my face flushed again, I welcomed the feeling. Memorized it. Let myself feel it in its entirety until it faded.

He brought his lips to mine, kissing me softly yet deeply at the same time. Our mouths touched as if it were the first time. That first night we went out to the bar. I wanted to remember every detail of that kiss for the rest of my life, all while praying we never had to encounter a last kiss.

As we pulled away, I spoke. "Date night?"

Decker gave me one of his infamous grins. "Absolutely."

"What do you have in store?"

He cocked his head to the side, signaling for me to follow. "Well," he started, grabbing the grocery bags off the floor and setting them on the counter, "it's kinda cliché, but I figured we could have a little picnic at Miller Park?"

My entire being brightened as if his words caused a massive white light to reflect off me. "I'd love that."

* * *

"You got wine too?" I squealed, grabbing the bottle.

"Duh," Decker lifted a brow playfully. "It wouldn't be a proper picnic without it."

"Can't argue with that," I agreed. "We don't have glasses, though."

Decker gave a tiny shrug, snatching the bottle out of my hands, popping it open, and lifting it to his mouth for a lengthy gulp.

My mouth dropped, yet the corners of my lips remained upright, my smile refusing to disappear. "Decker Lincoln!"

He lowered the bottle, lightly wiping his mouth with the back of his hand. "Yes, Kamryn Elizabeth?"

I narrowed my eyes at him, plucking the bottle from his grasp and taking a swig of my own. "That's really good wine."

"I made sure not to get anything bitter. I know you only like sweet drinks."

I grinned wider. Just knowing how well Decker knew me at this point was so soothing. I glanced him over, hooked on the view, unable to look away even when I tried to force myself.

If I'd looked away when I told myself to, then he wouldn't have caught my gaze. But he did, of course, causing his husky voice to pass through his lips.

"What?" he asked.

I shook my head. "I just love you," I muttered.

His fingertips trailed underneath my chin. "I love you more," he said. My head tipped towards his hand, as if I couldn't help but gravitate closer to him. "Now eat your dinner," he joked.

I let out a laugh. "You mean my gourmet meal?"

"Yes."

I rolled my eyes, picking up the peanut butter and jelly that Decker made for me and taking a bite.

"Best PB & J of your life, right?"

"Yep," I said sarcastically after swallowing. "You are quite the chef."

His astounding chuckle broke through the air as he picked his sandwich up. We ate in silence for a few minutes, both of us peacefully peering around the park.

Thankfully, the park wasn't packed by any means, but there was a decent amount of people here. There was a trail that led through the middle of the park, where a handful of people were casually walking. It was November, but still a little under seventy degrees outside, which made the perfect day for this sort of thing.

There was a cute couple on the other side of the park, also having a picnic, but with a tiny addition. Their baby couldn't have been older than a year, smiling wide as she swatted her arms around.

A million thoughts chased each other around in my head, all of which involving a future with Decker. "Do you want kids someday?" I blurted out.

He twisted around, surprise sitting on his face.

"I mean..." I corrected myself, "not necessarily with me. Just in general."

His expression melted from surprise to fondness. "Kam, if I have kids, then I hope it's with you."

I looked away before he could catch another blush, my hands reaching for the wine and taking another gulp. Decker's playful laughter rang in my ear.

"You do realize that the wine is going to make your cheeks pinker, right?" he simpered.

"Don't know what you're talking about."

"Oh, you know exactly what I'm talking about," he teased.

"I'm just sunburnt from the wedding."

"Yeah, if sunburns appear after two weeks, then sure."

I shot him a frisky glare, causing his modest smirk to grow into a mischievous one. He held his hand out, gesturing for the wine. I handed it over. Watching the way his lips curled around the bottle made my mind fantasize about other things his lips could be around— *should* be around.

Knock it off, Kamryn. We're in public, I thought to myself.

Luckily, Decker's voice snapped me out of it. "Tell me something about you that I don't know yet."

"Um," I shrugged, "like what? I feel like you know almost everything about me already."

"See, that's the problem. I know *almost* everything about you, but I don't know everything about you."

I scooted closer to him until our thighs were touching and I could smell his fresh scent lingering off him, the smell a mixture of rainwater and mint. "What would you like to know then?"

He chewed on his bottom lip in thought, staring off. "What's one of your favorite memories from when you were a kid?"

I didn't have to overthink it. Actually, I didn't really have to think about it at all. It was pretty much a no brainer for me. "When I was little, my parents took me to Disneyland. It was the most magical place. They really spoiled me on that trip." I smiled lightly at the memory, but before grief could set in, I turned the spotlight onto Decker to take my mind off the dark road it was heading down. "How about you?"

He tipped his head side to side in thought as if he were flipping through a book of memories and couldn't decide which page to read from. I was a bit jealous of him for that. Don't get me wrong, I had a wonderful childhood. But when my childhood became tainted by my parent's death, every happy memory I had of them was tainted with it, becoming nothing more than a painful image.

"When I was younger, my dad and I played baseball together a lot," Decker said.

"What changed?"

His mouth formed a hard line. "We hit a rough patch a few years ago and it hasn't really been the same since." He shrugged carelessly. "It's fine, though. He tries."

"I could kinda tell you get annoyed by him sometimes."

"Is it that noticeable?" he grinned.

"Pretty sure the whole office notices."

His smile faded and he scratched the back of his head. "Yeah, uh, I'm not surprised there."

"It doesn't seem like your mom really notices though. Or at least she just doesn't acknowledge it."

"My mom has always been like that, I guess. She chooses to be the positive one of the family, to always see the good in things, even the situations that are absolutely... horrid."

"I wish I was like that," I muttered.

He peered over at me with such honesty that it made my heart shake. "I wish I was too."

"So, I'm guessing your mom is your favorite then?"

His seriousness faded, replaced by another laugh. "Actually, if I had to choose a favorite family member, it would be Emmy."

"Really?" I lifted my brows in shock.

He nodded. "We've always been pretty close, but we've gotten even closer recently."

"I wish I had a sibling growing up," I admitted. "Or even a cousin. Just someone I could hang out with, ya know?"

His tongue brushed over his lips. "Yeah. As you know now, I have quite a few cousins," he chuckled.

"I know. I'm jealous."

Decker shrugged lightly. "There are good things and bad things about it."

I shook my head. "I only see the good things."

"Well, here's one good thing about not having any," he said. "You never had to share anything."

I bobbed my head side to side. "I guess, but that's such a small one."

He playfully nudged me. "Not when there's only one scoop of ice cream left. Or when you get a brand-new toy, and your parents insist that you share it. Or when you get in trouble because you wouldn't let your sister play with any of *your* birthday presents. Or when—"

"Okay!" I cut him off with a laugh. "Being an only child has some perks. I get it." His laughter followed suit, the most beautiful sound hanging between us. "If growing up with Emmy was such a pain, then why is she your favorite now?"

Decker's eyes roamed up towards the sky. I could see his chest expand with a deep breath as what looked like regret flickered across his face. "Emmy just gets me a little better than my parents, I guess. She doesn't really see me for my mistakes. She just sees me as her brother."

His aura had turned somber in the slightest and I felt the need to take that feeling away for him. I climbed onto his lap, burying my head into the crook of his neck.

I wasn't planning on speaking, but somehow between that moment and the next, the words slipped out before I could stop them. "I miss my parents," I confessed. The second I said it, I braced myself for Decker to ask when it happened. Why it happened. *How it happened.*

But instead of focusing on their death, he took the conversation in a completely different direction.

"What were they like?"

A tiny smile flickered across my mouth. "They were fucking awesome," I said. "My mom was the sweetest woman on the planet. She was an incredible cook. I used to be her little kitchen assistant. Both of my parents were pretty religious, but my mom especially. She dragged my ass out of bed every Sunday morning for church up until she died." I paused, taking a deep breath before I continued. "And my dad," I nodded along as I spoke, "he was the best. I was such a Daddy's Girl growing up. He was fun and playful and by no means were we rich, but he spoiled the heck out of me as much as he could. He always told stupid jokes, but my mom and I laughed at them anyway."

Great, now I was the somber one.

Decker's hand ran up and down my back, comforting me. As hard as it was to speak about my parents, it also felt kind of nice. I'd been avoiding the memory of their death for so long that I hadn't even allowed myself to remember their lives.

But as nice as it was, it was obviously still sad as hell.

"Sounds like they were incredible," Decker whispered.

"They were," I agreed quietly.

A moment of silence passed between us, followed by my own small sniffle.

"Want some more wine?" Decker offered.

"Please," I said, taking the bottle.

Chapter Thirty-Six
Decker

We stayed at the park until it was dark out, talking for hours about anything and everything that came to mind. I could tell Kam's glum mood hadn't fully faded when we got home though. I could still feel it in the air.

This was the first night that Kam spoke in-depth about her parents. Even though she still hadn't told me about how they died, I felt like she was finally getting closer to talking about it. And the closer we were getting to that point, the closer I was to telling her about my past as well.

I double checked to make sure the apartment door was locked and when I turned back around, Kam stood on the far side of the room, her gaze stuck on me. My mind instantly flicked back to the night we came home from the bar for the first time. The night we kissed for the first time. The night I admitted to her that I liked her.

This time, I didn't hesitate to stride over to her. Naturally, my hand threaded through her platinum locks. Her eyes hadn't left me, silently watching me like she was waiting for something.

"You okay?" I murmured.

She gave a tiny shrug. "I guess."

It wasn't until then that I looked directly into her eyes. The same feeling that I got once before overcame me again.

The feeling of familiarity.

What was it that gave me this feeling? Was it just the alcohol sizzling through my veins? Was it something more? Something less? Was I just fucking crazy, or did I subconsciously know her from somewhere long ago?

Instead of ignoring it like last time, I dug deeper.

C'mon Decker. Where have you seen these eyes before?

They didn't look like their normal shade at the moment. They looked a little darker, deeper, more sullen and more vacant.

But I still couldn't pinpoint it.

Kam's hand trailed over mine. "I'm gonna take a warm shower. Might help me decompress a little."

"Okay," I whispered, leaning forward and planting a supple kiss on her forehead.

As she walked towards the bathroom, I watched her, still trying to figure out why she only looked so familiar right now. It was strange how I'd looked at her hundreds of times by now, but rarely got this feeling.

I headed into our bedroom and took a seat on the edge of the bed, trying to sift through my thoughts.

Maybe I met her at one of Alaina's softball games back in high school. I tried to picture Kam in a Parkersville softball uniform, but the image didn't ring any bells.

I tried to think if I'd ran into her at a party back in high school, but after sitting there and sorting through my memories for five more minutes, I knew that couldn't be it either.

I let out a frustrated groan as I stood and aimlessly peered around our bedroom. My fingers ran desperately through my hair as I eyed the nightstand on Kam's side of the bed.

I glanced at the bedroom door for the briefest moment before rushing over to the nightstand and pulling it open. I knew I shouldn't have been going through my girlfriend's shit, but if taking a peek would possibly help me figure out this mystery that had planted a seed inside my head, then I had to do it.

Who knew, maybe I was wrong. Maybe the first time I ever saw her truly was when she showed up on that corner.

Either way, I was about to find out.

Chapter Thirty-Seven
Kamryn

I was trying my best to get my mind off everything besides Decker, but I was failing miserably. Even though the hot water was a nice distraction, it couldn't wash away my thoughts.

I squeezed my eyes shut, regretting it the moment that horrid night was waiting mercilessly behind my lids.

"It's almost midnight!" Arianna squealed, grabbing onto my arm excitedly. "Ten more minutes!"

I let out a chuckle, sitting beside her on the couch. Our friends Jessica and Luna accompanied us while the boys were off in the room next door, stuck in their own world of video games and whatever else it was that boys did.

Arianna's parents were kind enough to let all of us come over and casually drink here under their supervision, of course.

I sighed. "Ryan better get his ass back in here soon."

Arianna playfully rolled her eyes as she forced a smile. She tried to be the supportive best friend, but I knew how much she hated him. I was never quite sure why they didn't get along in the first place, but I was at least grateful that they both tried to be nice to each other for my sake.

"I'm gonna go get him," I said, standing.

Jess leaned forward. "Turn up the damn music!" she insisted to Arianna.

The second I walked out of the room, the music was blasted. I smiled to myself as I headed next door, peeking my head into the room.

"Hey," I said, announcing my arrival. All three of the boys were staring at the TV, engrossed in their game.

I could hear the smile in Ryan's voice as he responded, making my smile grow just knowing that he recognized my voice so easily. "Hey, beautiful."

I giggled with content. "It's almost midnight."

"Shit, really?" Sean asked.

"Yes. Now get off your stupid game and come hang out with us," I demanded.

Sean and Jeremy both groaned, while Ryan immediately stood. "You heard her, boys," he said, stepping over to the TV and turning it off. "Let's go."

I gave him a thankful smile as I extended my hand. He gladly took it, and we made our way back out to the living room.

My phone buzzed in my back pocket, and I slipped it out, reading the incoming text.

Mom: We're leaving the gala shortly after midnight. Are you staying the night at Arianna's or do you want us to pick you up?

Me: I'm gonna stay the night

Mom: Okay, sweetie. Love you!

Me: I love you too! Let me know when you guys get home safe

Mom: We will <3

I slid my phone back in my pocket as Ryan took my hand to spin me around. Everyone was on their feet, dancing as we anticipated the countdown.

210

The minutes ticked by and just as sixty seconds were left, Ryan hugged my midsection from behind. All seven of us counted down with the timer on the TV, our voices growing louder and louder as we got closer to zero.

"3... 2... 1!" we screamed. "HAPPY NEW YEAR!"

Ryan held me close as I twisted around to face him. He smashed his lips onto mine, letting his lips linger there softly for a New Year's kiss.

When he pulled away, I wrapped my arms around him, giving him a warm hug. Everything felt just right. I had all my best friends here with me, and nothing could ruin it.

Only another half hour passed when there was a knock on the door. Luna and I both heard it, and our eyes wandered over to Arianna, noting how strange it was for someone to be knocking on the door at almost one in the morning.

She shrugged. "My parents will get it."

We brushed it off, and laughter once again drifted through the air, but when Arianna's mom entered the room white as a ghost, everyone's laughter ceased.

"Kamryn?" she shakily said, lightly cocking her head towards the foyer.

I frowned in confusion as I stood, warily following. I could see Arianna and Ryan worriedly glance at each other as I walked past, and before I knew it, both had followed while everyone else stayed behind.

When I stepped into the foyer, two police officers were there, their faces sullen and dreadful.

The one on the left dipped his head lightly. "Miss Arliss?"

I anxiously shoved my hands into my back pockets, shifting my weight side to side. "Yes?"

The officer took a deep breath. "We're here to inform you that unfortunately, your parents have been in an accident tonight."

Panic immediately started bleeding out of me. It echoed as I spoke. "What kind of accident?"

The officer on the right finally spoke, his tone no less distressed than the other. "A car accident."

My heart twisted in another direction, heading from worried to paranoid. "Well, are they okay? What hospital are they at? Can you take me there?" I frantically said.

Both officers looked at each other for a moment, desperation and pity in their eyes as if they were silently arguing with one another over who was going to speak next.

Finally, the officer on the left took on the burden. "We're very sorry, Miss Arliss, but your parents have both passed."

The words sounded like Hell itself was coming out of his mouth. I stared at them in silence, my mouth agape. None of it registered in my brain. It was impossible that I heard him correctly, especially when my mother had been texting me less than an hour prior.

"What?" I muttered. Every breath that I exhaled felt like ice, the cold burning the back of my throat on its way out. "A—are you sure?"

"Yes," he nodded softly. "We're very sorry for your loss," he added with his head down.

When the words finally sunk in, I grew dangerously lightheaded. Every muscle in my body felt heavy, unable to maintain control as the realization rushed through me. I could feel my balance go, my legs giving out beneath me as I dropped backwards.

Ryan caught me as I let out a bloodcurdling wail, sliding down to the floor in his arms. He knelt beside me as Arianna fell onto her knees on the other side, both of them holding me in an attempt to comfort me.

But there was no such thing as comfort right now.

I couldn't stop screaming. The immediate grief and agony were overwhelming, maliciously caressing me like broken glass against my skin.

My head couldn't wrap around the idea of both of my parents being gone. They were the only family I had. My best friends. My protectors. My favorite people in the world.

Tears were blurring my vision, but I didn't need my sight in order to feel how different the world was now. The air didn't sit in my lungs quite right. The earth wasn't spinning the same as before. Everything looked different. Felt different.

I buried my head into Ryan's chest as Arianna's hand ran up and down my back. I was shaking like I'd been stranded in the Arctic for hours.

There was no worse feeling than knowing that neither of your parents no longer existed on this earth in human form when you were at the age where you needed them most.

I sat there grieving, encompassed in the arms of my boyfriend and best friend, whom, no matter how much I loved, would never be able to fill the void of my parents.

Although for now, since they were all I had now, their arms would do. But never could they feel like home.

Chapter Thirty-Eight
Decker

I combed through the lip balm, hair accessories, and headphones Kam had in her nightstand, and when my hand brushed along a small, laminated card, my spine stiffened and I stood upright, taking the card with me.

My mouth parted, hands shaking as my eyes jumped all over the memorial card.

In loving memory.

Jack & Eileen Arliss.

I took a good look at the photo. I couldn't identify the man, but I didn't need to, because I immediately recognized the woman.

The image of that night flashed into my mind, just long enough for my skin to run cold.

No. No, no, no. There was no fucking way.

I dropped the memorial card into the drawer as if it were covered in thorns and shoved the drawer shut.

My throat tightened, lungs struggling as an inescapable cloud of denial caged me in.

"Hey," Kam murmured from the doorway.

I spun around, nearly skittish, staring at her with a dire look in my eye as she stood there wrapped in a towel.

"Decks?" she asked worriedly, her brows furrowing. "Are you okay? You're really pale."

I couldn't respond. I was out of air. Out of clean blood rushing through me. I could feel my bones turning brittle by the second. The familiar feeling of remorse didn't just surround me, it clenched my heart and squeezed it inside of my chest. And just when it felt like my heart was about to explode from its grasp, my stomach flipped and I ran past Kam, straight to the bathroom.

I slammed the door behind me harder than intended, locking it before dropping onto my knees, barely making it to the toilet before vomiting.

How was this even possible? How could fate be this fucking cruel?

The sins were showing no mercy in their punishment, taking over every part of my body until I was gasping for fucking air on the bathroom floor.

Dear Lord.

It felt like I was swallowing burning coals and throwing them right back up.

The realization was too much to bear.

I was in love with the same girl I had destroyed.

Chapter Thirty-Nine
Decker

How had I not known? How had I not realized sooner? She told me her last name and I completely disregarded it.

My guilty eyes stared up at my father. "Did they have any children?"

He glanced away, tapping his fingers anxiously on the table. "No," he responded.

So, this was all his fault.

He fucking lied to me.

Unless he didn't?

Maybe this was all a huge mistake, a misunderstanding that I'd be able to forget about in a few days. Maybe this was just some joke that fate was playing on me. It had to be, right? Certainly, there was no way that she was who I thought she was.

The image of her mother popped into my mind. Cold, lifeless, nothing but darkness and vacancy in her blue eyes as I delivered as many chest impressions as I possibly could, doing everything in me to save her life.

That memory earned me another round of vomit.

There was a knock on the door. "Decker?" Kam's gentle voice called. "Are you okay?"

I winced.

"Decks?" she whispered.

216

"I'm alright," I choked out. "Just feeling sick."

"Do you need anything? Let me come in, baby."

"No," I croaked out in a panic. "I'm alright."

But I wasn't alright. Not in a long shot.

My mind was so jumbled, tugging back and forth between guilt and heartbreak. The one word that I hated more than anything crept its way back into my mind, just like it had a million times before.

Murderer.

It was a word that was impossible to change. Once it pertained to you, it did so for the rest of your life.

And now, it was worse. I wasn't just responsible for the death of two people. I was responsible for the death of the love of my life's *parents.*

That was a massive fucking pill to swallow.

There was nothing I could do to change that night, nothing that would make me anything other than what I was. It was devastating to know that I was responsible for Kamryn's life turning to hell. If it wasn't for me, she would still have her parents. She never would've ended up living on the street. She would've been happy, living with her family, instead of alone and scared, sleeping on a tattered blanket outside my apartment.

I thought about what it was like to see her for the first few times out there, covered in dirt and sweat. Hungry. Lonely. *Sad.*

More vomit.

"Decker? Babe, c'mon. Open up," Kam begged. "I can hear you throwing up in there."

Just hearing her voice made another tidal wave of guilt pierce through me. What was I going to tell her? How was I going to explain to her that this was what I'd been hiding all this time? She would never believe me when I told her that I didn't know they were her parents. If I'd known this entire time, then I would've avoided all of this to ensure that she wouldn't have gotten hurt more than she already was.

She was going to hate me, but I didn't blame her. She *should* hate me. She should want me to be homeless. She should want me dead.

There was no way around this. I had to tell her the truth. And the most tragic part was that nothing could be worse than the truth.

Chapter Forty
Kamryn

He'd been in there all night. I wasn't sure if it was something he ate. Maybe he had too much wine. I knew hard liquor made him sick, and even though he hadn't mentioned anything about wine making him sick, I assumed that had to be it.

I made eggs and toast for two, setting two plates on the counter before heading back over to the bathroom door. I knocked lightly.

"Decks?"

I could hear him let out a small groan.

"I made breakfast for us." I jiggled the doorknob for the thousandth time, hoping he'd finally unlocked it. And for the thousandth time, I was disappointed. I sighed. "Please come out. Please let me help you."

I waited a moment with my ear up to the door, and when I picked out the noise of shuffling, I grew hopeful.

The door slowly swung open, and I immediately gasped to myself. I'd never seen Decker look not only so sick, but so destroyed. His head hung low, as if he was afraid to look up at me. His body didn't look as strong and indestructible as usual. All his muscles looked brittle, as if the bones beneath them had shattered.

I reached out and touched his hand, but he instantly recoiled, his head still towards the floor. "Hey," I said a bit firmer, "are you okay?"

He didn't nod. Didn't shake his head. Nothing. There was no sign of a reaction from him. He was so still that if I couldn't pick out his shallow breaths, I would've been convinced he was just a statue.

"Decker, what's wrong?" I demanded.

He shifted his weight, finally shaking his head as he did so. "I'm sorry," he wept. "I'm so, so sorry."

And with that, he stumbled past me, straight into our bedroom without another word.

I stared blankly towards the door.

What the hell?

***

Decker wouldn't eat. I could tell he was trying to sleep off whatever sickness he was fighting, but sleep refused to take him. He tossed back and forth underneath the blankets, and even though he was absolutely covered from head to toe, he was shivering like crazy.

Maybe he had the flu or something. But then why was he apologizing? Why wouldn't he at least talk to me?

I grabbed a spare blanket from the living room and snatched the thermometer out of the medicine cabinet on the way back to our bedroom. At this point, I wasn't at all surprised to see Decker still fidgeting, unable to get comfortable.

"Hey," I whispered, climbing into bed. I draped the blanket over him before gripping his shoulder and turning him to face me. His eyes remained closed, still refusing to look at me as I ran the thermometer over his forehead. When it beeped, I glanced at it. My brows creased.

No fever.

Then why was he sweating?

"Decks, baby, I need you to talk to me," I said.

His frown lengthened, pain appearing across every feature of his face. "I just don't feel good," he muttered sadly.

"Okay..." I nodded. "Why don't you try to take a nap?"

"I can't sleep."

220

"Here," I said, scooting over to him. I rested my back against the headboard, directly beside Decker. It seemed as though he was trying to avoid being close to me, probably so that he wouldn't get me sick, but right when his forehead touched my leg and he could feel my body heat, assuring him that I was right beside him, his body relaxed.

His eyes flickered open and closed a few times before ultimately landing on closed, and after a few minutes, his breathing evened out.

I ran my hand through his damp hair, trying my best to comfort him while he slept. I reached over and grabbed the TV remote off the nightstand, turning on the first Marvel movie that I saw.

I didn't know how much time had passed before Decker sprung up, gasping for air as if I'd been strangling him in his sleep. He was sweating even more than before, his eyes darting around the room in a panic.

"Hey, hey," I said steadily, crawling over to him. "What's wrong?" I ran my hand across his forehead, unfazed when I earned a handful of sweat.

"Nightmare," he murmured, his eyes falling to the comforter.

"Do you want to talk about it?" I asked, trailing my hand down the length of his arm. Goosebumps rose on his arms from my touch.

"No," he gulped, shaking his head. "No," he repeatedly quietly.

"Okay," I muttered, thankful when he at least let me wrap my arms around him.

He was worrying the hell out of me. Whatever bug he'd caught over the past twenty-four hours, I just prayed it would leave as quickly as it came.

Chapter Forty-One
Decker

She thought I was just sick. And the truth was that I *was* sick, but not in the way she assumed.

I wasn't sick with a cold or the flu. I was sick with *guilt.*

It had taken years for me to stop thinking about the accident every second of every day. But just like the first few weeks after it happened, it was all I could think about. It had been five days since I realized who Kamryn's parents were, and each day was becoming harder.

I wasn't sure how to act around her at this point. All I could focus on was coming up with a way to tell her the truth, but there was no easy way to tell your girlfriend that you were the villain instead of the hero.

Every part of her was good. From her skin to the center of her core, she was good. But *me?* I was what I was, and she was too good for me. Too good for everyone, but for a villain especially.

There was no way to get out of this unscathed. Both of us would inevitably be destroyed when the truth came out, but I was less concerned about myself and more concerned about her. How would she handle it? Surely, she would leave me. No doubt. And I didn't blame her. But I was worried about where she would go. I couldn't let her end up on the street again.

I knew I should've told her the second I realized, but part of me was still in denial. As sure as I already was, there was a thread of hope I'd been clinging onto that I was wrong.

My deplorable thoughts were interrupted by my office door launching open to reveal my father. This was only my second day working this week since I'd been too sick to come in over the past few days. But apparently two days at the office was enough for me to do *something* to cause that look of rage on his face. I just didn't know what.

He slammed the door behind him, stomping right up to my desk and leaning forward, towering over me in my seat.

My father never really intimidated me, not anymore. But there was something about the change in atmosphere that he brought into the room that immediately told me something wasn't right. That whatever he was about to say wasn't just crucial— it was personal.

"Joseph called in sick today," he simmered, his jaw tense.

"Okay?"

"So, I had to do all the paychecks myself."

I stared at him in confusion, waving my hands around to tell him to get to the point.

A heavy breath blew out his nose. He raised a small paper in his hand and smacked it down on the table, shoving it towards me. "You didn't tell me her last name was Arliss," he seethed.

Well, shit.

I glimpsed down at the paycheck on the table, gulping at the sight of Kam's full name. "So?"

"So?" he repeated, his brows drawing inwards. "What do you mean, *so?"*

I dropped the pen that I'd been holding, using my free hand to cover my face. My denial took over, questioning what we both already knew. "It doesn't mean—"

"Yes, it does," he cut me off. "You and I both know who her parents were."

My eyes darted up at him, rage stirring. "Thought they didn't have any kids?" I challenged harshly.

He glanced away, blowing out a long, stiff breath. His fingers found the edge of my desk and anxiously tapped along it, the same way they had on the night he lied to my face.

"Hmm?" I dared, my jaw tightening. When he only shook his head silently, I pushed further. "Why did you lie to me?"

"I..." he paused, his voice turning from scornful to gentle. "I knew how broken you were. I knew how guilty you felt. You're my son. I wasn't going to make it worse for you."

I remained silent, chewing on my bottom lip. I could feel my eyes gloss over, welling up with tears, but I refused to let them fall in front of him.

"I'm assuming she still doesn't know?"

"No," I let out in a whisper.

"Decker," he disapproved, his head dropping as he shook it. His anger came back, overriding his gentle tone. "God, I know you've made some questionable decisions before, but I didn't think you were this stupid."

"I didn't know," I insisted sharply.

His eyes scanned over my face, trying to decipher if I was telling the truth or not. "Do you have any idea what's going to happen when she finds out? Because she *will* find out. There's no way around that."

Yeah, thanks for telling me the fucking obvious, Dad.

He ran a hand restlessly through his graying hair. "Do you know how difficult it was to keep your name out of the media? If your name gets out, it's going to absolutely ruin your reputation."

My teeth grinded together as I stared off, annoyed by his fucking audacity right now. As if my reputation wasn't already ruined in this town? Everyone knew, but since there was never an official release of my name, no one had the proof to point fingers. Either way, *they knew.*

"But," my dad continued, pointing a deadly finger at me, "that's the *least* of my worries at this point. Do you realize what it'll do to her when she finds out? It's going to completely gut her."

I slammed my palm against my desk, standing. "I know that!" I shouted.

"Keep it down!" he hissed through his teeth. "We don't need anyone in the office knowing about any of this right now. Not before you could tell her the truth yourself."

I glared at him, fuming. I could feel my body shaking with anger, knowing damn well that we wouldn't be in this position if he hadn't lied to me in the first place. I knew he did it to protect me at the time, but in doing so, Kamryn wasn't protected. And that was a fucking problem with me.

"You are going to tell her... right?" he asked.

My eyes narrowed down further. "Yes," I said firmly. "I haven't even known for a full week."

He dipped his chin towards his chest. "Is that why you called off all week?"

I nodded, hastily shifting my weight back and forth. A single tear trickled out of the corner of my eye, and I caught it quickly before my dad had the opportunity to catch sight of it.

"This wouldn't have happened if you'd told me they had a daughter," I muttered, my voice cracking.

"This wouldn't have happened if you hadn't driven that night," he blurted out.

I sucked in a sharp breath, my bottom lip uncontrollably quivering.

His face immediately melted with regret. "I'm sorry," he said. "That was harsh."

"Just get out," I insisted quietly.

He gave a tiny nod in defeat, stepping backwards towards the door. Once he left, there was nothing in the room besides the broken fragments of my soul scattered across the floor.

Chapter Forty-Two
Kamryn

Something wasn't right.

I needed to ask him what had been brewing in his head over the past week, but my fear was holding me back. My gut was telling me that whatever was wrong wasn't something I wanted to know.

I could feel Decker drifting away, but I knew it wasn't because he was beginning to love me less. The way he looked at me hadn't changed. He still gazed at me as if I were the greatest thing to him, but there was now a somber flicker behind his eyes each time he glanced my way.

I got dressed and made my way out to the living room. Decker was sitting on the couch, his posture weak. The TV was on, but his mind was seemingly off as he stared out the front window.

"Hey," I said softly, just loud enough to be heard.

His head snapped towards me, face full of sorrow. "Hey."

"I'm gonna head over to Arianna's now."

"Okay," he said.

I gave him a reassuring smile as I slipped my shoes on.

"Wait, Kam," Decker said suddenly.

"Yeah?"

His chin dipped as his voice shook. "Can I ask you something?"

My spine stiffened, alarmed by the seriousness in his tone. My feet moved sluggishly and warily towards him. "Yeah... What is it?" I asked, sitting beside him in slow motion.

I could've sworn I could hear his heart throbbing within his chest. As if taking precaution, he glanced away from my face. "You don't have to answer if you don't want to," he said, shaking his head.

"Alright..."

He paused, second-guessing himself before he finally spit it out. "How did your parents pass?"

The question knocked my mind off track for a moment. "Um," I staggered, nervously tugging on the hem of my shirt. I sucked in a sharp breath, my eyes jumping around the room. "They were, um, killed in a car accident." The words were tainting each breath I took, depleting my lungs. "It was a drunk driver. A couple years ago on New Year's Eve."

"A drunk driver?" he repeated quietly, almost angrily.

"Yeah," I murmured.

Those amber eyes went hollow, and before I could react, Decker's arms were around me, drawing me in for a tight hug. I could feel his body shaking slightly against me. "I'm so sorry. *I'm so sorry,*" he swore again and again in my ear.

As sad as the conversation made me, it left me more confused than anything. Because he seemed abnormally grief-stricken over two people that he never knew.

Chapter Forty-Three
Decker

She verified what I already knew.

What I wished I *didn't* know.

I'd been sitting in the exact same spot for nearly an hour after Kam left. My mind wasn't just swimming in guilt, it was drowning in it. The voices in my head were so loud, overwhelmed by the beat of the cold, hard truth the second it left her mouth. Any sliver of denial that I had was gone.

There was no way to make up for my sins now. No way to redeem myself by loving her. I was trying to brace myself for the inevitable heartbreak, the inevitable loss of her. I would not try to stop her when she left.

Because I didn't deserve her.

I didn't deserve anything that I had.

I didn't deserve my father's help.

I didn't deserve for the judge to take it easy on me.

I didn't deserve to be *alive*.

Maybe this was God's way of making me pay for my sins.

The same girl you ruined was about to be the one to ruin you. How poetic?

It felt like each day that passed was a growing mass of clouds looming before a storm. I knew the truth was on its way.

I wondered how long it would take her to figure the truth out herself if I kept quiet.

I couldn't keep quiet, though.

As much as that little selfish voice in my head wanted to duct tape my mouth shut and keep Kamryn forever, my conscience refused. My *heart* refused. I loved her too much to continue lying to her.

We had our Friendsgiving dinner tomorrow, then Thanksgiving with my family two days later. I would tell her right after. The day after. Immediately after.

I swore I would.

***

I wasn't sure how much more time passed before there was a loud bang on the door.

I took a moment to collect myself, pulling myself out of my petty thoughts before striding over to the door and tugging it open.

A sigh escaped as Benny's face appeared in the doorway.

"Is Kamryn home?" he asked, his jaw tight.

My brows pulled in, my body defensively going rigid. Why the hell was Kam the first thing he asked about?

"Nah," I said firmly. "She's at a friend's house." My eyes narrowed in the slightest. "Why?"

He chewed on his bottom lip. "Can I come in?"

I eyed him cautiously for a moment before stepping aside, allowing him in. He took a few steps into the apartment before coming to a halt, his back facing me. "Be honest with me," he insisted.

"About?"

"Kamryn."

Every muscle of mine hardened in suspicion. "What about her?"

He finally turned back around. A hushed, yet stressed breath left his mouth. "Well, she followed me on Instagram."

I shifted my weight around. "And?"

His hardened demeanor shifted to denial, seemingly hopeful that he was wrong about whatever he was going to say.

I hoped he was wrong too.

He shook his head lightly. "I saw her last name. She's not related to them, is she?"

That question was painted black like death. Before I could confess, I found my myself playing dumb without a second thought.

"To whom?"

He tilted his head, reading me like a goddamn book. "Decker, cmon. Arliss? Really? All of our other friends may be oblivious to that, but I'm not."

I folded my hands atop my head, once again struggling to get a full breath in. My throat was tightening as if Benny walked over and wrapped his hands around it.

"I didn't know," I managed to get out, looking everywhere other than at him.

I could feel his eyes on me, burning a hole into the center of my chest as I hastily shifted my weight around. "What do you mean, you didn't know?" he asked.

"I didn't..." I paused, wincing, "I didn't know that she was who she was when I met her."

"Decks," he said doubtfully, "you're trying to tell me that all this time you've known her, you never knew her last name?"

"I knew her last name, but I didn't know who her parents were."

His eyes bulged out of their sockets. "Her *parents?* What the fuck do you mean her parents? I assumed they were her aunt and uncle or some distant shit like that."

I let out a small grunt in pain, hitting the palm of my hand against my forehead repeatedly.

"I thought they didn't have any kids?" his voice raised.

"That's what I thought too," I muttered.

Benny's anxiety was rising alongside mine. He turned his back towards me again, as if he was afraid to face me for his next question. "She knows though, right?" His shoulders rose and fell with deep breaths as he waited for my sinful answer.

I shook my head even though he couldn't see, fighting back more tears as guilt once again surged through my bloodstream. "No."

"Decker," his voice hardened, "this is bad."

"I know," I agreed harshly.

"Do you love her?"

I stepped backwards as if he'd pushed me. What kind of dumbass question was that? "Of course, I love her," I said stiffly.

"Then stop ruining her."

Well, that was a punch in the gut. Benny was only the second person close to me that had figured out the truth, but he was also the second person to ensure I was bound to shatter Kamryn.

My harsh tone fell to a defeated one. "I've only known for a week."

As if that made it better. All it meant was that I've had a week to tell her the truth and I hadn't.

Benny whipped around with empathy across his face. "I'm only saying this because I think Kamryn is a nice girl and I don't think what you're doing to her right now is fair at all."

"I know it's not," I admitted, bringing my hands up and dropping them against my sides. "I'm going to tell her. I just wanted to wait until after Thanksgiving."

He studied my face, taking in every inch of my misery. After a moment, he sighed. "Okay."

"Just please don't say anything."

He nodded.

"I'm serious, Benny. *Please.*"

Benny stuck his hands up defensively. "I won't. But you've gotta tell her right after Thanksgiving."

"I'm going to."

He sighed again heavily, almost stressfully, as if he were the one in this shit position. After a quick glance at his watch, he looked back up at me. "I've gotta go. I'm heading over to Myra's."

"Okay," I muttered quietly, staring at the ground. "Hey," I stopped him just before he walked out. I waited for him to turn and look at me again so that he understood how damn serious I was being. "Please don't say anything."

"I won't," he promised.

With that, he walked out the door, leaving me with nothing but a bad feeling.

He may have been my best friend, but that kid had the biggest fucking mouth on the block, and I wasn't sure if I trusted him to keep that promise.

Chapter Forty-Four
Kamryn

"Hey, babe?" Decker's voice called. My heart fluttered in the slightest at the sound.

Ever since last night, Decker seemed to be getting back to normal. He let me touch him without flinching and finally began reciprocating by touching me back. His voice wasn't shaky when speaking to me, and although the agony in his eyes hadn't completely faded when he looked at me, it had lessened an extreme amount.

"Yeah?" I responded, wiping off the kitchen counter. Our friends would be arriving in just a few hours, and Decker and I were scrambling to get the apartment cleaned and get food cooked.

"We forgot to get dessert," he cringed.

My hand shot up to my mouth. "Shit."

Our friend group decided that we would each bring a dish to dinner, making it a fun potluck. Alaina and Nolan were bringing mashed potatoes and corn. Myra and Benny were bringing green bean casserole and rolls. Decker and I were in charge of the turkey and apple pie. Too bad we forgot half our assignment.

"What should we do?" I asked.

"Um," he stammered with a light wince, "I'll run to the store, I guess."

"Okay, I'll finish cleaning while you're gone."

"Alright, baby," Decker said with a shy smile. He made his way around the island to where I stood. His hand rested along my hip in the slightest as he leaned forward, planting a warm kiss on my forehead. His lips engrained themselves there, long and loving as if it were the last time he ever would.

"I love you," he swallowed as he pulled away.

I ran my thumb along the light stubble on his jaw. "I love you too."

The sorrowful look in his eyes returned for a moment, studying me, branding me with their unexplained pain.

"Are you okay?" I let out.

"Yeah," he murmured a lie.

"Decks," I stiffened. "Tell me what's up."

He took a deep breath through his nose, his eyes once again full of an unsolved mystery. I could tell he had a thousand thoughts rolling through his mind, but he refused to admit any. "It can wait."

"Is it something bad? Are you... breaking up with me?"

His eyes widened. "No. No, I'm not breaking up with you."

I sighed a breath of relief. "Are you sure you don't wanna talk about it right now?"

His frown lengthened involuntarily, bottom lip shaking in the slightest. "I'm sure," his voice cracked.

I swayed side to side uneasily, fear returning. "Decks," I pushed, on the brink of begging.

His hands cradled my face. "Baby, it can wait. Please, don't worry about it right now. I just want to have a good night with you."

"Alright..." I agreed reluctantly.

His fingers trailed along my cheek as he let go. "I'll be back shortly."

I nodded, unwillingly watching as he walked out of the apartment. I managed to take a deep breath, filling my lungs with as much air as they could possibly hold.

Whatever Decker had to talk to me about surely couldn't be that bad if it could wait, right? If it was something extremely important, it would be urgent. He wasn't breaking up with me, so that was a relief.

Get a grip, Kamryn. Everything will be fine.

I spun on my heels and strutted over to the to-do list that Decker and I made this morning.

All that was left to do was dust and sweep the floor. I nodded to myself as I opened the supply closet, searching for the duster and broom.

The closet was a mess and a half. I rummaged through, making a mental note that Decker and I needed to organize all this crap after Thanksgiving was over.

I spotted the broom in the back corner of the closet. I struggled, but managed to reach it, taking it out and resting it against the wall beside me. I narrowed my eyes back towards the closet, playing I-SPY with myself to find the damn duster.

Finally, I spotted it on the top shelf, besides a box that read *Decorations.*

My face lit up in the slightest as I went up on my tiptoes, grabbing at the box. I doubted that Decker had any fall decorations, but it would add a nice touch to dinner if he did.

I held onto the doorframe with one hand, leaning forward more and more into the mess of the closet. I grabbed at the open flap of the box, slowly tugging it towards me. Just as I thought I had a good grasp, it slipped, sending the decorations and the stack of papers it was on top of to the ground.

"Damnit," I muttered to myself.

I lowered myself to the floor, grabbing everything and shoving it back into the box. There were papers everywhere, more than half of them to seemingly be junk, but there was one that caught my eye. I slowly picked up the paper that was ripped in half, reading the bolded letters at the top.

PRISON RELEASE FORM.

My mind struggled to keep up with what I was reading.

I had to read Decker's name on it three times before it sank in.

Decker had been to prison. But for what? I was assuming the bottom half of the paper would've stated his charges, but after rummaging through the rest of the papers that had fallen, I couldn't find the bottom half anywhere.

What were you hiding, Decker?

Chapter Forty-Five
Decker

If I was being honest, I was trying to savor my last few days with Kam. When Friday rolled around, I would be telling her the truth. Which meant I only had forty-eight hours left with her.

Just that thought was enough to sever my heart in half.

When I got home with the pie, Kam was finishing up cleaning, but for some reason, she was the one that seemed off now. She was touching me normally, speaking to me normally, doing everything *normally*, but there was something different about the spark that lingered between us each time our hands touched. It was as if there was an unsaid disconnect between us, and even though I knew we were coming to an end, that disconnect still scared the shit out of me.

The six of us laughed throughout dinner before pulling out UNO and wine. We played for an hour or two, jokingly shouting at each other.

But all night, there was a strange tension radiating off Benny. Each time I glanced at him, his hard eyes were on me, stabbing through me like daggers. I ignored him, but after a while, it started bothering me. I wanted to ask what his problem was, but under no circumstance was I going to do it while anyone, especially Kam, was in the room.

"Alright," Alaina said, standing. She glanced back and forth between Kam and Myra. "I'm ready for some pictures."

Nolan playfully rolled his eyes. "You girls and your dang pictures."

"Hey!" Alaina pointed at him. "You know I love taking pictures."

"Oh, I know," he teased.

She rolled her eyes at him, trekking over to her jacket and slipping it on. Her red locks swayed as she shot another glare at the girls. "Are you guys coming?"

"You wanna take them *outside*?" Kam asked.

"Yeah," Alaina shrugged nonchalantly. "The brick wall on the side of the building is the perfect background."

Myra sighed loudly. "Fine," she said, "but only a few pictures."

Alaina tilted her head. "Oh, c'mon. Don't act like you guys hate taking pictures."

Kam walked over. "Alright, alright. I'm coming."

"Yes!" Alaina jumped up and down excitedly. "We can get some more pictures for your Instagram."

I swallowed, feeling Benny's harsh glare burning into me once again. What the fuck was his problem tonight? He seemed decent yesterday when he left.

I walked over to the kitchen island, pouring myself another glass of wine and avoiding Benny's scowl. Once the girls all walked outside, I finally looked back at him. I spoke before thinking about it, as if forgetting Nolan was also in the room.

"What?" I asked sternly. "You've been looking at me all night like you want to punch me in the face. What is it?"

The air in the room shifted from light to heavy in a split second. Benny's stringent eyes raked over me like flames lighting up a cornfield.

"I finally asked Myra out," he said, his tone uneasily still.

I froze for a second, my glass halfway to my mouth. That was not at all what I was expecting him to say. My eyes questioningly glanced around. "And?"

"And she said no," he spat at me. "You wanna know why she said no?" He stood. "Because apparently she's still a little hung up on *you* and she also thinks it would be awkward dating the best friend of the guy she used to hook up with."

"Okay," I unsurely nodded once. "How is that my fault?"

Benny's face twisted as his voice raised in the slightest. "Why did you have to hook up with her in the first place?" His brows rose as if realization hit, yet it was the sarcasm and animosity in his voice that told me otherwise. "Oh, wait. I know," he said. "This is all about Casey, isn't it?"

My eyes narrowed. "What?"

"If you weren't so caught up in getting back at fucking Casey—"

I cut him off, anger rising. "Getting back at Ca— What are you talking about?"

"Guys," Nolan attempted to butt in, but failed.

"That's probably why you're dating Kamryn, isn't it?" Benny accused.

My muscles went stiff, hand constricting around the wine glass so tight that I was surprised it didn't shatter in the palm of my hand.

There was something about her name coming out of his mouth right now that made me go on the brink of fucking feral. "Don't bring Kam into this," I spewed, my thread of control about to snap like a rubber band.

"*Guys*," Nolan warned loudly.

"You were never actually planning on telling her, were you?" Benny pushed.

"Tell me what?" Kam's voice echoed throughout the apartment, concern creasing her features as she tugged her jacket off and tossed it onto the couch.

Everybody froze.

My heart was beating so vigorously that I could've sworn it caused an earthquake throughout the apartment. Fear was a bitter flavor on my tongue, slithering down my throat like a snake through tall grass.

This was it. The ugly and bloody truth was about to make its debut. And when it did, Kam— the only girl in my world— would hate me.

Chapter Forty-Six
Kamryn

Even though the silence was only there for a minute, it seemed to pass by slowly, yet not slowly enough to prepare me.

Decker was completely still, seemingly in shock. I could feel the panic radiating off him, could see the dread in his eyes.

"Decks?" I quietly muttered under my breath. My voice snapped him out of his trance just enough for his shaking hand to reach behind him and place his wine glass on the counter.

I looked back and forth between Decker and Benny, waiting for someone to explain what the hell was going on. I shifted my weight back and forth restlessly, the silence finally starting to bother me. It felt like Benny just pulled the pin on a grenade and we were all anticipating the explosion.

"Go ahead, Decks," Benny dared. "Tell her what you did that night."

Decker's fear flipped to rage, his jaw hardening. "Shut up, Benny," he warned, the words erupting out of his mouth like molten lava.

Anxiety, so strong that it was painful, filled my core. Yet, I just stood there silently. Waiting for whatever was next.

Decker stepped towards Benny, his eyes a swirl of all different emotions. Benny was much smaller than Decker. If

Decker lost it right now, Benny wouldn't stand a chance. And Benny most definitely knew that, but for some reason, he wasn't backing down.

"Tell her," Benny said. He was taunting Decker, toying with him like a caged animal at the zoo.

But unfortunately for Benny, Decker wasn't caged. He was a free lion about to pounce on a gazelle.

"*Benny*," Decker warned again.

"You were never gonna tell her," Benny hissed in a whisper.

Decker grabbed two handfuls of Benny's shirt, shoving him back against the wall in a final attempt to get him to shut up.

It was too late though. At this point, I *needed* to know. And I needed to know now.

"Tell me what!" I shouted, stomping my foot like a child.

Neither of the boys glanced in my direction, their eyes scorching into each other with so much hostility that it made everyone else in the room squirm.

Decker's face was a mixture of a furious grimace and a plead, but Benny didn't currently give a fuck.

"You weren't gonna tell her until she figured out for herself that YOU were the one that killed her parents that night!" Benny screamed ruthlessly, the veins in his neck bulging.

I froze briefly as three gasps came from behind me. I stalked forward. "You know, Benny," I fumed, "it's really fucked up that you'd joke about something like that."

Once again, neither of them looked at me. Their silence made me uneasy. "You are *joking*, right?" I hissed in a shaky voice.

Benny's cold glare never left Decker. His teeth were clenched so hard that I wouldn't have been surprised if it was crushing his molars to dust. "Am I joking, Decks?"

Decker's bottom lip shook in the slightest, his hands shuddering as his grip on Benny grew weaker and weaker.

My face fell. "Decks?"

His hands opened, releasing Benny as his spine crumbled and his head hung between his shoulders. "It's true," he whispered reluctantly.

"What?" I doubted. "That's not possible."

Decker's skin turned ghost white from head to toe, his chest expanding so quickly and deeply that for a second, I thought he was about to faint.

"Everyone besides Kam," he struggled to speak, "get out."

I stared at Decker as everyone behind me scrambled to grab their stuff, not saying a word as they practically ran out the door.

"What the hell was he talking about?" I demanded.

His eyes glazed over with guilt.

"What was he talking about?" I repeated, my throat tight. He clutched onto his stomach, unable to speak. "Tell me he was lying."

Decker weakly shook his head. "I can't."

I slowly stepped forward. "Tell me the truth," I ordered. "Why did you go to prison?"

His eyes jumped up to me, taken aback by the question. It seemed like he was more horrified than I was at the moment. "You knew I went to prison?"

"I found your release form in the closet this morning," I said, my eyes knife-sharp. "*Why* did you go to prison?"

"I..." he stopped, as if he'd forgotten how to speak. "I went to prison because... I'm responsible for the death of your parents."

I stared at him, taking in every inch of his expression and trying to figure out what to do with it. There was nothing on his face to suggest that he was lying.

A wet diamond formed in the corner of his eye and trickled down his cheek. The sight felt like a bullet to my heart despite the grisly truth that I was still denying.

"I'm so sorry, Kam," he cried.

My brain was still struggling to get a grasp on reality. I felt numb, almost lifeless as my own tears slowly followed suit. "Why didn't you tell me?" my voice shook through anger.

"I didn't know," he insisted quietly. "Not until recently."

"How recent?" I demanded.

"A week ago."

I eyed him once more, speechless as my heart constricted. That's why he'd been sick over the past week. Why he'd been distant. Why he'd been so hesitant to touch me.

I could see his panic rising by the second alongside mine. It was as if our anxiety was racing, challenging each other to see whose body would collapse first.

"Decker," I said warily, "there's no way."

"I wish I could tell you it's not true," he sobbed, burying his head into his hands.

From everything I knew about Decker, he was so put together, so responsible and so considerate. I couldn't envision him doing this. "You're telling me that you drove drunk?"

He exploded in a loud cry, a blood-curdling wail leaving his mouth as his back fell against the wall and he sank down to the floor. "No," he wheezed. "I wasn't drunk. I was a lot of things that night, but I wasn't drunk."

It was slowly, yet surely registering that he was being serious. But how? I didn't understand how this was possible. I still wanted to believe that he was wrong, that maybe he had the wrong people in mind. But I could hear the grief behind his words, could see the suffering on his face.

This amount of truth wasn't enough for me though. If he was going to rip my heart to shreds, then he needed to do it thoroughly.

"You're going to tell me," I said.

His head whipped upwards, his mouth parting in realization of what I meant. He shook his head, pleading with me.

"You're going to tell me what happened that night," I said firmer.

"Please don't make me explain," he begged. "That was the worst night of my life."

"Yeah, mine too," I declared. "Now talk."

Chapter Forty-Seven
Decker

I bent over, panting as sweat beaded down my forehead.

"Shepley," Coach called.

"Yeah, Coach?" I straightened.

"Great job today." He patted me on the back.

"Thanks," I nodded.

"We're very excited to have you here next year," he said.

"I'm excited to be here."

He gave me a firm nod. "Alright, kid. It's New Year's Eve. Get outta here."

I gave him a shy smile. "Okay. Thanks, Coach."

"We'll see you in the spring!" he shouted after me as I jogged off the field, turning and giving the stadium one last look before heading to grab my stuff.

I hopped in my car carefully, my sore muscles aching as I did so. I'd spent the past three days at Stanford, training for next year. I already had my scholarship and my spot on the team secured, which meant I would be finding myself here almost every month, preparing for my next four years on Stanford's baseball team as their starting pitcher.

The ultimate goal was to play professionally, but I still needed a lot of work before I'd reach that level.

Only five minutes after I started driving, my phone buzzed in the passenger seat. I kept my eyes on the road as I grabbed it. I gave it a single glance before answering the call, putting it on speakerphone and dropping it into my lap so that I had both hands on the steering wheel.

"Hey," I said.

"Decks!" Benny exclaimed. "What's up, buddy? How was training?"

"Exhausting."

"Yeah, I bet," he said. "Are you gonna come out tonight?"

I frowned. "Ah, I don't know, man."

"Oh, c'mon, Decks! The whole friend group is going!"

I let out a small groan. "What time are you guys going?"

"Around eight, I think."

I shrugged even though he couldn't see it. "I won't be able to anyway. It's already a little past six. By the time I get home, eat, shower, and change, you guys will be there already."

"Just drive separately and meet us there," he suggested.

I stared at the road in thought. "I don't know..."

"C'mon. It's our senior year. It might be the last New Year's we get together. And plus, don't you wanna see Casey?"

A tiny grin surfaced on my lips at the sound of her name. He was right. I did want to see Casey tonight. Hell, I always wanted to see Casey, regardless of whether I should.

"Fine," I gave in. "But I can't drink then."

"Then don't," he said nonchalantly. "I'll send you the address. Cool?"

"Cool," I agreed, ending the call and tossing the phone back in the passenger seat.

As excited as I was to spend the night with Casey, it was more so my worry that had forced me to give in, because I knew in the back of my mind that if she wasn't spending New Year's with me, she would've spent it with someone else.

***

Robby Rink lived on the other side of town, about a fifteen-minute drive from my house. I didn't know Robby well at all. No one in our friend group did. But apparently his parents went out of town for New Year's and he had the house to himself, so he threw a party and invited the whole grade.

There weren't as many cars on the block as I imagined there would be. Either people didn't want to park too close to the house to avoid drawing attention or there were very few people that drove tonight just for the chance to get wasted.

I parked half a block away and walked the rest. Even though I'd never been to Robby's before, it wasn't hard to tell which house was his. Robby's mother used to be the governor of California and his father was a well-known doctor. So not only was it the biggest house on the block, but it was loud and rowdy from a quarter of a mile away.

So much for not drawing attention to the party.

When I walked up the driveway, there were people going in and out of the house. Some seemed fine, whereas others were already drunkenly swaying even though it was only nine o'clock.

Leave it to the high school kids to not know how to pace themselves.

I walked in behind a few people whose faces I recognized, but I wasn't entirely sure of their names. The second I was two steps through the front door, I could hardly take another step. The house was absolutely packed. It seemed like our entire high school was here rather than just the senior grade.

Since I didn't know the layout of the house, I had no idea which direction to head in. I slowly made my way through people, searching for any of my friends.

A hand wrapped around my wrist, yanking me. "Decker!"

I turned, relieved to see Myra. "Oh, shit. Hey," I said. "Where is everyone?"

"Over here," Myra said, cocking her head. She held her hand out, gesturing for me to take it so we wouldn't lose each other through the sea of people.

We didn't walk far before our friends' faces came into view. I scanned over all of them briefly, but none of them were a tall, dirty blonde with brown eyes.

"Decks!" Benny shouted, wrapping his arms around me for a quick hug.

"Hey, man," Nolan nudged me. "How was Stanford?"

"Yeah, how was Stanford?" Alaina smiled.

"Good," I nodded. "Really good."

"You're gonna have to tell me all about it," Nolan said. "Since obviously, I'm not good enough to join you..."

"Don't sweat it," I assured him.

"Nah," he shook his head, "it's fine. You know I didn't wanna go pro anyway."

I opened my mouth to respond, but I clamped it shut at the sound of a screech, loud enough to be heard over the music.

"DECKS!" Casey shrieked, jumping into me.

I chuckled, catching her in my arms and squeezing her tight. I buried my face into her hair. "Hey," I smiled.

She pulled away, glancing up at me with a grin that made my heart swell. "I missed you."

"I missed you too," I responded, running a hand through her hair. "How's your night?"

"It's been alright." Casey shrugged, casually swaying side to side. "Much better now that you are here." Her pearly whites appeared, sending a bolt of fulfillment down my spine. A lightbulb popped up over her head, and she reached out, clutching onto my hand. "Let's take a shot!"

I shook my head with a light wince, watching her face fall. "I can't. I drove."

"Oh," she frowned.

There was a tap on my arm, and I turned to see Benny standing in front of me with a handle of vodka.

"Alright," he started, "hear me out."

I tilted my head at him, already knowing what he was about to say. "No."

"No, no, no. Listen," he insisted, causing me to sigh. "I'm not telling you to drink and drive. I would never let you do that. All I'm saying is that if you wanted to drink, you could just come crash at my place with me tonight. It's only two blocks

away. We can walk back at the end of the night and come get your car in the morning."

I inhaled deeply, rubbing the light stubble on my chin in thought. "I'm not sure..."

Benny shrugged. "It's up to you. Just figured I'd offer."

I took in his earnest expression before tipping my head just enough to glance at Casey. She was jumping up and down, caught up in a conversation with Myra. As if she could feel my eyes on her, she peeked over at me, lightly batting her lashes.

I sighed in defeat, giving in to my first mistake of the night. "Fine," I said. "Let's take one."

"Aye!" Benny roared with a triumphant smile.

Alaina peeked her head around Nolan's large frame. "Your ass is not driving tonight, Decks."

"I know," I said, taking an empty plastic shot cup from Benny. "I'm gonna crash at Benny's."

"Good," she said, satisfied.

"You're gonna drink with us?" Casey asked hopefully, stepping back over to me.

I gave her a casual grin. "Guess so."

She smiled that beautiful smile once more, planting her hand on my shoulder to steady herself as she went on her tiptoes to bring her lips to mine.

I kissed her intently, acknowledging the magic that existed there. It was a darker magic, a sometimes painful magic, but magic all the same.

See. She loves you. She wouldn't betray you again.

I kept repeating it to myself as she pulled away, trying to soak the words in the best that I could and convince myself of them.

But in reality, I knew my hopeful heart just needed the white lie.

"Does everyone have a cup?" Benny asked, lifting a brow as he looked the group over. We all nodded, yelping eager yeses in his face.

He went around the circle, filling everyone's cup nearly to the rim. Six cups raised in the air, clinking in the slightest before we all dumped them down our throats.

My face scrunched from the aftertaste, but thankfully, it quickly went away.

"Decks," Casey called, gripping my hand with both of hers, "let's go dance."

"Okay, Case," I agreed happily.

"We're taking another one in a bit!" Benny called after me as the nightmare in the little black dress swept me away.

***

An hour and a half passed, and I still didn't feel drunk. Granted, I'd only taken two shots and I knew I didn't want to get absolutely hammered tonight, but I felt the need to be at least a little drunk in order to deal with this shitty party.

It would've been more fun if I knew more people, but since there were over five-hundred students in our grade alone, it was impossible to know each one.

Some of the guys from my high school baseball team showed up, so I was able to hang out with them for a while, which so far was the best part of my night. I just wished Casey was hanging out with me more.

She was hopping around, talking to anyone and everyone that she knew. Which was fine. I wasn't the type of boyfriend to put a leash on her and force her to stay by my side all night. It just would've been nice to be around her more, especially considering the fact that her best friend had spent more time with me tonight than she had.

I'd been hanging out with Benny and Myra for a decent amount of time now. I had no idea where Nolan and Alaina were at, but it was safe to assume they ran off somewhere to be alone for a while. Either way, I was growing sick of being the strange third wheel.

Benny and I were pretty open and honest with each other. I knew that if he liked Myra, he would've said something, but he hadn't. His actions weren't lining up with his silence though. It was hard not to notice the way he kept casually touching her and trying to dance with her. She didn't necessarily shy away from it, but she never initiated it either.

248

I couldn't quite put a finger on whatever weird friendship dynamic they had going on, but whatever it was, I needed a break from it.

I leaned towards Benny. "I'll be right back." I turned to walk off, but he grabbed the sleeve of my shirt and yanked on it.

His eyes widened in the slightest as he spoke. "Are you going to the bathroom? Because I gotta piss too."

"What? No," I said. "I'm going to find Casey."

"Oh," he said, blowing out a disappointed breath. "Fine. Guess I'll find the bathroom myself."

"The house is huge, man. There are probably a gazillion bathrooms. I'm sure you can find one," I assured him before trudging off.

Once again, I scooted through people as carefully as possible. After quickly scouting the crowd upstairs with no luck, I followed the noise of people down a long hallway, leading to a staircase that I assumed led down to the basement.

I wandered downstairs, for some reason surprised to find that the entire basement was full of people as well, but thankfully, it wasn't packed shoulder to shoulder like the upstairs was.

A dirty blonde head came into view on the far side of the room, and with all my confidence that it was Casey, I picked up my pace to make it over to her faster.

But I came to an abrupt halt when my eyes zeroed in.
She wasn't alone.

Tommy Pry was casually laughing alongside her without a care in the world. Did he know I was here at the party? He must not. If he did, then he probably wouldn't be risking another broken nose just a month after his previous one healed.

My jaw stiffened as I watched Casey flirtatiously flip her hair. Immediately, my mind started racing, searching helplessly for assurance.

Maybe the hair flip was casual. I mean, they weren't even standing close at all. Maybe she's only talking to him because she felt bad that her boyfriend broke his nose.

I watched with boiling blood as Pry reached out and lightly touched Casey's wrist before letting his hand fall back to his side.

My fists clenched, anger overwhelming my chest and I burned within the heat of it. I wanted nothing more than to stomp over, give him another broken nose and swoop her away, but I used every ounce of control within me to stop myself.

The last fight, even though it wasn't much of a fight with Pry's poor performance, was enough to get me suspended for two days. I couldn't risk getting in trouble again, especially since my last season of high school baseball was about to start and that the punishment would most likely be worse a second time around.

I gritted my teeth together before whipping around myself and stomping off, knowing that that was the only option possible unless I wanted another fight to unfold.

Luckily, Benny and Myra were still in the same spot, but now, Benny was double fisting with the vodka in one hand and a slice of pizza in the other.

He spoke with his mouth nearly full. "Where's Casey?"

It felt like I was contaminating the air with the words. "Downstairs talking to Pry," I snarled.

"What?" Myra yelped.

I nodded stiffly, avoiding eye contact with them. But out of the corner of my eye, I could see Myra drop her arm against her side as she rolled her eyes.

"I'm gonna go get her," she snapped, stomping off.

I turned towards Benny, eyeing him in indifference. "Where'd you get the pizza?" I muttered.

He threw a thumb over his shoulder. "There's a ton in the kitchen."

I gave a single, bitter nod as I stepped around him and roamed into the kitchen.

Benny was right. There were at least ten boxes of pizza scattered across the long granite countertop. I grabbed three slices and a bottle of water out of the case on the kitchen table.

I glanced around myself, relief filling me at the realization that I was alone. Finally. Alone for the first time since stepping into this fucking house.

I enjoyed the solitude as I ate, unsure of how much time passed before all three pieces of pizza and the water were gone. By the time I got back to Benny, I could tell that my body had relaxed some, but still, my shit mood hadn't faltered.

"Hey," Benny tapped me on the shoulder. "You okay?"

"No," I admitted.

Benny sighed. "I'm sure it was nothing. I know she's pulled some shit in the past, but she wouldn't be dumb enough to cheat on you while you were in the same house, right?"

I laughed without humor. "Who knows at this point? Her and Myra are still nowhere to be seen."

He swayed uneasily side to side, seemingly unsure of every single thing coming out of his own mouth. "Just trust Myra then. I'm sure she's found Casey and that they're just off doing whatever." He pulled his mouth over to the side, holding the bottle of vodka out. "Want another shot?"

"Yes," I said sternly.

Fortunately for me, the shot went straight through me without affecting me at all. Unfortunately for me, it was still enough to convict me.

Chapter Forty-Eight
Decker

It was already eleven-fifty.

Where the fuck was my girlfriend?

It was almost midnight, and I hadn't seen Casey in God knew how long. After Myra went looking for her, they came around for half an hour before disappearing again. It'd been so long that even Nolan and Alaina were back at this point.

I shifted my weight around, too antsy to stand still.

"Decks," Alaina said, placing her hand on my arm. "Relax."

"I'm trying," I assured her, "but like... what the fuck, Alaina?"

"I know," she nodded. Her face fell, and I couldn't help but feel the pity she was emitting. "Look... I really think you need to just break things off with her."

I sighed, sadness creeping in at the thought. "I just..." I stumbled.

Alaina nodded sympathetically. "I know, Decks."

I rubbed my forehead, tugging back and forth between looking for Casey again and just saying fuck it altogether. I inhaled deeply, trying to get my anxiety under control as a hand gripped my forearm and spun me around.

"There you are!" Myra said stressfully. "I've been looking everywhere for you!"

The tone of her voice and the troubled look on her face instantly made me grow wary. I tipped my head downwards. "What's wrong?"

Her eyes zipped away from my face as her mouth opened and closed, unable to form the words that I could tell were consuming her mind.

"Do you know where Casey is?" I asked.

"Decks..." she said prudently.

"Myra," I said a little firmer, stepping closer, "where is she?"

It looked like she was having an internal battle between protecting her best friend and protecting me. I gave her a few more seconds, my anxiety growing before spilling over completely as she spoke.

"She went upstairs with someone," she blurted out.

"What?" I exclaimed as if it were a surprise. "When?"

"Like ten minutes ago. That's why I've been looking for you," she said, gesturing to me.

My shoulders stiffened as I glanced at the staircase that led upstairs. "Did she go with Pry?"

"No," she shook her head. "I have no idea who it was. I didn't recognize him."

I went to step around her, but she planted a small hand strongly against my chest, stopping me in my tracks. "Decker."

"I need to go up there."

"Listen to me," Myra insisted. I forced myself to look away from the stairs and at her instead. "Don't you realize that you deserve better? You need to leave her, Decks. She may be my best friend, but you're too good for her."

"Myra..." I said delicately, my gaze wandering back to the stairs.

"No, I'm serious," she said, pointing a finger at me. But when I looked directly at her, her hard expression melted. "There are so many girls who would be lucky to have you. And who would actually treat you the way you deserve." Her eyes fell to her feet for a moment. "Don't go up there, Decks."

"Thank you, Myra," I said softly, pausing. "But I have to." Before she could stop me, I was gone, hustling through the crowd much less carefully than before.

I took the stairs two at a time, and when I got to the top, I came to a sudden stop, my head flipping back and forth between the right and left, unsure of which way to go.

I knew I was only standing there for less than ten seconds, but it was enough to be able to feel the adrenaline gushing through the chambers of my heart.

My gut told me to head to the left, so I did. All the doors were closed, and there were so many rooms that for a moment, I thought it was hopeless.

Until I noticed light peering through the cracks of a doorframe.

I strode heavily over and without thinking, I gripped the doorknob, relieved when it pushed open with no problem. I didn't even make it past the doorframe before halting like a car slamming on its brakes.

Casey and some guy that I didn't recognize were both shirtless, sprawled out on the bed, hands and lips everywhere.

"You've got to be fucking kidding me," I said, running a hand over my eyes.

Two heads popped up, but my eyes were solely on Casey, taking in her paralyzed expression.

"Decks," she finally let out in shock.

My gaze lingered over to the guy, who looked both confused and overly smug at the same time.

My body reacted instinctively— muscles coiling, anger rising, thoughts scattering.

But luckily, before I went through with the temptation of smacking that smug ass look off his face, I stopped myself.

It wasn't worth it.

I looked at Casey— the last time that I would ever do so. "We're done," I fumed.

I turned on my heels at the same moment that the entire party screamed "HAPPY NEW YEAR!"

I could hear Casey calling after me as I descended the stairs and I knew it wouldn't be long until she was chasing me, begging for forgiveness the same way she had before.

I needed to get the fuck out of here before she had the chance to catch up to me. I shoveled through people, eyes focused on nothing other than the front door. Everyone was still shouting happily, celebrating the start of the new year.

Happy fucking New Year to me.

My friends had all been right. I should've left Casey a long fucking time ago and I knew it this entire time, but for some reason, I hadn't been able to let her go. And now, the pain was the price.

The front door was in sight and just as I was five simple steps away from it, Benny blocked my escape.

"Hey!" he shouted. "Are you alright? Where are you going?"

"I'm leaving," I contended, trying to step around him, but he shifted over, once again cutting me off.

His entire face scrunched together. "What do you mean you're leaving? You've been drinking. You can't drive."

"Benny," I said firmly, impatience and anger laced into my voice, "I'm leaving."

"You can't drive," *he hissed.*

"Look at me!" I said, motioning to myself. "I'm fine. I'm literally fine. I am not drunk at all."

I was certain that I hadn't actually been drunk all night. Tipsy at some point, maybe. But definitely not drunk. Either way, any amount of alcohol that had been lingering in my system had faded at the sight of Casey and that guy. That shit sobered me up real quick.

"Decks," he winced, shaking his head, "no. I'm not letting you drive."

"Benny," I warned through my teeth.

"Alright," he nodded with his hands up, trying to reason with me. "We'll just go back to my place now, okay? We'll walk back. Let me just say bye to Myra really fast. I'll be back in less than a minute, I swear." He skirted around me, rushing away to find Myra.

The second he was out of sight, I scurried to the door and busted through it without looking back. I practically sprinted the half block to my car, ignoring how strangely cold it suddenly was for a Californian night.

I hopped into the driver's seat and blasted the heat but didn't bother to wait for my car to warm up before putting it in drive. The entire scene replayed inside my head over and over again, from the moment Myra came up to me to the moment I stormed out the front door.

The animosity and heartache cascading through me was weighing me down so much that it was making me dizzy. But in the end, it was partially my fault, wasn't it? Because I always let her get away with it. I allowed her to think it was okay to keep screwing me over.

Even though I saw it coming, the expectation didn't make it hurt any less. When you spend a year of your life with somebody, they become part of you. And when you lose them, you lose that part of yourself.

And at this moment, I felt a little lost. The world looked distorted, slightly different than it looked just an hour prior.

The longer I drove, the more the anger faded away, leaving only sadness in its place. Another flash of pain stabbed through me as I blinked tears away. I let out a small sniffle, thankful that I was less than ten minutes away from home now.

I turned onto the main road, accelerating until I was five over the speed limit. When the sky suddenly turned from black to white, my brows came inwards.

What the hell? *Was it* snowing? *In* California?

Within another minute, the pace of the white flurries had quickened, making it harder to see.

I'd never driven in the snow before. Hell, I'd never even seen *snow before in my life.*

I gripped the steering wheel tighter, leaning forward to get a better look at the road. My eyes were straight ahead, focused, but apparently not focused enough.

The light that I was approaching shifted from yellow to red, and I reacted too late to do anything besides slam my foot on the brake, sending my car sliding through the intersection at fifty miles per hour.

It happened so quickly, quicker than the speed of light when a single glimpse of a grey car flashed in front of me. The brakes screeched, followed by a loud crash of metal against metal that sounded like a firecracker.

The momentum mixed with the thin layer of snow on the road sent the grey car spinning, its tires crying out loudly as it crashed into a nearby lamppost.

My car had skidded through the rest of the intersection before coming to a complete stop. The front of my car was smashed like a boulder collided with it. The airbag had gone off but was already deflated.

Other than my frantic gasps for air, the world was so eerily quiet after the amount of chaos that had just taken place in the past fifteen milliseconds.

I took a single glance over my shoulder at the grey car before frantically undoing my seatbelt and leaping out of my car as I yanked my phone out of my pocket. I dialed 9-1-1 as I raced over there.

"9-1-1, what's your emergency?"

My adrenaline was at an all-time high, fight-or-flight kicking in as I spoke through a riptide of anxiety, words scrambling out as I glanced at the street signs.

"I need an ambulance at the intersection of Maple and Albany as soon as possible."

"Okay," the operator spoke, "tell me what happened."

"Car accident," I stammered, approaching the grey car. I zoned out from the call, dropping the phone from my ear as I took in the scene of what was before me.

There was smoke rising from the vehicle, mixing with the cold air. The driver's side door was detached, lost somewhere, and broken glass surrounded the car. There was a man in the driver's seat, the left side of his face looking nothing less than fractured, covered in blood.

The sight was traumatizing, but for some reason, I couldn't look away. I could feel the current of shivers as it cascaded down my entire body, absolute shock overwhelming every inch of me.

After thirty seconds of standing there like a deer in headlights, I leapt forward. "Hello?" I frantically shouted, desperate for the man to answer.

No response.

I needed something. Anything to signify that he was alive.

The sight of him already made me skeptical. I'd never seen so much blood before, never even realized there was that much blood within the human body.

My shaking hand reached quickly inside, hovering over the side of his throat. "Please," I muttered. "God, no."

I couldn't even feel my own heart beating as I held my breath, tears spilling over when all I received from the man was silence within the walls of his chest.

"No!" I screeched. "Fuck, no!"

I stumbled back a few steps, my lungs concaving.

I just killed a man.

Just then, there was a choking sound, almost like a small cough that echoed through the frozen night. My head immediately darted back to the car.

Was there someone else in there?

I sprinted to the other side, my eyes once again bulging at the sight. A woman was face down on the hood of the car. Or at least what was left of it.

She had been partially ejected. Her upper body was lying out the broken windshield while her lower half was still inside the car. She too was covered in blood, but the second I saw her arm move, I dashed forward, panic rushing helplessly through my bloodstream.

As carefully as possible, I scooped her up, doing my best to guide her away from the broken glass. She was limp in my arms as I held her bridal style, carrying her quickly over to the grass. She was wearing a long, elegant dress that had been torn to shreds, but by the amount of blood she was enveloped in, I couldn't even tell what color it was.

"I'm so sorry," I cried as I delicately laid her down on the white-tipped grass.

But she wasn't moving now. Her sky-blue eyes were halfway open, peering into me, but they were vacant. I tapped her face lightly. "Please, no," I muttered. "Please, God, please."

I leaned down, pressing my ear against her chest and waiting a moment to hear anything. A single breath. A single pulse. Any single sign of life.

When I didn't get one, I didn't hesitate to kneel above her, tipping her chin back before planting my hands in the center of her chest.

I began giving her chest compressions, counting under my breath until I reached thirty before giving two breaths and repeating. Over. And over. And over again.

"C'mon!" I shrieked as tears slipped off my skin and onto her, mixing with her blood. "Please breathe."

Where the fuck was the ambulance at?

I didn't stop delivering CPR, even when my hands started cramping unbearably. Her blue eyes were still dark and empty, her body still lifeless before me.

A little out of breath and a little wobbly from the adrenaline, I could start to hear a siren in the distance, approaching quicker by the second.

But I still didn't stop.

The snow had slowed, but the chill of the air was no match to the chill within me. It was a strange, paralyzing feeling to witness someone's death. Especially at the palm of your hand.

She couldn't be dead though, right? I mean, I just saw her move minutes ago.

I could feel the life getting sucked out of me, leaching away the same way it had for this woman and who I could only assume was her husband.

The phantom echo of the siren had finally grown louder, a blaring anthem as blue and red flashing lights flew up beside me, coming to a sudden halt.

I didn't take my eyes off the woman, didn't take my hands off her chest as countless medics piled out of the ambulance, half of them running over to check the cars and the other half coming to me.

"We'll take it from here," one announced.

I tried to stand to get out of their way, but the earth beneath me didn't seem quite steady. My legs gave out and I tumbled onto the ground a few feet from them, letting out a deafening wail as I buried my face into my hands before collapsing completely. I curled up, becoming a grown man screaming in the fetal position.

The guilt and remorse didn't just trickle in, but it completely engulfed me like a tsunami hitting shore.

I rolled over onto my knees, planting my hands on the ground and covering the snow with vomit. I emptied my stomach until I was dry heaving.

I stayed there, panting as I stared at the ground. My chest hurt. My brain *hurt as it tried to wrap itself around the reality of what the fuck just happened. Devastation sat deep in my bones, spreading like the venom of a rattlesnake.*

I could see a pair of black shoes appear next to me out of the corner of my eye. A man knelt beside me, lightly touching my shoulder. "Are you alright?"

It felt like I couldn't draw in a full breath. I was shaking, heart hammering, blood freezing, stomach turning. It felt like my body was failing. As if at any moment, I'd drop dead right on the pavement.

"N—no," I stuttered, unable to look at him.

"We're going to need to talk to you about what happened," he said softly.

I forced my head to turn. It wasn't a medic in front of me. It was a cop. His frown was accompanied with pity.

"Son, have you been drinking tonight?" he asked gently.

My bottom lip quivered, and I let out a wince. "Yes," I admitted.

"Okay," he gave a small nod. "The medics are going to check you out, and then we're gonna have to breathalyze you."

My head fell between my shoulders. "Okay."

In a better world, this entire thing would've been a horrific dream. Even though I was still in denial that it was *real at all.*

But it wasn't until I blew a zero-point-zero-three and the cuffs dug into my wrists that the ghastly truth finally settled in.

Chapter Forty-Nine
Kamryn

Silence. Denial. *Sorrow.*

Reality slowly consumed me as if I were breathing in a toxic vapor. All I could do was stand there, letting it assault me.

Darkness had woven through the only light I'd known. The same man who gave me everything was the same one who took it all away in the first place.

Decker had always had the power to make me blush, but right now, the blood was drained from my face. I couldn't wrap my head around how someone could be both the safety and the danger.

We were still in the same room. Still breathing the same lethal air. Both strained hearts still hammering in sync. But the amount of distance that this one truth had just created between us was gut-wrenching.

Decker was on the floor, curled up against the wall as I stood five feet from him. Both of us were enveloped in an ocean of tears and sobs, but neither of us said anything.

As fucked up as it was, I wished he was holding me. Comforting me. Telling me that everything would be okay. But I didn't have to read his mind to know that he was internally killing himself.

If none of this involved my parents, I'd have more pity for Decker than I'd ever had for anyone before because I could tell how sorry he was. Could see how much the guilt had devoured him over the past few years. I was torn between wrapping my arms around him and quite honestly— punching him in the face.

Decker's red-rimmed eyes slowly peered up to meet mine. "I'm so sorry," he muttered between shallow breaths. I stared at him in silence as he spoke. "I would do anything to change it."

I tucked my thumbs into my palms, squeezing them with the hope that it would cause me to wake up. But the harder I squeezed, the more the tears flowed.

I didn't know what to say. There were no words to express that feeling of betrayal. All I could do was let out a whimper. My eyes remained on Decker, vision clouded as if I were peering through thick gauze.

I wasn't sure what was happening inside of me at the moment. I couldn't describe it in any word other than *pain*. I hadn't experienced shock or grief like this since finding out my parents died.

Hearing Decker tell me what happened made it so much worse. Because it made it so *real*. I almost wished I hadn't asked so that I wouldn't have to know what my parents' last few moments were like.

After hearing about the details of the accident and piecing it together with what I previously knew, it was a relief to know that my parents didn't suffer. But at the same time, I shouldn't have been relieved about their death, because they still should've been alive.

What if I had been in the car that night? What if my parents picked me up from Arianna's like they'd offered to? Should I have died that night along with my parents?

There were too many things going through my head, too many possibilities and ghastly images. I envisioned Decker hovering above my dying mother, attempting to save her life.

I thought about how much I looked like my mother, and I couldn't help but wonder if that's who Decker thought about every time he looked at me now. Did he visualize hovering above *me*? Trying to save *my* life? Did the image hurt him just as much as it hurt me?

When my legs buckled, I found myself on the floor just like Decker, burying my head into my hands. That same feeling of the world crashing down came about, and when I looked back up, once again, *nothing looked the same.*

But this time, it was the pain of feeling like everything I knew was a lie. I had never been more sure of anyone or anything than I had been of Decker. He was supposed to be my hero, my saving grace. He was not supposed to be the villain.

Now, the only thing I was sure of was that fate was cruel by leading us into this twisted love story. All our love and hope crumbled to dust in that moment, scattering along the floorboards.

Decker was usually my antidote to pain. I wanted to reach for him. I wanted him to numb the pain, but that was the issue— he was not currently the antidote. He was the pain.

"Kam," Decker struggled to breathe, forcing my gaze to meet his. "Are you okay?"

He knew what the answer to that question was. I was not okay. And he was not okay. But I was certain this was his way of attempting to comfort me since he was so uncertain of whether it was okay to *physically* comfort me or not.

Which he was right to assume.

Mentally, I could not bear to be too close to him, but there was somehow still a pull coming from within me, begging me to go to him. I was confused with how this could possibly be, considering how cold and horrific the truth of our love was.

My mind was still partially stuck in the past, and although I was positive I couldn't handle any more from Decker, I asked anyway.

Chapter Fifty
Decker

"What happened next?" she let out in a whisper.

My teeth dug into my bottom lip. My body felt so frail after having to relive that night, detail by detail. If I had to think about it anymore, my heart would surely give out.

"What happened after you got arrested?"

I winced as my head fell towards the floor once more. Even with all that pain fresh in my mind, I knew she deserved to know everything. If she was strong enough to hear the words, then I needed to be strong enough to speak them.

Other than a few cuts and bruises, I was fine. Maybe if I'd gotten brutally injured, I'd feel less guilty. A few broken bones or brain damage or internal bleeding. Anything. But there was nothing.

Now I sat in silence at a table in some type of interrogation room.

I'd hardly spoken since the cuffs went on. People kept asking me questions, trying to understand what happened, but I couldn't get any words out.

Some other people in my situation would simply be relieved to be alive, but I was not. My brain was swarming in possibilities.

What if I hadn't driven at all?

What if I'd reacted sooner?

What if I had been the one to die?

I was numb from head to toe as the distressing words kept repeating inside my head.

I'm a murderer.

They were the right words, the truthful words, but they were also so horrid.

I would never be able to take back this night. And I would never be able to unsee the blood on my hands. How could I live with myself after this?

My head shot up when I heard voices outside the door. The familiar timbre of one made my brows crease inwards.

"Where is he?" my father asked frantically.

"Scott," a man's firm voice called. It was the forcefulness and confidence in his tone that told me he wasn't a cop. He must've been the prosecutor. It was silent for a moment before the man started speaking again. "I hope you know he's getting charged."

"With?"

"DUI vehicular manslaughter."

"DUI?" my father questioned. "He wasn't drunk. I was told he blew a point-zero-three. That's not even halfway to the legal limit."

"He's a minor," the man shot back. "His legal limit is zero.*"*

My father went quiet, and I could only envision the look of anger on his face. "Where is he?" he repeated stiffly. "I'd like to speak to my client."

I waited impatiently as the door opened and my father entered, a frenzied mess. He was wearing a suit, of course. The only man on earth that would arrive at the police station at four in the morning wearing a damn suit.

He let out a stressed huff as he sat at the table across from me. There was only silence as he looked over my tired, bruised face.

My father took a deep breath. "Decks," he started softly, "are you okay?"

I shook my head in the slightest.

"What the hell happened?"

I opened my mouth to respond, but nothing came out besides a rush of forlorn air.

"Decker," he said, a little firmer, "I need you to tell me what happened."

I stared at one of the squares of cement on the wall past his shoulder. When the image of the woman inevitably went through my mind again, I finally spoke. "The woman," I blurted out. "Is she alright?"

My father looked down, his heart undoubtedly heavy.

"Is she alright?" I repeated sternly.

"She was pronounced dead at the scene," he said sorrowfully.

A sob immediately left my mouth. My voice came out muffled as I covered my face with my hands. "There was nobody else in the car, right?"

"No."

Suddenly, it dawned on me that I'd been forgetting to ask about the people who weren't in the car. My guilty eyes stared up at my father. "Did they have any children?"

He glanced away, tapping his fingers anxiously on the table. "No," he responded.

That part at least brought me a little relief. "What's going to happen now?"

"Apparently you're going to be charged with two counts of DUI vehicular manslaughter," he said matter-of-factly. "I'm not sure if you'll be charged with anything else. They're going to hold you here until your bond is posted. Once I know it, I'll get you out and—"

"No," I interrupted.

His brows creased. "No?"

I shook my head. "I deserve to be in here, Dad."

"The bond will only get you out until your court date," he assured me. "I'm assuming you're going to plead guilty?"

"Of course," I croaked. "There's no other option anyway, is there?"

He winced moderately, as if trying to hide it. "Not really." There was no doubt he was currently torn between father and lawyer. "Decks, I'm going to do everything that I can to make sure you get the lightest charges and shortest sentence possible.

I tipped my head in the slightest, shaking it. "Dad," I said through emotional and physical exhaustion, "just let it happen."

"Decker—"

"I killed two people, Dad," I snapped, my voice cracking. "I deserve to be in here."

His bottom lip shook in the slightest, a clear sign that his fatherly side had won the battle. "You're just a kid."

"I'm a kid that fucked up," I said. "Bad." I'd never sworn in front of my father until now, but that was the most innocent part of this entire night.

"Decker, I don't believe you were drunk. I believe it was the weather conditions that..."

"It doesn't matter," I shrugged. "I shouldn't have been driving anyway."

My dad's eyes glossed over, unable to hold it back any longer. "I'm going to get you out of here."

"Dad..."

"I will," he promised, just as the door opened to reveal a guard. "I love you, son."

"Love you too, Dad," I muttered as he stood and left the room.

*****

Fifteen days later, I sat in the courtroom beside my father, awaiting the judge to tell me my fate.

The prosecution had already spoken, but I zoned out during most of it, my mind circling repeatedly on how different everything could've been if I hadn't driven.

When the judge gave my father permission to give his statement, my father stood, buttoning his suit jacket as he did so. He stepped up to the podium at the head of the courtroom.

"Your Honor," he began, "I'm requesting that the court gives Mr. Shepley three to five years for his charges. Before the accident, Mr. Shepley was an honors student with a clean record and a full scholarship to attend Stanford University. He was planning on playing baseball there with hopes of eventually becoming a Major League Baseball player. After the accident, Mr. Shepley's senior year of high school has

been cut short, he's already lost his scholarship and dream of playing in the MLB, and he will forever have to live with his immense remorse. In my eyes, Your Honor, that is already a heavy punishment." He paused for a brief moment before continuing. "On the night of the incident, it snowed for the first time in San Francisco in nearly a decade. Mr. Shepley was not familiar with how to drive in these conditions, and unfortunately, this resulted in the death of two innocent people. But that's not to say Mr. Shepley did not take immediate action after the accident took place. He made the responsible decision to call 9-1-1 and deliver CPR to the best of his ability, which are two things that not all teenagers in his position would have done." Another pause, but this time, there was a small waver in my father's voice when he began speaking again. "Mr. Shepley is young and has a lot of potential to do good in this world," he stiffened, "which is why I'm requesting that he has access to a library and online schooling during his sentence."

My head popped up. "What?" I muttered quietly. Did he seriously just do that without my permission? Not once was that ever discussed between us.

I could hear the prosecutor let out a small scoff across the aisle from me. I didn't blame him. I supported the prosecution more than I supported my own defense team.

After my father finished, I gave him a harsh side eye when he took his seat beside me. Since there were no victim impact statements to be read, I was up next.

It's not required for every defendant to speak during their sentencing, but I wanted to. I knew Jack and Eileen Arliss didn't have any children, but if they did have any other family in the courtroom, I needed them to know how sorry I was.

I stood, taking the deepest breath I could manage to compose myself, but it wasn't enough. I was crying before I even reached the stand.

"Your Honor," I started, choking down a small sob, "I'd like to start off by addressing the family of the victims. I know that nothing could ever bring back Mr. and Mrs. Arliss, but if trading my life for theirs would bring them back, I'd do it in a heartbeat. I cannot put into words how incredibly sorry I am. I'm not going to stand here and beg for forgiveness because I don't deserve forgiveness." I paused, eyes burning.

"I take full responsibility for my actions, and I deserve the maximum sentence allowed."

I could hear my father spit out what sounded like a cross between a gasp and a growl.

I had more prepared to say, but I was worn out. I couldn't get anything else out, standing there for nearly a full minute with my mouth hanging open. My head fell and as I stepped away from the podium, it lifted just enough to see my mother in the front row of the gallery, hysterically crying against my fourteen-year-old sister's shoulder.

I swallowed, taking in Emmy's red-rimmed eyes. For the rest of her life, she would have to be known as the girl whose brother killed two people.

I squeezed my eyes shut as I took my seat. This time, my father was the one giving me a harsh side eye.

We waited for the judge to make his decision, and when he was ready, everyone in the room stood. The judge's attention was solely on me, pity resting in his eyes.

"Son," he said, "I want to start out by saying I truly believe you are sorry for your actions. I have taken a substantial amount of time to review the facts of this case, and through red light camera evidence, a lack of evidence convicting you of intoxication, and by taking weather conditions into consideration, I've concluded that your charges are not quite correct. I have also reviewed your grades, athletic career, and clean record prior to the incident. With that being said, I agree that you have a lot to offer this world, and therefore, I grant the request to have access to the prison's library and online schooling. I am a firm believer that the punishment should match the crime, and in this case," he shrugged, "this seemed like a complete accident. Regardless of the faint amount of alcohol in your system, and regardless of the fact that you are under twenty-one, I do not believe you were intoxicated when you got behind the wheel. But unfortunately, since you already pled guilty to these charges, all I can do is give you the best sentence in the eyes of the law."

He paused, looking down at the papers in front of him. I could feel my father's heart beating in double time, mine right there with it. He grabbed onto my hand, and if I weren't so focused on the judge, I would've ripped my hand away.

"For the deaths of Jack and Eileen Arliss," the judge spoke, "Mr. Decker Shepley, the state is sentencing you three to five years in the San Francisco County Prison."

"What?" I murmured.

In my mind, that was not enough for what I'd done.

My father let out a lengthy sigh of relief, a triumphant smile overtaking his face. I, on the other hand, was more disappointed than anything.

<u>*Chapter Fifty-One*</u>
Kamryn

My eyes were narrowed at Decker, burning a hole into his head like a cattle brand.

Before hearing about his sentencing, I was struck with sadness. A burning, torturous, treacherous sadness. And now? *Anger.*

There was no image violent enough to describe the force of what happened to me in that moment. Being crushed by a semi filled with fury would be an understatement.

A twitching jaw had replaced my tears. I pushed myself to my feet, standing above him. "Look at me," I demanded.

Decker's ashen face slowly lifted, and the moment his grief-stricken eyes met mine, I had to look away. If I looked at them for too long, I knew my anger would fade and that I'd fall right beside him to comfort him.

"You're telling me that I lost both my parents and my life went to shit, and you got three years and special treatment in prison for it? What the fuck is that!" I shouted.

His expression was so tortured you'd think he'd been stabbed in the gut. I'd never seen Decker look like anything less than a man, but right now, what he resembled most was a boy. A scared, young boy.

Another haunted tear trickled down his cheek. "I'm... I'm so sorry," he struggled to get out.

But the word had lost all meaning.

"It doesn't matter, Decker! Nothing can bring them back!"

"I know," he muttered, running a shaking hand over his face.

I squatted down in front of him, my voice eerily steady. "Do you know why I wasn't at the sentencing?"

He shook his head.

"Because my bitch of an aunt never told me about it."

I didn't stay there long enough to gauge his reaction. Instead, I stood, pacing back and forth, my thoughts reeling.

I wished I'd known about the sentencing. I wished my shitty aunt had told me everything that was going on, because chances were, she knew about it all but chose to keep it from me.

If only I'd been there. I would've known who Decker was and none of this would've happened. I would've read an impact statement on my parent's behalf so the judge could see how much their deaths affected me.

Either way, the system failed them.

I stopped in my tracks at what I'd just thought.

Did I really just wish Decker had been in prison longer? That more of his life would've been taken from him on top of what he'd already lost?

I gritted my teeth together, almost angry with myself for wishing something so cruel upon someone I loved.

What about my parents though? What about the justice they deserved?

My heart plummeted as I stood there, tugging back and forth between Decker and my parents. My blood was running weak, overwhelmed and unprepared with this level of pain. If Decker was listening closely, I was sure he could hardly make out the sound of my feeble heartbeat.

The longer I stood there, enveloped in heavy silence, the stronger the anger got. I glimpsed around at the apartment, taking in every item.

I shook my head slowly, my back facing Decker. "Do you see all of this?" I said, holding my arms out. When there was no response, I turned. My brows raised. "Do you?"

He gave a frail nod.

"Look at everything that you have."

For the first time since he confessed his sins, Decker's voice was still sad, but steadier, his tears finally slowing. "None of the things in this apartment matter to me..."

I stood quietly, his gaze holding me captive.

"Besides you," he finished. "Nothing in here matters besides you."

I shrugged, my voice cracking in the slightest. "What do you want from me, Decker?"

His eyes fell from mine with so much shame.

"What do you expect me to say to you right now when you are the reason I have no parents?" I said, my voice beginning to rise. "You are the reason my life changed for the worst! You may be the one that took me off the street, but that means nothing when you were the one that put me there in the first place!"

Only a small sniffle escaped as he nodded along while I spoke, agreeing with everything I was saying.

I circled around to the other side of the kitchen island, my eyes once again wandering from corner to corner of the apartment, taking in the family photos he had scattered along the walls. "Look at you! You have a family. A family that is alive and well. You have a mother, a father, a *sister!* And what do I have? Nothing! I have nothing!"

"You'll always have me," he muttered quietly.

"I don't want you!" I snapped, but immediately recoiled. I could've sworn I heard the crack of his heart, another shard of it tearing off. I could see how much I'd just hurt him, and at the moment, my greatest dread was the expression on his face.

It felt like I was getting whiplash from jerking back and forth between emotions. On one hand, I wanted Decker to know how mad I was. How unforgivable his actions were. How much he'd affected my life before he even knew me. But on the other hand, I couldn't bear to see him hurt.

A shocking contrast between love and hate.

Each time I looked at him, the love and sympathy took over. But each time I looked *away* from him, the rage simmered deeper.

So, I stopped looking at him.

My hands smacked down flat on the counter, exhales blowing rapidly out my nose. I leaned into my hands, eyeing the dishes and decorations spread across the island.

Before I knew it, a drinking glass was in my hand one second and across the room the next.

Chapter Fifty-Two
Decker

She was destroying the apartment and I let her.

It was like watching an inferno consume the room.

Bottles were being pushed off the counter. Plates tossed across the room. Decorations ripped apart.

But through it all, she would not look at me.

I finally found it in me to stand. "Kam," I stammered, but it was easily drowned out by the sound of glass shattering.

"I just wish you hadn't driven that night!" she screeched.

"Kam," I said louder, but still, her attention remained everywhere other than on me. "Kam!" I finally yelled.

She halted, her eyes shooting over to me for only a moment before they fell to the floor.

"Stop," I demanded softly, raising my hands in front of me. "This isn't you."

I could see her chest rise as she inhaled deeply, pressing a hand against the ache in her heart. "You're right," she declared.

We both just stood there for a moment. My eyes on her. Her eyes on the floor.

I didn't know what I was thinking when I started to step towards her.

Too bad I couldn't take more than three steps before she was practically sprinting past me and into our bedroom.

The door slammed and I could make out the sound of the lock clicking as I jogged over. "Kam," I pleaded.

The only response was the sound of rustling and our dresser drawers opening and shutting. I let my forehead fall against the door in defeat. My dry eyes burned as more tears formed, a few trickling down.

I knew what was coming next.

I would have to watch her leave and endure it.

"Kam," I begged through the door. I tried to think of how to say goodbye in a way that would tell her exactly how much I loved her, but there seemed to be no words for that. Not in our particular situation at least.

The door swung open, revealing an unsettled Kam with her duffel bag thrown over her shoulder.

"Kam, please," I cried, the tears rushing faster as she strode past me. "You can stay here. I will go."

She paused with her back facing me, a mere five feet from the door.

My heart stuttered knowing I had her attention. "You don't have to go. I will leave and you can have the apartment."

No response. Neither verbal nor physical.

"I don't want you to end up on the street again. *Please*," I pleaded. "Let me be the one to go."

When she spoke, it sounded like it was partly through gritted teeth and partly through tears. "Decker..."

"Kam," I wept, "I love you more than anything. I meant it when I said that you are the only thing in this apartment that matters. The only thing in the *world* that matters. I'm not going to beg you to stay with me. Because I shouldn't. Because I don't have the right." I paused just long enough to hear her let out a whimper. "But *please*... I need to make sure that you are safe and have a roof over your head."

For ten gruesome seconds, the room was so silent that I felt like I was going deaf. It physically hurt to breathe, as if someone took a dull razor blade to my lungs.

Everything was wrong with this picture— soulmates being torn apart at the hands of calamity.

The thud of Kam's duffel bag hitting the floor gave me false hope. She stumbled over to me, her ocean eyes finally looking at me.

Ever so softly, she brought a hand up to my cheek. It was second nature for me to lean into it. The weight of her gaze was so heavy, so urgent.

"I love you," she promised, stroking my cheek with her thumb. "But God, I hate you," she whispered as a tear fell.

It was as if I'd handed her a gun and those words were the trigger.

I watched in utter disbelief, my feet cemented to the ground as Kam grabbed her duffel bag off the floor, and with one deep breath, walked out the door.

Chapter Fifty-Three
Kamryn

Two weeks had already passed since I arrived at Arianna's unannounced, collapsing on her doorstep as she comfortingly rubbed my back the same way she had nearly five years prior on the night my parents died.

I'd spent the first three days staying there bundled up on the couch in tears, lost in the fog of it all. There was so much pain I was trying to sort through. From the loss of my parents to the loss of Decker to the pain that I'd inflicted upon him myself.

Even though it had been two weeks since the last time I saw him, I still couldn't get the image of his brokenhearted face out of my mind. I had nightmares of it when I was asleep and daymares of it when I was awake. It seemed to be haunting my every move.

"Good morning," Arianna softly said as she opened her bedroom door and wandered into the kitchen. Her apartment was only a one-bedroom, so I'd been sleeping on the couch, which I didn't mind. I was just grateful to have a roof over my head.

"Morning," I murmured.

"Are you still meeting up with your friend for coffee?" she asked, pulling out her coffeemaker.

"Yeah, I think so."

"Do you want some coffee now at all?"

"Yes, please," I said, welcoming the thought of as much caffeine as possible. A few minutes later, she joined me on the couch, handing me a mug of hot coffee. I inhaled the aroma, the smell reminding me of *Joe's Coffee Shop*. A tiny, comforted grin drew up on one side of my mouth, but when my mind drifted to the apartment directly across from the shop, the smile disappeared. "What are you up to today?" I asked, desperate for a distraction.

"I think I'm gonna go visit my mom in the afternoon. Do you want to come with?"

"I would, but I've got my interview after I grab coffee with Lydia."

"Oh, that's right!" Arianna squealed in excitement. I gave her a forced smile.

I was absolutely not excited for my interview. When I didn't show up to Thanksgiving dinner with Decker at the Shepley's house, it was no secret that we'd broken up. I texted Mr. Shepley the next day, telling him that I'd be resigning from my position. Of course, it was unprofessional to quit over text, but there was no way in hell I was stepping into the office to do so. Mr. Shepley sadly agreed, but thankfully, didn't ask any questions.

Then again, how could he have the audacity to ask questions when he already knew the truth?

Maybe if he hadn't lied to his son about my existence in the first place, Decker and I would've stayed far away from each other.

But then again, maybe not.

I had a very strong feeling that no matter the circumstances, no matter if my parents were still alive or not, no matter if Decker had been responsible for it, that our paths would've crossed regardless.

Either way, here I was now. Half a day away from a job interview for a new receptionist position at a chiropractic office.

"Well, you'll have to come with me next time I visit then. My mom misses you like crazy!" Arianna said.

"I know," I gave a friendly grin. "I miss her too. I haven't seen her in so long."

She nodded. "It's been quite a while."

"Yeah," I said solemnly, checking the clock on the wall. "Well, I'm gonna start getting ready," I stood.

"Feel free to use any of my stuff if you need it."

"Thanks, Ari," I said with a shy smile before shuffling into the bathroom.

***

Lydia and I skipped our weekly coffee date last week, and I was thankful that she was kind enough to meet me at a different coffee shop today, since I knew I wouldn't be able to handle being that close to Decker's had we gone to Joe's.

Lydia asked me several questions about what happened between Decker and me, and I gave her the shortest answers possible before diverting the conversation back onto her.

After a bit, I could tell she'd given up, clearly getting the hint that if the subject was on me for another minute, I'd break down right then and there.

We were only at the shop for an hour and a half, and since I still had two hours before my interview, I decided to kill the time by walking down the small strip of stores nearby. There were plenty of boutiques and bookstores, all of which my mother used to take me to when I was younger.

I waved goodbye to Lydia as she wandered off in the opposite direction. The sidewalks were crowded, a normal occurrence in San Francisco. I weaved in and out of people for a few blocks, turning the corner, but coming to an immediate halt.

My eyes were glued to the pure white chapel across the street, watching as groups of people walked up the front steps and inside, all wearing nice clothes.

I stared at the building like it was an alien spaceship, but the truth was that I was familiar with the building. More than familiar.

This was the building that I spent every Sunday morning at until my parents passed. The building that my mother would drag me out of bed to go to. The building that I had my first Communion in. The building that I practiced my faith in up until the age of sixteen. The building that I said goodbye to my parents in.

People were rushing around me, giving me dirty looks as they passed since I was in their way. I followed the herd of people crossing the street, and within another thirty seconds, I was standing in front of the chapel, my neck cranked back as I stared at the top.

I glimpsed at the time on my phone. *Ten-fifty-five.*

Which meant eleven o'clock mass was about to start.

My eyes trailed down to my white sundress, debating on whether to walk inside or not.

"Go," I could hear my mother's voice telling me.

She didn't have to tell me twice.

I sashayed up the steps and walked through the massive wooden doors, instantly hit with both a sense of comfort and awe.

The church looked the same. From the wooden pews lined on either side of the center aisle and the stained-glass windows to the large crucifix at the head of the room and each articulated arch in the ceiling.

I took a seat in one of the pews in the very back. Smoothing out my dress, I waited for the service to start.

The church was practically filled from front to back, with my pew being an exception. There was only one small family sitting on the opposite end. A mother, father, and young redheaded girl in a blue dress.

Typically, the sight would bring jealousy to the forefront of my brain, but there was something about the air in the room that brought warmth instead of pain.

At precisely eleven o'clock, the service began. After the opening songs and prayers, and Communion was served, a preacher took the stand at the head of the room.

The preacher must've been fairly new to the church since I didn't recognize him. Then again, I hadn't been here in nearly five years.

"Today, I would like to focus on a scripture that I believe we are all familiar with, whether we have read it directly from the Bible or not. And that would be *One Corinthians Thirteen*," he said. He began reading the entire verse, stopping to emphasize the message of today's sermon.

"Love endures all things," he repeated slowly. "Surely, each and every one of us has questioned it before. Is there truly a type of love that endures all things? Even the painful, tragic, and ugly?"

He undoubtedly had every ounce of my attention. It was as if I could not hear the little girl on the other end of the pew scraping her feet against the floor. I could not hear the loud breathing of the man across the aisle from me. I could not hear the dog that was barking outside.

I was zoned out from every noise besides the preacher's voice.

"Love can," he answered his question with assurance. "True love, the type of love that surrounds your entire being, is not only a long-lasting feeling, but it is consistent and compassionate to the real you. The for-better-or-for-worse you. The you that is worthy and welcomed and treasured simply for being you. Forgiven for every sin out of love. Now, is this type of love an easy thing? Of course not. Is it always filled with the happy endings you see in movies? No. Love is beautiful, but it can be costly. Real love can cost everything you have in your heart. Sometimes it fills your heart and sometimes it breaks it."

It wasn't until I felt a wet droplet hit my arm that I realized I was crying. But it wasn't an ugly cry. It wasn't the type of crying caused by pain or sorrow. They were tears of comfort. Relief. *Love.*

"The worst part about this type of love," the preacher continued, "is the pain that it brings upon loss. Love makes loss hard. This comes with every type of loss. Whether it be having a fallout with a friend. Or when a family member moves away. Or worst of all, death. What makes the death of a loved one so hard is just that— love. It's what makes grief so hurtful. But no matter how much grief there is, love endures it. Love lies beneath it. It is the foundation. The beginning and the end."

I wiped underneath my eyes, letting out the smallest sniffle in the history of sniffles. There were three people on a loop in my mind.

My mother. My father. And of course— Decker.

I was listening thoroughly, but my mind, or perhaps my heart, was the one wandering off.

Three smiling faces.

282

Three warm pairs of arms around me.

Three hearts that filled yet also broke my own.

Before sitting right here, in this very spot, I felt like a terrible daughter. Like I'd betrayed my parents for loving Decker. But right now, I somehow felt calm, peaceful. It was clear that whether they were on Earth or not, they could never hate me. Because they love me.

The same went with Decker. I may have been angry with him, may not have been able to forgive him, but I could never truly hate him.

That realization sent a small trickle of guilt to drip down my skin, because how I felt now was not what I said then.

"No matter how hard it might be sometimes, no matter how much love opens us up to pain, without it, we have nothing. We gain nothing. We are nothing," the preacher stated. "Love bears all things, believes all things, hopes all things, endures all things."

I nodded lightly, letting the words soak in.

And when the service came to an end, I walked out feeling much better than when I'd walked in.

My mother was right. *I needed that.*

Chapter Fifty-Four
Decker

I hated how fucking quiet it was.

Not even my prison cell was this quiet.

Even though it had already been two weeks since I last saw Kamryn, it felt like it happened yesterday, because the pain wasn't ceasing. At all.

Forget drugs— you want to know what real withdrawal feels like?

Lose the love of your life.

I was currently lying on the floor. The fucking *floor.* Because no matter what piece of furniture it was, every time I went to sit, it burned. And I mean, physically burned. From my ass to the center of my chest. I could feel the absence of her in every square inch of the apartment.

It was a Tuesday. I should've been at work. Instead, I spent the day lying here, staring at the ceiling, reminiscing my favorite moments spent with Kam, since truly, that was all I had left.

But all those moments simply added up to a future that was entirely impossible.

I was worried about her. I knew she had a few options of places to go, like Arianna's or if worse came to worst, her crazy aunt's. Either way, I worried, and until I had confirmation that she was safe, I would continue to be worried.

I should've chased after her that night. I should've insisted that she stayed at the apartment and allowed me to leave instead, but I didn't.

That was just another thing added to the list of things I regretted.

I'd tried contacting her a few times since she left, just to make sure she was safe, but she ignored me every time.

My phone buzzed beside me, and like every other time it had done so over the past two weeks, I dashed to grab it, for some reason still having hope that Kam's name would appear on the screen.

Once again, it was just another disappointment when Benny's name was there instead. He'd been texting and calling every day, trying to apologize and ask to talk in person, but I ignored him every time.

Did he not understand that our friendship was over? He broke the worst fucking promise he ever could have. If Kamryn had found out the truth from me, she definitely still would've left. And I definitely still would've been heartbroken, lying on the floor right now, but at least I would've told her myself.

A light knock sounded on the door, and I let out a groan as I stood. I swore to God if Benny was at my door, he would be greeted with a gracious fist to the face and a kind "fuck off."

When I swung the door open, my tense muscles relaxed at the sight of Emmy. I leaned against the doorframe.

"Hey," she said, her eyes swimming in worry.

"Hey," I said, stepping away from the door. She followed inside, closing the door behind her. "What're you doing here?" I asked, lowering myself onto the couch. The second my ass hit the cushion, I popped right back up.

I could've sworn it burned me.

"Haven't seen you in a while," she shrugged.

I gave a nod. "Yeah."

She took a tiny step towards me. "Are you doing okay?"

My eyes swept over everything other than my sister, trying my absolute best to avoid her sympathetic gaze. My hand lifted aimlessly and fell to my side as I spoke. "I mean..." I trailed off.

"Decks," she pushed.

"What do you think, Em?"

She chewed on her bottom lip. "Is there anything that will make you feel better?" she asked in a small voice.

"Kam," I blurted with no hesitation, my voice shaking in the slightest. Less than five seconds after it left my mouth, a low whimper followed. And that whimper turned into two, then three, and before I knew it, I was bawling.

"Decks," Emmy said sadly, wrapping her arms around me as I sank to the floor.

I buried my head into my little sister's chest. How ironic was this? A big brother was the one that was supposed to comfort his little sister when she had a broken heart. It didn't typically go the other way around.

"Maybe she'll forgive you," Emmy hushed.

"She won't," I cried. "And she shouldn't."

"Maybe she will," she said, rocking me. "Just maybe."

Chapter Fifty-Five
Kamryn

I walked into the beautiful white chapel the following Sunday morning, heading straight to the same pew I'd sat in the week prior.

After attending my first church service since my parents' passing, I'd been feeling a bit more at ease. Was I healed from everything that had happened? Absolutely not. Would I ever be fully healed from it all? I doubted it. But if attending church again continued to comfort me and somehow make me feel closer to my parents, then I was dedicated to making it a weekly occurrence, just like my mother had.

The service began the same way as before, but it was when the preacher from the previous week took the stand that I really zoned in.

"For those of you who were not able to be with us last week, we discussed unconditional love and how love endures all things. Today," he paused, scanning over the filled pews, "I want to discuss something that ultimately goes hand and hand with that unconditional love. Something that's easier said than done, but when it *is* done, it can be the most rewarding, fulfilling, and healing thing." Another pause. I found myself leaning forward, eager to hear what the topic was. "Forgiveness," the preacher said confidently.

I sat back, nearly rolling my eyes. *Oh Lord*, I thought, before chiding myself.

First love and now forgiveness? Was he kidding? It was as if the entire church was pointing at me and saying, *"Yeah, you, Kamryn. Listen closely."*

"First, what is forgiveness? Let's start with what forgiveness is *not*. It is not forgetting. It is not denial. It is not brushing off someone's betrayal as if it never happened. Forgiveness is not fair. It's not a feeling. It takes faith."

I shifted around in my seat, contemplating sneaking out when no one was looking, but it was as if I could hear my mother's voice again, scolding me for even considering it.

"As much as it may hurt, I'd like everyone to take a moment of silence to think about someone who has betrayed you, someone whom you have not forgiven, at least not yet." He did exactly that, taking what felt like a small eternity to pause. The church was so silent that I could hear my own breathing. Which was not a good thing. Because although my mind had already been lingering on Decker *before* the silence, now it was amplified. His voice. Face. Smile. Tears. Everything. Clear as day.

The preacher continued, "Whatever it was that came to mind, just know that it did so for a reason. No matter who betrayed you or how they betrayed you, we are all faced with the same dilemma. Forgive or not forgive? It's easy to hold a grudge. Easy to wish the worst upon someone who deserves something bad. So, if *not* forgiving is what's easiest, then why should we forgive? And even more so, *how?"*

At this point, I was trying to zone out just for the sake of ignoring the pain his words were causing. But whether I listened or not, Decker was still there. In the forefront of my thoughts.

"When the sin is small— a simple lie, perhaps— it's fairly easy to forgive. But when it's something that happens more than once, or a betrayal that's very big and very hurtful, especially by someone you trusted, someone you believed had the best intentions, someone who should've protected you, someone you loved dearly..." he drifted off for a moment. "It becomes much more difficult. So, why forgive this? Why should we forgive something that seems so unforgiveable and so unfair?" Another moment of silence. I gulped, waiting for what he was about to say, even though I had a pretty good idea of what was coming. "Because it's what we ask for every day."

And there it was. Of course.

"We ask for forgiveness but we ourselves are not willing to forgive. It's a little hypocritical of us. A little selfish of us. And that's okay. Because if the betrayal wounded you, then you have the right to feel wounded. If someone came up to you and stabbed you in the stomach when you least expected it, then you have the right to fall to the ground, holding on desperately to the wound to stop it from bleeding..."

This was where I zoned out, lost in a train of thought. For the first time since the preacher began speaking today, it wasn't Decker that was occupying my every thought.

It was my parents.

If they were here, what would they say? Would they tell me to forgive those that had done me wrong, or would they tell me to move forward and try to forget? Would they forgive Decker themselves?

I chewed on my lip for the rest of the service, chewing and chewing until I could taste blood. The moment the final prayer was over, I sprinted out of the church and waved down a taxi.

There was someone I needed to see.

Chapter Fifty-Six
Kamryn

The house hadn't changed over the past six months. It was still the same tiny yellow house that it was when I last stomped out of it.

I slowly made my way up the front steps, hesitating as I brought my hand up to the door.

Turn around. You shouldn't be here, I thought. My teeth gritted together. *Shut up,* I silenced myself, knocking before the dubious voice in my head could change my mind.

I shifted around, merely uncomfortable in my own skin as I waited to see who was going to open the door.

The familiar creak of the old hinges sounded, and Ryan's face came into view.

His jaw dropped to ground, and he gave a visible shudder. "Kam," he shook, staring at me as if I were a ghost appearing out of thin air. Without a hint of a falter, he swung his arms around me. "Where the hell have you been?" he croaked.

I surprised myself by hugging back, but I remained silent.

He pulled away, holding me by the shoulders so he could see my face. The astonishment in his eyes hadn't faded. He kept studying me, but I wasn't sure what he was looking for.

Was he looking for any physical injuries? Was he analyzing my face even though he'd seen it a million times prior?

I took the opportunity to stare back at him, searching for any changes to make a mental note of, but I couldn't find one. His brunette hair was still in its regular crew cut. His eyes were still the same shade of grey. He was still right under six feet tall and had the same freckle on his cheek.

"Kam," Ryan repeated, "where have you been? Do you not understand how worried I've been?"

I glanced down at my feet, and when my gaze swept over his face again, that warm glimmer in his eye that I'd come across so many times before wasn't making me feel anything. There was no spark in my core. No color in my cheeks. No flutter of my heart. Then again, I wasn't quite sure if Ryan ever gave me any of those feelings to begin with.

I didn't know exactly what I came here for. Did I come to grant Ryan my forgiveness? Did I come to see how being in his presence would make me feel? Or maybe both?

"I went looking for you," he muttered quietly.

"I know," I murmured back.

"Your aunt wouldn't tell me where you were."

"That's because she didn't know."

His expression went stiff for a moment before softening again. "Why don't you just come in for a bit?" he proposed.

I took a deep breath through my nose, giving him a hesitant nod. He led the way as if I was a guest, as if I'd never stepped foot in this run-down house.

The air was stale, bitter almost. I glanced around, expecting to see some of Sadie's things, or really anything that looked different or out of place, but once again, I couldn't find anything.

"Before anything else..." I blurted out. "My mother's jewelry box. Where is it?"

Ryan eyed me for a moment too long, just enough for my mind to head in the worst direction.

"Ryan," I insisted, "you didn't do something to it, did you?"

"No," he immediately shook his head. "No, of course not. It's upstairs. I'll go get it." I let out a sigh of relief as he trotted up the stairs.

When Ryan reappeared with the box unharmed in his hands, a sense of ease came about. "Are you, um, leaving already?" he asked.

I raised a brow. "Do you want me to?"

"No," he said, carefully setting the box on the table beside the front door. "I mean, I'm not gonna hold you hostage, but I'd like if you stayed for a bit."

My teeth dug into my bottom lip, and I nearly winced. There was already an open cut from gnawing at it earlier.

"Where's Sadie?" I questioned.

His brows knitted together. "What do you mean? She doesn't live here."

Now, *my* brows were knitting together. "She doesn't?"

"No," he shrugged.

"Why not?"

He let out a playful sigh, his lips twitching.

"What?"

"You're just as adamant as always," he teased. "I have a feeling we've got lots to catch up on. You want something to drink?"

I pulled my mouth over to the side, becoming more and more comfortable as the seconds ticked by. "Tea?"

He gave a nod. "Coming right up," he grinned, strolling into the kitchen.

Ever since I could remember, Ryan was a tea drinker. He never really liked coffee much, but tea? He could drink it day in and day out. Morning? Night? Didn't matter. There was always a kettle on the stove.

I took a seat in the small front room that served as a seating area just as Ryan returned with two cups of hot tea. I gave a small smile at the sight.

"Thanks," I said as he handed one over and took a seat on the couch adjacent to me.

"Can you please tell me where you've been now?" he asked kindly, bringing his mug up to his mouth. "You haven't been staying with your aunt then, I'm assuming?"

"No."

"Arianna?" he guessed, but I didn't miss the meager edge in his tone when he said her name.

"I'm staying with her *now*, but..."

"But?"

For some reason, I was finding it hard to look directly at him. I'd always been bad at eye contact when a conversation made me uneasy, but I'd never had that issue with Ryan. I'd practically grown up with him. He was so familiar to me that even his presence now was making me comfortable despite everything that happened.

But I still stared off as I responded. "I was staying with my boyfriend for a while."

Out of the corner of my eye, I could see his mouth draw up into a content smile. "You have a boyfriend? What's his name?"

Inevitably, I smirked as I responded. "His name is Decker." But the smirk faded completely when I corrected myself. "He's an ex-boyfriend now, though," I said, finally finding the courage to look back at him.

He leaned forward in the slightest, and I tried to pick up on the expression on his face. His brows were slightly creased, mouth had flipped to a gentle frown, eyes glossed with warmth. But none of it spelled out jealousy to me.

"Tell me everything," he said.

I shook my head. "You first," I demanded. He briefly glanced over my face, then nodded. He knew damn well I deserved for my questions to be answered. "Why doesn't Sadie live here?"

He shrugged. "We're not dating."

"Why not?"

"Because it was a mistake," he said without hesitation. "Yes, I slept with her once, but from the second it started, it was a mistake. It was my bachelor party and I was fucked up and it just happened and I'm sorry. Do I regret it? Yeah. Am I going to take care of the kid because it's my responsibility? Of course. Do I feel awful for hurting you? *Absolutely*. But I can't change it."

I took a sip of tea, allowing his words to brew inside my head for a moment. Why did this conversation not hurt more?

Ryan sighed. "Kam, this isn't a long sob story slash apology to guilt you into taking me back. I mean, absolutely it's an apology because I feel like shit about it still and probably will for the rest of my life, but either way, I don't think you and I getting back together would be the best thing either."

Typically, when your ex tells you they don't want to get back together with you, it should sting. But it didn't. Once again, I felt nothing.

I envisioned Decker sitting in front of me, and had those same words come out of his mouth that just came out of Ryan's...

Just the idea of it fucking stung me. Not even stung— *electrocuted.*

I gave Ryan a nod, agreeing with him, but I still wanted his reasoning. "Why?" I asked softly.

His head tipped in the slightest. "You've been my best friend since freshman year of high school," he said with a smile. "I'll always love you and I'll always, *always* care about you. But no matter how fucked up I was that night, it's the fact that I was still able to betray you two months before our wedding..." he shook his head, shamefully scolding himself. "People who are meant to be together don't do that to each other." I glanced down at my lap, nodding. His tone became much lighter, teasing almost. "Not to mention the way your face lit up at the mention of this Decker guy."

A laugh popped out of my mouth even though the situation wasn't humorous at all. "Yeah, well there's no going back with that."

"What do you mean?"

I swished my mug around, watching as the liquid circled around in the cup. I wasn't sure if I had it in me to explain everything again. It was already difficult enough explaining it to Arianna.

I remained quiet, prompting Ryan to softly push further. "Kam, what happened?"

I shook my head, my bottom lip trembling.

"C'mon, don't make me pry it out of you," he taunted.

Pry.

Suddenly, I was laughing.

Ryan's laughter accompanied mine. "What? You looked like you were just about to bawl and now you're laughing? Kam, you've gotta give me something here cause I'm genuinely confused."

"Okay, okay," I said, placing my tea on the side table. "I'll start from the beginning."

I told him everything, from the moment I saw Decker for the first time to the last moment I saw him at all. And when I was done, there was a solid minute of silence hovering over us.

Ryan stared at me, his mouth agape. "H—hold on," he said, leaning forward and resting his elbows on his knees. "You're telling me that he was the one that—"

"Yes," I cut him off, refusing to hear the words again.

"And you're both sure?" he lifted a brow.

"Yes."

"I don't understand how this is even possible. What are the chances of the two of you meeting, let alone falling for each other?"

"Apparently the chances are higher than one would think."

I'd expected this conversation to be more difficult. By no means was it an easy one, but somehow, I got through it without crying. I could feel the waterworks about to hit though.

"Holy shit," Ryan muttered.

"Yeah," I croaked.

The tightness of his eyes softened. "Hey," he whispered, standing. He made his way over to me and sat, his arms snaking around me. I buried my head into his chest the same way I had on the night my parents died, unleashing a river of tears that would without a doubt leave his grey t-shirt soaked. "I'm so sorry," he said, repeating it over and over.

After a few minutes, my tears slowed, and Ryan's gentle voice rang in my ears again. "So, what are you gonna do now?"

"What do you mean?"

"Are you gonna forgive him?"

I pulled away just enough to see the actual wonder on his face. My face scrunched together as I stared at him. "You're being serious?"

"I mean..." he shrugged. "Yeah?"

"How could I forgive someone for that?"

"Kam—"

"I don't understand how you'd think I could possibly even—"

"You love him," he said surely.

"So?" I questioned sharply. "I love my parents too."

His voice remained calm, steady, arms still comfortably around me. "I'm not saying you don't. But I know you, and I knew your parents."

I stared at him, hoping my gaze was slicing into him. My mouth lightly hung open in utter shock.

"And?" I finally disputed.

He sighed. "We dated for over five years. Not once did you *ever* look at me the way you looked at *midair* when you were talking about Decker. You are absolutely in love with this guy and if he makes you that happy, then I'm rooting for it." He gave a shrug. "And about your parents? Your mom had the kindest heart in the world. Your dad too, but your mom especially. She was the most compassionate person I'd ever met and ever will meet. With that being said, what would she want you to do?"

Without a doubt, my mother would choose forgiveness. She was all about being gracious and good-hearted. She looked past every horrible thing that my crazy aunt ever did or said to her, and even forgave my aunt for stealing nearly five *grand* from her. My mother shook it off as if it never happened.

On the other hand, this wasn't just five grand. This wasn't just money at all. It was her *life*. And my father's life.

I looked up at Ryan, and once again, there wasn't a single romantic feeling that came about in any way. Looking at him now or even thinking about us back then, I didn't feel the way towards him that I felt towards Decker.

I wasn't sure what I was expecting to feel when I showed up on his doorstep, but I sure as hell wasn't expecting to feel nothing. There wasn't even a flush of anger. It was just *nothing*. As if he'd been my best friend for five years and nothing more. As if I never planned on marrying him. As if he hadn't cheated on me two months before our wedding.

Perhaps I'd already forgiven him before I even walked through the door.

Whatever the reason was, Ryan was right. He and I weren't meant for each other in a romantic way, and that scared the hell out of me, because it was just more reason to believe the one person who truly *was* meant for me, was the same one who watched my mother take her last breath.

I inhaled deeply, mentally spent. "I'm gonna head out."

"Okay," he reluctantly said. He walked me to the door, holding it open for me as I picked up my mother's jewelry box. "Hey," Ryan said, causing me to turn. "It was really nice seeing you. You're welcome here anytime. Please don't fall off the face of the earth again."

I gave him a friendly grin. "I won't."

"And Kam?"

"Yeah?"

"Whatever you decide to do, just know I'm rooting for you."

***

I sat on the couch, staring at the jewelry box in my lap.

Arianna wasn't home, which meant that besides the sound of my own loud, pulsing thoughts, it was quiet.

I hadn't opened this box in years. When I was shy of my seventeenth birthday, my aunt asked where some of my mother's jewelry was, which could only mean one of two things. Either she wanted the jewelry for herself, or she wanted to sell it. Neither of which were okay with me.

So, I pretended like I had no idea what jewelry she was referring to, and the next day, when she wasn't home, I brought the box over to Ryan's and hid it there for the next year and a half until we moved in together.

I traced my fingers across the intricate designs on the box, avoiding undoing the latch because I was too nervous for too many reasons.

For starters, I was worried that things would be missing. I didn't believe— or at least, I didn't *want* to believe— that Ryan would be capable of doing anything malicious to any of my parents' belongings. But I was also scared of what my reaction would be if everything *was* there.

My fingers tapped along the side of the box, stalling some more.

Just open it. It's not going to open its damn self.

My mouth went dry as I rolled my shoulders back, bringing my hand to the latch. It gave a superficial clink as I popped it open.

One by one, I began pulling everything out. The first thing I grabbed was an old charm bracelet of my mother's. I held it up between two fingers, giving it a light rattle before slipping it on my wrist.

There were dried flowers— daisies, of course— that my mother had kept for the remainder of her life. I wasn't sure when they were from, considering the number of daisies my father bought for her over their marriage, but I carefully plucked them out and laid them on the couch beside me.

There was a small stack of letters that my parents had written to each other back in college, long before I was born. I wasn't currently brave enough to read them, so I simply ran my fingertips across the ink and set them beside me as well.

There was a crucifix, no bigger than my hand, and a sterling silver necklace that had a cross pendant. In the center of the pendant was a tiny blue dot. My thumb skimmed along the top of it.

"Blue topaz," I whispered to myself. *My birthstone.*

I shut my eyes, focusing vigorously on keeping my tears at bay. I wanted to put the necklace on, but it felt like it was almost too important to be worn. It was one of those things where you were afraid that wearing it would somehow cause you to lose it or break it. So, I carefully laid it beside me.

There wasn't much left in the box, and the next thing that jumped out to me was the sparkle of a diamond ring and its counterpart beside it.

My hand shook as I reached in, and I pulled back, worried that touching the rings would somehow taint them. The purity and certainty of my parents' love for each other was within those two rings, and I wanted to protect that at all costs.

But I found myself reaching for them again. I plucked out my father's gold wedding band and delicately set it in the

298

palm of my free hand, then did the same with my mother's diamond ring.

I held them there, not doing anything besides staring at them. The longer I stared, the more it hurt.

Because the heartbreak was setting in again.

Reality was sinking deeper and deeper. I would never have this with Decker the way I wanted to. We would never have the exquisite wedding we talked about. I would never have a ring chosen by his hand. I guess not all soulmates got a happily ever after.

My eyes closed and my mouth clamped shut, trying to suppress the sob that wanted to escape. My throat felt like it was closing as my body shook helplessly.

I was hurting everywhere. In my head, in my heart, in my soul.

I inhaled purposefully, focusing on calming down. I shook my head as I placed the rings beside me, turning back to the box to retrieve the very last thing there.

Photos.

My hands were still shaking when I grabbed them. I brought them up to my face to take in every detail as I flipped through them.

A photo of my father holding me for the first time in the hospital after I was born.

A photo of my mother sitting on the doorstep with me on her lap as a child.

A photo of all of us together.

A photo of my parents, Ryan, and me before Ryan and I headed off to prom.

There were dozens and dozens of photos, and as I looked through them, each one seemed to bring more and more grief.

I was missing my parents extra right now, enveloped in tears and remorse and physical pain. I wished they were here, and what sucked the most was that I loved the same man who took them away.

I could never unlove him. But I could not forgive him.

Chapter Fifty-Seven
Decker

"Decks," Nolan sighed through the phone.

"I told you, I'd think about it," I said, seated on the corner of my bed as I slid my socks on, getting dressed to grab lunch with Emmy.

"I know today is hard for you," he said sincerely, "but it will never get better if you never try."

"I told you I'd consider going if Benny wasn't gonna be there."

Nolan's voice grew agitated. "You *know* there's no way he's not gonna be there."

"Well then it's settled," I shrugged. "I'm not going."

"You can't avoid him forever."

I scoffed. "Watch me." I tapped the speakerphone button and tossed the phone on my bed. Turning towards the closet, I began skimming through my shirts. When my fingers trailed along an ocean blue t-shirt, I hesitated, nearly skating past it. But instead, I tugged it off the hanger and lifted it over my head. If I was never going to see Kam again, then wearing the color of her eyes was the closest I was going to get.

"You know, I'm honestly really surprised he hasn't tried showing up at your place."

"So am I."

"I think he's scared."

"He should be," I growled.

Nolan sighed again, and I knew him well enough to know that he was probably shaking his head right now, holding the phone up to his ear with one hand and stressfully rubbing his face with the other.

"Does he know you invited me?" I asked.

"I don't give a shit if he knows or not."

"I want him to know," I said.

"Why?" he asked, disdainful.

"Because if he really is scared of me and knows I might go, then maybe he *won't* go."

"Well Myra is for sure going, so I don't think there's any way Benny won't."

I rolled my eyes as I slipped my shoes on. "She already turned him down. Does he really think she'll change her mind?"

"Apparently."

I snorted. "She's too good for him anyway."

"She's too good for most people," he agreed. "Except..."

"Don't even think about it," I shook my head, grabbing my phone and wallet before heading out of my bedroom. Emmy was going to be here any second to pick me up.

"Alright, alright," Nolan said. "I get it. You're still not over you-know-who."

"No, I'm not," I admitted firmly. "And I never will be." There were a few silent beats that followed before I spoke again, my tone much softer than it was a minute prior. "I gotta run. I'll let you know about later."

"Okay," he agreed. "I really hope to see your ass there."

***

I sat across from Emmy in the café as we waited for our food.

"Be honest," she said over the rim of her coffee cup.

"Mhmm?"

"Are you doing alright?"

I gave a meaningless shrug.

"You guys still haven't spoken?" she asked, setting her cup down.

"No," I said sharply. "I ruined her life. Why would she talk to me?"

Emmy tipped her head towards her shoulder, her voice soft. "She loves you."

"She hates me," I corrected her. "She even said so herself."

Emmy shrugged, wrapping her hands around her mug. "Well, I don't think she meant it."

I shut my eyes, giving a lengthy exhale. "Can we please talk about something else? *Anything* else?"

"Fine," Emmy huffed. "Do you have plans tonight?"

"Nope."

She narrowed her eyes incredulously. "Decker."

"What?"

"I know you're lying. Your eyebrow just twitched."

I gave her a blank stare. "What does my eyebrow have to do with anything?"

"Your eyebrow always twitches like that when you lie, and don't try to deny it because it'll just twitch again. So, why are you lying?"

I leaned forward with a bothered frown. "My friends are going to Westside, but I already decided not to go."

"Why not?"

"Because today is already hard enough for me, and if I get a single glimpse of Benny's face, I'll lose my damn mind."

"Yikes," she muttered. "Still haven't spoken to him either, I'm assuming?"

"Nope and I never plan to ever again."

A laugh flew out of her mouth. "Good luck with that! He's the pushiest person on the planet. There's no way he'll leave you alone forever." She took another sip of coffee. "I think you should go tonight, though."

I scoffed, staring out the window of the café. "No."

"Why?"

"I already told you why."

She sighed. "You can't hide on this day every year for the rest of your life."

"And why can't I?"

Her voice stiffened. "Because it's not good for you!"

At this point, I cared more about what would keep me sane rather than what was necessarily good for me.

"If you don't go out," she threatened, "then neither am I."

I tipped my head at her, trying to decipher if she was bluffing. "Don't do that."

"I'm serious," she warned. "Do you think I like this day? Do you think today is all glitter and excitement for me like it is for everyone else? Well, it's *not*. But I'm going out because I can't allow myself for the rest of my life to view this day as the day my brother's life got messed up."

I swallowed, my eyes funereal as I looked at her. I mindlessly brought my fingers to my mouth and ran them across my lips in thought. "Alright," I said hoarsely, "I'll go."

Chapter Fifty-Eight
Kamryn

Today was my least favorite day. If I could erase today's date from every calendar, I would.

From the moment I woke up today, I instantly wished the day was over already. Couldn't we just skip December thirty-first? New Year's Eve as a holiday was overrated anyway. And while we're at it, could we erase January first, too?

My birthday was earlier in the month, which meant that I was officially twenty-one. I wouldn't have to sneak into the bars anymore. Go me.

Too bad I hadn't been to a single bar since I turned twenty-one. Arianna begged to take me out for my birthday, but I refused. Instead, I requested a nice girl's night with plenty of wine. She reluctantly obliged, but since it was *my* birthday, she didn't really have a choice.

And now here we were, seated on the couch, while Arianna, once again, was begging me to go out with her.

"Just hear me out," she said softly, scooting closer to me. "I know how much you hate today, and by no means do I blame you... But I know you," she urged, giving my hand a gentle squeeze. "I know you well enough to know that if you don't get your mind off everything, you're going to self-destruct. We don't have to be out late," she assured me. "We could even come home before midnight if you want."

I toyed with my mother's charm bracelet that rested on my wrist. "*If* we went out, and emphasis on the *if*," I stressed, "where would you want to go?"

Ari's eyes lit up in the slightest with hope. "Well, I really, really, *really* don't want to go to Red Lion because I'm there constantly," she said, referring to the bar she bartended at almost every night during the week. "So, how about Westside?"

I couldn't help but cringe. "Uh, yeah, I don't know about that."

She jutted her bottom lip out, pouting. "Why not?"

"Because that's where Decker and all his friends go."

All of our *friends,* I wanted to correct myself, but wasn't sure that was still the case.

After Friendsgiving, or to better describe it— the second-worst-night-of-my-life— Myra and Alaina both texted me, checking in on me every few days. Nolan even sent me a message at one point, telling me how sorry we was, and that he wished the best for me. But ever since then, the only one I'd been keeping close contact with was Alaina.

"I mean, Red Lion doesn't sound absolutely awful, right?" I hesitated, my voice skyrocketing with doubt.

Ari tilted her head, giving me a snide look. "Please don't drag me to work on my day off." She studied me for a moment, taking in the pleading gleam in my eye and ultimately sighing. "We could go somewhere else if you really wanna, but Westside is like the only other bar around here that's never filled with creepy old men."

I stared off at the corner of the room, chewing anxiously on my bottom lip again. I'd been doing that so much lately. If I kept it up, I was going to need stitches on my damn lip.

"Can I think about it for a bit?" I requested.

She nodded softly. "Sure. It's only three, so you've got plenty of time."

"Thanks."

She reached out, amiably squeezing my hand with a benevolent smile before standing and walking out of the room.

I fidgeted, running my hands through my waved hair. Gosh, I couldn't decide what to do.

I knew the best option for me mentally would be to go out. I wasn't going to force Ari to stay in with me, and if I stayed here alone, I truly would self-destruct like she'd said.

Shortly after midnight would make it five years since my parents' passing. Even though I remembered it like it happened yesterday, five years really was a while.

There was no way in hell that my parents would want me to spend every New Year's Eve for the rest of my life alone and crying the night away. I'd already spent the past four in bed with numerous boxes of tissues, bawling my eyes out while Ryan rubbed my back until I passed out, which was usually well before midnight.

I snatched my phone off the table and typed out a message to Alaina.

Me: Hey, are you going to Westside tonight?

Alaina: Yes!

Me: Is Decker going?

Alaina: Nolan invited him but he was iffy about going because he doesn't wanna see Benny. So I really dunno at this point

I stared at her message, contemplating what to do. This time, instead of biting my bottom lip, I found myself subconsciously nibbling at the inside of my cheek while rattling the charm bracelet on my wrist.

Even though I was already holding my phone and staring directly at it, for some reason, I jumped when it buzzed again.

Alaina: Are you going?

Me: Not sure

Alaina: Pls come!! I miss you ☹

In lieu of responding to her text, I tossed my phone aside and stalked over to Arianna's bedroom. Her eyes peeked up at me from over her phone as I appeared in the doorway.

"What are you wearing?" I asked.

"Huh?"

"We're going out tonight."

Chapter Fifty-Nine
Decker

I couldn't believe I was actually taking advice from my eighteen-year-old little sister.

The weather was decent, around forty degrees, a stark difference to how cold it was on this exact night five years ago. I was wearing a long-sleeved black shirt and blue jeans, accompanied with a hard expression as I sighed, muttering an expletive under my breath as I waited in line at Westside since it was so busy.

I sure as hell was not in the mood to see Pry's stupid ass face, or Benny's for that matter. My patience was thin tonight, and if either of them did some shit to tick me off, the chances of me controlling my anger were slim.

The line died down, and content washed over me when a random bouncer was at the front instead of Pry.

Hearing his snarky comments would be the worst way to start off my night. I could just envision it.

Where's your girlfriend, Shepley? Why isn't she with you? Is she single now? Can you give me her number?

My jaw tensed just from the thought.

I wasn't sure where Nolan and Alaina were, but after one step inside, they were no longer the first thing on my mind. I didn't get a whiff of any alcohol, but I got nauseous almost immediately, unsure of why at first.

My hands began shaking, heart beating a little faster. I closed my eyes for a moment and recognized the familiarity of a specific soul.

She was close by.

I knew how much it would hurt to even get a single look at her, but that didn't stop me. With no hesitation, I began rummaging through the bar, praying for my brown eyes to catch a glimpse of her blue ones.

I didn't know what I'd do if I saw her. All I knew was that I wanted to see her.

Kam, where are you?

The bar was so crowded that I was surprised they hadn't reached capacity yet, unless they had and just didn't care. People gave me dirty looks as I pushed past them, but I didn't give them a second glance.

Who did Kam come with? Did Alaina know she'd be here? Was Alaina the one who invited her?

I was starting to second-guess myself. Would Kam really go out tonight even though tonight was her least favorite night on the calendar? I doubted it.

It's your least favorite night too and you came out, I reminded myself.

I kept searching, my eyes desperately scanning over every face, when suddenly, a familiar one came into view.

I raced over to her, not caring that I was interrupting her conversation with some guy. "Arianna," I called, desperation in my tone.

All her attention turned onto me as if the other guy was never there. After a moment, he stalked off.

Arianna's mouth parted, pale white washing over her face. There was a crossover between panic and guilt as she blinked at me. "D—Decker," was all she said.

I sounded out of breath, as if I'd just competed in the damn Olympics. "Where's Kam?"

She held her breath, nervously wringing her hands. "She's not here."

I stared at the ground for a moment, blowing out a breath. I spoke softly, pleadingly. "Arianna, please. I respect that you're trying to protect her, but... I *know* she's here. I can feel her."

I could see the reflection of myself in her eyes as she studied me, the way I resembled a man getting burned at the stake. She took in my tortured expression, silently fighting with herself as she opened her mouth, shut it, and then gulped.

"God, Decker, I..." she trailed off, the war within her seemingly getting worse. She winced.

"Please," I croaked, on the verge of tears.

She tipped her head at me, eyes battered and unsure. What if she wouldn't help me? What if she ran off to Kam right after this, told her I was here, and they left before I got the chance to even catch a flash of her?

Just as I was about to get on my knees and beg, she let out a lengthy exhale, looking down at her feet. "She's sitting at the bar, talking to some guy."

I went from panicked to jealous, even though I didn't have the right. "What guy?"

Arianna shrugged, just as confused as me. "I don't know. It seemed like she knew him though, so I stepped away for a minute."

Someone she knew? Maybe Nolan ran into her, and they were catching up. Or perhaps Benny saw her and was trying to apologize?

I wouldn't be at ease until I knew for sure.

I headed towards the bar, Arianna on my heels. The moment I had a straight line of sight to the bar, I stopped in my tracks, picking out the back of her head immediately.

I didn't know if Arianna was still behind me at this point, but I didn't bother checking. I was completely unaware of everything in the room besides *her*.

I soaked her up with my eyes. Her bright and healthy platinum hair was in a loose braid, lying perfectly in the center of her back. The sight was both a gift from Heaven and a punishment from Hell.

The stitches of the unhealed wound in my heart burst at the seams. I was bleeding out, my body growing weaker and weaker as I stood there.

Did she feel my presence the same way I felt hers?

Did she know I was here, that I was this close?

A few more steps and I'd be able to touch her, and maybe in another lifetime, I could've. But not in this one. This lifetime was tainted.

When she began uncomfortably leaning to her right, my eyes shifted over to who was seated next to her. In the matter of five minutes, I'd managed to go from panicked to jealous to *fucking furious*.

My nostrils flared, fists clenched as I gave a murderous glare at the back of his head.

Fucking Pry.

Chapter Sixty
Kamryn

Arianna was right about Westside not being filled with creepy old men, but in my opinion, Tommy Pry was just as bad.

"I'm good," I insisted, leaning away as Pry drifted closer and closer to me.

"Let me just buy you a drink. Really, I insist," he pushed for the tenth time.

I grinded my teeth together. Where the hell was Arianna? I wanted to hop off this damn stool and go find her, but I was scared that she'd be coming back here to find me, and that if I didn't stay put, we'd both be on a wild goose chase to find each other all night.

I slipped my phone out of my purse to shoot her a text, surprised to find that she'd texted first.

Ari: SOS. We need to leave. Now.

I stared at it, wondering and worrying what her SOS was about. I took a troubled breath as I realized how clammy my hands were. My throat felt dry, heart fluttering before quickening its pace completely. Which could only mean one thing.

He was nearby.

Me: Where are you?

She needed to hurry up and either find me or answer before my heart exploded. I could not handle seeing his face tonight.

"Kamryn?" Pry raised a brow, and I suddenly realized he'd been trying to talk to me this entire time.

"Sorry, I have to go," I said, hastily throwing my phone back in my purse. I dug around, frantically trying to find my wallet and wave down the bartender at the same time to pay.

"You're leaving?" he questioned. "It's not even midnight yet. You should stay."

"No," I snapped, unsuccessful in getting the bartender's attention and just throwing a twenty-dollar bill on the bar top.

Each second that passed made my anxiety grow. Arianna needed to answer, or else I was going to run out of this bar without her. I couldn't handle being in the same vicinity as Decker. Just being able to feel that he was close was sending my body into shock.

"Why not? I'll buy your next drink. Do you wanna take shots?" Pry pressed more.

"No!" I shouted.

"Oh c'mon, let's—"

"She said no, Pry," a voice growled from behind us.

I froze, my blood running cold as I quite literally held my breath. I didn't want to turn around. Seeing his face every night while I slept was painful enough. And tonight especially, I was extra vulnerable.

If I turned around right now, there was a strong possibility that I'd stomp over to him with a tight jaw and punch him right in the face. But the possibility that I'd run into his arms was just as strong, and I wasn't sure if I was willing to take that chance.

I gasped for air, my lungs strained as if someone were sitting on my chest.

Fuck this.

I turned, keeping my head down as I practically sprinted out of the bar. It took longer than I'd like considering how many people were in my way, but the second I was outside, I finally felt better.

Until I didn't.

"Kam!" Decker called after me.

"Go away," my voice shook.

"I just wanna make sure you're alright," he insisted, trailing behind my brisk steps.

"I'm fine," I lied, keeping my eyes ahead of me. I had no idea where I was walking, but I refused to stop. "By the way, I didn't need you to save me. I was perfectly capable of handling it myself."

"I know."

It went quiet between us other than the sound of our footsteps, and after a few unbearable moments of silence, I groaned— no, practically *growled.* "Why are you following me?"

But regardless of my harsh tone, Decker's stayed soft. "I don't want you walking alone at night."

"Don't worry about me," I muttered.

"I've been worrying about you since the second you left."

"Well, stop it."

"I can't."

"Why?" I spat.

"Because I love you."

Those words were so beautiful coming from his lips, yet so devastating. I halted, somehow finding the courage to turn and look at him. My heart rate tripled, blood pounding loudly in my ears. This kind of pain was unendurable.

"Please don't make tonight harder for the both of us," I said.

I was trying to be strong, trying to keep myself together, knowing damn well that if I let a single tear fall, that it'd be like opening a door that led straight to Niagara Falls.

But my armor was chipping away at the misery on his face. Those eyes of his that I loved so much were run-down, and I could tell that even though he hadn't expected for me to say the words back, that it still hurt that I hadn't.

314

Decker shook his head slowly, his eyes glued on me. "I'm not trying to," his voice cracked like the words were being ripped out of his throat.

Walk away, Kamryn. Walk away. Walk away. Walk away.

I knew I needed to, but I could feel my heart tugging towards Decker, trying to keep me near him.

I forced myself to release a sigh. "Just go back to Westside, okay? I'm going back to Ari— fuck!"

"What's wrong?" he stepped closer.

"Arianna's still there." I tugged my phone out once again.

Ari: I looked for you by the bar but couldn't find you. Did you leave?

Me: Yes, I'm so sorry. I'm coming back for you.

Her response was almost immediate, as if she'd been waiting for me to answer.

Ari: It's ok, you don't have to. Luna and Jess just showed up. You can head home if you want. I know tonight has already been a lot for you

Relief washed over me, but there was something about reading the word "home" that made me unsettled. I loved Arianna and appreciated her so much for taking me in, but although her apartment was where I'd been staying, it was not *home*.

"Are you gonna go back?" Decker asked.

"No," I said, turning on my heels and continuing to walk.

Sure enough, Decker was right behind me. His presence was both comforting me, yet frustrating me, but above all, it was *breaking* me.

Seeing his face, hearing his voice... It was all just a reminder of how much I loved him. How much I wanted him. How much I wished things were different. He needed to go away or else my strength to resist him was going to cave like a house of cards.

I kept walking as quickly as my legs would carry me. I took a glance at the street signs, noting that I was only a couple more blocks away from Arianna's.

"Kam, stop," Decker called desperately. I ignored the sharp clench in my chest as I continued to walk. "I know you hate me, and I know you'll never be able to forgive me, and I don't blame you, but—"

"We've both said everything we needed to say," I said, trying to keep my tone stern, but anyone with working eardrums could hear the pain laced into my voice. "There's nothing more for us to discuss. It's all said and done."

"If this is possibly the last time I'll ever see you, then please just listen," he begged, trying to keep up with my pace.

I winced at the words, choking back a sob. The thought of this encounter being the last time I ever saw Decker was soul-crushing.

"Decker, please," I forced myself to speak. "It's almost midnight. All I wanna do is lay down and cry."

"Will you at least let me walk you home?" he hoped.

There was that word again. *Home.*

"I don't need you to."

I needed to cross the street so that I could take the next left turn. Typically, I'd wait until I was at the crosswalk, but I was so flustered that I didn't bother. I looked both ways, being sure that no cars were in sight before striding across the street.

"Do you really hate me that much that I can't even make sure you get home safely?" he sobbed, causing me to stop mid-step in the street.

I turned. "I don't hate you," I let out, tears finally spilling over. It was pitch black out, the only source of light being the various streetlamps lined along the road. But even with the shitty lighting, I could still pick apart every detail of his appearance.

I saw the agony in his eyes. The few tears that had escaped down his perfect skin. The uneven rise and fall of his ragged breaths. The light quiver of his lips.

I wrestled my gaze away from him, forcing myself to walk the rest of the way to the sidewalk. When I realized the

316

only sound of footsteps that I could hear were that of my own, I turned back around, sucking in a sharp breath to see Decker still standing in the middle of the street, not having moved an inch.

"Get out of the road," I said.

"No," he responded.

I clenched my jaw, tears still falling. "Get out of the road," I repeated, firmer.

Decker stood there, frozen. His tears matched mine, and his eyes fell to his feet. "My feet won't move."

I wasn't sure if it was anger or sadness or panic that caused me to start yelling. "Get out of the road before you get hit by a fucking car!"

"I deserve to get hit by a fucking car!" he shouted back. "You should want me to get hit by a fucking car!"

"Decker," I warned. After a moment, my voice turned softer. "Please," I cried.

It was as if that had breathed life back into him. His steps were slow, but I was glad he was at least moving.

Unfortunately, he wasn't moving fast enough.

Maybe if the asshole had his headlights on, we would've seen it coming. Or maybe if I'd handled things differently, Decker wouldn't have been standing there.

Either way, it was too late.

My blood-curdling screams echoed into the night as a car came out of nowhere, slamming into Decker.

Chapter Sixty-One
Kamryn

When I was four, I was convinced there was a monster under my bed. I refused to look under my bed or sleep without a night light. I was too scared.

When I was seven, I lost my mother in the grocery store. I cried and cried until an employee found me and brought me back to my mother. I'd been so scared that I was never going to see her again.

When I was sixteen and saw the police in Arianna's foyer, I immediately knew something was wrong. And I was *beyond* scared to hear what that something was.

But I'd never been more *terrified* than I was now.

"Where are you taking him?" I demanded through tears, running alongside the doctors and nurses as they pushed Decker's stretcher frantically down the hallway.

"Emergency surgery," someone said.

"Why?"

None of them seemed to be paying attention to me, and it was their panic that was causing me to panic even more. They were shouting things to each other and motioning for everyone to get out of the way.

I kept up with their pace, holding on to Decker's right hand, since his left arm and leg had both been deemed broken. He was floating in and out of consciousness, his breaths seemingly slow and dragged out. One of the nurses was holding something that looked like an oxygen mask over his mouth.

"Why!" I repeated loudly as they opened the doors to take him to a different wing of the hospital. The second they practically ripped his hand out of mine, I let out a grisly sob.

One of the female nurses stayed back after they went through, her hand held up to signal me to stay behind.

"No," I cried, trying to peer around her to see where they were taking him. "Please let me go with him."

"Miss, I'm sorry, but you have to stay here," she said gently.

"Please!" I screeched.

"We'll come out to update you as the surgery goes on," she assured.

I stepped closer to her, distraught with blurred vision from being unable to stop my flow of tears. I wasn't sure if she could even understand me from how jumbled my words were. "Why are they doing surgery on him?"

I assumed she was only remaining so calm to try to calm me down, but it was absolutely impossible to take me out of the hysterical state I was in. "As you already know," she said, "in addition to X-rays of his arm and leg, we took a chest CT because he was showing symptoms of a chest injury. The results were enough to conclude he has cardiac tamponade."

I shook my head, not understanding. "What is that?"

"It's a condition where the pericardial sac that surrounds and protects your heart begins filling with fluid, which causes your heart to not have enough room to pump."

My voice cracked, "Fluid?"

She broke eye contact with me, filled with remorse as she explained further. "In this case, blood."

"He's bleeding around his heart?" I screamed, eyes wide. "What are they gonna do?"

She motioned slowly up and down with her hands to try once again to calm me. Did she not realize that the love of my life was potentially dying? Calm was not in my artillery of emotions right now.

"They're going to perform surgery to remove the excess fluid," she said.

I covered my mouth with both hands, shoulders slumping as I bawled. My eyes squeezed shut as I stood there, trembling in the hallway.

The nurse placed a hand on my shoulder. "Do you need anything?" she asked softly.

"I need to be with him," I struggled to get out.

A pained expression overcame her face. "Honey, I'm so sorry but I can't let you back there." She brought a hand onto my lower back, leading me to a chair against the wall. "Why don't you take a seat and I'll go get you some water, okay?"

I gave a weak nod as I sat, gasping for air between each sob. I brought my knees up to my chest, burying my head into them.

I could not even describe the hysteria that stretched across every cell in my body when I saw Decker lying on the ground after getting hit. Every time I closed my eyes, I saw it.

I'd raced over to him immediately, screaming and crying as I hovered above him, trying to keep him awake as I called an ambulance.

He was bleeding, wincing, in so much pain that I winced alongside him.

I would never be able to forget that image.

And now? The anxiety was still at an all-time high. My mind went to the worst possibilities.

I wasn't a damn doctor, but I didn't need to be to know that bleeding around your heart wasn't fucking good. I didn't know anything about the surgery they were performing on him, didn't know survival rates or mortality rates, but I was too scared to look them up.

If he didn't make it through this surgery... I cowered at the thought.

I sat there, shaking my head at myself. I wasn't a fan of my own thoughts, but they wouldn't stop coming.

I'd been so cruel to him. On the night I left, and tonight too, I'd treated him like an unwanted pest. I had hurt him so bad, not because I wanted to, but because I felt like that's what I was supposed to do.

Even after finding out the truth about Decker's past, there was never a moment where I didn't want to be with him. It was the guilt that I felt about loving him and wanting to be with him that made me stay away, but the anguish of being faced with the possibility of losing him was swallowing that guilt whole.

I thought about what it would be like waking up each morning knowing that Decker wouldn't. I thought about what it used to be like to lay my head on his chest and listen to his heartbeat, then imagined if that same heart was no longer beating. I thought about what it would be like to live in a world knowing he no longer existed.

A chilling wail got caught in my throat.

If I dwelled on these thoughts for a fraction of a second longer, I would surely start bleeding around my heart too.

When I heard a group of feet trampling down the hallway, my head whipped over to find Scott, Shannon, and Emmy Shepley hurtling towards me. I stood, stepping towards them as Shannon threw her arms around me.

"Oh goodness," she whispered through a cry. She pulled away, holding me by the shoulders. "Are you alright?"

I trembled under her touch, shaking my head. "No," I murmured. She hugged me again, this one quicker before letting go and looking around.

Decker had always talked about how optimistic his mother was, even in the worst situations. The first time he'd ever witnessed her break down was in the courtroom during his own sentencing. But if that was her first ever breakdown, I was fairly certain right now was her second.

It was easy to make out the speedy rise and fall of her chest as she spun around in a circle and glanced in the nearby hospital rooms, and although she wasn't crying hysterically like me, the wet droplets on her cheeks were reflecting under the bright lights in the hallway.

"Where is he?" she asked to know one in particular. The second a nurse was in sight, she ran over, seemingly firing a hundred questions at him.

Scott turned to me, worry settled in the deep crease of his forehead. "The people at the front desk said he's in surgery?"

I gave a powerless nod. While Decker was getting his X-rays, I'd called his parents to let them know what was going

on, but that was before they rushed him into surgery, and now, I
didn't have the ability to explain the rest to them.

Even though Scott wasn't actively crying, he didn't
seem far from it. He took in my miserable expression, and when
he headed over to meet his wife, sparing me from an
explanation, I'd be lying if I said I wasn't grateful.

Now it was just Emmy and me, mirrored tears in our
eyes. She was wearing a short, emerald green silk dress, her
hair straightened. Clearly, she'd been out celebrating the New
Year before she received the call about Decker.

Instead of continuing to celebrate, she was standing
here in front of me, barefoot with her heels in her hands and
mascara running down her face.

The moment I stepped towards her, she did the same,
and we collided in a heap of tears and fear. Neither of us spoke,
but we didn't need to. There was an unsaid echo of emotion
between us as we held each other.

Although it was comforting to not be alone anymore, I
would not be at ease until Decker was alright.

***

Fifteen minutes passed since Decker's surgery began.
The four of us sat in the hallway, the only sound being the eerie
beeping of monitors and the quiet conversations of nurses
around us, tending to their patients.

I'd done nothing other than sit there, my eyes
wandering aimlessly around the hallway as my morbid thoughts
showed no mercy. My body felt heavy, tired and overwhelmed
from both exhaustion and anxiety. It was already shy of two in
the morning, and I wasn't sure if Decker's family was planning
on staying here all night, but I sure as hell was. Even if I were
to go back to Arianna's, there would be no chance of me falling
asleep.

When the double doors opened and the same nurse that
had helped me earlier appeared, all four of us shot up.

She gave us a promising grin. "They just started. So
far, so good."

"How long will it take?" Shannon asked.

The nurse brought her mouth over to one side. "It'll most likely be a while. At least an hour." She found my eyes, then gave my hand a firm squeeze. "Hang tight, okay?"

Scott, Shannon, and Emmy seemed to relax a little at her words, but I didn't. Was it good to know that the surgery was going well so far? Definitely. But I still wouldn't feel okay until Decker was safe and beside me.

It finally occurred to me that I hadn't touched my phone since I used it to call 9-1-1. As if in slow motion, I dug it out of my purse, my eyes growing at the number of missed calls and texts I had.

Two missed calls from Ryan. Twelve missed calls from Arianna. Four missed calls from Alaina.

Ryan: Hey, I meant to call you earlier in the day but got sidetracked. Just wanted to check in on you today. Are you doing okay?

Arianna: Did you make it home safely?
I just got home. Where are you??
Are you alive??
Um hello??????
Kam, you're freaking me out! Pls answer

Alaina: Hey, have u seen Decker? He was supposed to meet us at Westside and never showed

I winced at the last one, squeezing my eyes shut. I sent Ryan a text back that I'd call him when I had the chance, then called both Alaina and Arianna. I wasn't surprised when both of them insisted on coming here, and within twenty more minutes, the hallway wasn't just occupied with the Shepley's and myself, but now Arianna, Alaina, Nolan, Benny, and Myra were here as well.

I didn't speak to any of them. I just sat quietly, ignoring everyone. Not that there was much to ignore anyway. Everyone else was fairly quiet, other than the occasional question or comment.

Once again, the double doors opened, but this time, the returning nurse didn't offer a smile. Her face was an alarming shade of white. I held my breath as she approached, but that didn't stop a few sluggish tears from trailing down my cheeks.

She cleared her throat, preparing to give us whatever terrible news was about to come.

"Unfortunately," she began, "they've run into some complications. It—"

"What kind of complications?" I cut her off with a voice so hoarse that it sounded like I'd been chain-smoking for weeks straight.

Her eyes remained on the floor. "Try not to worry. You've got some of the best surgeons in California working on him."

"What kind of complications?" I demanded.

She breathed heavily, stuttering under the pressure. "It seems that his condition is worse than they originally thought."

"How bad?" Shannon murmured, taking a small step forward.

The nurse's mouth pushed further into a frown. She fidgeted, eyes skimming over the nine pairs of eyes on her.

"You can say," Shannon said softly.

The nurse gave a tiny nod, eyes filled with sympathy. "He wasn't rushed into surgery as soon as he should've been, so unfortunately, the fluid has put an extensive amount of pressure on his heart..." she swallowed, "leading to an acute myocardial infarction."

"What is that?" Emmy asked with glossy eyes.

Absolute silence filled the hall for a fraction of a second.

"A heart attack," the nurse said.

I grew faint, gripping onto the handle of the chair. "Is he going to make it?" I demanded.

"The doctors are doing everything they can," she assured.

That was *not* the answer I wanted.

I could see Shannon bury her head into Scott's chest. Emmy faced the floor as she cried. Arianna covered her face with her hands. Alaina slid down the wall with a sob, Nolan following her lead. Benny and Myra were hugging, their bodies shaking together.

But me? I did not sob. I *screamed.* A scream so nightmarish that you'd think I'd been getting butchered in the middle of the hallway.

Through blurry vision, I could make out Arianna's hand reaching towards me, but I swerved it, turning on my heels and running into the nearest bathroom.

Thankfully, it was a single-room private bathroom. I practically slammed the door behind me before falling to the floor.

I knew I wasn't the one driving that car, and I knew I hadn't physically pushed Decker in front of it either, but that didn't take away the guilt I felt.

I was trying to brace myself for his death if it were to come tonight, but I just couldn't. I couldn't accept the possibility that he may not survive.

I wouldn't be able to live with myself knowing he died under the impression that I hated him. I'd told him that I didn't hate him, but I saw on his face that that wasn't enough.

I attempted to clear my mind and began praying to God or my parents or whoever it was that might be listening until there was a light knock on the door. "Kamryn?" Emmy said weakly.

I felt bound to the floor by fear, but I forced myself to stand and open the door.

"Kamryn," Emmy said, her head dropping towards the floor as her voice dropped to a whisper. "First... I needed to tell you that I'm so sorry about your parents. None of us knew." She shook her head. "I hope you know how sorry he is."

I gave a weak nod.

"And if he doesn't make it..." she said, "I want you to know how much he loves you."

I covered my mouth with the back of my hand, stifling another sob as Emmy wrapped her arms around me.

I knew how much he loved me. And I needed him to know that regardless of everything, I loved him.

Chapter Sixty-Two
Decker

I was dying. That much, I was sure of.

Despite being unconscious, I was inexplicably aware of my surroundings.

I was in a strange limbo, similar to the realm you'd be in when you weren't fully awake, but you weren't quite asleep either.

I knew I was lying on an operating table. I could hear the frantic shouting of the doctors and nurses alike, even though I didn't understand half of the terms they were yelling.

I'd never really wondered what it would feel like to die, but I never expected it to feel so peaceful. I wasn't in pain, or maybe the anesthesia was just numbing it all.

It felt like I was floating, as if my body had become a light feather rather than the bleeding, dying mess that it actually was.

It wasn't the typical or cliché near death experience where I saw a white light and was in Heaven just long enough to realize I needed to come back to Earth. But honestly, it may have reached that point had I let it.

I didn't see my entire life flash before my eyes, but I did see the last five months. It was like watching a movie on fast forward, from the moment I saw Kam for the first time to this very moment right now. And all I knew was that I didn't want to let the movie end that way.

I was still unconscious, and even though it seemed impossible, I was miraculously focused.

Do not stop breathing.

Keep your heart beating.

Fight, Decker. Focus.

I would fight. Because I'd be damned if I never saw her again.

Chapter Sixty-Three
Kamryn

Another torturous hour.

I couldn't take it anymore. I was about to burst into that operating room and see what the hell was going on in there.

It was three in the morning. Everyone else was practically falling asleep in the hallway, but I was wide awake despite my fatigue.

When the doors opened again, I could feel my heart beating so fast and prominently that it felt like it was about to jump out of my chest and explode on the floor.

The nurse was not smiling, nor was she frowning. Her skin was not golden, nor was it pale. She seemed almost detached as she took a deep breath.

I was sweating, practically panting. I gripped a handful of my hair, unprepared to hear the words. Tears of grief were already streaming down my face and pooling on my lap.

But the nurse's lips twitched, forming a small grin. "He made it," she said. I wheezed, bending over as I wallowed in relief. "The doctors have him all stitched up and stabilized. They're going to move him into the ICU to monitor him closely."

Arianna knelt in front of me, her hand rubbing my back. I jumped into her arms, and within seconds, her shoulder was wet from my tears. "He's gonna be okay," she assured me.

Ari pulled away as the nurse began speaking again. "He's most likely going to be asleep for a while longer," she explained, turning to me. "He was awake for a moment before going back down. He was asking for you."

"For me?" I pointed a finger to my chest.

She nodded a gracious smile to me before bringing her attention back to the group as a whole. "We typically only let one or two visitors in the ICU at a time, so whoever would like to go in first, let me know."

Everyone's gaze slowly shifted onto Decker's parents, but to my surprise, their eyes were on me.

"Go, honey," Shannon said.

"Are you sure?"

"Yes," she grinned through exhaustion of her own.

"When he wakes up, your face is the first one he's going to want to see," Scott spoke with the lightest chuckle, hand in hand with his wife.

"Thank you." I gave them an appreciative smile before dashing down the hallway with the nurse. I would've given them a massive hug had I not been in such a rush to see Decker.

When she directed me to his room, I paused in the doorway. Decks was asleep in a hospital bed, surrounded by monitors. His broken arm and leg were already in a splint, carefully elevated. I could make out the steady rise and fall of his chest, and I brought my palm flat against my own, feeling the gratitude swarming through me.

There was already a chair beside his bed, and I slowly made my way over, taking a seat. As gently as possible, I picked up his right hand and held it between mine.

It calmed me to feel how warm he was, to see how full of life he still was. I used one hand to trail delicately through his hair, admiring his beautiful face as I did so.

"I love you," I muttered, thanking God for the chance to tell Decker when he woke up.

***

I hadn't moved in the past two hours. It was five in the morning, but I still refused to sleep, determined to be awake for when Decker came to.

The staff approved us to have two people in here at a time, so everyone else had rotated one by one to see him for a bit. I stayed here the entire time, grateful that no one asked me to leave. But by now, everyone had gone home to sleep, all saying they would return in the morning.

I hadn't let go of Decker's hand, and when I felt a light squeeze, I sprang forward, closer to him. He stirred in the slightest, his eyes gradually peering open.

He groaned. "Kam?"

I brought his hand up to my mouth, cradling it there as I cried. "You scared me," I whimpered. "You scared the hell out of me."

"I'm alive," he grumbled weakly, but it sounded more like a question than a statement.

"I'm so sorry," I wept.

"You have nothing to be sorry for."

"I'm so sorry this happened to you," I repeated.

His small moan made me cringe. It seemed like every move hurt him. "I guess this is just my karma, isn't it?" his gravelly voice spoke.

I shook my head. "Don't say that."

He took a deep breath through his nose, his eyes never leaving my face. "I was worried about you."

My brows shot up. "*You* were worried about *me*? Decker, you gave me a heart attack. I thought—"

"Hey now," he joked, "I'm pretty sure I was the one with the heart attack."

I gave a light chuckle through tears, amazed at how he could possibly have a sense of humor so soon after almost dying. Once my laughter faded, I shook my head at him, relief and shock and love all mixing through my bloodstream.

"I didn't mean anything I said that night about hating you." I cupped his cheek with my hand, stroking his velvet skin with my thumb. "I hate what you did, but I could never hate you." He gave a feeble nod, finally believing the words. "I love you," I cried, seemingly unable to stop crying. It was a miracle how I even had water left in my body to cry after the amount I'd expelled over the past five hours. "I love you so much. You have no idea," I said, squeezing his hand again. His subtle smile sent a current of fulfillment and ease through me.

Decker looked at me admiringly. "I love you too. Thank you for being here."

He once asked me where I would be if I could be anywhere in the world. I responded with no real answer, because at that point, I didn't have a person or a place or a home. But if anyone asked me that same question today, I knew what my response would be.

I held his hand against my chest, refusing to let go of it. "If you could be anywhere in the world right now, where would you be?"

He took the deepest breath that his sore body could manage, his eyes scanning around the room before looking back at me. "On the beach in Malibu," he smiled, "with you." I brought his hand up to my mouth and kissed it through a smile. "How about you?" he asked.

"Anywhere you are."

He gave me a tender grin. "You don't have to stay here though, you know."

"I'm not going anywhere."

He tilted his head at me, and the way he was so concerned about me while being in the state he was currently in was something I would never be able to understand. "Why don't you go home and get some rest?"

Before tonight, I had a very different outlook on forgiveness— on what could be forgiven and what could not. But this strange, compelling story of fate was both inexplicable and unavoidable.

It was hard enough to live in a world where my parents no longer existed. But to live in a world where neither my parents nor Decker existed? I couldn't even fathom the thought.

I shook my head. "I am home."

The End

Acknowledgments

First, I'd like to thank my talented cover designer, Rachel McEwan for creating this gorgeous cover.

To my bestie for the restie— Antonella, thank you for your love and support. I'm blessed to have you as my number one fan.

This book would not be what it is without my incredible editors. Liv and Shogs, you both are rock stars! I cannot thank you enough for all the time you've put into not only *Home*, but all my books. I would not be the writer that I am without you.

To all my roommates— Josie, Natalie, Emily, Kat, and Sydney, I appreciate each one of you. Thanks for cheering me on and celebrating with me every time I reach a bookish milestone.

To my siblings and parents— thank you for supporting my every move, even when you think my moves are crazy and a little out of reach.

To my dear sisters of *Sigma Kappa*— you all brighten my life. Thank you.

Jazzy, Kate, Sums, Sher, Chloe, Taylor, and Christina— I love and cherish every single one of you. Thank you for being the best!

To Maddy and Olivia— nothing will ever compare to our book talks, wine nights, and movie marathons. On top of that, thank you for being just as weird as me. I wouldn't want to reenact *Twilight* scenes with anyone else.

I will forever be grateful to the sweetest person on the planet— Sarah Sutton. My writing buddy! Thanks for all your advice and words of encouragement.

To my Heavenly angels— my grandparents, Maggie, and Kaylee, I love you all. Thank you for watching over me.

And most importantly, to my readers— you are the greatest reason why I love what I do. Thank you for reading. Thank you for reviewing. Thank you for loving my characters. I appreciate all of you and everything you've done for my career and me.

Lastly, thank you to my characters. Tatum, Axel, Kamryn, and Decker— you hold a special place in my heart. Thanks for being my muse and allowing me to bring my stories to life.